dream HOME

A BLUESTONE LAKES NOVEL

JENN MCMAHON

Author's Note

Hello friend.

Thank you so much for picking up book two in the Bluestone Lakes series. This little fictional town has become so real to me. The same way these characters hold a special place in my heart.

Through this series, you will find second chances and found family. Bluestone Lakes is an ideal location for those looking to escape everyday life or whatever problems you're facing back home. In our secluded town tucked between the mountains with a lake as far as the eyes can see, you will find peace and solitude during your stay. However long that may be..

If you want to see more, you can visit the town website. This will be updated regularly *wink wink* as the series progresses.

http://jennmcmahon.com

While this book was created to be light and easy to read—I understand there are some elements that may be triggering to some readers.

My goal is to respect and honor that before you dive into this story.

Please be aware that this book you has explicit language, alcohol consumption, and explicit sex scenes. It also has mentions of death of parents and grandparents, as well as a character who has depression and PTSD. I worked diligently and with an amazing group of people to help me ensure the pieces inside the pages were handled with care.

The experiences you'll read are deeply personal to the characters—and in many ways, personal to me as well. Mental health is something many of us live with quietly. Sometimes we speak about it. Sometimes we don't.

In this book, I chose to let it be seen.

If parts of this story feel close to home, I want you to know you're not alone. You're never alone. If you feel you need support, I encourage you to reach out to someone you trust or a mental health professional.

Thank you for reading and thank you for being here.

I hope this story meets you wherever you are.

I hope you end up swooning through this book the same way I did writing it. As always, my Instagram DM's are always open for your reactions, favorite moments and to chat as you read!

xo, Jenn

If you are in need of help or someone to talk to, please contact a crisis hotline in your area.

*For the ones who stayed when it would've
been easier to leave. Who rebuild even when
no one is watching. Who believe if someone sees
the cracks, they'll walk away.*

*May you find someone
who sees them and steps closer.*

DREAM HOME

BLUESTONE LAKES

BOOK 3

PROLOGUE

ALL GREAT LOVE STORIES START WITH A CORNY PICKUP LINE.

SCOTTIE

I feel like I'm two seconds away from hyperventilating into a paper bag from nerves, now that I'm in San Francisco for this interview tomorrow.

But at least I look good.

Swiping through the dozen timed selfies I took a bit ago in front of the view at the Golden Gate lookout, I know my social media followers are going to eat this up. I'm dressed in a neon yellow blazer, black ankle-length dress pants, statement earrings, and a pair of matching neon yellow heels sharp enough to be registered as weapons.

It's bold, bright, and unapologetic.

I pick my top three selfies and upload them to social media with the caption: *Big things are coming.*

After I upload it, I switch to a map app and find I'm only one block from the burger bar I found while doom scrolling at the airport. Apparently, it's a must-visit when visiting San Francisco. As luck would have it, it's so close to my hotel, too.

And what I need right now is a drink to take the edge off.

Tomorrow, I have an interview with a panel of producers who could offer me a dream job to be the feature for the next season of my favorite home renovation show called *Nailed It or Failed It.*

On a whim, I submitted an application when I heard they were looking for someone. They must have received thousands of submissions from actual professionals and people with real portfolios or larger followings. Somehow, they still picked me for an in-person interview. I've been sick with nerves ever since because I want—no, I *need*—this chance to prove I'm more than a face behind bright colors, some brand deals, and a decent editing app. I want a chance to prove I belong in this industry.

It's also a shot to finally get out of my parents' house.

I've spent the last few years doing DIY project tutorials with paint-stained nails and plaster dust in my hair before spending late nights video editing, all for this moment. So, naturally, instead of rehearsing my answers to the interview questions they sent over in my hotel room, I'm headed to drown the nerves with booze.

"You have arrived at your destination," the GPS says.

I look up at the sign, and it's…not what I was expecting. The outside looks weathered, but I pull the door open anyway. This bar is essentially a hole-in-the-wall establishment. I'm not one to wander into a bar like this alone, especially one that smells like old wood, spilled beer, and someone's questionable cologne.

I scan the room and it's busy. My eyes land on an open bar seat and I take it. My phone rings in my purse, pulling my attention. Looking down, I reluctantly swipe to answer.

"Hello, Mom."

"Scottlyn? Can you hear me?" she practically yells through the phone, causing me to pull the phone away from my ear while I cringe at the use of my full name—which she knows I hate.

"Yes. Can *you* hear me?"

"Barely. There's so much shouting and music around you. Where are you?"

"I'm at a little spot in San Francisco called *Between the Buns* to grab dinner."

"Shouldn't you be preparing for your interview?" my mom asks, full of judgment. "And did you bring the notes I gave you? The ones about how you should explain the remodel we did?"

"I was just grabbing some food. And—"

She scoffs, cutting me off. "Haven't you heard of room service? You should be in your hotel room preparing and, most importantly, figuring out what to wear. These producers are going to want someone polished and put together."

And there it is.

The only thing my mother ever worries about is appearances.

But that's how it's always been.

If I fail at anything, it reflects back on her.

"You're right," I lie to keep things at bay. "I'm going to grab my burger to go and head back to the hotel. Thanks for calling to check on me."

"Just…try not to get your hopes up, Scottlyn. These shows tend to go with someone more established."

"I know," I say, even though I don't want to. "Love you."

"Love you too," she replies flatly before hanging up.

I release a sigh, pocket my phone in my small purse and rest it on my lap. At the same time, the bartender stops in front of me.

"What can I get for you today?"

"I need something that says, *I have my life together.*"

"Good luck," a man beside me says, and I snap my head in his direction. "I don't think any bartender has been able to figure out *that* drink for years."

Piercing blue eyes stay fixed on me, leaving me speechless. I think my mouth is open, so I make a point to close it. He's dressed in casual jeans and a deep brown Henley shirt, showing off forearms that are tan and muscular. His messy brown hair peeks out from the sides of his backward baseball cap.

A freakin' backward baseball cap.

Christ. He's good looking.

As if he knows what I'm thinking, a grin spreads across his face. I remind myself to breathe as my eyes trail where he stands. A glass already in his hand, amber liquid catching the bar light. I feel my lips curling into a smile, too.

I arch a brow. "Whiskey guy?"

He shakes his head. "More like a bourbon guy. Whiskey makes me feel old."

"And how old are you?"

"Twenty-four next week. And you?"

"Twenty-four now."

"And she's funny too," he says, nodding repeatedly in approval as he turns to face the bartender. "I'll have another bourbon. Whatever you decide to make her, you can put it on my tab."

The bartender acknowledges him and then moves around behind the bar to make both drinks.

"What are we drinking to this afternoon?"

I lift my chin, straightening my spine. "If I go down in flames tomorrow, I may as well start the journey with this delicious drink, a bacon cheeseburger, and fries loaded with cheese sauce."

His grin widens, and it almost makes my stomach flutter as he takes the seat next to me. "Then we can go on it together."

"Together?"

He nods. "We're ordering drinks together, are we not? We'll need a second round for the fun we're about to have. Then we can order burgers—two different ones, obviously, to split and try both..." He pauses, deep in thought before lifting a pointer finger in the air as if a lightbulb just went off. "And the cheese fries to share."

"Who said I want to share my cheese fries with a stranger?"

He holds up a finger again. "One, I like you already for the fact that you want your own. My kind of girl." He winks and then narrows his eyes as if he's thinking. "Now that I think about it, I might not want to share if they are as good as the internet says they are." He holds up a second finger. "Two." He extends the same hand in front of me. "I'm Tucker."

I look at his hand and back to his face, realizing I've already been smiling this entire time.

Then he grins broadly, with his hand still extended. "See? Now we're not strangers anymore."

I reluctantly take his hand in mine. The moment our palms connect I feel a shock to my system. Call it an electrical current or a lightning strike—whatever it is, it almost knocks me off my barstool. There's a chance he felt it, too, with how his eyes just snapped to my hand in his.

"I'm Scottie," I tell him, forcing his eyes to meet mine again.

"Scottie." He pauses, processing it. "I like that. It suits you."

"How so?"

"You look like a walking ray of sunshine in this dingy bar. I was drawn to you the moment I walked in here." I look down at my bold outfit choice. "In a good way," he adds with a laugh.

I shrug. "I figured if I spilled some cheese sauce on it, you wouldn't be able to tell."

"Dammit. I wish I had thought to wear a yellow shirt, too," he says in a serious tone, as if he really was wishing he had.

The bartender stops in front of us, sliding our drinks across the bar. "Bourbon for you," he says to Tucker. "And a tequila sunrise for you."

"Ah, good man," I say, taking the drink between my hands and sipping it. My eyes practically roll behind my head at how good it is. "Tequila is like the duct tape of the soul."

The bartender laughs. "Can I get you two something to eat?"

I point a finger between the two of us. "Oh, we're not together."

"We are," Tucker says too quickly.

"No...we're not."

He shrugs, but that damn smile doesn't leave his face. "I'm going to have the barbecue cheeseburger, and then we'll take a bacon cheeseburger, too. Best of both worlds," he says, winking in my direction. "And two orders of cheese fries." He snaps his head to face me. "You're not allergic to barbecue sauce or bacon, are you?"

I laugh and shake my head.

"Whew. That would have been a deal breaker."

I wish I could wrap my head around what is happening right now.

The bartender leaves to plug our order into the register, and I do nothing to stop him or defend that I'm not actually *with* this stranger.

Tucker is the most unexpected thing to happen, but it's also come at a time when I need it the most. Like the universe knew I needed this distraction to take my mind off the stress.

"So, Scottie, what brings you to San Francisco?"

"I have a job interview." That's not a lie, but I won't give him more than that. If I start diving deeper into it, it stops being light. And I really need light right now. "You?"

"Leisure. My best friend works for the San Francisco Staghorns, and I tagged along to keep him company."

"That's really nice of you."

"What can I say, I'm a nice guy."

I roll my eyes playfully, fighting off the laugh. It's a foreign feeling for me to be smiling this much when I'm not creating perfectly curated social media content. I spend so much of my time editing the rougher edges of who I am and polishing myself into a version that will please everyone. Especially my parents.

This feels good with Tucker.

This feels free with him.

And it's only been a short period of time.

"And if I had to guess, you're a nice guy from a little small town in the middle of nowhere, and you ride horses into the sunset?"

"Close, but no. How did you guess small town?"

"You have lumberjack arms."

"You noticed my arms?" He grins. "If you must know, these are working man's arms. If you did what I do every day, you might chip that manicure," he teases.

"And what is it you do?"

"I build houses…in said small town."

"Please. I could out-hammer you any day."

"Yeah?" His eyes sparkle with mischief, sitting up taller for the challenge. "Name three kinds of nails that aren't on your fingers."

"Finishing. Casing. Brad."

His eyebrows rise, and he pauses, staring at me. "Marry me."

I laugh and lift my drink to my lips, reveling in the booze hitting my system. "You said before that no one has been able to figure out that drink," I say, not even acknowledging what he just said. "But I think our friend behind the bar has nailed it. No pun intended."

Tucker studies me. His eyes remain fixed on my face as if memorizing me—the color of my eyes, the tone of my skin, the crinkle around my eye. It's uncomfortable but also exhilarating.

I've never had a man look at me like he's captivated by me.

"I like you," he says.

"We're still strangers," I say in a tone that says he is *not* having an out of body effect on me.

"I'm like a fast pass in the amusement park. We can get past the stranger-danger zone and into friendship territory *very* quickly."

This time I laugh hard—full on, bending over the bar top with laughter.

"Did you really just say that?" I ask, catching my breath. "That sounds like a corny pickup line."

"All great love stories start with a corny pickup line."

I don't have time to respond because the server drops our food in front of us. But my cheeks feel warm, and I hope it's not obvious. I can't believe he just said that…but I kind of like it. It's bold. *He's* bold. Tucker didn't even flinch when I called him out on how corny it sounded. Most guys would have backpedaled, but he doubled down. I'm not sure if it's cocky or charming.

Maybe both?

I find myself staring at this man next to me, and he seems like the kind of guy who knows exactly what he's doing, standing here with that smirk on his face, and slowly sipping his bourbon. Still…there's something in the way he just said that, like he actually believes it.

Like he's daring me to believe it, too.

"So, you said you've got an interview tomorrow," Tucker says, thankfully changing the topic. He picks up a french fry, bringing it to his lips. "What's the interview for? Anything I can help you with?" he asks, before taking a bite.

"It's a TV thing." I shrug.

"Damn. So you're not just some girl walking around the city in a bright yellow jacket, huh?"

"Nope. I'm a girl in a yellow *blazer* who might be on your TV one day."

He smiles so wide that for the first time since he sat down next to me, I see a dimple form. Dammit, I'm supposed to be acting completely uninterested here, and he's making it very difficult.

"I don't watch TV," he replies, eyes laser focused on me. There it is again, the steady stare that makes my stomach flutter like champagne bubbles rising inside of me. "But if you're on it? I'd learn your schedule, set reminders, and make it my new favorite show."

Heat prickles my skin, and suddenly the air around us feels heavy.

Trying not to show how his words have affected me, I decide to accept his offer to help with this. Maybe he can even give me a better answer than I've come up with for one of the interview questions they gave me ahead of time.

I turn in my chair, fully facing him. "Maybe you can help me with an interview question since you build houses for a living."

"Shoot."

"What does *home* mean to you?"

He doesn't answer immediately. I watch as the smile on his face fades just enough for me to notice, but I can tell he's hiding it. He reaches for his drink, taking a sip before placing it back down. I immediately regret asking because it seems to have triggered a memory for him, but the words have already left my mouth. I can't take them back.

"A lot of people think a home is composed of walls and a roof where you live. A structure that you fill with belongings and memories. But it's more than that. It's who's inside those walls. It's a place where you're seen without needing to explain yourself. A place where you can breathe and your flaws don't need to be hidden. It's where you don't have to pretend. You can just... be."

The final words land like a sharp sucker punch to the gut.

I didn't realize until hearing it from him that I want that. Someday, I want a home that feels exactly like what he just described. A place that's mine. Where I don't have to perform or impress or earn my right to take up space. Somewhere I finally get to just...be.

"Sorry." He laughs, breaking the tension. "That was way too deep—even for me. But in conclusion"—he clears his throat, and the funny guy I know from just moments ago is back— "home isn't just about the structure. It's less about where you live, and more about where you feel whole."

"That's...wow. That's a good answer."

"Feel free to use it to nail your interview." He winks. "I need a reason to start watching TV again."

For the next half hour, we each order another drink, leaving behind the unintentional deep conversation we just had, to eat our meal. Tucker splits both burgers in half and we share them to get a taste of the two different kinds. It feels like we've slipped into our own bubble at the bar, the kind where the noise around us fades away and it's just the two of us. My cheeks hurt from laughing so hard as he holds up the burger like he's presenting a case in court about why this burger is the best he's ever had.

I can't decide if I'm more full from the meal, or from the way he makes me laugh.

"My jaw officially hurts from laughing this much," he says, relaxing, but then his eyes widen and he turns to face me on the barstool. "Do you think we've exceeded the legal limit for laughing at a bar?"

My smile falls, and I offer him a serious look. "Do you think the bartender will write us a citation?"

"Fuck," he says, equally serious—matching my sarcasm. "I hope not. I'm not good with fines. You think we should make a run for it?"

I lean in, keeping my voice low. "Are you suggesting we flee the scene?"

He nods. "It's a *very* serious crime."

I laugh, shaking my head. "You're ridiculous."

He smiles playfully, placing cash on top of the receipt to pay for both of our meals. I should protest. I usually do. I'm careful about owing anyone anything or about letting moments get misread into something more than they're meant to be.

But there's something about him.

The way he's so casually gotten under my skin, like it didn't require effort or strategy or a perfectly timed smile.

"I never thought I'd say this but…" I glance at Tucker, my voice softer than I expect it to be. "I don't want this night to end."

His eyes lock with mine, and goose bumps pebble across my skin from the intensity of his stare. "Same."

One word, barely above a whisper.

A stark contrast to our playful laughter moments ago.

"Do you…maybe…want to come back to my hotel room?"

Oh god. I can't believe I actually said that out loud. Since when do I do this? Since when do I risk rejection instead of hiding behind silence? Instantly, I wish I could rewind to ten seconds ago and swallow the question, but the braver part of me is already blushing, waiting to see what he says.

"Yes."

One word to make me completely unravel. Heat rushes to my neck and my pulse sky rockets like it doesn't know what to do now. He stands from his barstool, extending his hand to me. I take it and feel the heat of his palm in mine all the way to my core.

I remind myself that this is just one night.

One night to let myself go and forget about tomorrow.

One night without rehearsing who I need to be or thinking about how I'll need to prove that I deserve this show.

One night with a stranger that I won't ever see again.

"Lead the way, Scottie."

CHAPTER 1
WHO THE HELL IS NAN?

SCOTTIE

I'm halfway through a bag of Sour Patch Kids when my phone buzzes on my nightstand. Quickly picking it up, I see an unknown San Francisco number, and my stomach immediately drops like I'm riding the tallest roller coaster.

This is it.

For the last week, I've spent every waking moment refreshing my emails. I've been waiting for the rejection email because the producers told me they would call *if* they were going to choose me. But the tone they used that morning was less than promising.

I wouldn't blame them if I don't get picked because I went into my interview on less than three hours of sleep, completely hungover, and an aching body from the greatest sex of my life the night before.

With shaking fingers, I finally answered. "Hello?"

"Hello. I'm looking for Scottie Monroe."

"I might know where she is," I say, shrugging, even though they can't see me. "But if this is a telemarketer, she's currently in witness protection and not taking phone calls at this time."

There's a laugh on the other end. "This is why I like you. It's

Andrea from the *Nailed It or Failed It* production team." I suck in a sharp breath. "We want to officially offer you the spot on season seven."

I can't breathe all of a sudden.

Me? They want me?

They want me!

"Scottie?" Andrea says through the phone.

"Yes. I'm here," I say quickly. "Sorry. But wow. Thank you."

I sound as shocked as I feel. There wasn't an ounce of confidence in me during the interview. I blame it on two things… waking up alone in my hotel room without a fucking word from the man who swept me off my feet, and texts from my mom asking me what I was wearing and then telling me it wasn't good enough.

Even after that…they want to offer me the spot.

"We're so excited to work with you," Andrea says cheerfully. "You have the perfect spunky and fun personality we're looking for. I will send you an official email in just a few minutes with all the necessary information from us and details on how we'll cover the entire cost of this project. After that, we will need the location of the home for the show from you."

"Location?"

"Yes, for the renovation project. You have a house to fix up, right?"

My excitement fades instantly, and I feel my stomach drop to the floor. I look around my small bedroom in my parents' house. The same one I've already renovated top to bottom over the last year that got my social media presence up and running. No one has mentioned anything about *me* needing to find a home to renovate.

Or have they and I totally missed it?

"Yes. Of course," I lie, biting the inside of my cheek. "How long do I have to get the location information for you?"

"The sooner the better. We start filming in two weeks."

I can feel my heart rate pick up speed. "That fast?"

"This whole process will be fast."

I can hear the smile in her tone. This is her job, so she's used to this. Me, on the other hand? I'm freaking the fuck out that I don't even have a place to present them.

"Awesome."

Andrea squeals with excitement. "I can't wait. It's going to be an epic *Nailed It*, if you know what I mean."

That or an epic Failed It.

"Yup. Can't wait," I squeak out with a fake smile, even though she can't see me.

We hang up, and I stare down at the phone, my excitement turning quickly into panic.

Getting this show is my big break—not because I want fame or my face on a big screen. I need it because I'm tired of being seen as just another girl with a glue gun and a ring light. This is my chance to be taken seriously as a professional in the industry and not a hobbyist who got lucky online.

My mom insisted I go to college to be able to land some successful corporate job. So I did. I earned a degree in marketing and communications while spending my free time dragging discarded dressers home and refurbishing them in the garage. I started filming the process because it was the only thing that actually made me feel like myself. I've built a social media presence around independence and the idea that women can do anything a man can when it comes to a drill or a hammer.

When I graduated, I knew I couldn't do the office life that my mom wanted for me.

I wanted to build things.

I wanted to *fix* things.

When I opened up to my dad about how I felt, he gave me one year to try. One year to turn our house into my portfolio and see if I could make something real out of it.

But my mom never stopped judging me for it. She never stopped reminding me I should aim higher and that what I did wasn't enough for a sustainable career. It's hard to tell the difference when the message is always the same—that what I choose is never quite enough.

Especially when there's Kali.

My older cousin who's wildly successful living in New York City and climbing the corporate ladder as an editor for a major magazine. I've spent *years* being quietly measured against her. A part of me envies her success and the close friends she has, but I've never wanted that career. I love what I do—the same way she loves what she does.

The problem is, my mom doesn't see it that way.

She worries about my image, how this looks, and the money I'm making.

Does my gig on social media make me money? Yes, but it's not nearly enough to get out of this house and be on my own.

This show is supposed to be the thing that changes that.

But renovating a home I don't even have?

I should have asked more questions during the interview.

Because there's no way my mom is going to think I can tackle this.

I groan, falling back on my bed, staring up at the ceiling.

This is the offer of a lifetime, and I'm going to have to let Andrea know in a few days that I don't have the means to do this.

"Scottlyn?" my mom says from the doorway. "Was that the producer on the phone?"

I turn to face her. "Yep. I got it. They want me for the show."

"Oh…good," she says, relief flickering through her smile. "That's wonderful."

Just as I'm about to open my mouth to say more, she continues.

"But…they do know the only big project you've done is this house, right?"

My stomach churns. "They've seen my work."

"I know. I just mean…those little affiliate things you do aren't quite the same as a real renovation schedule."

"I—"

"I'm just saying," she continues gently. "It helps people take you more seriously when they understand where your experience really comes from."

I sit there, still, taking in every word before I nod automatically.

Because that's what I always do when she makes my work sound smaller than it is.

"I might not get to keep the show anyway. I need to provide my own fixer-upper." I face the ceiling again, fighting back the emotions threatening to spill out. "Like, hello, I don't just have a fixer-upper home lying around like some people."

"Actually," my dad's voice says, forcing me to snap my head toward the doorway again. "Maybe you do."

This time, I smile when I see my dad.

"Billy," my mother warns. "We talked about this."

He nods, placing a hand on her shoulder. "I know we have, Laura. But this is a big opportunity for her. I want to see her take it."

I sit up in my bed, staring at them, confused.

"Do you remember your grandmother? My mom? I know it's been a while, but you used to call her Mimi Millie," he says through a soft smile at the memory.

My gaze falls to the floor, searching for a memory. I try to piece together a face, a voice, or a laugh. But for the most part, it's all a blur to me. It's been so long since anyone's even mentioned her.

"I don't remember, why?" I ask, looking back up at my dad.

"Well, when she passed away years ago, she left you her house. You were only thirteen and obviously had no means to have your own home. But it's in Bluestone Lakes and only about an hour from here."

My eyes widen with shock.

I try to think deeper into my memories of her. But still, I barely remember Mimi Millie or her house. I know my grandfather passed away before I was even born and she lived alone, but I had no idea Mimi had died.

But a memory hits me the longer I stare at my dad, shock still all over my face and unable to speak yet. I was young the last time we went there. Then one year we just…stopped going. There was no explanation or dramatic fight that I know of. I never received birthday cards from her, and even my parents stopped saying her name.

So why did she leave her house to me?

Better yet, why am I just finding out about it now?

"I know you have a lot of questions," he says, reading my mind.

"Yeah, you could say that."

He laughs. "This is long overdue. Your mother and I wanted to find the right time to give this to you."

What is even happening right now?

My mom leans into him. "Are you sure this is the right time?" she whispers, thinking I can't hear. "She still barely has a stable income to survive on her own."

"I'm in the room," I announce.

"Yes, Laura. It's been forever since any of us has seen the place and it's been abandoned since she passed. Which means it'll need a *whole lot* of work."

"There's a big difference between renovating *this* home," my mom says with her arms out showcasing the room. "And renovating an abandoned one. I don't think she's ready for that kind of work."

"Still *right here*," I try again, forcing a small, tight smile. My jaw tightens in aggravation, because even though I haven't seen this house or remember it, I *know* I have what it takes.

"She's ready," my dad answers for me. "The house is yours. Use it for the show. Make it yours and do whatever you want with it. You can even stay there when you're done, or sell it to buy something here." He steps fully into the room for the first time placing a hand on my shoulder. "You're ready. Your grandmother always wanted that house to shine again after Grandpa died, but she didn't have it in her. I know you'll make her proud."

My mom exhales slowly. "I just hope you don't end up in over your head with this, Scottlyn."

"She won't," my dad says with confidence before my mom turns to leave.

A tear escapes and I wipe it quickly. I rush for my dad, wrapping my arms around his neck for a hug. "Thank you."

"Of course, honey." He returns my embrace and presses a kiss to my forehead before pulling back. "Make sure you let the producers know you have a place and you'll be ready."

I'll be ready.

In the last half hour, I've shifted from buzzing with excitement to feeling like the rug was pulled out from under me, then to anticipation for the future and what's to come.

It's a fixer-upper for the show, but it's so much more than that.

It's my house—a potential future home for me if I want it.

I have no idea what kind of work it needs, but my mind is already racing with possibilities. Even if the house is rough, it's mine to shape and dream into something tangible.

My dad rests a reassuring hand on my shoulder. "I'll call Nan and figure out the logistics."

I tilt my head to the side, narrowing my eyes. "Who the hell is Nan?"

CHAPTER 2
I JUST ABOUT STARTED STREAKING DOWN MAIN STREET WITH EXCITEMENT.

SCOTTIE

Apparently, "one hour" is road trip math for "forever."

It's funny how it can feel like forever when I'm the one behind the wheel on a trip that could change my life. The road feels endless and like a dark tunnel of trees, even though I know the sun is shining on the other side. About twenty minutes ago, I was convinced that the road was just some cruel loop designed to trap me.

As soon as I'm ready to pull over and call my dad to ask if I'm even headed in the right direction, the road opens up and the trees part almost like a curtain. I pull myself closer to the steering wheel, taking it all in. Bright blue paints the sky while mountains sit in the distance. I almost laugh, because after a ride that felt like eternity, this feels worth the wait.

A lake off to the left comes into view, and it's so perfect that it doesn't look real.

That's when I see the sign I've been waiting for.

Welcome to Bluestone Lakes.

I inhale and exhale, tightening my grip as I steer the car straight down the single-lane highway. "This is it," I whisper. "This is where I decide what I'm doing going forward."

A smile forms involuntarily.

My dad showed me as many pictures as he could find of my grandmother's house to prepare me before I left. They were outdated, but I could still see the bones of something beautiful. I emailed the producers immediately after and told them the location of the property and included some pictures that he showed me. They approved everything within hours.

My dad pulled out all the old photos he could find, telling me stories about my grandmother and a few of the memories I had forgotten along the way. I asked him why we stopped going there. He didn't say much, but that there was a falling out years ago. Mostly between my mom and my grandmother. Something that never fully healed before Millie passed away. He didn't offer more than that, and I didn't push. But the way his voice softened when he changed conversation told me everything I needed to know.

He quickly went into telling me all the ways Mimi Millie wanted the house to shine again. How it felt dull when my grandpa died. The light went out inside the home and never came back on.

And I knew right then and there that I want to make it shine again.

For her.

And for me?

I can't say for sure because I don't know what the future holds for me. I can't seem to remember a single thing about this town or if I can see myself staying here when the project is over. I'd love a place to call my own—a place where I can just…be.

Another sign that reads *Welcome to the Heart of Bluestone Lakes* comes into view, and I scan the area for a large tree and a bench my dad told me to look for. When I find it, I see the mystery woman named Nan sitting with one leg crossed over the other. She honestly looks the same as I had imagined from how my dad explained her to me: short white hair, tiny frame, and retro-style glasses. Just looking at her through the front window of my car, I already know she's a total vibe wearing a pair of hot pink, straight-leg jeans with a loose white T-shirt tucked in.

Pulling my car off to the side, I exit and round the hood of my car and make my way to where she sits. "Hey. Do you happen to be Nan?"

She smiles. "Normally, this is where I give some smart-ass response to someone lookin' for me, but not today." She smiles widely, looking me up and down. "You've grown up so much."

Tipping my head to the side, I study her, trying to see if I can remember her.

She waves me off. "You wouldn't remember me. You were about three feet tall last time you were here to visit Millie."

"You knew my grandmother?"

She stands from the bench and meets me where I stand. "I did. She was one of my best friends here in town. And when Billy called me up and told me they finally told you about your inheritance and that you're coming to fix up the place, I just about started streaking down Main Street with excitement." I press a hand over my face to hide my giggle. "But I thought better of it. I heard people pay big money to see a pair of tits online these days. I can't risk someone taking a video to give out for free." She winks and retreats toward my car.

She's *definitely* a total vibe.

"Get in," she says, waving from the passenger side of my car. "Let me show you the place."

I hesitate for half a second, because letting a woman I barely know get into my car feels wildly out of character for me. But I guess today is about doing things I normally wouldn't do.

I jog to my driver's side and get in quickly.

"What's with the plastic cup of green and yellow candy?" Nan asks, buckling her seat belt.

I chuckle. "I only eat the red, blue, and orange Sour Patch Kids. I have an aversion to the green and yellow ones for some reason. You're welcome to them if you'd like."

She reaches in and pops a yellow in her mouth. "They all taste the same to me."

She's wrong, but okay.

Nan guides me with a mix of lefts and rights—she's not good at it. She seems to tell me at the last second to turn, which has only made this drive feel very erratic.

I can feel my stomach twist as we get closer. Not from car sickness, but from a mix of nerves and curiosity. Every corner we take I wonder if it's the street, or if the roof will peek out from behind the trees.

What if it ends up being bigger than anything I'm capable of?

What if I can't pull it off the way everyone expects me to?

That's the part that scares me.

We make another right on a street called Redwood Ave. when Nan finally points through the window at an open lot coming into view. "This is it on the left."

When I pass the row of trees lining the edge of the property, my car slows to a stop in the middle of the road as I stare.

"Best views in town," Nan adds.

I swallow, suddenly overwhelmed by how real this just became.

A two-story farmhouse looms at the end of a long gravel driveway, hidden between wild grass that claws around the edges, mixed with weeds and wildflowers as if they are locked in some kind of messy battle for dominance over the property. I put my car in park, unable to take my eyes away from the view in front of me as I exit and start to make my way up the driveway—if that's what you even want to call it anymore.

The closer I get, the more I see the paint peeling in strips from the side as if it's shedding its own skin. The windows are clouded over with age with an old wooden frame and paint cracked around the edges. There's a mix of crooked and missing shutters, and a porch sagging just enough to make me hesitate to even step foot on it.

To anyone else, it probably looks like a burden.

To me?

It looks like potential.

"The house isn't livable right now," Nan says behind me, cutting through my thoughts.

I turn around to face her, not realizing she's following me closer to the house.

"I assumed so," I reply, reaching for my phone in my back pocket. "I think I have an email somewhere in my inbox about them handling lodging."

Swiping through all my never ending emails, I finally find it. Only to feel my entire body tense because I never replied back to the email from them asking if I needed a place, or if I was finding my own.

Shit. Shit. Shit.

I look up at Nan. "I know it's kind of last minute, but do you know where I can find a place to stay in town? I never replied back to them about lodging."

"The film crew took up all our rentals and the few bed and breakfasts we have in town." She pauses, but she must register my disappointment. "I thought that might be an issue and have already made some calls. I have a friend who was nice enough to let you stay in his house. He has a small apartment over his garage that he's going to stay in while you film."

"Oh no," I say, waving my hands. "I can't do that, Nan. I can stay in the garage apartment since I'm the one who messed this up. And maybe tomorrow when I meet the team at the house, they can squeeze me in somewhere with them."

She shrugs. "I'll tell him, but I think he's going to insist."

I force a smile, but a quiet, familiar shame curls in my gut. The kind that whispers I should've planned better. I should have responded to the email immediately. I should admit now that I can't handle things on my own.

"I just don't want to put anyone out. Please."

She nods. "I'll talk to him. Let me take you there to get settled."

We walk back toward my car, still parked in the road. Thank god it's not a busy road, otherwise I would have made a solid first impression as the girl who just leaves her car in the middle of the road.

I turn around one more time, taking in the home where my grandmother used to live, and smile to myself. "I'm going to make it shine for you, Millie," I whisper to the wind and get back in the driver's seat.

Thankfully, the place I'll be staying is only one turn away on a street right off Redwood Ave., so it was a much less erratic drive with Nan and her terrible delivery of directions from the passenger seat.

"Here," Nan says, pointing to a house on the right tucked away into the trees.

This time, I pull into the driveway leading to the house. The gravel is cracked and moss-dotted, like no one's paid attention to it in years. I scan the open space and see the driveway is wide, with one side leading to the home, and the other to the detached garage with the apartment over the top, half hidden by trees.

I refuse to let the owner of this home uproot his life for me.

I *will be* staying in this apartment.

Once I get out of the car, I look around. It's a cozy place—tucked away off the road. The main home isn't flashy, but you can tell it's well built. It's a small craftsman-style home with weathered wood siding and a low, inviting porch. The porch is swept clean, but the rocking chair, withered flowers, and muddy boots by the door show he doesn't care about appearances.

Nan holds out her hand. "Here are the keys to the garage apartment or loft, whatever you kids call it these days. I can't make promises about him kickin' you out of there to stay in the house. He's persistent and a gentleman like that."

I take the keys from her. Looking down, I roll them around in my hand, feeling the cold metal in my palm.

"You should know…he works *a lot* and he's gone most of the day. If you need anything, you can call me."

She hands me what appears to be a business card. I take it, narrowing my eyes when I notice it's nothing but her name, phone number, and a note that says *I don't know how to email.*

"Thank you. I really appreciate all of this."

"Anytime." She nods, placing a hand on my shoulder. "One more thing you should know about this town is that we look out for each other."

I smile, acknowledging her words.

But deep down, they sting.

Due to my commitment to making everything work out on social media, and the fact that I'm swamped, I don't have friends who look out for me, and vice versa. I've always kept to myself because the few I've made along the way have been surface level and only needed me when they needed something. I have no idea what it's like to have people outside of my immediate family look out for me, and even then, I sometimes wonder if my mom has my best interest at heart.

Just as I'm headed toward the stairs that lead to the apartment, I turn around again. "Hey, do you need a ride somewhere? I just realized I drove you here."

She waves me off, keeping her back to me. "Walking's good for ya. Don't you worry about me, Scottie."

I laugh as she walks away, looking down at the keys in my hand again, and then make my way up the stairs. The staircase groans under my sneakers, each step telling me this is definitely not the chic loft I was envisioning. When I get to the door and turn the lock, I attempt to push it open, but it's stuck. With a few shoves using my full body weight, it finally swings open. The apartment is dark and smells faintly of old pine and stale air. Flicking the light on, the sky lights buzzed like it was the start of a scene in any horror film.

"It's functional," I say to an empty room.

This place completely lacks any personality that I thrive on. This feels like I'm being shoved into a sad beige shoebox.

I scratch my forehead, exhaling.

Okay, it's only temporary.

This is just a stepping stone—a place to stay while I fix up my grandmother's house.

I have no idea how I'm going to make *that* happen.

But at least I get to try.

With a little help from power tools and a lot of wishful thinking, what could go wrong?

CHAPTER 3

YOU KNOW I DON'T WATCH TV.

TUCKER

The bell chimes overhead as I enter Seven Stools for my lunch break, and I immediately find Griffin scowling behind the bar.

I hold up my hands in defense. "I haven't been here all day. Maybe you should learn how to disconnect it yourself if you hate it that much."

He rolls his eyes, which only makes me laugh.

My coworker, Levi, chuckles next to me, shaking his head. "I love watching you piss him off."

"It's the best part of my day."

While Griffin may technically be my cousin, he's been more like a brother to me since I moved into his parents' house when I was younger. Even though I love pissing him off and seeing him get angry, it's all out of fun and games for me to keep the people around me laughing.

I take my seat at one of the seven barstools lining the bar. "Any specials today?"

"Tucker," he warns. "You literally work behind this bar every night. You know we don't do specials, and today is nothing new."

He's right. This is my second job and my second favorite place to be. There aren't many places in town to grab a bite to eat, so Levi and I try to come in a few times a week to grab lunch between construction projects. But one day, I hope to walk in and see that Griffin has changed his mind about adding specials. He's spent years in a grumpy mood to the point that he was barely tolerable. But not long ago, he fell in love again. The kind of love that's head over heels and makes me sick to my stomach. Yuck.

But Blair makes him happy, and that makes me happy.

I smirk. "Well, do you have a menu then?"

"It's the same as it's been since we opened."

"Maybe I want something different today." I shrug.

Griffin leans in close, resting his elbows on the bar before crooking a finger as if he wants to tell me a secret. I lean in, smiling, ready for whatever he's about to say to me. "This is how it's gonna go. I'm going to give in to your request, as I always do when you come in here on your short lunch break. You're going to look over the menu and then you'll order the same chicken sandwich, with extra bacon, and the spicy ranch on the side."

"Maybe this week I want r—"

"Ranch on the sandwich," Griffin and Levi both finish for me at the same time.

"Fine," I concede. "I'll take the chicken sandwich, extra bacon, and the spicy ranch on the side."

Griffin nods, standing up again. "Good choice."

"I'll have the same, but regular ranch," Levi tells him.

Griffin writes down the order and places it in the small window leading to the kitchen staff so they can start preparing it.

"Are you two busy today?" Griffin asks.

"Not too bad," Levi answers. "But it's definitely about to get busier."

"Shit. The film crews are showing up today, aren't they?"

Levi nods. "Yep. They're doing that old abandoned house on Redwood Ave."

I groan, letting my head fall to my arms crossed on the bar top dramatically. "It's my dream to live on that property." I lift my head again, pouting. "The views are immaculate and the land is perfect. I want it."

"I have to agree," Levi says. "But that project is going to be a mess. That house needs to be bulldozed and rebuilt from the ground up. I can't imagine that structure holding for much longer."

My body tenses at his words.

Not enough that anyone around me would notice, but it's just enough to spark memories of my past. Memories I wish I could erase from every part of my brain.

Levi may be one of my best friends in town because we work so closely together building houses and fixing things up around town, but even he doesn't know the shit I've been through. He doesn't know that even one statement can cause me to spiral to the point where guilt churns in my gut.

It's been over a decade, but the day replays like it was yesterday.

I shake off the thoughts, nodding. "It's not going to be easy, that's for sure. I'm curious to see what the new owner has planned for the house. And hey," I say, my tone even more chipper. "Maybe the plans will be just that—knock it the fuck down and start over."

"Do you know anything about the show?" Griffin asks, grabbing our food from the window and placing it in front of us.

"You know I don't watch TV," I say as I take a bite of my sandwich.

He rolls his eyes. "I only found out about it because Blair was bouncing up and down when she heard *Nailed It or Failed It* is coming to Bluestone Lakes. I've never heard of the show before, but apparently, it's a fixer-upper type thing. They take something old and update it, basically judging it as a win or a fail when all is said and done."

"I think we're going to nail it. Pun intended." I wink between bites. "And I think the star of the show is renting my apartment space above my garage. At least I think that's what Nan said," I say, thinking about it for a moment before I shrug. "Or maybe it was someone from the film crew. Either way, someone is staying there."

"Whoa." Griffin's eyes widen. "You really let a stranger stay on your property? In your sanctuary? In your personal space?"

I roll my eyes jokingly, but he's right.

I don't ever let anyone in close enough to see through me. I don't host parties, dinners, or events. If I date, it's always casual. And they never come back to my place.

My home is where I can breathe and don't need to hide.

My home is where I don't need to pretend.

My home is *my place*.

I wipe the corner of my mouth with a napkin. "Nan practically *begged* me. And then she said she would let me have first dibs on the pretzel twists shipment when the General Store gets some in."

"You can't be serious," he deadpans.

"I'm so serious. It was an offer I couldn't turn down. Besides, they're only staying there temporarily. Hell, I even offered up the main house and I would stay in the garage loft." I chuckle. "You know, since maybe he'd let me get more airtime. My face deserves to be on TV, don't you think, Griff?"

He narrows his eyes, giving me a knowing look as I finish off my sandwich.

"Anyway, filming starts in a few days, and according to the producers, they have a strict deadline on everything. I think it's part of the show? Which I'm sure Blair knows."

"Yeah, she said they have a one month to complete the renovation from start to finish. If it's not done, it's considered a fail. If they get everything done and it's livable, they say: *Nailed It.*"

"Nailed it," I say, fist-bumping the air.

"This is going to be a long month," Levi says, laughing next to me.

"You're telling me," Griffin agrees. "You should ask for bonus pay every time Tucker says that throughout filming."

"I'd get to retire by the end of it."

I look down at my watch, leaping off the barstool. "Shit, we're going to be late. We have to meet at the house to go over everything with the crew."

"You running late? That can't be right."

When I snap my head to Griffin, he's got a smirk on his face. Asshole.

"I hope everyone from the crew comes in here one at a fucking time and the bell doesn't stop all day," I say, turning around to leave the bar. I take the extra few minutes to leave dramatically, only to walk right back in to hear it go off again.

"I hate you," Griffin calls across the bar.

"I love you too," I shout as I exit for the last time, with one more chime.

***

Pulling my truck into the gravel driveway, I put it in park and round the hood to take in the abandoned house.

It's not my first time here.

Sometimes I come here and think—dream.

It's completely different from my property around the corner covered by trees. This one has a vast landscape of mountains in the distance and trees lining the property line. Every time I come here, I think about what it would be like to own this property and wake up daily to this view and go to bed without obstruction of the stars above. I could never pinpoint why I've been drawn to this particular place when there's so many amazing wonders in Bluestone Lakes, but it's stuck. I like to think it's the stars. They shine so fucking bright here at night.

I've always said if I could pick my dream home, this would be it.

Well, it's not a home. At least not yet.

It's nothing but a list of problems pretending to hold itself upright. The siding is shot, the porch sags like a tired old man, and the shingles have been begging to be replaced for ten years. I've pictured how much work this house needs a dozen times before today, long before I even got into construction.

When I was a teenager and first moved to Bluestone Lakes to live with the Barlow family, I started by taking on small jobs around town. From fixing fences, patching roofs, to any other tasks that kept my hands busy. Along the way, I discovered I had my father's knack for fixing things. Growing up with a mom being a nurse and a dad working in construction, I was taught two important things.

Work hard with your hands, and care for people even when it's hard.

There was something about having a hammer, a saw, or a drill in my hand that grounded me and gave me control when everything else had been taken away.

I know Levi sees this place as a structure waiting to fall, but when I look at this place…I see good bones, a solid frame, and a steady foundation.

This place isn't hopeless, it's just worn thin.

Like most things worth saving.

"Tucker," I hear my boss, Frank, call my name from the patch of lawn where there used to be overgrown weeds. They seemed to have cut it down to make room for this to get started. "Over here."

I jog over to where he stands, abandoning the thoughts so no one asks questions.

"This is Tucker," Frank introduces me to a woman dressed in a pantsuit, as if she's just come from a board meeting in the city. "This is Andrea. She's the producer of the show and is in charge of everything here."

"Nice to meet you," I say with a nod.

"Likewise," Andrea says, staring at me with intensity like she's assessing me. It's uneasy. "Thank you for being here for this meeting this afternoon. Frank says you're the best contractor in town."

"Must be a short list."

She laughs. "This is going to be perfect." I tilt my head to the side in question. "I'm not sure if you've ever watched the show before or not…"

"Every episode," I lie, because this isn't the moment I admit I don't watch TV. "It's my favorite show in the entire world. I've been looking forward to this season since the last one ended."

Frank glares at me knowing I'm full of shit, and I wink back at him.

"Amazing." Andrea claps her hands together. "This season will be a little different. We usually have a couple working together on a project. It really drives drama for views sometimes because not all couples can agree on everything, even happily married ones." She laughs lightly. "But this season we're show-casing our star solo."

"Sounds good."

"We've asked for a team to help with this because, as you know, there's a strict one month deadline. We will film a lot of main content, but there will also be a lot of work done when the cameras aren't rolling to help drive things along quickly."

"Works for me."

Andrea turns to Frank. "He really is the best, huh?"

"He's a hard worker. Whatever you need, him and the rest of the team can get it done. No questions asked."

I nod in agreement.

"Our solo star," Andrea says with a bit of shimmy in her body like she's excited. "Is doing her first walk through of the house as she hasn't seen what the inside looks like yet. This way, she can plan what she wants to do. After she's done, we can get the meeting and introductions started with everyone present.

Does that work?" Andrea asks, gaze bouncing between Frank and me.

Her?

My brows lift before I can stop them but clear my throat and school my expression. I mentally prepared for some guy with a beard and a hammer to be staying in my apartment. Definitely not a woman. Interesting.

"Yep," I say.

"I have to go check on some projects on the other side of town," Frank says, looking down at his watch. "But Tucker here will be in charge, and whatever you need, he's your man."

Frank's words hit me harder than they should have.

It's just a simple compliment, but it's lodged in my chest like it belongs there.

I've always been good at being the extra set of hands. The guy who shows up early, stays late, and fixes whatever needs fixing without being asked. I'm the helper. The one who tries to make things easier for everyone else. The funny guy who makes everyone laugh to keep the energy up.

I'm good at that.

I help Dallas coach a kids' baseball team.

I help Griffin behind the bar so he doesn't have to work nights.

But what I'm not used to is being in charge of anything. It makes my chest feel tight that Frank sees the ability in me to run the crew for this project.

When I turn to face Andrea, she's staring at me with a smile on her face, like she might believe it, too.

Laughter flows from the house, and Andrea turns around. "Oh, good, they're done. We can get this meeting started."

When I follow her stare, the world around me stops spinning.

Of all houses, *she* has to walk out of this one.

Scottie, with her bold blazer and a strut that could stop traffic, is the very last person I'm expecting to see standing in the doorway. The universe really has a messed-up sense of humor.

My brain immediately travels back to that night in San Francisco. That night, when I heard her laugh echo in the dark room and how she tasted like tequila and trouble. The memory hits me and I clench my fist at my sides, remembering how her skin felt under my hands and the sound of her voice screaming my name in the hotel room.

Now she's here. Standing in broad daylight, looking like sin wrapped in sunshine. And *dammit,* if it doesn't knock the air right out of me and make me feel like my chest is caving in.

Because I left that next morning.

I left without a word while she was still sleeping. Never expecting to see her again.

CHAPTER 4
ARE YOU SUGGESTING I FAKE DATE HIM?

SCOTTIE

"Before we get started, can I see the inside of the house? I haven't been inside yet," I ask Andrea's assistant, Jade.

"Of course. By the way, I love this look on you," she says, looking me up and trailing her finger in the air from head to toe. "You're literally a walking ray of sunshine."

I look down on instinct and take in my rosy pink wide-legged jeans. An outfit that my mom would *definitely* not approve of. In fact, she wanted me to wear a maxi dress. A dress! While we're not actually doing work today, I was not showing up to an abandoned house wearing a fucking dress because she said it would help beat the summer heat. So I kept it casual. My pink jeans paired it with a tucked in, ivory T-shirt that has a picture of lemons gathered on the front, and a bright yellow sweater over my shoulders to look professional.

"Thank you," I offer with a smile.

I take a calming breath, feeling nervous for what mess I'm about to walk into as I follow Jade to the front porch. Jade has been very nice since I arrived half an hour ago. She's technically part of the camera crew but also assists Andrea on the production team.

She opens the door for me and I step in. Once I cross through the front door, the air hits me first. It's dusty but sweet, like old wood and forgotten perfume. The hallway leading to the back of the house is narrow, with wallpaper curling at the seams and shadows in random places where family photos used to hang. There are no frames with photos in them left behind, just faint outlines on the walls like ghosts of something that was removed. I feel like I stepped into a time capsule that's caught between nostalgia and neglect.

The floorboards creak under my sneakers with every step I take. Looking down, I see how scuffed and dull they are, but my mind is already sanding, staining, and polishing them to shine again. The house isn't empty exactly. An old umbrella leans in the corner and a cracked lamp sits on the side table. None of it feels personal. It feels like the leftovers no one bothered to carry away.

When I enter the living space, my eyes widen because I don't know where to look first. The living room stands out the most on the right. There's no furniture arranged like someone meant to come back for it. No photos. No books. No signs of a life paused. It's just filled with things that didn't matter enough to take. Looking up, I notice the ceiling has a huge water stain like a bruise spreading from a potential leak. As I continue scanning the space, I see the old fireplace sitting in the corner, cold and soot-streaked.

Even with the disaster of this room, I can still see it coming to life.

I can see warm cream walls, the mantle decorated with fresh greenery, and a cozy sectional draped with a throw blanket. Turning to the left, I step through a narrow archway into the kitchen, and I practically gasp in horror. It's filled with yellow linoleum and chipped cabinets.

As the cloud that must've been covering the sun outside moves away, I see the light pour through the window above the sink, and I suck in a sharp breath. Dust mites fill the air like glitter, but still…*I can see it.*

It will be the kind of house that looks good on camera, but feels even better in person.

It feels like proof that imperfection isn't the end, but just the beginning.

I pause where I stand, circling to take one last look at the first floor, deciding I'm overwhelmed enough and don't need to see the second floor right now. My brain is already ten steps ahead thinking about the walls to knock down, blowing the budget and the timeline of the show.

It's clearly the largest project I've ever done, but instead of wanting to back away out of fear, I feel myself leaning in—embracing the hard, because this is everything I could have wanted.

I feel myself smile even when my stomach is filled with nerves, because this is an opportunity to make everything I want happen. A chance to prove to my mom that I am enough to take on something like this.

When I make my way back toward the front door, Jade is standing in the foyer with a raised eyebrow, waiting for me to say something.

"Well. It needs a whole lot of work," I tell her. "This is definitely going to be a long month."

She nods. "We thought the same thing."

There's a beat of silence before we both burst into laughter as we step onto the front porch. I feel like I can finally take a deep breath now that I'm out of the dust-filled house.

But it doesn't last long.

Because standing across the yard, smiling with Andrea, is the one person I never thought I'd see again.

Tucker.

One night of letting him charm me to the point I was naked and tangled in the sheets all fucking night with him back in San Francisco, only for him to vanish before sunrise. I understand if he had to go, but at least wake me up and say goodbye. No, I felt like nothing more than some kind of pit stop on his road trip through life.

And now he's here.

As if he can sense my eyes on him, he turns his head to where I stand. His eyes widen momentarily, before one corner of his lip twists into a smug grin. I'm too mad that he's standing here, on *my* property, for *my* show, to register and let that smile affect me the way it did the night he swept me off my feet.

I wonder if he thought about what he would say *if* he ever saw me again? I know I have. The chances were slim because neither of us are from San Francisco, and neither knew where the other was from.

Well, if he can be so cool about it, then so can I.

Stomping down the porch and across the yard, I make my way to where he and Andrea stand with the rest of the production team. When I stop in front of everyone, Andrea is the first to break the silence. "All right, let's get this quick meeting started. It's nothing major, more so just some introductions." She holds a hand out toward Tucker. "Tucker here will be your lead contractor on site."

"What?" I practically choke out, eyes darting between the two of them.

Of course, the universe would play this joke on me. Of all the contractors in the world, it just has to be him? It just has to be the man with *that* smile and *those* arms?

It's rude if you ask me.

Andrea is taken aback momentarily by my tone, and now she's looking between the two of us, assessing as if she's missed something. "You two should get to know each other because you will be working closely—"

"Oh, we've met," I interrupt, my tone sharp and a fake smile plastered on my face.

Tucker grins. "Briefly. She made quite the first impression."

"And he made none."

He takes a step closer to me, and my body tenses as he eyes me up and down. The smell of cedar and fresh soap hit me almost instantly, which is wildly unfair because he should not be smelling like temptation wrapped in denim when I'm this mad.

"I see you've traded the blazer that looks like you've been attacked by a highlighter for something else."

He's one to talk, wearing a white T-shirt hugging his sun tanned skin and a tool belt hung low on his hips. The smirk on his lips makes me wish I had a boiling cup of coffee in my hand to throw at his head.

I shrug, unbothered. "I didn't want to be responsible for distracting the crew on my first day with my good taste."

Avoiding seeing whatever look he has on his face after that, I look to Andrea, who has her hand covering her mouth and whispers something in Jade's ear. Jade is silent as she talks, looking from me to Tucker and back to me before nodding in approval for whatever she's telling her.

"So," Andrea says, clasping her hands together in front of her. "In past seasons, we've had a couple doing this together. It usually helps with B-roll content in filming."

"B-roll?" Tucker asks.

"That's the stuff that isn't related to actually fixing up the house. A little insight into who the people are outside of the project. It helps the viewers fall in love with them. And when viewers fall in love with the couple, they cheer them on from the other side of the TV and hope the project ends up being a win."

"Sometimes it adds a touch of drama," Jade chimes in. "Even the happiest couples argue over paint colors or the placement of a wall when the deadline is so tight. And we get to watch them overcome it together on screen."

"The viewers eat it up," Andrea emphasizes.

"Well, we knew going into this I'm doing this on my own," I say.

Andrea and Jade exchange a look before both of them smile widely, and my stomach flips.

No.

"We're thinking…a little on-screen romance subplot," Andrea says.

"I think the viewers will love it," Jade adds to encourage the idea. "You two have some weird chemistry happening here, so it works. And," she continues, voice higher to really sell it, "you already know each other. It's perfect."

My brows practically shoot up to my hairline and I scoff. "Me and him?" I shake my head in disbelief. "Are you suggesting I fake date him? No, thank you. He has the personality of a rusty nail."

"Rust adds character. You should appreciate that, no?" Tucker grins.

With my hands on my hips, I turn to face him. "You're enjoying this, aren't you?"

"So much," he says, drawing out the words while his smile only widens. "It's the only time I've been accused of being irresistible while standing in a field of weeds and sweat dripping down my back."

"No one said you're irresistible." I face Andrea again, hand out toward Tucker. "See? He's impossible."

Jade bounces where she stands, clapping her hands together. "This is so perfect."

"Listen," Andrea starts, stepping between Tucker and me, resting a hand on each of our shoulders. "You don't need to decide right now. We start filming in a few days, so you can sleep on it, talk through it, whatever you need." She removes her hand from Tucker's shoulder and faces me completely. "But from the few minutes we've been standing here and listening to you two together, I already know this is precisely what this show needs."

I swallow, my anger subsiding and nerves setting in again. "I'll think about it," I decide on.

I can't fake date Tucker for the cameras.

Not when my body still remembers how easy it was to let him in.

That night, I let myself believe one reckless, perfect night could be harmless and easy to forget. I didn't ask for promises. I didn't ask for more. But when I woke up, he was gone without a note or a quick apology scribbled on hotel stationary.

I tried to tell myself it didn't bother me.

But seeing him again…it isn't nothing.

He doesn't get to casually reenter my life like I won't remember how quiet it felt afterward.

There's no way in hell I can do this.

CHAPTER 5

WE DON'T BLUR THE LINES.

TUCKER

Seven Stools is quieter than usual for a weeknight, which is odd given that we have a couple of dozen people now scattered across different rentals around town. I'm not complaining about it—as long as they don't start arguing over the jukebox or convincing me that Fireball is considered top-shelf whiskey.

But I love entertaining them when that argument starts.

I enjoy working at the bar after a day of construction work. I started here the day after I turned twenty-one to help Griffin. He *hates* working evening hours because it attracts a different group of people that he doesn't have the patience for.

Me? I don't mind because I fit right in with them.

I'm good at both of my jobs and it keeps my hands busy.

When my hands are busy, it means my head is quieter.

I'm halfway through wiping down the pint glasses fresh out of the dishwasher when the bell chimes over the door. Griffin hates that bell, and every time it goes off, I smile to myself and add one more person to the count in my head.

Looking over, I see Nan strutting through the door like she owns the place. Some days, I wonder if she thinks she owns the town. She's everywhere; a gossip queen and professional meddler. She somehow always seemed to know things before everyone else does.

"Talkative Tucker." She beams, taking a seat at the bar. "Don't you look chipper this evening."

"I'm always chipper." I laugh. "What are you doing here so late? Don't you have your recorded soaps to watch?"

"They're recorded, Tucker. Means I can watch 'em whenever I please."

"Valid point."

"I'll take a glass of water, two lemons, and extra ice." She nods, and I shake my head, laughing. I fix her drink, setting it in front of her, then brace myself. Because if there's one thing about Nan we know, it's that she never shows up out of the blue without a hidden agenda. "So, how's your new tenant doing?"

And there it is.

"Don't know. I've been working."

Which isn't a complete lie. Between finishing up some projects around town before this big renovation starts, and working here every night, my hours blurred together.

"You mean to tell me that *you*—Talkative Tucker—haven't gone over there, knocked on the door, and introduced yourself?"

I sigh. "Nan, I worked all day yesterday finishing up a house then meeting the crew at the house on Redwood Ave for the show in the afternoon, only to wake up at the crack of dawn again today to lay foundation for Frank across town. Then I came right here. I don't know what to say other than I haven't even been home."

I know I'm the one who agreed to let someone stay at the apartment above my garage after Nan begged me, but deep down, seeing my new tenant will only make it clear that I'm no longer alone on my quiet property. Which sounds dumb, but for years it's been my sanctuary. It's the one place I can let my guard down. The one place where I can sit in my own grief without judgment or pity. The one place where I don't have to hide behind being the guy who makes people laugh.

No one has any idea how much time I spend actually trying to fool those around me.

I will never let anyone close enough to see through my jokes, to the mess underneath.

That would be dangerous.

Because if anyone really saw the cracks in my armor, there's no chance they'd stick around.

"Tucker," she groans, drawing out my name. "She's very sweet. Very pretty. The type of gal to bring sunshine into this town. You'll like her."

I freeze at her words. Not at the word *she*—I'd already swallowed that surprise. But at the rest of it.

Sweet. Pretty. Sunshine.

Only one woman in bright colors comes to mind. The one who seemed to slip under my skin before I could stop it. Truth be told, I haven't been able to stop thinking about her since the night we met. In any capacity. Scottie rocked my world in San Francisco—and again yesterday when I saw her at the house. It only confirmed that the spark I felt was something no one could deny or try to hide.

"That's nice," I settle on, grabbing the dish rag and wiping the counter.

"Careful," Nan warns. "You're coming off like Grumpy Griffin. Sometimes I think you prefer the company of your tools over—"

"At least they don't talk back."

She points a finger in my direction. "You can't fool me."

I feign shock. "I'd never try to do that."

"Pull out your phone so you can take her number down, smart-ass," Nan says. "And at *least* check in on her since she's been there for *well over* twenty-four hours now and the owner hasn't so much as stopped by." She dramatically rolls her eyes dramatically.

Nan tells me her number from memory like she's known it her whole life, while I type it in my phone.

As I'm about to put it down, Nan stops me. "Whoa. You didn't text her."

"I will when I leave here."

"That's like midnight."

I tip my head back, and exhale a sigh. "Fine."

ME

Hey. Nan gave me your number. Since you're staying at my place, I wanted to check in on you. Sorry, I've been busy with work and haven't stopped by.

I hold up the screen toward Nan. "Happy now?"

She shakes her head. "Real smooth. You're just as bad as Griffin with texting."

I scowl in her direction because there is no one in the world as bad as Griffin at texting. He doesn't even spell out full words and leaves you to decipher every message he sends. The word you, is literally "u."

"What do you want me to say? You asked me to check in on her, so I am."

My phone buzzes almost immediately.

UNKNOWN

Hey there. Thank you so much for reaching out. Your text came at the perfect time because I was hoping to get a chance to meet with you about the door to the apartment. It keeps getting jammed.

ME

Sorry about that. I meant to take care of it. I'll get it fixed tomorrow.

"Done," I tell Nan. "We had a conversation. *Now* are you happy?"

Her lips twitch like she wants to smile, but she stops herself. Sitting back on her stool, she crosses her arms over her chest.

"Almost. But she's a busy girl. Since she's awake and texting you, maybe you should bring her a burger from the bar on your way home. I doubt she made it to the General Store."

My phone buzzes again just as I'm about to concede to Nan's idea.

My fingers go numb around my phone and my chest drops so hard it feels like gravity just doubled. Hearing that Scottie is the one staying in the apartment above my garage is a whole new feeling.

The woman who laughed into my neck in a hotel room in San Francisco as I tore the bright yellow blazer off her.

A woman I left in tangled sheets because I didn't trust myself to stay.

A woman who stood in front of me yesterday morning and looked at me like I was nothing more than an inconvenient memory.

A woman I have not been able to get out of my head for a single fucking day since.

Nan clears her throat but I don't look at her. If I look at her, she'll see it—the shock. The way my pulse is suddenly everywhere.

Before I can write back or save her name in my contacts, my phone buzzes again.

I turn my phone again toward Nan. "Are you telling her to ask me this?"

"No." Nan covers her face with her hands and laughs. "You know I don't carry that cell phone with me anywhere. I don't need it when I remember numbers right here." She taps a finger to her temple as she stands from the barstool. "Let's just add this to the list of all the times I'm right. Which is always."

"I wouldn't go that far."

"Bring that girl some food and be a good landlord. They're harder to find than good lumber," she says, walking toward the exit. She pauses just before the doors and faces me. "I know you try to hide it, but I see you, Tucker. You have a habit of trying to keep to yourself. Try not to do that with her."

I don't get a chance to respond before she's out the door.

I look from the closed door and back down to the phone in my hand, staring at her message.

Would it be so bad if I just brought her home some food?

Not because Nan pushed and not because it's the polite thing to do. But because I know what it feels like to be dropped into a strange place and act like you're fine when you're not.

If I'm honest, it would give me an excuse to stop pretending I'm not already thinking about her. About the way I heard her laugh coming out of the old abandoned house.

It's just food, I tell myself.

Nothing complicated.

But the truth in my thoughts settles in my gut. I don't want this to be just about being a landlord. I want to see *her*.

ME

I can bring you something on my way home. It'll be late though...close to midnight.

SCOTTIE

Are you serious? That sounds perfect. You're a lifesaver. I'm swamped with work so I'll be up for a while.

ME

How does a burger sound?

SCOTTIE

So good! I can give you cash when you get here.

Yeah. I won't be taking her money.

For the first time in a long time, I can't wait to get the hell out of here.

It's just before midnight when I pull into my driveway, parking closer to my garage than I usually do. My headlights illuminate the gravel as I park my truck on the side of the driveway closest to my house. The air is cooler than usual for the summer, and the world is quiet. Exactly what I crave after working all day. The porch light I left on this morning casts a light glow across the yard. My body aches, and I smell like a mix of wood, whiskey, and grease from the kitchen. All I want to do is shower, grab a beer, and sit in the dark like a man twice my age.

Working two jobs means I'm barely home long enough to sleep, but now feels different. It feels like coming home to *someone*.

Except I don't go toward my door.

I grab the takeout bag from the passenger seat and look toward the apartment on my property that hasn't ever had anyone there.

The light is on, and my chest tightens before I even see her.

I make my way up across the driveway and up the steps, my pulse racing with each one I take. Stopping at the top, I hesitate for half a second. I know she's awake because she said she would be up late working.

Finally, I lift my hand and knock. The sound feels too loud in the quiet night.

I hear a shuffle on the other side of the door and see the doorknob jiggle, but the door doesn't open. She curses on the other side of the door as the handle rattles like she's fighting it.

"Step back. I got it," I tell her.

Reaching for it, I give the door knob a little twist and push it, and it finally gives way. The momentum forces me through the doorway and fully into her space. I stumble but catch myself as my eyes trail from the ground, to her exposed legs from the shorts she has on, and up to her face. Our eyes meet at the exact same time and for a suspended second, neither of us move.

It hits me all over again how unfairly beautiful she is.

She's not styled for an interview or a meeting with the production crew. That blonde hair I remember tangled in the hotel sheets, is now twisted into a messy bun. There's a softness around the edges that I didn't get to see that night in the city, when everything between us has been loud and fast and reckless.

Not long ago, she was a stranger I didn't allow myself to imagine a future with. Now, she's here and I don't know where to put the awareness of her without letting it show.

She's like an angel in the night that's just waiting to burn me alive.

I clear my throat. "Hi."

The air shifts between us the longer she stares at me. She finally blinks, as if coming back to the moment after learning *I'm* the one she was texting. Her shoulders relax a fraction and I can visibly see her breath. "Hi."

"I'm sorry about the door. I'll get that fixed for you tomorrow."

"So you're my temporary landlord?"

I extend my free hand in front of me, a smile on my face. "I'm Tucker, nice to meet you."

She raises a brow. "You're serious right now?"

"Deadly," I say. "I'm trying to build a reputation. Starting with a door apology and a handshake."

She laughs. And it's the type that makes me want to hear it again just to be sure it's real.

I lift the bag in my hand. "Oh, and a burger delivery."

Her laughter dies down, but the smile doesn't waver. "Thank you."

She steps forward to reach for the bag in my hand, and a mix of vanilla and something floral hits me, like her skin carries springtime with her. It draws me to her, but I try not to step too close. When she grabs the bag, our fingers brush for half a second. The contact is light, yet it sends a quiet shock through me, like my body remembers something my brain never fully forgot. It's familiar and dangerous as it settles into my skin.

"You're saving my night with this," she says, lifting the bag. "I haven't made it to the store yet."

"I figured."

She narrows her eyes and tips her head to the side. "Nan told you that, didn't she?"

"She heavily implied it."

A soft laugh slips out of her, and it loosens the tension in my body.

"So..." she draws out, biting down on her bottom lip and rocking back on her heels. "I'm sorry. I just can't believe that of all the people in this town, *you're* my landlord?"

I shrug. "It could be worse. I hear the other side of town has a moose that looks through your windows while showering."

She laughs, louder this time and its music to my ears. "Yeah. That's definitely worse."

All I can do is stare at her, feeling the smile widen on my lips as I take it all in. We both still stand here in the entryway of the apartment, unmoving, staring at each other while the air between us crackles. It's different from being at the house yesterday.

She's different.

"Do you...want to come in?" she asks.

It's casual, almost careless. Something in the way she says it feels like she's testing herself. The clipped answer and controlled distance on site earlier is gone. In place is something more uncertain, like she's deciding in real time how close she's willing to stand to me. And I don't know what shifted between yesterday and now. I only know this is the first time we've been alone since our night in the city, and the weight of it settles into me in a way I didn't expect.

"If you're sure."

She nods, stepping back to make room for me. "Just ignore the chaos. I haven't unpacked my bags."

I follow her to the small kitchen table I had put in when I first moved here, thinking I'd have it in me to allow someone to rent this, but never did. Until now. Until her. She has her laptop open and papers scattered beside it. She moves it all to the side to place the takeout bag down.

She pulls the container out of the bag. She looks at me and then gestures to the other seat. "Sit, Tucker." And the way she says it makes me melt. Like I'd obey anything she told me to do at this point.

This is so fucking dangerous.

Moving to the drawer, she brings out a knife and a plate before cutting the burger in half and sliding the other half to me.

"Oh no. This is for you."

"I'm not eating this entire burger at midnight." She chuckles. "We can share."

"Wouldn't be the first time," I say before I can stop myself.

Her breath catches. Just barely, but I see the way her cheeks pink.

"I've been thinking about what the producers told us." She looks from her plate to me. I feel the tension creeping into my body again because I know what she's talking about. I've been thinking about it nonstop myself. "I don't know what to do. I don't know if it's going to work."

"What do you mean?"

The edges of her eyes soften just a fraction. "Us doing that whole dating thing in front of the cameras. I just want to focus on doing this house, and…" Her voice trails off as she averts her eyes from me. "Doing it right." Then she faces me again. "But I keep thinking about it since she brought it up. About what it would look like."

Little does she know, I *could* do this with her—for her.

I can be whatever the producers want me to be. I might be too broken for a real future with anyone but faking it? That I can do.

I already do it every day.

I shrug. "I think it's your show, not mine. I'm just the guy making sure the house doesn't collapse on national television."

"I hate that it matters this much, but…" She trails off, as if thinking of her next words carefully. "This show…it's my shot. I can't afford to be stubborn about every little thing."

I watch her carefully. The way she takes a steady breath, I don't say anything more to allow her to keep going.

"I don't want the story of the house to disappear behind something messy or fake." She sighs, looking down at the plate in front of her. "But I also don't want to spend the entire season fighting them."

I sit here. Frozen. Because I didn't expect any of this.

With how she acted toward me earlier today, I thought she'd shut down their idea. I thought it would be a hard no.

When her eyes meet mine again, I see it.

That familiar spark.

That reckless softness I remember from the bar in the city.

"I think…" She clears her throat. "I think I'm done pretending I don't already know what my answer is." My pulse kicks hard against my ribs as she continues. "I don't love the idea. But I don't hate it either."

"If this is what it takes to help you, I'll do it."

Her head tips to the side. "Just like that?"

"Just like that."

She narrows her eyes, curiously. And it hits me. The difference between seeing me on the property to seeing me here. She doesn't trust me because I left her. I fucking left that morning without a goodbye or asking for her number like it didn't matter —like *she* didn't matter. At the time, I thought keeping it casual would protect me, but now all I feel is guilt.

And I carry enough of that with me through life.

But if this is a chance to show her that I'm not that guy, then yeah, this is the least I can do.

"I'm not a complicated person," I continue when she doesn't say anything back. "I'm also not the type to flake when it comes to my agreements. Just tell me what you need, and I'll be there."

She searches my face with a long look, trying to figure out what my angle is, but there is none. She exhales a breath that resembles relief, brushing the loose strands of hair that have fallen from her messy bun out of her face. "If we do this, we keep it simple. Professional. No mixed signals like last time."

And there it is. Confirmation of my thoughts just moments ago.

No mixed signals like last time.

That hurts more than I want it to, because there were no mixed signals that night. If it wasn't already late, and I wasn't exhausted, I'd open that can of worms and tell her exactly how I felt about her that night—how I didn't want to leave, but Dallas was eager to get on the road and back home to Bluestone Lakes.

I nod anyway. "Got it."

"On camera, we give them what they want. Off camera..." She trails off, still staring at me. "We don't blur the lines."

I smirk. "I'll do my best."

The corner of her lip twitches like she's fighting a smile. "You're impossible."

"But I'm reliable."

Her gaze softens, just for a moment. She picks up a french fry and pops it into her mouth. I can see by the way she's sitting there in silence that she has a dozen questions.

"Scottie?" I say, forcing her to look at me again. "I might not be the guy you'd want with you in front of the camera, but I am the guy who can keep things together. I'm hardworking and a good friend. If you'll allow me to be that," I say with a wink, keeping the conversation light when it's anything but. "But I want you to know, you can count on me for this project, for this arrangement."

Her expression is unreadable as her eyes flicker over my face like she isn't sure if she wants to believe me. But I can tell she does. I see the shift in her eyes.

"That's all this needs to be," she says. "I'll let Andrea and Jade know we're in when I talk to them in the morning."

I nod, standing from the chair. "I'll see you soon, Scottie."

I have no idea how I'm going to make this work when the cameras are rolling.

But as I head back to my house, I tell myself I can do this.

Fake is safe.

Fake is easy.

If I ignore the hollow ache sitting in my chest, maybe I can almost believe it.

CHAPTER 6
HE'S LIKE A LABRADOR IN WORK BOOTS.

SCOTTIE

After three hours of tossing and turning last night, I ended up in the little kitchenette with my notepad and paper, drawing rough sketches of the house and the way I envision it when we're all done.

It wasn't the best idea to skip sleep, but knowing I'm staying on *his* property and that he agreed to date me for the show, there was no way I was drifting off anytime soon.

It's absurd, really.

People run into exes and one-night stands all the time.

But Tucker isn't just anyone.

And most people aren't in a position to pretend to date their one-night stands.

That night felt like it meant something, even though I knew better. He kissed me like he meant it. He memorized every inch of my body like he didn't want to forget, then disappeared the next morning.

Now, the two times I've seen him, my stomach turned over so hard I could barely breathe. He looks the same as he did the day I met him. He's got this charm I can't fucking escape, no matter how hard I try. My body and my brain seem to be in a constant battle when he's around. One is begging to touch him again—let him in. While the other hates him for making me feel used that night.

No wonder the producers see chemistry.

There's no way I'm going to be able to make this look real for the cameras, feeling this way about him.

I laugh out loud in the empty room. "Get it together, Scottie. It was a one-night stand." I roll my eyes. "What the hell did you expect from a stranger?"

Now I'm talking to myself. Great.

Exhaling, I reach for my phone on the table to send Andrea a text about our decision to go ahead with her idea, only to pause when I see a flood of notifications waiting from my recent post revealing the news about the season and start of filming.

This is amazing news! I'm so proud of you!

Can't wait for this next season now!

You are goals! I can't wait to watch you Nail It!

The comments don't stop. Hundreds of affirmations from strangers who think they know me, but truly only know the perfectly curated, bright-and-bold version I let the world see. The version that makes me feel like I'm enough despite what my mom always reminds me of.

It's only then that my smile falls. If only everyone could see me now—hair sticking out in three different directions, mascara smudged, and an old baggy tee with the neck stretched so taut that it looks like a U-neck.

Oh, and shaky hands at the thought of pretending to date *someone.*

I shake off the negative thoughts and send the text to Andrea before I can go back on my decision, because I have to start getting ready to head out to be at the house on time. It's day one of filming, and we're doing all the before shots of the inside and outside of the home, plus a few short interviews needed for the first episode.

Once I'm showered and hair done in loose waves around my

face, I rummage through the clothes I brought with me. I hold up a solid light green V-neck blouse and shake my head. My eyes widen when I look down, and I smile when I see I remembered to pack one of my favorite shirts.

It's a vibrant button-down blouse that bursts with painterly shapes in hues of coral, violet, teal, and tangerine. Its colors come alive in the outdoor sun but remain bold indoors. Since we're going to be walking around the broken down home, I settle on wearing a pair of light wash, high-waisted denim jeans that are loose enough to move freely. Finishing the look with a pair of all-white sneakers, I step back to assess myself in the mirror.

It's nothing my mom would approve of, which means it's perfect.

Squaring my shoulders, I give myself one last look. "Let's do this."

I need caffeine and sugar. So, with time to spare, I decide to detour to Batter Up, the bakery and Cozy Cup, the coffee shop next door to the bakery, which Nan had told me was a must.

My nerves are staging a full-scale mutiny over filming today.

When I step through the front doors of Batter Up, the scent hits me first—butter, sugar, and something that resembles caramel. While the woman with long copper-red hair, tied back in a ponytail, helps another customer with a friendly smile, I take that moment to browse the display case. Rows of muffins, croissants, and cupcakes gleam under the glass.

"Hi, what can I get for you?"

"Everything," I say before I can stop myself. "Everything looks too pretty to eat and I could use a hefty dose sugar and zero judgment."

She laughs, and it's soft and welcoming. "Lucky for you, we

specialize in both," she answers proudly before the kitchen door swings open, slamming against the counter behind it. The woman behind the counter and I both snap our heads in that direction.

"Oops, sorry. Swung the door a little too—" The woman stops, taking me in, her eyes widening. "No way! Are you Scottie? As in my favorite DIY influencer, Scottie?"

I blink, caught off guard. I'm used to being one of many names on someone's feed or an account you scroll past, but not the one you single out. Not someone's *favorite*.

"Your favorite?" I say with a small, disbelieving laugh slipping out. "I'm glad you like my stuff. I just…wow. That's really nice to hear."

"Are you kidding? Some of those accounts out there make everything look…unrealistic to attempt. Yours feels doable. Like real people could pull it off."

Her words are opposite of what I normally hear. Where my mom says things aren't polished enough or impressive enough, this stranger just told me that's what she loves most about it. And that's what I've always tried to show. If I can do it, anyone can.

"I appreciate that."

"And," she continues, "I saw your post announcement for the upcoming season of *Nailed It or Failed It* and saw it was going to be filmed here, and I squealed!"

"I'm excited about it," I say, smiling wide and matching her energy. "I'm just trying not to throw up on my first day of filming."

The first woman hands me a box filled with six assorted muffins. "Then you need the breakfast of champions."

Looking down through the little window hole of the box, my mouth waters thinking about how good these will be. "Thank you. How much?"

She waves me off. "On the house." She extends her hand across the counter. "I'm Lily, by the way. I own the bakery."

"Wow, thank you. This place is so cute," I say, looking around. "I feel like I can get lost in the smell alone. You need to bottle it up and put it in a candle."

She puts both hands on her hips. "You know what, we should!"

"And I'm Blair," the other woman says, extending her hand across the counter. "I promise I'm not really a crazy person. My sister and I both follow you and love your work. I'm just so excited you're here."

"Me too. But definitely nervous," I admit.

"Oh, that's right, you're working on that old abandoned house on Redwood Ave., right?"

I nod. "It's actually my grandmother's old place. The house is in rough shape."

"You're not kidding," Lily says. "But word around town is you have a good crew!"

Blair faces Lily. "If Tucker is part of that crew, she's going to need a steady sugar drip to keep up with him."

"Facts," Lily says with a finger pointed in Blair's direction.

My stomach twists at the sound of his name. I hate how quickly my brain thinks of his easy grin, full confidence, and the feeling I felt every time his eyes met mine last night. The easy way out of this and pretending his name doesn't do something to me, would be to change the subject or bring up muffins or something. But the words tumble out of me anyway.

"You…you two know Tucker?"

"He's my cousin," Lily says, facing me. "He's a pain in the ass, but the good kind. And he's really good at his job."

Blair nods in agreement. "You're either going to want to laugh at him or throw something at him. Oftentimes it's both."

A short, surprising laugh slips out before I can stop it, and I press my lips together like I can shove the sound back down. Apparently, I'm not the only one who's noticed his talent for getting under someone's skin.

"Don't worry," Lily says, noticing my expression. "If he gives you any trouble, remind him that I'm the only reason he gets free cinnamon buns."

"And if he gets grumpy," Blair adds, "just feed him. He's like a Labrador in work boots. Carbs will calm him down."

I smile. "I'll have to keep that in my back pocket."

"Good. And in case you need the reminder, you'll do great today."

"You think?"

The smile that spreads across Lily's face is proud—too proud maybe, for someone who only knows me through a screen. It makes me feel off balance and caught somewhere between unease and comfort.

"You have that look people get before they do something that scares the hell out of them," Lily says. "Scary means it's something that matters."

My throat tightens, and I don't know what to say back because she's right.

This isn't just nerves about a strict schedule or a camera crew following me around. It's the aching hope deep inside of me that this might finally be the thing that changes my life around. That changes how people see me—how my mom sees me. This isn't just a successful renovation if I pull this off; it's proof that I didn't make the wrong choice when I didn't go down the corporate path and chose to follow my heart.

It's proof that I can build something solid enough to be able to stand on my own.

That's actually what's at stake.

Not the house.

Me.

"And if you need a place to hide from the cameras, we've got you," Blair chimes in.

I blink, gaze bouncing between the two of them. "But you barely know me."

"Town rule." Lily shrugs. "If you stay here, even for a short period, you're one of us. Which means we have your back."

Some of the tension in my shoulders ease and warmth surges through my chest at the idea of a friendship blossoming with these two. I don't really have true, good friends back home. I have the type of friends who reach out when they need something from me. When they need help with refinishing a dresser, or questions about how I got a particular brand deal online. Other than that, I never hear from them. And it hurts. It really fucking hurts to feel like you don't have anyone.

A smile crests my lips. "Thank you."

Lily reaches into her back pocket, pulling out her cell phone. "Here, put your number in and I'll text you so you have mine."

"Send it to me, too, Lil," Blair says, leaning over her shoulder before looking at me. "I was once the out-of-towner here too. We have to stick together." She smiles brightly.

Normally, I'd hesitate. I'd tell myself it's too soon to trust people who feel this kind so quickly. But coming here already meant saying yes to something out of the ordinary for me. So I push past the instinct to keep my life small and type my number in her phone before handing it back to her.

"Have the best first day filming, girl," Lily says with a wave. "You're going to do amazing."

"Agreed," Blair says with a curt nod.

"Thank you," I say, smiling as I turn and leave the bakery.

When I step onto the sidewalk again, I breathe in the mountain air.

I still don't know for sure if I'm about to change my life.

But I do know I'm ready to try.

EPISODE ONE

BACK TO THE FOUNDATION

Welcome to season seven of Nailed It or Failed It.

Last season, we successfully Nailed It *in the Big Apple with the renovation of Ollie's Dining. It's now time for us to visit the cozy, small town of Bluestone Lakes, where one home isn't the only thing getting a fresh start.*

Scottie Monroe is a DIY influencer and queen of color. Her first big project was fixing up her parents' home while still living in it. Now, she's taking on her most personal project yet: her late grandmother's old house.

Tucker Daniels, local contractor and the man who knows his way around a power tool, is going to help make this happen.

Together they'll tackle a house that's seen better days. You'll see laughter and a whole lot of drywall dust as they discover that love, just like any great renovation, takes vision, patience, and a little demolition.

So grab your hard hat and maybe a box of tissues, because this season we're not just rebuilding this old, abandoned house—we're building a dream home.

CHAPTER 7

IN THREE, TWO—

SCOTTIE

When I pull into the driveway, vans and cars line the road leading to the property. The film crew is busy setting up cameras and standing in small huddles, discussing whatever they need to.

My eyes scan the land, trying to take everything in. People are scattered everywhere. Cables run through the overgrown grass like veins through the heart of chaos. The land isn't a quiet oasis anymore. It's more like a living machine where every sound is competing for attention. The buzz of the generators, the radios crackling as people talk into them, and everyone moving with hurried purpose.

My nerves spike as I take it all in.

You're in over your head, Scottie.

What the hell were you thinking, taking this project on for national TV?

I hate that my mom's voice is in my head right now.

I've been in front of a camera before at my house for tutorials and livestreams, but this is so much different. This feels bigger. Louder.

"Scottie!" a voice cuts through the commotion. Andrea's

making her way to where I'm rooted at the top of the gravel driveway with a clipboard tucked under her arm and a coffee in each hand. She looks composed, which must be a requirement in television because how can she be this calm in the chaos. "Ready for your close up?"

"Define ready?" I say, forcing a smile I hope looks steadier than it feels.

She giggles. "This is perfect. Stay just like that—charming and terrified. It looks great for the camera."

She hands me one of the coffees in her hand and I take it despite having one with my muffin on my way over here. She adjusts the clipboard in her now free hand before guiding us toward the porch. I follow her, looking past her at the old house standing quiet and still, waiting for the first hammer to break the silence.

My next big project.

My everything or nothing moment.

"Okay," Andrea says, flipping through papers on her clipboard, before she does a double take over my shoulder. "Oh, good. Tucker is here, too."

I turn around to look over my shoulder and find him already staring at me. He's leaning against the side of a work truck in worn boots, dark jeans, and a gray fitted T-shirt stretched across his broad shoulders. His tool belt sits low on his hips, and he looks exactly like you'd picture a small town contractor to look when showing up to work.

God, he looks good.

When I texted Andrea that we would go forward with the fake relationship subplot she had pitched, she was ecstatic. I still can't stop overthinking what we're doing here. Even though we agreed not to blur the lines, I'm terrified he's going to try to cross all of them. The longer I stare at him, the more I have to remind myself that it's just for the cameras. Nothing more.

He starts walking toward us like he owns the ground, and I instinctively grip my cup tighter. The world seems to slow down the closer he gets, like the air thickens around us to mess with me. My stomach does a flip, and I hate that it does. I shouldn't feel *anything* when it comes to him. But every time he's close, I have the unsettling thought that rebuilding this home might not be my biggest concern.

He stops in front of me and smiles. "Hi."

"Hi," I say back, my words softer than I intended them to be. Like he's sucked all the air from my lungs just standing here.

"All right, lovebirds," Andrea says in a playful tone and we both turn to face her. "For the intro episode, we'll introduce both of you before filming a thorough walk through of the home. You can also give us a sense of what you see in each room as we go and give the viewers something to look forward to."

Tucker shifts next to me, crossing his arms over his chest and listening to every word.

I nod. "Got it."

"Make them fall in love with you early on. Big chemistry, and maybe a little playful arguing. Viewers eat that up."

"We can make that work," Tucker says first. "But the main focus will remain on the house and its story, right?"

My knees nearly give out on me with his question. We *just* started, and he immediately remembered my worries about how the fake relationship in front of the cameras would take away from the house. And here he is asking the question I was too afraid to ask myself.

"Yes. Of course," Andrea says quickly. "But if the viewers fall in love with you, it'll be great for the ratings."

Tucker doesn't reply, and I look from Andrea to him. His eyes are fixed on her as she looks down at her clipboard. He looks as if he's assessing her motives and searching for something he can't seem to place in her.

He turns his body to face me, his gaze finally leaving Andrea. "So, what's the plan, boss?" he asks quietly. "Are you walking them through first, or do you want me to stay in the background until you call me in?"

The word boss shouldn't do anything to me.

But it does.

I straighten my spine. "I'll start the introduction to the house out here. Once we get inside for the walk through, I'll bring you in. Structural, load bearing walls…you know, all the things I'm not allowed to pretend I know so you have your part in this."

His mouth curves into a grin. "I appreciate your commitment to honesty."

Andrea claps her hands once. "Perfect. That's exactly what we want. Easy and natural."

Tucker grins to the side of me, crossing his arms over his chest. "Oh, you'll still get arguing though. She's got plenty of experience pretending to like me. Should be easy."

"I don't pretend," I say sweetly. "I just work really well with difficult material."

"I'm, uh, going to let the film crew know you're ready and we can start rolling in a few," Andrea says, giving us a quick, approving look before walking away.

The moment she's gone the space feels different.

Like we're trapped in a bubble and the rest of the world faded back a step.

"So," I say, breaking the silence between us. "Is your crew here?"

"Nope."

"Don't you need to wrangle them up or something?"

He glances down at me with a half-smile tugging at his mouth. "I'm good right here."

There's something in his voice that makes me feel fully at ease. As if my body knew I wasn't before and just hearing that solidified it for me. He studies me for a second, my grip tightening around the cup in my hand. Instinctively, I roll my shoulders like I'm trying to shake something loose.

"Are you nervous?"

"A little," I admit. "It…feels weird."

"How so?"

I don't answer back right away, because my thoughts can't even be put into words. When I look at this house, all it is to me is a project. My one opportunity to catapult me into something more and be taken seriously.

Reality is, it's more than that.

I've been here before—spent time here before.

This house is part of a family I don't remember.

But I can't tell him all that.

Not yet.

"It feels different when it's not just me and a tripod with my phone," I continue.

He studies me for a moment, and this time his features soften. There's an understanding in his eyes that wasn't there before, despite barely knowing me. "You'll do amazing," he says with certainty.

I feel the heat creep up my neck at the confidence he sees in me and avert my gaze to avoid letting him see. Deep down, under the voices telling me I can't, I *know* I can do this. I *know* I have what it takes, even if the house is worse than anything I've worked on. Even if the deadline is so tight. I have to believe I can do this.

Andrea jogs up to us with a few crew members trailing behind her. "Ready?" she asks, her tone chipper and excited.

I look up to Tucker and he's already smiling at me. "She's ready," he answers for me.

"Perfect." Andrea claps. "Let's start out here with just Scottie. And before we go inside, we can set up on the porch and introduce Tucker. Does that sound like a good plan?"

I nod in agreement.

Tucker raises a pointer finger in the air like he's in class and has a question. Andrea chuckles and waves a hand for him to ask. "So...like, what am I saying?" he asks, looking around. "Is there a screen with a script for me? Or whatever you call those things?"

"A teleprompter?" Andrea confirms.

He snaps his fingers and points to her. "That's the one."

"They're a bit of a pain to carry around the renovation sites so we've always gone without one," Andrea says with an easy shrug. "Will that be a problem?"

Tucker opens his mouth to answer, but stops. His jaw tightens, and he rubs the back of his neck as his eyes flick once toward the camera crew.

Placing a hand on his shoulder, I feel my palm burn through his fitted T-shirt, and offer him the same confidence he offered me moments ago. "He's got this."

"That's the spirit."

She waves over two crew members, who clip a mic pack to the back of my jeans before discreetly placing the mic inside my blouse. Closing my eyes, I inhale and exhale a calming breath while straightening my spine. I allow myself to exude the confidence I know I have deep down.

The camera operator takes their position, pressing a button and adjusting the camera toward me. "In three, two—" He points at me, and a little red light blinks on.

Showtime.

"Hi, I'm Scottie Monroe, and welcome to *Nailed It or Failed It.*" I smile, probably a little too wide. "This season, we're taking on a home that's not just another project to me. This one is personal." I turn, angling my body to face the home. "This house belonged to my grandparents. It's filled with memories and the kind of charm you can't buy in a store." I face the camera again. "But it's also…well, let's just say it's seen better days."

Nervous laughter escapes my lips, and when my eyes do a double-take, I spot Tucker behind the camera. There's enough distance between us that he's not hovering, but just enough that he can hear. His arms are crossed over his chest, muscles popping as he stands there tall and strong.

When the corner of his lip twists into a lopsided grin and he offers me a slight nod, I feel a calm wash over me as if his mere presence is what I need to get through this.

I prepared all night for what I'd say today, but the longer I stare at Tucker, the more everything I rehearsed goes out the window.

I avert my gaze to look back at the house. "My goal is to honor what was, while creating something new. This project won't just be about making it look good on the outside, but also about making it feel whole again. A place to fill with memories," I say, swallowing as I remember Tucker's words from the night we met. "When I think of this house, I'd love to see it shine again. To bring it back to life. I want this house to represent second chances. Every wall we rebuild, every color we choose… it's about reminding ourselves that broken and weathered things can still be made beautiful again," I say, facing the camera again.

And this time, Tucker isn't standing behind it.

We wrap up this first part, and as I turn to make my way to the front porch, I find Tucker again, standing off to the side leaning against his work truck, watching from a distance now. Our eyes meet, but it's hard to read what he's thinking.

Then…just the corner of his lips twists up in that lopsided grin again.

Just when I was starting to breathe again, he has to go and look at me like *that*.

Keep it together, Scottie.

No distractions.

No feelings.

I almost laugh to myself at how easily I believe my own rules.

CHAPTER 8

DO YOU EVER STOP ARGUING WITH ME?

TUCKER

I had to walk away.

I just needed one minute to catch my breath after hearing her talk and do her first segment for the cameras. She's…captivating. The way the light catches her golden blonde hair—bright and soft at the same time. Just watching her in front of a house that's standing on its last leg, she somehow manages to bring life back into the property again.

I mean, hell, if anyone can bring this place back to life, maybe it's her.

Watching from off to the side, I see the crew gathering up their things to make it toward the front porch. Andrea scans the front lawn, finds me, and waves me over. It takes me a minute, but I push off the old work truck and allow my feet to cross the yard to where everyone stands.

With every step I take, my mind can't help but travel back to that night with Scottie. I know I agreed to do this whole fake dating on screen thing with her, but I'm struggling to stuff down the way my body reacts to her. The need to be near her—to look at her.

"We're going to start your segment out here," Andrea tells me. "Let's get a mic pack on you."

They waste no time tucking a mic pack into the back pocket of my jeans and snaking it up the front of my shirt to clip onto the neckline of my T-shirt. I can't help but smirk when I notice Scottie's eyes trailing to my exposed abdomen when they lift my shirt.

"See something you like?"

Her gaze snaps up to mine, glaring. "Just figuring out how I can grab hold of that cord and strangle you with it."

I laugh. "You wound me, Scottie."

She rolls her eyes, and we both face Andrea. "You two act like you've been married for years. It's wild."

I almost snort. Married? Hell, I don't even date. I don't build anything with someone that can fall apart in my hands. I'm much better off keeping my life simple and unattached to anyone, otherwise I risk someone knocking down every wall I've ever put up.

This arrangement with Scottie…it's nothing more than that.

The film crew gives us the signal they're ready. We both set up, and the camera faces us. "We're rolling in three…two…" And they point toward us, and a red light flashes on.

"This here is my…contractor, Tucker Daniels," Scottie says. Andrea rolls a finger in the air, urging her to continue. "But he also happens to be my boyfriend," Scottie adds hesitantly, and Andrea nods in approval.

I lift a hand to the air in greeting. "Hey there. Guess I'm the lucky guy who gets to turn all this"—I gesture behind us at the house— "into whatever she's dreamed up."

Scottie tilts her head to look at me. "You mean whatever *we've* dreamed up."

"That's what I said, babe."

The crew behind the camera chuckles.

Looking down at her, I smile when I see her eyes still on me, so sharp I swear they can shoot daggers right through me. "You didn't," she says through gritted teeth.

I wrap an arm around her, pulling her into me, and I laugh. "No, but it sounded better when you said it."

Scottie clears her throat, and I don't miss the way her cheeks pink as she looks back to the camera. "For our walk through, let's start with the porch. It's supposed to be the most welcoming part of the home, and as you can see," she says, gesturing around us. "It's kind of scary to be honest."

She laughs and just like every other time I've heard that sound from her, it settles into me. In an easy and familiar way, doing nothing to help my focus on the cameras in front of me.

"When I picture this porch finished," she continues, "I can see a hanging loveseat swing off to the side here." She smiles as she looks from the empty space to the small roof above us and back to the space. "A nice throw blanket over—"

"A swing won't hold."

Her eyes widen briefly, as if taken back by the suddenness of my voice. "What do you mean?"

I point to the roof over the porch. "This structure is very old. And I can't see what's under those panels yet. But based on what I can see from here, it won't safely support the weight of a swing and two people."

Her face falls and her shoulders dip for a second before she catches herself, smoothing it out like it never happened.

"I don't want to put something here that could hurt some-one," I add.

"Okay," she says, nodding once.

"But talk to me about the rest of it," I say, tilting my head toward the porch under our feet. "If the swing's off the table for now, what's your plan for the space itself?"

She straightens her posture, relief threading back into her expression. "I'd like to refinish the entire thing: clean white slats and wider posts. I'm going for the classic but polished look."

I shrug. "Polished often means expensive. It also means impractical."

"Practicality isn't the goal for the porch, *Tucker.*" She says my name with a warning tone. "A welcoming beauty is what I'm going for. You can tell a lot about the inside of the house from the outside."

I hold up my hands in defense. "I get that. All I'm saying is we should consider using treated lumber."

She exhales, closing her eyes and pinching the bridge of her nose. "Do you ever stop arguing with me?"

"Nope. It's part of my charm." I wink.

"You're insufferable."

I lean in close, and the faint smell of coffee and vanilla hits my senses. I let it linger before I cover the mic on my shirt with one hand and let the other rest on the small of her back. "Yeah, but you secretly love it," I whisper.

She doesn't step away from where my hand rests on her back, but turns to look directly into the camera. "Like I was saying, this porch is one of my favorite spots," she continues, her voice steady. "I want to create a place that feels cozy yet welcoming. A place where someone can sit, enjoy their coffee, and just breathe in the fresh air."

The cameras cut out for a moment as Andrea tells us we're going to head inside now. I don't register much of anything she's saying because the only thing I'm thinking about is how I can't seem to keep my hands off Scottie, and how she's *not* pushing me away.

And right now, I'm taking every minute I can.

Because standing next to her, watching her talk about bringing light to something broken, and turning this old house into something worth saving…

It makes me wonder if I could be saved.

She wants this house to represent second chances.

And maybe I do, too.

The camera crew follows us in as we head through the front door. Dust fills the air as we walk through, kicking up everything in the process.

I've thought about the inside of this place a dozen or so times whenever I came to this property for quiet and to look at the stars. I built this image in my head that the inside was perfectly put together, and it was just the outside that was weathered. But standing here now, I realize there was never anything to preserve. It's hollow—like someone packed up the memories of the place and left the shell behind.

I understand that more than I'd like to admit.

I follow Scottie through the house, stepping carefully over the warped floorboards.

Once we enter the open living space, Scottie stops and faces the camera. "This is the living room. It has great bones, but I want to open up this wall," she says, tapping the one to the side of her. "It will create a more open-floor concept, and I'd also like to add custom built-ins around the fireplace with modern lighting," she says moving around the space. Then she stops in the middle and points a finger at the ceiling—and I cringe. "And most definitely investigate the water damage in the ceiling before replacing any drywall."

The longer I stare at the ceiling, I wonder if any second now will be the moment it decides to give way and fall on top of everyone in this room. It looks dangerous. It looks ready to cave.

She finishes by telling the camera about the type of couch she can see and where she would place a TV before crossing the room and heading toward the archway leading into the next room.

"As you can see, this is the kitchen."

The tone in her voice pulls my attention away from the mustard yellow scattered around the space and onto her. The last time I saw this exact look on her face was back in San Francisco. It's one that radiates pure joy.

"If you can't tell, it's a total gut job. It's wildly outdated with mismatched cabinets and old linoleum flooring. But even with it looking like *this*…there's something about a kitchen that makes me feel alive." She pauses, looking around and closing her eyes as if she envisions everything in this one space. I'm transfixed by the way she looks right now that I can't tear my eyes away. "When you think of a family gathering, it's usually in a space like this. Everyone surrounding the island and enjoying appetizers over the holidays."

And then just like that, something shifts in her features.

A sadness takes the place of the spot where joy just lived. I know what she's thinking because I've gone through the motions a hundred times myself.

A memory just hit her.

One she can't place, but hits just the same.

She shakes her head, looking at the camera and you can see by the way her eyes suddenly widen that she's nervous they caught that raw moment of vulnerability.

"I have to agree on the sentiments of the kitchen," I say, forcing the film crew to swivel the camera on their tripod to where I stand off to the side. "However, we can't get rid of this wall."

"Of course we can't," she says lightly, but there's a tight edge under the smile she flashes for the camera. "But every great kitchen renovation starts with the sentence *'we can't do that.'* Which basically means, we can."

A laugh ripples from behind the camera.

"Every great kitchen also starts with the house still standing," I say, crossing the kitchen. I knock on another wall off to the side. "But this one definitely has to go."

"We can't just rip out any wall, Tucker. I want that one gone," she says, pointing to the first one, then points back to where I stand. "That one gives the room character."

"Mold is a kind of character?"

She glares at me. "You're infuriating sometimes."

"And yet…devastatingly handsome."

I hear more snickers off from behind the camera and we both turn to face them. Andrea is whispering something to Jade before directing their attention back to us.

"Perfect. Let's keep that flirty and playful vibe."

Scottie rolls her shoulders like she's resetting herself, then turns back to the space around us. She then carefully steps closer to me. "Is there anything we can do to make this work?" she asks quietly.

The cameras are still rolling and the crew is practically breathing down our neck, but suddenly it doesn't feel like a show anymore. She stops performing for the lens, and starts looking at the room like it might actually matter what happens to it.

"Talk to me, Scottie."

She faces me, and there's a sudden sad and pleading look in her eyes. "I don't know much about this house, but before I came here, my dad told me how, ever since my grandfather died, a light went out in here. My grandma tried for years to bring it back, but she was never able to. I know it sounds silly, but I really think that opening up the space will help make this place feel alive again."

Something about the way she says it makes me want to rush out the door, find any tool I can and cut windows everywhere just to bring the light back for her.

I move closer without thinking, stopping at her side and letting my hand settle on her lower back again. She doesn't flinch. "How about this," I start, pointing to the window over-looking the sink and she follows. "We can widen that window into a farmhouse style that stretches longer than the length of the sink. We can even frame it out higher since we have some over-head room to work with."

"Yeah?"

She looks up at me and I nod. "And we can definitely talk about the wooden pillars over the beams."

"You sure?"

"Yep."

Her mouth curves, subtle but real. "See?" she says to the camera. "This is why you bring in someone who actually knows what they're doing."

"Only when it comes to beams."

"And mold."

"And mold," I agree with a laugh.

For the next hour we keep moving through the house, falling into an easy rhythm. We disagree just enough to make it interesting and agree often enough that it feels natural.

Which is exactly what this is supposed to be.

Pretend.

Except standing close to her in every room we stopped in and watching her light up when an idea clicks into place. Or the way her hands move when she's mapping something invisible in the air—it feels dangerously close to something real.

EPISODE TWO

THE FRONT PORCH SHOWDOWN

This week on Nailed It or Failed It, *Tucker and Scottie are tackling the sagging front porch, or as Tucker likes to call it, the death trap with charm. Years of neglect have left this once-stunning porch drooping so severely that even the crew has been hesitant to step onto it.*

But fixing the porch isn't the only thing at stake here.

Between sawdust and second chances, there's something else lingering in the air.

Last week, sparks flew faster than a power sander when these two shared the screen. This week? Let's just say the sparks aren't cooling off anytime soon.

Scottie is determined to keep the aesthetics, while Tucker is convinced the whole thing needs to be rebuilt. We can't tell for sure if Scottie would rather keep their relationship off screen, but the banter and chemistry between the two is hard to deny.

Let's get to work.

CHAPTER 9

BUT CAN YOU HIT THE NAIL?

SCOTTIE

We're wasting no time getting this project started.

After filming the intro pieces and the walk through two days ago, I walked through the house the next day, without the cameras or crew, to remove some old things left behind. I was hoping to find some personal belongings from my grandparents, but I couldn't even find a single photo.

Last night, I spent the entire evening holed up in the apartment drawing sketches and layouts for each room. I had a general idea of what I wanted after the first walk through but I've figured out exactly what we need to do and the best way to execute it so we can finish this project on time.

As I was finishing my last set of notes, my dad called. He didn't ask for numbers or timelines. He didn't question whether I was ready. He just wanted to hear how it felt to be at the house. He ended the call telling me how proud he was of me, like it was already a given. Sometimes that kind of uncomplicated faith in me has made my chest aching in a way I don't know what to do with. There's been times I've resented him for it and how easily he believed in me and how much simpler it would be if my mom was able to do the same.

After the call with my dad, I emailed all my plans to Andrea. She asked me to break it down by episode, and I did. Her reply reminded me that much of it will take place off camera, but if we can highlight the big stuff, my plan will work beautifully.

Pulling up to my grandmother's home today feels different.

I feel ready.

It probably has something to do with the award-worthy pep talk I gave myself this morning. *Focus on the house.* That's it. Smile for the cameras, laugh when Tucker tries to put on the charm, and absolutely *do not* let my heart, hormones, and other uninvited emotions get involved.

I basically had a full-blown staff meeting with my brain, heart, and body before arriving today.

My brain is on board—she's rational. Sometimes.

My heart's on probation.

And my body? She RSVP'd yes and then didn't bother to show up at all.

So, yeah, today's focus is the house. If it's not, I lose the only shot I have at proving I can do this. I need to stop focusing on the man currently standing on the other side of the yard, staring me up and down with his stupidly nice smile, who somehow makes every scene we've recorded so far feel a little too unscripted.

Now would be a good time to bring my body up to speed on the meeting.

What a traitor she is.

Of course, he got here before me, leaning against the porch railing like he owns the place. The sun hits his stupidly perfect and messy hair that looks like he just rolled out of bed. It's unfairly attractive. He's infuriatingly handsome. Smug. And yet every time he grins, I feel like he's chiseling away at my armor. For half a second, I forget why I promised myself I wouldn't notice him like this. He's wearing a pair of dark denim jeans that roll at his ankles and sit just above the rim of his work boots, paired with a solid white T-shirt. Both of which look well-worn, like he's built dozens of houses in this uniform of his.

My pulse skips as I start to walk to where he and Andrea stand at the house. I reach into my pocket and pull out my pack of Sour Patch Kids and empty a few into my palm. I stuff the bag into my pocket and pick through them, placing the yellow and green in my other pocket and pop the others in my mouth one by one with each step I take.

Looking up, I make eye contact with Tucker. He raises a hand to wave with that Labrador in work boots energy. Suddenly, it feels like my heart is auditioning for the town marching band.

Nope. We are not doing this today.

I'm supposed to be focusing on the blueprints tucked under my arm, but somehow all my focus is standing a foot away from me with a hammer and forearms that should be illegal.

"Good morning," I say, coming to a stop next to them before popping a blue Sour Patch Kid into my mouth and dusting the sugar from my hands in front of me.

"Oh good, you're here," Andrea says, looking at me and then assessing me with a narrowed brow. "You look different today."

I feel my cheeks turn red. Today's vibe was to look like I belong here, as if I'm ready to handle anything thrown my way. I wore my oversized overalls that have years of wear, from paint splatters to wood stain. I've paired it with a plain white tee and a hot pink headband that matches the pink work boots my dad got me as a gift for my birthday one year.

"I'm ready to get my hands dirty so I dressed for the part." I smile at her, before glancing at Tucker.

"Porches don't care about your outfit," Tucker says with a smirk.

I know he means it practically, but his words still land like a challenge. And something in his tone gets under my skin like he's not talking about the porch at all. It feels as if he's daring me to prove I'm more than the outfit I'm wearing. Or he just wants me to fire back.

But I don't.

I'm here to be taken seriously. So I straighten a little and remind myself that I'm here because I can do this.

"Okay." Andrea claps her hands. "Let's get the porch segment started. Scottie, you're going to start by briefly reminding us of your vision for the space. After that, you two will get started on what you need to do and pretend the cameras are not on you. Essentially, we'll be recording all day, taking clips, and cutting them for the episode."

I nod. "Got it."

"I'll get everyone ready," Andrea says, walking to where the film crew is huddled off to the side.

Tucker moves to stand even closer to me, facing the house the same way I am.

"Are those boots made for construction?"

I look down at them before turning my head to look at him next to me. His eyes are fixed on the home, but I don't miss the smirk on his lips. "For your information, they are very versatile. I can build a house *and* post an outfit-of-the-day in them."

He shakes his head, laughing, as the crew comes back to mic us up for the day.

We settle into a stance as if we've done this together for years, even though it's only the second day with the cameras on us.

When a member of the crew lifts Tucker's shirt to expose his abdomen, I suck in a breath. I can't help but take him all in again. Six foot something of broad shoulders, rough hands, and maddening muscles that make him look like a lumberjack catalog model without the beard. My body reacts to the sight in front of me, remembering my hands roaming along every ridge of muscle when I was on top of him in that hotel room. I adjust my stance, tightening my legs together because I feel it right to my fucking core. When our eyes meet, he's caught me staring—again.

How can one look make me feel this way again?

My eyes trail up to his face. He's got a smirk that almost tells me he can read my mind. I want to smack him for it, but the ache between my thighs stops me from feeling anything else. With our eyes locked together, I reach up to unclip the one side of my overalls, exposing my crop top to let the crew work on my mic pack. His eyes trace the movement of the crew member's hands brushing against my skin. It's in a professional way, but Tucker's eyes darken, nonetheless.

"Arm's up," the man says so he can snake the wire through my crop top.

I lift my arms, meeting Tucker's stare again. It's hot and burns through my skin. He bites down on his bottom lip and I feel my body coil at the way he's equally devouring me and the way he hates someone else is touching me under my shirt.

"All set," the crew member says, completely oblivious to everything happening right now.

"Thank you," I choke out.

Chancing a glance back at Tucker, his eyes never leave me.

This is fake—strictly for the cameras.

That's what we agreed on. That's what I repeat to myself like a mantra every time he looks at me like that—like he knows me in a way the cameras never will.

Taking a breath, I face the camera, away from him. I *have* to look anywhere but him to will this tightness in my body go away. I pull out a few more Sour Patch Kids, filter them and pop an orange one in my mouth before putting the few yellow and green in the other pocket.

"It's a little early for sweets, don't you think?" Tucker says.

I shrug, emptying a few into my palm and picking out the yellow and green. "Sour Patch Kids are good all hours of the day. Besides, they keep me from saying something I'll regret."

His gaze flicks to my mouth. "Does it work?"

I feel my breath catch in my throat and I almost choke before I swallow down a mix of sweet and sour. "Sometimes."

"Hmm. Good to know."

"Okay, we're getting ready to roll," Andrea shouts to the entire crew, before looking between Tucker and me, voice lower. "Now, just…do what you do."

Which is reality TV code for *please flirt without acknowledging that we're asking you to flirt*.

I move closer to Tucker without thinking—clearly my body is more than willing to cooperate after all that. The air around us shifts, and even without touching I feel the heat of him through my entire body. I try like hell to ignore it, focusing on the man standing behind the camera giving us a countdown with his hands before the red light turns on.

I start by sharing a summary of what I said when we filmed our first walk through about the porch. Once I finish, I glance toward Tucker. "What do you think, Tucker? Can you work your magic?"

He smiles at me, and it feel so fucking real that it almost knocks me backward. He's looking at me as if cameras are not even on us. Or he's just really damn good at faking this.

"Depends. Are you planning to help, or just tell me where to swing the hammer?"

I narrow my eyes. "I have plenty of experience swinging a hammer."

He stares at me, not responding. I'm about to turn my head back to the camera to talk more about the porch when I see his eyes dip, tracking from my face to my hands, and lower, like he's mapping something he shouldn't be thinking about.

"But can you hit the nail?" he finally says with an even tone, but there's something underneath it now—something deliberate.

Heat creeps up my neck.

I know *exactly* what he's implying.

What's worse is that he knows I know.

I straighten my shoulders anyway, refusing to give him the satisfaction of seeing me flustered. I smile sweetly. "I don't miss. I'm *very* precise."

The corner of his mouth twitches and he fights a smile. He

steps closer into me, not enough for the cameras to notice, but enough that I can feel him all around me.

"Good," he murmurs. I feel his breath against my neck as he's leaning in. My pulse stumbles and my body reacts in ways I absolutely did not approve during this morning's staff meeting. "I would hate to have to show you how it's done."

The crew loses it behind the camera, and I faintly hear Jade murmur, "This is gold."

Tucker doesn't look away or move.

Neither do I.

"Okay," I say, forcing myself to step out of this bubble he's put us in, and force myself to keep smiling for the camera. "Then why don't you walk me through it. Front to back. What's the plan from the contractor's perspective?" I cross my arms over my chest.

He puts more space between us. *Thank god.*

"The first thing should really be removing this entire thing and starting from scratch."

I shake my head. "Not happening. Next."

He narrows his eyes briefly before releasing a sigh. "This porch isn't safe, Scottie."

The way he says my name and the stark change in his tone pulls something in my chest. I think it's the first time I've ever really heard him get serious. And this isn't him doing this for the show. It's not the cameras on us right now. This is all him, looking at me like he's responsible for what happens next when it comes to my safety.

I've spent years learning how to smile through pressure and spin hesitation into confidence. But the way he's standing here now with a pleading look in his eyes, makes it harder to tell myself this is just a creative disagreement.

When I don't answer, he shakes his head. "You say the porch is the first impression of a home. Well,"—he extends a hand to the space around us— "this home's first impression is going to land someone right in the hospital with a broken ankle. If this was up to me…we'd start by replacing the damaged boards and then reinforcing the steps. Structure always comes first. Yes, you will need new railing. I know you want this to be the perfect farmhouse, but you need to keep it practical."

His serious tone slaps me as if he intended to hurt me with his words, and I feel my mouth part in shock. "That's—" I stop myself, looking from him to the camera and back to him. I cross my arms, anchoring myself in the familiar resistance. If I give in too easily, it looks staged. If I dig in too hard, it looks personal.

Under it all, there's a quieter truth I don't want to name.

It's that Tucker knows where my weak spots are. Not because he's trying to find them. But once—just once—I let him see me without the polished confidence.

I clear my throat, moving away from him and placing my hand on the worn railing that's currently there. "I think…we should start by assessing the structure. That way, we know what actually needs to be replaced."

"All of it will."

"Stop exaggerating."

Just to prove my point, I give the porch railing a light tug, barely more than a test. The wood groans in protest, and I hear a sharp snap before I can register what I've done. The railing gives way completely and my balance goes with it. I open my mouth to let out what I assume would be a scream as my foot slips back, scrambling for something solid.

Tucker moves on pure instinct.

So fast I barely see him. His hand shoots out, gripping my waist and I feel the air shift where his palm lands.

In this moment, there're no cameras. It's just the two of us frozen in place—me teetering and him with two hands holding me upright. I can see the exact moment he realizes where his hands are. His jaw is tight as his eyes trail down to where he's touching me and then he pulls back.

I steady myself and straighten slowly.

I realize I'm still holding the broken piece of railing in my hand. Releasing a breath and averting my stare, I toss it to the ground before turning to face him again. "Okay, maybe you're not exaggerating."

When I clap my hands together to brush off the dirt, I expect him to have a smug and satisfied grin, but it's the opposite. It seems as if he didn't want to be right. There's something unspoken in the way his eyes look distant, as if he's lost in another world while staring at me. It feels like he's not really seeing me. He's seeing something else.

He moves without speaking, making his way to the railing that just broke off. He crouches down, running his hands along it as he inspects it. I feel myself hovering, watching the way his shoulders move and the way he mutters construction type things under his breath. But I can't make any of it out because my brain is transfixed on how beautiful this man is.

I'm not supposed to think my fake boyfriend is beautiful.

If circumstances were different between us, then maybe I could.

He moves with ease—assessing and thinking before standing to full height and facing me again. "This porch isn't the worst I've seen," he admits. "But it's not safe long term."

"Is there anything that can be saved? It has character."

"It has rot," he counters. "Different vibe. Let's try to go for safety first?" he says skeptically, raising a brow.

I tilt my head to the side as if thinking it over, but he's right.

I know he's right.

And just because I want the playful Tucker back, I smirk. "And aesthetic second?"

His eyes warm, and I visibly see the way his shoulders relax. The corner of his lips turn up just the slightest bit and I know it's working. "I can build you the prettiest porch in town, babe. I just need you alive to enjoy it."

My heart skips a beat at the way he so casually calls me *babe*.

That traitorous little thing.

He reaches behind him into the back pocket of his jeans and pulls out a pair of work gloves. "Here. You can use these."

I step over the broken railing carefully, until I'm standing in front of him. Our fingers brush when I take them, and the contact lingers longer than necessary. "Are these your extra pair?"

He shakes his head. "But you need them."

And just like that, the faint smile falls and he's back to having that distance in his demeanor. I can't make out why, but it's weird and unsettling. It's like he cares about what I think all of a sudden, and he hates that he's right about needing to trash the entire porch and start fresh.

I'm ready to step away from him when I feel his shoulder brush mine as he points to the railing. "Now…if we rebuild this with heavier posts, it'll hold. You want classic whitewash, right?"

I turn my head to look at him, but his eyes are still fixed on the porch.

"Uh, yeah," I say, stuttering over my words because I feel like I'm getting whiplash. Is he working with me here? "Something warm, like a soft white, maybe ivory. I want it to feel cozy."

He nods. "I can do that."

This time the grin that takes over my face is unstoppable. I've spent so much of my life believing that what I wanted wasn't possible, and having Tucker say it so easily feels like someone quietly rewriting a rule I've lived by for a long time.

Looking over my shoulder, I directly face the camera, ready to lighten the mood again. "See? He can be agreeable when he tries."

I smile up at him as he looks down at me, eyes glinting from the sun.

There's a pause, and my heart thrums in my chest with each second his gaze stays locked on mine. "Keep smiling at me like that and I might start agreeing more often."

CHAPTER 10

THINK YOU CAN HANDLE FINISHING WHAT YOU STARTED?

TUCKER

By mid-afternoon, the front yard looks like a lumberyard and a war zone had a baby. Even though Scottie was reluctant to see the safety hazards of the porch, she agreed to getting rid of almost everything, and I agreed to give her the vision she sees without anyone getting hurt.

The old porch is finally gone, with boards stacked in neat piles.

Scottie stands in the middle of all of it. The messy bun she showed up with earlier today somehow messier with pieces angled around her face. She looks like sunshine in pink work boots. All brightness and warmth, but tougher than she looks.

Her cheeks are flushed, and she reaches up to wipe her forehead with the back of her wrist, leaving a streak of dust. "Looks good."

I step closer to her, brushing a piece of hair away from her eyes. "You mean, *we* look good."

"You've been holding that line all morning, haven't you?"

"Maybe." I shrug, and look down at my watch. "Levi should be back with the materials any minute now."

I sent Levi and two of my best crew members off earlier to

grab the supplies necessary for the porch after assessing how bad the structure really was. It felt easier this way. It keeps the cameras focused on us while the real logistics happen behind the scenes.

"We're doing this all today?" Scottie's eyes widen. "You can't be serious."

I laugh. "You're the one on a time crunch. This will be likely one of the easier projects compared to the inside of the house. We can bang it out in one go."

Her cheeks flush instantly, and I catch it before she can smooth it away. She looks like she's deciding whether she wants to murder me with a two by four or pretend she didn't hear it at all.

She chooses the second option when her gaze slides past me and she squares her shoulders. I clock all of it—every controlled movement and how she's trying like hell to prove my words don't have any effect on her. Watching her pretend she's unaffected has been my favorite game since she showed up here in town.

I step closer, just enough that my breath brushes her ear. "Is that what you want, Scottie?" My voice stays low, lips grazing the shell of her ear. "To bang it out in one go?" Her body tenses, but she doesn't move—doesn't pull away. "Think you can handle finishing what you started?"

"Professional," she says in a warning tone. "Remember?"

I should stop.

This is her giving me the chance to pull it back and laugh it off.

I can't find it in me to take it, though.

My eyes stay on her, unblinking, like if I look away now I'll lose something I didn't know I was holding.

"Yeah. I remember." I step a fraction closer—just enough for her to feel it. Just enough that the space between us closes more. "But let's not pretend," I add, keeping my voice low and honest. "That word doesn't make you any less distracting." Her breath stutters, and I see the exact moment she forgets what she was about to say. "I'm trying to behave. But you standing here like that? Acting like you don't know what you do to me?"

Her lips part in shock, and it takes all the restraint I have not to press my lips to the spot I remember drives her crazy on her neck. The one where I can feel her pulse on my lips and know that the effect we have on each other is mutual.

But I step away and shrug. "I can't help it."

My hands curl into fists at my side because the urge to reach for her and touch her is so strong.

She opens her mouth to say something, but stops herself. There's this part of me that wants to hear her say my name—in a whisper, a plea, *anything*. But the sound of the truck beeping behind me pulls both of us from the moment. We both snap our heads to find Levi backing up the driveway.

I turn and make my way toward the truck before I can dig a deeper hole for myself. But I don't miss the way she's still standing there when I move away.

Like she felt it, too.

Helping Levi and the rest of the crew unload the truck, I keep my hands busy. It's the only way I've managed to ever work through anything I'm feeling. I tell myself that physical work has always been my way out when my head gets too loud.

Right now, it's screaming.

And it has everything to do with the woman standing a few feet away from me, popping Sour Patch Kids into her mouth before putting on the gloves I gave her. I don't want my stomach to flip when I see her or have this urge for my hands to touch her. That's not what this fucking is. So I shove every feeling and thought down. It never makes it disappear, but it gives it somewhere to wait.

"Scottie," I say, and she tips her head up to look at me. "We can get all of this started if you need a break."

She shakes her head. "You can't tell me we're going to bang this all out in one go, and then tell me to fuck off."

Well, so much for shoving everything down.

I hold up my hands in defense, smirking. "I'm just saying, most people don't volunteer to keep going when they don't need to during the hottest hour of the day. Levi and I can handle this part."

"I'm not most people," she says, tilting her chin up.

Yeah. No kidding.

"Besides," she says, stomping to where the circular saw is set up, reaching for it like it's a dare. "I can handle myself."

And then she winks.

She fucking winks—and it takes everything in me to keep my hands to myself.

When she reaches for the trigger of the saw. "Whoa. Hold on," I say, my feet rush to stop her. Not because she's incapable, but because I don't trust myself to stay calm if she gets hurt on my watch. "Have you ever used one of these before?"

"I'm a fast learner."

"And you like your fingers, right?" I lean in close to whisper. "You know, to handle yourself."

Fuck.

She's making me feel completely unhinged.

But the glare in her eyes tells me she could cut the wood in half without the saw just by looking at it. "You're impossible."

"I'm whatever you need me to be," I say, holding the saw. My words carry a double meaning. "But I'm also in charge of keeping you from cutting off a limb on national television."

"It's my show."

"Then let's keep you around for all the episodes, yeah?"

The camera crew chuckles in the background, pretending not to listen. Honestly, we've been so lost in the work that I keep forgetting they're recording the entire day to clip the pieces together for the one-hour episode.

Scottie removes her gloves, and crosses her arms over her chest. "If you want to take charge of cutting the wood, then fine. What can I do?"

"You can measure and mark the boards for me."

I reach into my tool belt and pull out the measuring tape. I step closer and place it directly in her hand. Our fingers brush— barely. It's enough that I feel the warmth of her skin before she curls her fingers around the tape.

She looks down at it, then back at me. "You can't be serious."

"Measurements are the backbone of construction," I say, grinning as I crouch down to organize everything where I need it to go.

What I don't say is that this puts her right here with me.

I want to feel her in my space, distracting me up close and not far away.

"Please," she scoffs, rolling her eyes before leaning forward as if taunting me. "You just don't want me using power tools because you're afraid I'll outshine you."

She doesn't back away, and I know I have to look away before instinct takes over and I start memorizing every detail of her, but I can't do it. I trail her body—the line of her neck and the way one side of her overalls falls over her shoulder. I can't fucking look away.

"You caught me," I deadpan, trying to keep my voice even. "Your skills deeply threaten me."

She smiles, and for a second it doesn't feel like teasing.

It feels…easy.

We fall into a rhythm.

She measures. I cut.

Every time she leans over a board, hair slipping loose from her messy bun, I have to remind myself to look anywhere else. I have to remind myself not to reach for her and brush the strands away from her beautiful eyes.

I'm literally going insane.

And to think, this was my fucking idea to keep her close to me.

What's driving me crazy the most isn't the heat or the long day we've already had. Because I'm used to this work day in and day out. But it's her. She's a mess of sweat and sawdust, and somehow she's still trying to keep that perfect image together for the cameras. Every time I glance up in her direction, she's checking her reflection in her phone camera or making sure her mic is sitting just right, like if she slips for even a second, the world will see something she doesn't want them to.

And the worst part?

I get it.

I see it.

"So how long have you been doing this?"

She glances up. "Construction?"

"No. I mean, yes. All of it. Renovating things. The show." I spread out my arms to showcase the yard around us. "All of this."

She pauses, as if trying to think of what to say, clocking the camera aimed in our direction before straightening her spine. "I can't remember when I first discovered my love for it. But I remember it started when I found an old dresser on the side of the road and wanted to refurbish it for my bedroom. After that, I wanted to redo my whole room to match. I gutted the entire thing and learned everything from the internet. My dad thought it was the greatest room in the house." She smiles down at the memory, looking down at the wood and measuring tape in her hands. "He let me do more rooms in the house. I shared *one* before-and-after picture on my private social media account and it went crazy with people loving it. He had this idea that I should start my own DIY design page, and I ended up doing our entire house."

I nod, smiling, trying to focus on the work in front of me.

But all I'm registering is the passion in her voice for what she does.

"I didn't really have a niche at the time. It was a mix of design work and projects. I wanted to do it all," she emphasizes with a bright smile, like she's tryly talking about something she loves. "It took off like crazy. I started getting some brand deals with it, too. Turns out I liked the challenge of making something feel like home when it wasn't yet."

"What made you stick with it?" I ask, adjusting the saw blade even though it doesn't need it.

"I like proving people wrong." She sighs, as if it hits too close to home for her. "And I like fixing things people give up on."

I turn to face her. She's still looking down at the boards.

"I like it," I say.

She faces me, a hint of a smile on her lips. "What about you? Building houses isn't easy either. How long have you been doing this?"

I stiffen, just a fraction, keeping my eyes on my hands as I slide the board through the saw. "A long time," I say.

She waits for me to say more. I can feel her eyes boring into the side of my head, but I don't elaborate.

"What got you into it?" she presses gently.

There it is. The question I always dodge. It's not that I don't want to talk about it—okay, I don't want to talk about it. All it does is stir up old memories I don't want coming to the surface. Old wounds that will never heal.

Just when I think about some bullshit excuse to say, the generator coughs, sputtering once before roaring back to life. I seize the moment and hold up a finger to Scottie before turning to Levi off to the side. "Levi, can you check that?"

"Yep," he says, jogging to the generator.

I don't turn back to Scottie as I bend down, resetting the saw and moving lumber around my work station. She doesn't go back to the topic or press the issue, and I'm thankful. Some things stay buried not because they're forgotten, but because digging them up would cost more than I'm ready to pay.

After a few minutes of silence, Scottie cuts through my thoughts. "So…how precise do you want these cuts?"

"Within an eighth of an inch."

She looks at the measuring tape closely with narrowed eyes, and then at me. "I was thinking more like…a general vibe."

I bark out a laugh. "A vibe? Are you planning to eyeball all the measurements?"

"Please, Tucker. That's how I've always worked. All vibes."

"Sounds chaotic."

She sticks out her tongue playfully. "I call it art."

I stare at her for a moment, before shaking my head and laughing. "You're lucky you're cute."

The words are out before I can stop them.

The air around us goes quiet and Scottie freezes with the pencil in her hand, hovering over the board. She doesn't look up, and her shoulders draw in a fraction. I should tack on a 'kidding' or 'don't read into that.' But I don't.

I let it sit there between us.

Cute is the safest word I could've chosen. Anything more honest would've cracked this thing wide open.

"What?" she says, barely above a whisper before looking up at me. "You said I'm cute?"

I tilt my head. "Did I say that?"

She nods. "Pretty sure that's what I heard."

Instead of saying anything more, I grab a stack of lumber I just cut and bring it over to the porch where we'll use it. If I stay close to her, staring at her, I won't stop.

Cute doesn't fucking come close.

Cute is a lie I tell myself so I don't say beautiful, or perfect.

When I come back for another pile, she's still standing in the same spot with the pencil in her hand and looking like she's deep in thought.

That's when I know.

I didn't just flirt with her, I shifted something between us.

"Babe," I say like a fool but the word feels too natural in my mouth. She snaps her head in my direction. "Ready?"

"Yeah." She snaps out of it. "I'm ready." She moves quickly in a jog to catch up to where I stand. She quickly morphs into a ready stance, inhaling and exhaling a breath as she looks at the clean slate in front of us now that the old porch is gone.

She picks up a board, and I follow with another.

I don't even know what her plan is here, or if she's ever built a porch before, but I'm following her regardless.

"Can you pass me the drill?" she asks, holding her hand out without looking at me. I hand her the drill and her fingers curl around the handle, and for a second we're both holding it. I pull my hand away. This is too much for one day. She volleys it around in both of her hands, assessing it. "Thank you."

"Do you need me to show you how to use it?"

She stands, turning around to face me and pops her hand on her hips. "If you even think about trying to mansplain a power tool to me, I will staple your mouth shut with the nail gun."

I laugh. "At least I know you know how to use it."

She narrows her eyes before walking away. I let my eyes trail her body. Even with the slightly oversized overalls, I can still make out the roundness of her ass with every step she takes. I have to force my head not to let my thoughts travel to the way it felt in my hands that night.

But it's too late.

"Are you sure you don't want me to do this?" I ask as she walks back. She has that sour candy in her hand, popping two in her mouth before crouching down to get started.

"Nope. Got it."

"Don't strip the nail, babe."

Her head snaps to face me, and the moment she sees the amusement on my face, her eyes narrow. But it only lasts a moment before a flicker of defeat flashes on her face. If I blinked, I would have missed it. She squares her shoulders and looks around to see where the camera is, and the confident woman I know is back immediately. She lines up the bit, presses the drill to the wood and squeezes the trigger. The sound is wrong immediately. The metal shrieks and the screw spins uselessly.

"Dammit," Scottie mutters under her breath.

I move before I can think.

Then I stop.

I pause just behind her—close enough to feel the hesitation ripple through her body and enough that if she says no, I'll hear it.

"Easy," I say quietly. "You're forcing it."

"I'm not. I've used a drill a million times before today."

"I know. Just…hold on."

I lift my hand slowly, not touching her yet. I give her the choice of accepting my help. When she doesn't pull away, it's all the permission I need. My hand settles over hers and her breath catches the instant our skin connects.

"You have to let it work for you. You need to add pressure, but not too much."

My voice drops without permission and my body remembers things I shouldn't be thinking of at the moment.

She swallows. "Is that supposed to sound dirty, Tucker?"

The air between us hummed louder than the commotion and generators around the property. I should step back, but I couldn't seem to get myself to move.

"Did you want it to sound dirty, Scottie?"

She doesn't answer. Instead, she clears her throat, adjusting her grip beneath mine. I guide her hand again as the drill hums without a shriek and the screw sinks perfectly into the wood.

"See?"

She exhales, turning her head to look at me over her shoulder. She sucks in a sharp breath at the proximity. My eyes trail to her lips. I'm so close that if I lean in just enough, I can taste the memory of the last time my lips were on hers and experience it all over again.

But she backs away, standing up and away from me. "Are

you always this bossy?" she asks, running her hands down her overalls.

I wink. "Only when I'm right."

"Well," she says, taking the drill fully from my hands now to reclaim her space. "Don't get used to it."

"I wouldn't *dream* of it."

The porch is finally starting to look like something worth standing on. We spent the entire day replacing every rotted board, rebuilding the steps, and framing out the new railing.

Unclipping my tool belt from my waist and tossing it into the passenger seat of my truck, I turn around and find Scottie staring at the house. She has her arms crossed as her eyes roam over every inch of the work we've put in today. The setting sun catches her hair at just the right angle, lighting the blonde to a gold, stopping me dead in my tracks.

I'm proud of the work she did today.

It's not just about the porch and watching her get her hands dirty. It's the way she held her ground when I fought her to gut the whole thing. The way she didn't give up when the boards fought back. The way she listened, learned, and adjusted without giving up control of the vision.

She didn't just imagine this place.

She's building it.

And watching her do that does something dangerous to me.

I look down at my watch and wince. I'm now late for my shift at Seven Stools. I live on Griffin's bad side, even though I know it's all fun and games, he can never truly be mad at me.

"Do you have somewhere to be?" Scottie asks, and I snap my head up, not realizing she moved from where she was standing.

"Yeah." I gesture toward the road. "My shift at the bar starts soon."

"You have two jobs?"

I look toward my truck, hesitant to admit why I work so much. Saying it out loud would mean revealing my cracks, and I'm not sure I'm ready for that yet.

But maybe if I told her, she'd stop hiding behind that perfect smile for a second.

All day, I've caught myself wanting to ask questions I shouldn't ask. Why does she need this show so badly? Why does she put on that polished act for the camera, but when it's off, she relaxes as if she's been holding her breath the entire time we're recording? It doesn't sit right with me. Not because I think she's fake, but because I see the parts she's trying to bury.

"Keeps me out of trouble," I settle on, turning to face her with a smile on my face.

"You don't strike me as the trouble type."

"That's because you haven't spent enough time getting to know me."

Her cheeks turn that perfect shade of pink as she averts her gaze to the ground. There isn't a single camera on us right now since they're packed up and being put away. She opens her mouth to speak, but stops herself. She stares at me for a beat, and I'm frozen in place, waiting with bated breath for whatever she wants to say back to that.

Say something—anything that opens up to me, Scottie.

"You should go. I wouldn't want you to get fired for helping me," she says instead.

"I don't get fired." I toss her a wink. "I just show up late and work faster."

"That doesn't make any sense, but sounds very responsible for someone like you."

"Someone like me?" I feign shock. "I'm a model citizen. You're the one who wanted to flee the scene of the crime after exceeding the legal limit of laughing at the bar."

She laughs and, for a moment, it feels like we're inside a bubble no one else can reach. The memories of the night we shared, lingering between us. It's an unfiltered laughter, the kind that doesn't match the polished version of her that the world gets to see.

It's a laugh so real that it knocks the air right out of me.

"Have a good night, Scottie," I say, making my way to my truck.

Just as I open the door to jump in, she stops me. "Hey, Tucker?"

I turn around and see she's exactly where I left her. "Yeah?"

"Thanks for…everything today."

The corner of my mouth lifts, and there's that grip in my chest again. "I told you I'll be whatever you need, Scottie. I'm here to help you. I…*want* to help you."

She grins and gives me a quick nod before turning back to the porch.

"And I'm sorry," I add, forcing her to face me again.

"For what?"

"That we can't do the swing on the porch you wanted."

She waves me off. "I think it's coming along perfectly. It would have been nice to have the hanging swing as a place to relax, but hey, that's what they make rocking chairs for, right?" She smiles and it nearly takes me out, before facing the house again.

I stare at her for another moment, taking her in. I'd stand here all day just looking at her if I didn't have a shift at the bar. I've been late to work plenty of times and walked away from plenty of things that mattered less.

This is the first time that walking away feels like the hard choice.

CHAPTER 11

THE ONLY THING I'LL BE
SIGNING IS A LIABILITY WAIVER.

TUCKER

"You're late."

"Griffin," I say, shaking my head and making my way around the back of the bar. "My shift starts at five, which means I have four minutes remaining before you start paying me."

He eyes me before looking me up and down before the bell chimes over the door. Griffin groans, but I ignore him and turn around to see Dallas walking in with Poppy and Lily beside him.

I smile—a cheesy one—seeing my best friend and my two cousins walking in. Dallas Westbrook moved here with his daughter at the end of last year when he needed a break from the major leagues. He was looking for a breather, but ended up coaching the kids here in town. I've had the honor of assisting him in coaching the kids. It gives me something else to do— something else to keep my schedule packed during the season.

Dallas is also the only one outside of my family that I've ever opened up to.

It was after one of the little league games. The date on the calendar always weighs heavily on me but it felt even louder than the crowd that day. He noticed before I could try to hide it. He was calm and patient. Not wanting to break through my walls if I wasn't ready. Instead, he just stayed and listened. He's the kind of person who sees your worst days and doesn't turn away.

Now, he's dating my cousin, Poppy. They're happy—like, *really* happy. Which is great for me because he's like family now.

"Well, well," Dallas says with a lazy grin, headed for his usual stool before he takes a seat. "Look who's slumming it with the rest of us mortals."

"Can someone fill me in?" Griffin says, arms out wide.

"Talkative Tucker here is the lead contractor for that little fixer upper show," Dallas says.

Griffin moves to grab a bottle from behind us to pour Dallas a drink, and then narrows his eyes at me, so many questions floating through his head. "That part I know."

"Which means he's going to be a bigwig TV star now."

Poppy laughs. "You're going to be signing autographs behind the bar in no time."

"The only thing I'll be signing is a liability waiver."

Everyone laughs, including Griffin, which makes me smile. Hearing my family and friends laugh is the only thing that keeps me going most of the time.

"We met Scottie a few days ago," Lily says. "Well, Blair and I did when she stopped in for muffins. She is exactly what the internet says she is…a walking ray of sunshine. I wanted to bottle it up." She laughs. "And I know this sounds nuts, but even just the few moments she spent in the bakery, I felt like my day was better just from meeting her."

She's right. That's exactly what Scottie is—a walking ray of sunshine. I think about how I spent the whole day with her in a house so dull and lacking any sort of shine, yet she somehow made a place that should have been condemned a long time ago, feel alive. I don't even think Scottie realizes she does it.

"She's…easy to work with," I say casually.

Dallas laughs. "That's the most suspicious compliment you've ever given."

Lily smirks, raising an eyebrow. "And from what I hear, you two were bickering like an old married couple before lunch."

I groan, running a hand over my face. Of course the whole town already knows. If one person saw and told Nan, everyone knows.

"It's not like that."

"Right," Lily draws out. "I'm all ears for you to elaborate on that. Do you know her or something?"

My eyes snap to Dallas on their own accord. He stares at me for a beat before his eyes widen, as if he immediately knows what I'm thinking. I've never talked to Griffin, Lily, or Poppy about my one-night stand in San Francisco. But, poor Dallas, he had to hear about it the whole ride back to Bluestone Lakes.

Sixteen fucking hours of me bitching.

Mostly about my regrets for not leaving my phone number, and how I fucked up so bad. At one point, I even asked him to turn around. I needed to find her again, but it was too late. We were too far from the city at that point and Dallas needed to get back.

"No," Dallas breathes out in shock.

I nod my head once.

Dallas runs his fingers through his hair, taking it all in. "You're serious?"

"Dead serious."

"Fuck."

I see Griffin and Lily looking between the two of us, and Poppy has a hand over her mouth, chuckling—no doubt she knows, and Dallas has filled her in on the details after that long drive.

"Anyone want to fill the rest of the class in?" Lily says.

I pause, staring at her, trying to figure out how much I want to tell them.

"Well…" I sigh, deciding fuck it, they're going to find out anyway. "I had a one-night stand back in San Francisco."

"Not unusual for you," Lily says. "You do that—" She stops herself, eyes wide as realization now hits her. "No."

I nod again.

"This is torture, guys," Poppy says, sitting up taller on her barstool. "Let me give you all a quick rundown so we're all on the same page. Tucker had a one-night stand, and her name was Scottie. He didn't know much about her. Just her name and that she was there for something work related. They hit it off instantly—no, they *ignited*. Sparks, fire, static in the air. The whole damn cliché, and then some."

I look to Dallas. "Is that how you described it to her?"

He shakes his head, laughing. "No, but I think that's pretty spot on based on your rant the entire drive back to town."

They all think this is funny. The small-town contractor falling into the orbit of a now TV star with bright clothes and big dreams, but it's not.

It's something else.

Something that makes me feel awake again.

And I don't know if I'm ready for that.

"And now Scottie is the star of the season? And you're the lead contractor?" Poppy asks.

"And her fake boyfriend," I say quickly and calmly, as if it means nothing.

But it also means everything.

Dallas and Griffin must've been taking sips of their drinks because liquid sprays across the bar in different directions before they both shout. *"What?"*

"Let's not make a thing of it," I say as casually as possible.

"We absolutely are," Dallas adds.

"I want all the details," Lily chimes in. "How the hell did that come about?"

I shrug, trying to remain indifferent. "The producers thought we had chemistry. Claims it's good for the subplot."

Lily exhales, hands flat on the bar. "Wait, wait, wait. So the woman you hooked up with is now in charge of renovating the home you've had your eye on since you moved here, and the producers decided, hey, let's trap them together on camera all day?"

"It's a coincidence," I mutter.

"So, what's the deal, Tucker?" Griffin asks. "You don't like her?"

I hesitate for a moment, trying to decide what to say.

It's not that I don't like her. It's that I like her way too much. More than I should for someone I barely know. In the short time she's been here, she's already getting under my skin and makes me forget there are cameras rolling just a few feet away. One moment, she's laughing and it feels like sunlight. The next, she's glaring at me.

It's chaos.

Pure fucking chaos.

And I can't help but continue walking straight into it.

"I never said I don't."

"Translation," Dallas says, pointer finger in the air. "He likes her."

"I didn't say that either."

Lily smirks. "But you're not denying it."

"We're working together. That's all it is."

Lily gives me a look that only I would understand. "You know you're allowed to let yourself have something good once in a while."

I busy myself drying glasses from the dishwasher rack as I take in her words. I can't. Even if she's right, *I can't.*

"I have everything I could want in life," I say to the glass in my hand, before lifting my eyes to meet hers. "I have you all. I have a job. That's all I need."

That shuts them up for a second. Not in an awkward way, just the kind of silence people who know you well enough leave space for.

Lily busies herself with clicking away on her phone and Dallas clears his throat. "I think this is great. I'm willing to bet you two do have chemistry, and it will be good for both of you. She gets her show and the best contractor in Bluestone Lakes, and you get to showcase your skills for more work when the show is over."

"Nan says it's the most exciting thing to happen in town since the water tower got repainted," Griffin says.

We all stare at him before we break into a fit of laughter.

"I believe it," Poppy says first.

"If it keeps you busy and gives Scottie someone to boss around, I'm all for it. She seems nice," Lily says next, standing up from the barstool and grabbing her purse.

"She's all right," I say, and even I notice how flat that sounds as I say it.

Griffin raises an eyebrow. "That's the exact tone you use when you're trying not to admit you like something."

"Or someone." Dallas grins over the rim of his glass.

I throw the dishrag at him. "You two take your psychology degrees and hit the road."

They laugh at my response.

It feels good—easy.

"*I'm* hitting the road," Lily announces. "I have to run and grab something from the bakery, and I'll be back for Nan's karaoke night in twenty minutes."

Griffin rolls his eyes. "That's my cue to leave before it gets loud in here."

"Come on, Grumpy Griffin," I say with my arms out to my side. "The fun's just getting started."

"What he said." Lily waves over her shoulder at me as she walks away.

I clap my hands together. "Let's have a good night!"

CHAPTER 12
TRYING TO GET ME DRUNK SO I FORGET HOW MUCH YOU ANNOY ME?

SCOTTIE

LILY

Hiiiii, Scottie. Do you have plans tonight?

ME

I wasn't planning anything.

LILY

Do you want to go out tonight?

ME

I still need to shower after working outside all day. What time were you thinking?

LILY

I can pick you up at seven. It's karaoke night at Seven Stools!

ME

Seven Stools?

LILY

My brother's bar on Main Street! Nan organizes it and it's the best night!

I didn't plan on going out tonight.

After a full day of filming, my body wants nothing more than to collapse in bed, close my eyes, and forget that I'm renovating a "dream home" on television with the man who once made me forget my own name.

But the idea of having a friend in Bluestone Lakes is something I don't want to pass up. So, instead of rotting in bed, I'm dressed and ready for karaoke night.

I start to gather my stuff in my purse and my mind drifts to Tucker. Why am I *still* thinking about him right now? All day, Tucker was…infuriating.

He was funny when I didn't want him to be, and calm when I tried to argue. It was as if he knew exactly what to say to get under my skin—the right mix of teasing and charm. He has the kind of confidence that doesn't need to prove itself. It was also the moments when he didn't say anything, like when his hand guided mine over tools, branding my skin like a tattoo.

The cameras caught exactly what the producers wanted—the chemistry and banter between two people working on a house together. But what they didn't catch were all the feelings I shouldn't have when he's around.

Tucker made me lose track of what was real and what was for show.

This shouldn't mean anything.

It's supposed to be fake.

So why does my chest tighten every time he smiles?

Why does his voice still echo in my head hours later?

My phone buzzing in my hand snaps me back to reality.

LILY

I'm here!

I give myself one last look in the small bathroom mirror, running my hands through the soft curls I added, before tucking the front of my navy blue V-neck shirt into the front of my jeans. I settled on casual tonight since the bar doesn't sound upscale.

Locking the door behind me, I make my way down the stairs to where she's parked.

"Ready?" Lily asks as I'm halfway into my seat.

Once I'm settled and click my seat belt on, I notice she has a giddy smile on her face, filled with excitement. "You're way too excited for karaoke."

"It's the best night of the week. Everyone in town goes to cut loose." She reaches across the center console and places a gentle hand on my forearm. "And don't worry, there are no cameras or pressure. Tonight is just small-town fun."

No cameras. That sounds like heaven.

"Besides, you're probably been inhaling sawdust all day, or whatever it is you were working on. You need a drink and a break from pretending with my cousin."

I snap my head in her direction, and she has a sly grin on her face. "I never said—"

She holds up her hand and chuckles. "Full transparency here." She laughs as she drives. "We know about the little fake dating thing."

"Oh."

"You're safe with us." She winks. "And you know Blair and I have your back if he drives you crazy."

Little does she know, he's already driving me crazy, but not in a way that makes me want to escape. In a way that makes me hyper aware of his presence when he's close to me. In a way that feels inconvenient and distracting for something that's supposed to be pretend.

"We're here." Lily's voice cuts through my thoughts just as the neon barstool flickers over the corner of Main Street.

"That was quick."

She chuckles. "Small town."

The parking spaces lining the sidewalk are full, but Lily finds a spot close enough. The moment I open the car door and get out, I can feel the thump of the music through my body. With each step toward the bar, the music only grows louder and louder.

Lily hooks her arm in mine, guiding me through the front doors. My eyes widen because she wasn't lying. This place is packed to the brim. Looking around, I take in the fancy strobe lights and mini stage set up in the corner, where someone is singing "I Want It That Way" by the Backstreet Boys.

"Now let's get you a drink, girl," Lily shouts over the music.

She pulls me toward the bar, but we don't make it far because I crash right into a brick wall. Well, not exactly. The man feels like a brick wall of muscle.

He turns around holding the glass in his hand up so it doesn't spill, and I immediately widen my eyes. "Oh my god, sir. I'm so sorry."

"Please don't call me sir. It makes me feel so much older than I am."

Lily steps between us, poking the man in the chest. "Dallas. You almost broke my friend."

He laughs, deep and gravelly. "I didn't almost break anyone."

"Oh, there you are," a female voice sounds from behind Dallas. "I was wondering where you went, Lil."

"I'm here" Lily says, wrapping her arms around the woman. She's beautiful—long strawberry blonde hair wrapped in a ponytail behind her head and a few freckles painted on her cheeks. "And it got busy!" She pulls back from her and hooks her arm in mine again. "This is Scottie." She looks at me and places her other hand on the woman's forearm. "This is my sister, Poppy. And the wall you ran into is her boyfriend, Dallas."

"It's so nice to meet you two," I say.

"Scottie," Dallas says. "You're the one doing that project over on Redwood with Tucker."

I nod, straightening my spine and feeling nervous all of a sudden. "That's me."

"He told us all about it," he adds.

I'm not sure how I feel about Tucker talking about me with people in town. First, Lily's brother, and now this man I just met three seconds ago. It puts an uneasy feeling in my gut and makes me wonder what else he's saying.

Does everyone know we're in a fake relationship for the show, too?

And more importantly…*do they know our history?*

Lily must catch my nervousness, because she smacks his upper arm with the back of her hand, forcing Dallas to raise both hands in defense. "What? He didn't say anything bad. He just told us all about the project and that his team is working on it with Scottie."

"Correct," Lily warns, sticking her pointer finger in his face. "You guys better not mess with my friend."

I turn to face Lily and a warmth fills my chest. I've never had anyone defend me like this, despite there being nothing to defend. They were only talking about the show, which I expect in a small town like this.

I place a hand on Lily's shoulder and laugh to break the tension. "It's all good. I'm sure this show is pretty big for a town like this. People are going to talk."

"Apparently, Nan says this show is the most exciting thing to happen in town since the water tower got repainted," Dallas says over the brim of his whiskey-filled glass before taking a sip. "And to clear the air and remove the elephant in the room, we know you two are pretending to date for the show."

"Dallas," Poppy and Lily say at the same time.

"What?" He shrugs. "I can feel the weird energy around us. Like we're all hiding something from her. I don't want to start a blossoming friendship on lies."

The three of us stare at him for a beat before we all bend over in laughter.

Without even trying, he successfully breaks the "weird energy" in the air.

"Thank you for that," I say as my laughter dies down. "We're pretending because the producers say it works well for the plot. That's it."

Something shifts across his face. That almost grimace people get when a truth bumps too close to the surface. Like Dallas knows something he can't say out loud. It's not judgment or pity burning my skin the longer he stares at me. It's the protectiveness of his friend. And suddenly, I feel that weird energy we just joked about coming back.

When my eyes narrow in question, Dallas looks away, schooling his expression fast as he forces a smile.

But that look?

That isn't about me.

That's about Tucker.

"Well, now that that's out…we need drinks. Stat," Lily says.

The moment Dallas moves to the side to allow Lily and me to make our way to the bar, I almost trip over my feet. Standing behind the bar, sleeves rolled to his elbows, and pouring drinks like it's second nature to him is Tucker. The dim amber light of the bar catches on the curve of his jaw, and my breath hitches.

Of course, the universe would throw me into another version of him I'm not prepared for.

As we approach the bar, I try to look casual, like I'm not having an internal crisis over seeing him here. Tucker is making a drink for someone on the other end of the bar, and I find myself unable to take my eyes off him.

"This is the best bar in town," Lily says. "And I'm not just saying that because my brother owns it."

"Noted," I say, barely registering anything she's saying because all I can focus on is the way Tucker's forearms flex with every move he makes. He's not even lifting anything heavy, just bottles of liquor. Yet, I'm transfixed on everything he's doing.

He slides the drink across the bar, then turns to face us.

That's when he sees me.

His whole body stills and the easy rhythm he was moving with seconds ago stops like someone flipped a switch. He stops breathing, or I imagine he does, because I feel like I've forgotten how to breathe, too. The music dulls into light background noise, and the laughter at the bar turns to static. All I can see are his eyes—wide and shocked that I'm standing here. But it's short-lived as a smile reaches his eyes and he moves to stand across from us at the bar.

"Well, look who wandered in here to see me," Tucker says, his voice low and impossible to ignore.

"Don't flatter yourself. I came here for karaoke, not you."

He leans forward, forearms bracing the counter. "And here I was hoping you'd say you missed me."

"I did." I smile sweetly. "Like a root canal."

He laughs—entirely too easy. I latch onto it like a lifeline because this...I can do. This back and forth with him is safe territory where nothing has to mean more than what it looks. If we keep things light, then I don't have to explain the way my heart stumbles or why his attention still affects me. I can't help it when my mouth mirrors his naturally warm smile. The way he looks at me does that—past be damned.

Then it hits me...*this* is why he's so late to get home every single day. Not that I'm stalking him, but living on his property and hearing the truck come in so late had me wondering.

Does Tucker work construction all day and the bar all night? Seven days a week?

Why does he work so much?

And why do I care?

Lily leans over the counter, and that's when Tucker breaks our stare. "I'll take a vodka cranberry, please. And whatever Scottie wants."

"I'll have..." I pause, looking at the shelf of liquor behind him. The moment I see the tequila my attention shifts back to Tucker. One arm drapes across the table, the other tucks under my chin to keep it casual. *At least that's what I tell myself.* "Tequila sunrise."

He shakes his head. "How did I know?"

"I knew you'd order something like that." Lily laughs, oblivious to whatever is happening between Tucker and me right now. "This girl loves sweet things."

"I know," Tucker says matter-of-factly. "I'm willing to bet she has a package of Sour Patch Kids tucked in her bag right now, and a second package to discard the yellow and green ones."

My lips part and I blink, unable to comprehend how he already assumes I have my all-time favorite snack *and* that I pick out the two colors I can't stand. He says it so casually, like it's no big deal.

Except now I'm the one spiraling, because if he remembers something as small as that from the *one time* I did it in front of him, when I didn't even think he watched me do it, what else does he remember?

"How do you know I discard those colors?" I ask.

Tucker huffs in amusement as he makes both of our drinks. "I'm very observant."

A little too observant.

He passes Lily her drink first and then moves effortlessly around the bar to make mine. Poppy steps up to the bar on the opposite side of her and says something to Lily along the lines of Griffin and Blair not coming, but I barely register what they're saying because, again, I can't fucking stop watching Tucker.

God, what is wrong with me?

When he's done mixing my drink, he takes an orange slice and places it on the rim. When I reach for it, our fingers brush, and my pulse jumps. My eyes snap to his, and neither of us move. Somehow, even with the music and chatter around us, the air between us feels static.

"One, *I Have My Life Together*. On the house."

This is the second time he brought up the memory of that night.

I tried so hard before coming here to file it away, but he keeps tugging it back into focus with a memory disguised as a joke. I remind myself it doesn't mean anything, however, the way my heart rate is spiking indicates otherwise.

I arch an eyebrow, ignoring it. "Are you trying to get me drunk so I forget how much you annoy me?"

He smiles. *That smile again.* The one that needs a warning label. "You make it really hard to remember why I'm supposed to be keeping my distance outside of our…arrangement."

I take a long sip of my drink, swallowing it down. "Who says you're supposed to?"

He tilts his head to the side, eyes flicking down to my lips and back up again. I can't breathe all of a sudden. I can't think from one simple look on his face.

"You did, remember?" He winks.

Ugh, this man is infuriating.

And infuriating looks really, really good under these lights.

I try to look anywhere but at him, but the truth is written in every heartbeat. I think…no, I know I was mad because he didn't stay. For one night, he saw past the performance and still chose to leave. And maybe that's the bruise that hasn't healed. The part that always comes back to not feeling like enough. Tucker might not even realize it yet, but he's the first person to look at me like I'm not pretending.

When I don't answer, he clears his throat. "I didn't think you were the going out type."

"Lily is very persuasive. Besides, when she said karaoke night, I couldn't miss the small town chaos."

"If it involves Nan, it's most definitely chaos."

"Not so fast," Nan interrupts, showing up out of nowhere, forcing me to turn my head to face her. "I'm not the only one around here who brings the crazy wherever I go."

Tucker raises an eyebrow. "You sure about that?"

She huffs in annoyance and crosses her arms. "Tucker, you live and breathe chaos."

"I guess that is kind of my specialty, huh?"

I laugh. "You? But you're all about control, Mr. Blueprint."

He raises an eyebrow. "And you're not?"

Well, he's got me there.

I don't even bother trying to deny it because control over this project is the only thing that's ever been mine. When you grow up with a mom like mine who tried like hell to choreograph every step I took and every choice I made, it's what you do. So when it comes to this show, I'm holding it tight. Maybe even a little too tight, but at least I know it's mine.

When I don't answer, Tucker tends to another guest at the bar who needs to order a drink. I take another sip of my drink, but when I turn my head to the side, Nan is still standing there with her eyes on me.

"There's something there," she finally says.

"Huh?"

"You can't fool me, girl." She grins. "I now see *exactly* what those little producers were talking about with the chemistry. It's…electrifying!" She emphasizes with her whole body like she's part of *Grease* the musical and ready to break out in song. "Oh, I should sing that one tonight."

"I don't know what you see, but that's not it."

She stands from the stool. "Like I said, you can't fool me. Besides, I see the way he looks at you."

I open my mouth to ask more, but the song someone was singing ends. "Hold that thought," Nan says and she walks away.

I'm still looking where she was standing, when a man who was sitting on the opposite side of her moves one stool over to get closer to me.

"Hey there." He flashes me a grin. "You from out of town?"

I smile politely. "Something like that."

"Then you're new. That means I get to buy you a drink."

Before I could answer, Tucker's voice cuts in, sharp and low. "She's good."

The man snaps his head to Tucker, narrowing his eyes in annoyance. "I didn't ask you. I asked her."

"Still answering, Jeffy," Tucker says smoothly.

There it is, the edge under all of that confident charm he always has. The protectiveness he'd never admit to makes my chest feel tight, while also sending butterflies right to my stomach.

The man mutters something under his breath, and I watch as he walks away without another word.

When I turn back to Tucker, I arch a brow. "Jealousy doesn't suit you."

"I wasn't jealous," he says, leaning closer as his voice drops lower. "Just didn't like his face."

I shouldn't do it, but I can't help the laugh that escapes me. He's got that grin plastered on his face again. The one that could sell trouble in bulk. It's ridiculous how easy it is for him to pull off. Tucker knows what it does to me, no question about it. My pulse trips, and I tell myself it's the few sips of tequila, and not him.

It's definitely the tequila.

Taking another sip, I don't take my eyes off him as I place my glass back on the bar top.

"You've got a dangerous smile, Tucker Daniels."

"You think my smile is dangerous, Scottie?" He leans in even closer, if that's even possible. "Good thing my contract only covers what happens on camera."

CHAPTER 13

IS CHAUFFEURING A WOMAN HOME YOUR THIRD JOB?

TUCKER

The crowd has died down and left the bar with just a few stragglers still singing off key despite Nan closing up the karaoke machine over an hour ago. The floor is sticky and smells like whiskey and fried food, and my back is sore as hell. But somehow, I can't stop smiling because Scottie is here.

I'm not ashamed to admit I've been watching her all night. Laughing with Lily and Poppy at the bar. She didn't get up to sing karaoke, but the three of them belted the songs—badly, but full of life.

She lights this whole damn place up.

Like she doesn't even realize how much space she takes up just by being herself.

I'd be lying if I said I don't like having a front row seat to it.

Lily leans against the bar, sipping the last of her drink like she's savoring it. She has a look on her face like she needs to ask me something, but thinks I'll say no.

"Having a good night?" I ask with a raised brow.

"Great night," Lily says, dragging out her words. She turns to face Scottie and Poppy, who seem to be engaged in a deep conversation. "Scottie's got potential."

"At karaoke?"

"Life, Tucker," she answers, still looking at her before she faces me again. "Not everything is about the music."

Scottie laughs at whatever she and Poppy are talking about, and I face her again, wiping down the bar top. Her cheeks are flushed, hair a little wild, and eyes bright in a way that makes it hard to look away.

"A part of me is envious of her," Lily continues. "But that's how it starts."

"How what starts?"

"Believing in the what ifs," she says, voice barely above a whisper, as if she doesn't want anyone to hear her saying it out loud. She glances at me and knows I heard it. "Believing in something like that will get you every time."

I laugh, thinking she's joking around. "You sound like you're speaking from experience."

"Or deep regret."

I stand there silently, because I haven't heard Lily talk like this before. I have a strange feeling that Lily knows what it's like to want something she never let herself chase. It makes me wonder how many people settle into a muted version of life because they're too afraid to want more.

I think she's going to walk away, but she turns back to me, the smile from before on her face like that conversation never happened. "Do you think you can give Scottie a ride home? I mean, since she's staying with you anyway."

I freeze mid-wipe of the counter and give her a knowing look. "Really, Lil?"

"Uh-huh. Why would I go to the other end of town when you're going that way anyway?"

I glance at Scottie, who's hugging Poppy goodbye, before she walks to where Lily and I are at the bar.

"Ready?" she asks Lily.

"Actually..." Lily pauses, extending a hand toward me. "Tucker is going to take you home, if that's okay? Since he's going that way."

Scottie looks at me, and her expression is unreadable.

Honestly, it's a welcoming look. It's not a death stare like I'm the last person she would like to get a ride home with. It does something to me I can't quite explain.

"Sure," she says.

I nod. "I just have to close up here. Are you okay to wait like fifteen minutes?"

"Yeah."

She takes a seat on the barstool and pulls out her phone. I move around, closing out the last two tabs, wiping down counters, and pretending I'm not rushing just to have a reason to be near her.

By the time I'm done, the bar is empty.

When I finish up and grab everything from the kitchen, I come back out and find myself staring at her for a moment. She sits there under the low glow of the lights dangling over the bar. Her hair is loose, and she's the most relaxed I've ever seen her.

Right now, it's just her—no audience. The version of her that doesn't need to perform, and god, that version wrecks me, but everything about Scottie does. The way she bites her bottom lip, the little frown when she's thinking, and the way she looks way too good under bad lighting.

She's supposed to be my fake girlfriend, not the reason I forget how to breathe.

"Ready?" I ask, clearing my throat and rounding to her side of the bar.

She stands from her stool and follows me wordlessly.

I lock up the front door behind me. The night air is thick and quiet, the kind of silence that makes my thoughts too loud. I open the passenger door for her, and she smiles as she slides in, crossing her legs and tugging her seat belt into place. Rounding the hood of the truck, I hop in and immediately notice her perfume everywhere. It's something soft, like vanilla. It throws me off kilter because it's a smell that doesn't match her bold lipstick and sharp words.

The engine rumbles to life, and Scottie breaks the silence. "Thank you for the ride. Is chauffeuring women home your third job?"

I turn to face her with a smirk before pulling the truck out onto the main road. "Nope. I only do it for you, Scottie."

Even with the street lights illuminating her face every few seconds, I can see the way her cheeks flush the perfect shade of pink before she looks away quickly, like she knows I see it. It's a simple proof that I'm not imagining the pull between us.

She clears her throat. "Is this…normal? Lily inviting people out and then dumping them on you?"

Her tone is guarded, wondering whether she misread the whole friendship she's forming with Lily.

Shit.

I tighten the grip on the steering wheel because the last thing I want her to feel is out of place. "She's only done it twice. And it's not—she's not ditching you. She has this theory."

"About what?"

I turn onto the long stretch of road that leads toward my house. "Before Griffin and Blair got together, Lily did the same thing with them," I say slowly. "And with Dallas and Poppy. She thinks she's this quiet mastermind, nudging people toward their happily ever after."

Her brows lift. "She's matchmaking?"

"She thinks we don't notice."

"And what does she think she's doing with us?"

I can feel her stare on the side of my face. I shouldn't answer that. I know saying it out loud will make it real in a way the cameras haven't yet.

I exhale. "She thinks because you're staying on my property, it's fate. She's trying to speed it along."

I take my eyes off the road for just a moment to see her reaction. She blinks once, and then two times. Her lips part like she wants to say something, but close again.

Suddenly, the air between us feels heavier, like a door we didn't realize was cracked just swung open.

She turns away from me, facing out the window as she whispers. "Oh."

She's not disgusted or annoyed.

Just…shocked.

And there's something that resembles hope in the sound, even if she didn't intend it to come out that way. Or maybe it's just me wanting to go back to the first time I met her, when she didn't loathe me.

When I turn into the driveway, the crunch of the tires on the gravel breaks the quiet. I wish she would say something more. But she doesn't. We both get out of the car and she's already retreating from where I stand in front of my truck. I watch her, scanning her body from head to toe, and fully plan to watch her until she disappears up the stairs and inside.

But she stops, turning around to face me.

"She's wrong, you know," Scottie says across the driveway. "About us. I mean…we're just—"

"Working together?" I offer.

"Right." She nods, biting down on her bottom lip. "Working. Fake it in front of the camera. But that's…yeah. Nothing more." She says it like she's convincing herself as much as me.

My chest tightens for a second. Not painfully, just sharp. Like a reminder that she isn't mine.

Closing the distance between us, I stop in front of her. "Lily doesn't think she's wrong," I say softly. "But she never considers the parts she doesn't know."

"What parts?"

I lift my hand before I can talk myself out of it, slowly, like I'm giving her every chance to pull away. My finger slides beneath her chin just enough to tip her face up toward mine. The contact is light, but it lands heavy. She freezes, not startled, but aware as her lips part on a breath she didn't mean to take, and I swear I feel it everywhere.

"Like the fact that you've spent enough time with me to learn I'm not actually as unbearable as you pretend I am." My hand moves from her chin to cup her neck. Her pulse jumps under my touch, but she doesn't move. "And you still look at me like this."

"Like what?" she asks with an unsteady voice.

I lean in, hovering close to her lips. "Like you're trying to remember why you decided I'm off-limits when the camera isn't on us."

I want to kiss her. Hell, I want everything with her right now. I'm completely sober and clearheaded enough to know exactly what I'm feeling—and that somehow makes it worse. Being this close to her again sends a rush through me that I can't explain. It's like a high that only she can give me.

I feel her hands lift at my sides, but she drops them. Like she's afraid if she reaches for me or touches me, she won't stop.

"We're not supposed to be blurring the lines," she breaths against my lips.

I press my body into hers without even thinking, and every part of me lights up. Tipping her head to the side, my lips find the shell of her ear. "They've already been blurred," I whisper, letting my hand move from her neck to the back of her head, tangling my fingers in her hair, before pulling her hair lightly to allow me full access to her neck.

She releases a breath that sounds like a muted moan.

"You haven't backed away, Scottie. Tell me one more time this doesn't mean anything. Tell me your body doesn't remember mine, and I'll walk away right now."

She steps back, panting as she puts distance between us like it's a safety measure. Her eyes are on the ground in front of her, chest rising and falling. The distance does nothing to undo the tension. It only sharpens it.

I don't move.

Neither does she.

"Scottie," I say, softer than I mean to.

"This is a bad idea," she whispers, looking up at me.

I don't answer—I can't.

Deep in my bones, I know she's right, but I don't want her to be right. When my mouth curves into a smile, her cheeks turn a shade of red in the soft glow of my porch light. She turns her head again like that'll keep me from seeing it, but it's too late. I'm already memorizing her. The way you study a structure before you ever swing a hammer because you know one wrong move changes everything.

I've never wanted to kiss someone I shouldn't so damn badly.

I could tell her that—the truth.

That I can't stop thinking about her laugh.

Or the way she looks when she's not putting up her walls.

Instead, I step closer again. Just enough that I can feel her warmth and smell that vanilla again. Close enough that the line between real and fake starts to blur in a way that scares the hell out of me.

Her hand lifts like she's going to stop me.

Instead, it lands on my chest, fingers curling into my flannel like she needs something solid to hold onto. As soon as my hands come up, ready to take her face in my hands and claim her with my mouth to hers, she steps back. She pauses, shaking her head, only to put more distance between us, thinking it will save us.

"Good night, Tucker," she whispers.

I nod because if I say anything, I'll ruin everything we're pretending isn't happening.

She disappears up the stairs and into the loft, while my feet stay planted where she left me, with only one thought on my mind.

One of us is going to get hurt when this is all done.

I already know it's me.

EPISODE THREE

THE KITCHEN CLASH

Previously on Nailed It or Failed it, *Scottie and Tucker rebuilt the front porch and nearly took each other out in the process.*

This week, we're cooking up chaos in a kitchen so outdated that it may qualify for historical preservation. These two will tackle a kitchen soaked in 1970s mustard yellow with crackled cabinets and peeling linoleum. They're armed with sledgehammers and a plan that was never stress tested as they prepare for what's ahead. Tension is thick and the question isn't what will break, but who will snap first?

Can these two keep it together long enough to demo safely?

Or will the biggest blow not come from a hammer at all?

CHAPTER 14

TONE IT DOWN, ROMEO.

SCOTTIE

The kitchen looks even worse under the studio lighting the producers insisted we use.

Which does nothing to ease the anxiety that's been building up inside of me.

It has been raining non-stop all week, causing delays and issues with getting the materials we need to complete projects. I kept insisting there has to be *something* we can do inside to keep things moving along, but Andrea was adamant that we would be fine and we're still on track to complete the house on time.

So instead, I filled the time.

I took a trip to the General Store to stock my fridge and spent a lot of hours back in the apartment, spreading the same floor plans I drafted up across the table and making sure they are absolutely perfect for the rest of the episodes.

Even with the dreary weather still lingering today, it's let up enough that we can move forward. They needed to brighten up the space with studio lights so the cameras can capture every-thing. However, it only makes every stain brighter, every crack louder, and every crooked cabinet door feel like it's mocking me.

No matter what lighting it's in, though, this room is a

disgrace. The entire kitchen is painted mustard yellow. Old, stained linoleum floors and cabinets painted in multiple shades of white with mismatched handles. Ideally, I'd like to gut the entire thing, install all-new cabinets, and completely reshape this space. But it's not feasible. Not for the timeline to get this done on time.

Instead, we're pulling the doors off the existing cabinets and replacing them. The base of them is sturdy and could use a good cleaning, but it works.

Even though my mom's voice in my head tells me I can't fix this, deep down, I know I can.

I plant my hands on my hips, trying to channel my bold confidence for the camera, rather than my rising panic.

The camera starts rolling, and I circle the space to take it all in one more time before announcing my plan to the camera for the start of the episode.

"I'm very excited about this space in the home. I believe this will be one of our biggest projects to tackle, but once it's finished, I see it becoming the room everyone wants to be in." I extend an arm to showcase what is there now. "I know we went through this in one of the earlier episodes, but as you can see, these cabinets really need a facelift." I move to the wall and cringe in front of the camera. "And this color...needs to go." I laugh lightly, letting my eyes travel to each corner of the room. "When I picture this room completed, I see creamy white paint on the walls to make the sage green cabinets I envision really pop."

"Are you sure about that?" Tucker says, catching the end of my sentence as he walks into the kitchen.

Just seeing him sucks all the air from my lungs.

Because of the rain, I haven't seen him since the night he drove me home from the bar, which was almost a week ago. I had to put some space between us before I let my body follow what it wants, versus my head telling me to keep my distance so I don't get hurt again. We were so close to doing something neither of us could take back. I almost let myself fall into him when my desire was loud enough to drown out every warning. I chose distance over instinct. Staring at the ceiling all night, I don't know if I saved myself, or walked away from something I wanted.

"What do you mean, am I sure?"

He shrugs, stepping into my space, making the kitchen feel way smaller than it is. "I'm just saying, you should consider something neutral. Something timeless."

"Sage green is neutral."

"It's also going to look like leprechauns threw up on the cabinets."

I narrow my eyes. "You know you're only funny when you're wrong, right?"

"Then I must be hilarious around you, babe."

The camera guy snorts, and I turn on my heel before Tucker sees the way he so casually calls me babe makes my cheeks heat.

"Let's just start by removing the doors," he says, his tone shifting into that infuriating practical contractor mode. "These need to be gone before we figure out anything else. And there's no sense in doing the flooring until tomorrow if the cabinet debris is going to fall on it."

"That works, and then we can work on widening the window before we demo this wall that I want to get rid of." I gesture to the wall behind him.

His eyes narrow. "Window, yes. Wall, no."

"No?" I cross my arms over my chest. "Last I checked, this was my project. And if I want to open up this room, then I should be able to open up this room."

Something that resembles annoyance flashes across his face, but it's gone before I can even blink. He turns around, placing a hand on the wall and running his fingers along the old paint—assessing the entire thing.

"I told you before, this is a weight-bearing wall. It needs to be here," he says, his back to me. "I double-checked it and it's not safe to tear it down," he whispers, more for himself to hear than me.

I want to protest more.

I want to offer a solution like a pillar or something.

But I can't find the words.

The way he says it, tells me that the wall is a trigger for him. I know it in my bones. I may not know what or why it is, but my gut tells me he's carrying the weight of something far greater than he wants anyone to see.

"Okay," I say, clapping my hands together to snap him out of wherever his head just went. He turns to face me, almost startled by my clap. "We keep the wall. Let's get these doors off and tackle the plan for the day. Minus your misguided thoughts on cabinet color."

He laughs, shaking his head as he moves toward one of the cabinet doors. I exhale a sigh of relief that whatever that was moments ago has vanished, as if it never happened. I stare at him—muscles exposed in his white tank top, tool belt hung low on his hips over his dark wash jeans. As much as it pains me to admit it, Tucker is hot, and I can't even deny that.

My attention drifts before I can stop it. I watch his forearms flex and something warm curls low in my stomach, shooting right between my legs. I shift my weight, suddenly thinking about how small the kitchen feels with him in it.

I hate that my body remembers him even when my mind is trying to forget.

He works effortlessly to remove one of the upper cabinets and then another. Still, I haven't moved from where I stand in the middle of the kitchen as I watch him work. I know I need to move, I need to do something, but he has me in a trance right now.

"I like it when you watch me work, Scottie," he says with his back to me. Slowly, he faces me, dusting his hands off with a grin on his face. "But we'd get closer to the leprechauns moving in today if you help me out here."

"Right," I say quickly, hurrying to the lower cabinets on the island in the center of the room. "But for the record, I wasn't watching you."

"If that's what you need to tell yourself."

Reaching down, I grab hold of one of the doors, ignoring the tremor in my hands. I can't keep letting him throw me off balance like this because everything needs to go perfectly—the show, the house…me.

If everything comes together perfectly, I'm safe.

If I succeed in this project, people will trust me and see me as a professional.

If I do this right, my parents will—

The cabinet door slips from my grip, and the pointed corner slams down right on top of my foot. "Shit," I hiss, hopping back.

Tucker is behind me instantly. "Are you okay? Let me see."

"No, it's fine," I protest, sitting down on the ground and waving him off even though the tears sting the edges of my eyes.

Not from pain, but from humiliation.

"Scottie," he says, his voice so low that even the cameras won't be able to pick it up. He places his palm on my thigh, and my body burns, in a good way, from the contact. "I'm here. Let me help."

The softness—God, the softness in his voice disarms me more than the pain.

When I no longer protest, he crouches low, lifting my foot gently into his hand and removing my sneaker with his other hand. His thumb sweeps over the top of my foot. The contact sends a sharp pulse through me that has nothing to do with pain. My breath catches and I clamp my jaw shut, because if I don't and allow myself to react, I'm not sure I'll ask him to stop.

My eyes track the way his fingers assess the red mark, then up to his face, where I see worry etched in every feature.

"I don't think it's broken, but you're going to get a pretty nasty bruise."

"Great," I mutter. "Maybe the bruise will distract me from my embarrassment."

He laughs under his breath. A warm, rumbling sound that pulls something buried deep inside of me. He reaches a hand down, and I look from his face to his hand, and then back to him before I accept his help to get off the floor. He lifts me effortlessly, using one hand on my upper arm to brace me.

We stand inches apart. His gaze drops to my mouth, and I feel it like a pull. I tilt my chin up without thinking, drawn forward by something stronger than reason. He inhales sharply and stills, like he's hit an invisible wall that I'm glad is there. Instead, with his free hand, he reaches up, brushing his fingers through my hair to get it out of my face before his fingers trail down my neck over the pounding pulse.

"You have to stop looking at me like that," I whisper, letting my eyes flutter closed.

He leans in, lips hovering over the shell of my ear as his voice drops low. "Like what?"

I swallow, before I pull back as our gazes lock again. "Like I'm yours."

The corner of his mouth ticks up, and that look—*fuck, that look*. It sends my pulse into overdrive. I want to take back the words, and I feel myself bracing for whatever his next words will be.

"That's because you are, Scottie." He winks, bringing his hand under my chin to force me to level with him. He swipes his thumb across my lower lip, and I swear my insides combust on the spot. "You just haven't caught up yet."

I swallow hard, stepping back to put some space between us. I cannot let him know the effect his words have on me. I cover my hand over the mic clipped to my shirt. "Jesus, Tucker. Yes, we're faking this thing between us. But…" I whisper. "Tone it down, Romeo."

"I'll try, but I don't think my charm comes with volume control."

A throat clears behind me. I turn around to see Andrea behind the camera, pointing at her clipboard. "Back to the cabinets," she whisper-shouts.

When I turn back to face Tucker, neither of us move. Because Tucker still has his eyes on me. He looks at me like he's trying not to do something incredibly stupid.

And I'm looking at him like I might let him.

I've already fought this off once; if he tries again, I'm not sure I'll be able to show the same restraint.

Before we can act on it, he steps away from me, clearing his throat as he picks up the cabinet that fell on my foot to toss it into the pile of other broken cabinets off to the side.

For the next half hour, we work in silence.

He removes all the upper cabinets, and I remove all the lower. By the time we finish taking them all off, there's a pile in the corner of the kitchen that Tucker and his crew begin to take outside to the dumpster sitting at the top of the driveway.

Andrea comes up beside me. "This will be amazing when it's done. You're making good time despite the delays we've had."

"I am?"

She nods. "Tucker's crew has worked well together to get ahead on things in the rest of the house. We might be a day or two behind, but seeing them hustle today, I have no doubt we'll catch up."

"I hope you didn't just jinx it."

"I hope not either." She laughs. "We're going to film some mid-work content here in the kitchen with Tucker's crew if you want to step out and grab a snack or take a break."

"Perfect."

Making my way through the house feels like a full construction zone at every step. Tools buzz in different rooms that need to be done but won't be filmed, sawdust piles sit randomly throughout the first floor, and small, handheld tools are scattered everywhere. I didn't notice how much had gotten done today because I entered through the side door that leads directly to the kitchen when I got here.

When I step through the open front door, I feel like I can breathe again. The clouds still hide the sun, but I can feel it. I tilt my head back and close my eyes, letting the breeze cool the sweat caked on my skin. My muscles finally relax because out here, there are no cameras.

I open my eyes, exhaling slowly and ready to pull myself back together when something catches my eye to the left. I gasp and my hand flies to my chest. My other hand reaches out when I step closer and I run my fingers along the white wood finish of a swing on the front porch.

It's the front porch swing I wanted but was told couldn't happen.

When Tucker and his crew explained it to me, they went into detailed discussion about how the roof over the porch is very old. There was no way for it to support a swing that could hold two people. Lifting my eyes, I notice that the panels are all… new.

I feel tears sting my eyes and I fight back the emotions.

It shouldn't feel this big. It's just a porch swing—one small detail in a house full of bigger problems. But standing here staring at it, I realize it isn't about the swing at all. It's about the fact that someone heard me. I've spent so much of my life learning to compromise my vision and shrink my ideas into a box that's easier to accept. It's proof that sometimes, someone will meet me in the middle.

And there's only one person who could have made this happen.

"Do you like it?" Tucker's voice behind me forces me to spin around quickly.

I swipe at the tear that escaped and clear my throat. "Yes. Did you…"

He nods. "I know how much you wanted it. Part of my job is ensuring you get exactly what you want."

"How? When?"

"Levi and I snuck over here a few times this past week when we had a break between the heavy rainstorms. The beams under the panels were a lot worse than I thought and the whole thing needed to be removed," he says, looking up at the space above us. "I tried to make it look exactly the same as it was. Once we replaced them and checked that they were secure and safe, we attached it to that and put the panels in around it."

"I…" My voice trails off, looking at the swing again. "I can't believe you did this for me."

"I didn't do it *for* you," he says softly. "I did it because it matters to you."

Dammit. My heart flips on itself, and everything I've tried to keep down settles on the surface. I don't know what to say, because *thank you* doesn't feel enough when he's given me proof that my voice didn't disappear into the air like it usually does. Proof that someone listened to what I wanted and acted when I wasn't looking.

"You don't have to believe it yet," he continues. "But if you want something, and it's safe, I'll figure out how to make it happen. Seeing you disappointed over something like that?" His jaw tightens, and he looks away from me to the swing. His expression shifts to something I can't make out. "Some things don't get a second chance and not everything can be saved." He exhales, looking back to me. "This wasn't one of them."

I move without restraint, wrapping my arms around his waist. He's momentarily startled by the contact, but his body relaxes at the same time he wraps his arms around my neck, pulling me into him. My fingers curl tighter into his shirt and for a second, I'm painfully aware of how easily this could turn into something else.

Some things don't get a second chance.

I feel the truth of it in the way his arms tighten and in the careful breath he takes like he's holding more than just me.

Whatever he's lost, whatever he couldn't save, it still lives in him and shapes the way he moves through life.

I can tell now, Tucker fixes things he can before it slips away.

"Thank you, Tucker," I say into his chest. Pulling back, I look up at him, arms still around each other. "It—it means everything."

My emotions are all over the place as a tear slips down my cheek. He catches it with the back of his finger. I feel the shift before I see it. For a heartbeat, I think he might close the distance and kiss me. The air is thick and charged with all the unspoken words we both want to say. Instead, he unwraps his arms and steps back.

"And look...I'm sorry," he says quietly, voice rougher as he looks down at his hands. "About earlier...the sage green? I wasn't trying to shoot you down."

My throat tightens. "I know."

"I'm not used to bright and colorful," he admits. "Color, beautiful chaos, all that stuff. It wasn't really something I grew up with."

This is the first time Tucker has given me a piece of himself, a real one.

"I'm not used to...safe," I say before I can swallow the truth back down. "And I'm not used to people having my back like this. I learned how to make things look fine long before they actually felt that way."

His eyes flicker to me again. Something dark and understanding passes through them. Suddenly, we're both standing here on a porch we built together, carrying wounds neither of us have confessed to.

It's in this moment that something between us shifts.

He notices.

I notice.

Anyone with a pulse would notice.

"Scottie," he whispers to the ground between his legs. "I've never wanted to kiss someone I shouldn't so damn badly."

My heartbeat launches into a sprint. "Tucker—"

"I won't do it." He shakes his head. "I won't cross the line, even though it's been tempting me since driving you home from the bar that night. Hell, since you arrived here in Bluestone Lakes."

The problem—the terrifying, exhilarating problem—is that I want him to cross the line now. I didn't then because I wasn't sure, but now, I've never been more sure. I know this isn't the time and place, though. Not when emotions are so high over the incredible gesture from Tucker and cameras could come back outside at any minute.

"We should get back inside," I settle on.

The muscle in his jaw ticks as he looks far into the distance, avoiding making any eye contact with me. It stings when I know I have no right to allow it to sting.

"Fine," he says. "I'll have my crew bring in the new doors." He finally faces me, a smirk forming—dangerous. "And then we can get to work painting them that sage green."

I try my hardest not to smile, but fail miserably.

"I'm ready if you are, Tucker."

He reaches out, circling his hand around my wrist to pull me closer to him. My eyes widen, but only for a second, because the smile on his face when he looks down at me is enough to melt me on the spot.

"Careful, Scottie. The way you say my name...like that? It'll ruin me."

I'm unraveling, piece by careful piece.

And the worst part?

He's the only reason I haven't fallen apart already, and the reason I know I eventually will.

CHAPTER 15

NEW PLAN. WE BURN THE HOUSE DOWN.

TUCKER

Scottie is different today.

Not in a way that the crew would notice, but I do. I'm finding I notice everything about her way more than I should.

Her laugh isn't like it has been in the days before, and her smile doesn't quite reach her eyes. I watched her trembling hands on multiple occasions as she removed old cabinets and flipped through her design booklet. She's quick to hide it, but I see it.

And it does something to me I don't want to examine too closely.

Scottie stands off to the side of the kitchen with her hands on her hips, surveying the room like she's about to conquer it with sheer optimism. She's wearing her signature overalls, which I'm learning are strictly for construction work on this project, and underneath she's paired them with a soft yellow crop top. She's also wearing those damn pair of pink work boots today, and I assume it's because of the cabinet door falling on her yesterday.

Smart girl.

She's looking around the kitchen and taking in all the work

she did yesterday in a new light. The sun is shining outside today, casting a glow through the window.

The space is bright, like her.

I move to stand next to her, nudging her arm with my shoulder. "Green was a good choice."

She turns her head, looking up at me. "I can't tell if that's sarcasm or if you mean it."

"I mean it," I say quickly, not wanting her to think otherwise. "I may joke about a lot of things, but I mean this."

She eyes me curiously, and it leaves an uneasy feeling in my gut. It's not the kind of look you toss at a coworker or a fake boyfriend for the cameras. It's the kind that lingers too long, like she's lining something up in her head and realizing it fits. That shouldn't matter, but it does. She's looking at me the same way I've been looking at her. I don't know what scares me more. The possibility that she sees me or the fact that part of me wants her to.

Something changed yesterday.

I feel it in her stare.

She's silently listening to the things I don't say out loud, like she knows there's more under the surface and isn't backing away.

Is Scottie catching all the tiny details about me the same way I see hers?

The way her smile starts on the left.

The way her tongue sticks out when she's focused on a project or with a tool in her hand.

The way she pretends she's unaffected when I know she is.

It's all just wishful thinking.

But I want it—I want her to notice me. Not the version the producers are going to edit together, and not the man I pretend to be when I need to survive the day. I'm craving for her to see *me*, despite the fear that she could discover the dents and bruises of my past.

She opens her mouth to say something, but heels clicking on

the floor draw our attention to the archway leading to the kitchen. Andrea is clicking away on her phone when she comes to a stop, then looks up, takes it all in, and faces us with wide eyes and a smile. "Wow! This looks incredible."

I turn to face Scottie again to let her answer. I watch as she straightens instantly, shoulders back and chin lifted like she's flipping on that bright influencer switch—bubbly and effortlessly confident.

"Okay," Scottie says, clapping once. "Who's ready to rip up this…flooring situation?"

"It's linoleum."

She points to the floor as if it had personally offended her. "It's a crime against kitchens everywhere."

I chuckle. "We can add that to the demo notes."

The camera crews follow Andrea, setting up where needed, while I gather the tools we need.

Scottie talks to the camera for a few minutes, telling them about the progress we made yesterday and what the plan is for today, but all I can think about is how much I'm enjoying doing this with her. When we started, I was dreading how much she hated me for leaving her, on top of the fake dating scheme we're doing for the show.

But the cameras love her.

They love our chemistry.

It's something that can't be faked.

When she's done, she comes to kneel next to me on the floor. We begin by prying up the old linoleum that hasn't been updated since disco was alive and well. The smell is…something out of my nightmares.

Scottie yanks up the first strip, lets out a squeal, and drops it quickly. "What *is* that?"

I look down. "It looks like subflooring mixed with some glue residue."

She wrinkles her face in disgust. "It looks like something crawled under here to die, Tucker. That's a biohazard."

I laugh. "You said you wanted rustic charm. Congratulations."

She groans dramatically, throwing her head back. "This isn't the kind of rustic charm I meant."

I bite back a smile.

She's beautiful in a way that shouldn't make sense when pulling old floors up and finding possible mold underneath.

My heart slams in my chest hard enough to hurt. She catches me staring at her and narrows her eyes. "Are you seriously smiling at moldy subflooring?" she asks, using air quotes to emphasize the last word.

"It's not the mold," I say under my breath, and direct my attention back to the flooring I'm pulling up to do anything to keep my hands from shaking.

"What's that?"

I clear my throat. "Nothing."

I watch from the corner of my eye as she studies me for a beat. "You're distracted."

"You're loud," I counter.

"You like it."

I do. More than I should.

When I don't answer her, she turns her head to hide the blush on her cheeks and pretends to study the pry bar in her hands like that'll keep me from noticing.

I pull up another piece of flooring, and Scottie moves to do the same. The cameras zoom in, capturing her frustration as the flooring refuses to budge. She mumbles something under her breath involving creative violence and swearing at the use of glue.

I stifle a laugh, and she shoots me a warning glare. "Don't laugh at me."

"You're cute when you're mad."

"Don't." She pauses, swallowing, covering the mic clipped to her shirt and keeping her voice low. "Say things like that."

"Why not?"

"Because you…say them like they're true."

They are.

But I don't say that out loud, not when the crew is hovering over us and watching our every move.

Instead, I pry up more flooring and reveal a larger chunk of subfloor, and Scottie stands up, backing away.

"Absolutely not," she gasps. "Nope. This is disgusting. It's a crime scene under there."

"It's just wood."

"It's moldy."

I look down and smirk. "I guess it is a little moldy."

"A little?" She gestures wildly. "That's an entire civilization of mold. That's—"

I stand quickly, gently placing my hand in hers to stop the tornado that's about to tear through her. She freezes at my touch.

"Breathe," I whisper.

She does, shakily, but she breathes, nonetheless.

And something in me goes soft in a way I didn't know could. Neither of us move as my thumb brushes over the pulse in her wrist, back and forth until I feel it steady under my touch.

Scottie talks like chaos and works like sunshine, and I'd tear down every wall I've built if it meant I got to stand in the light with her because she's the kind of mess that makes a man want to roll up his sleeves and stay a while.

Not to fix her, but to smooth her out.

Just…stay.

And I don't ever stay.

But with her? I'm already half rooted without meaning to be. And maybe that's what scares me the most. I'm starting to crave the parts of her she hides. The shaky inhale when the cameras stop, the tight smile she uses like armor, and the way perfection is her shield.

She clears her throat, pulling her arm from my touch. "Okay. New plan. We burn the house down."

I freeze.

Only for a second.

Just long enough for something old and sharp to drag its claws up my spine. I shove it down—fast and hard. Like I always do.

She doesn't know.

She wouldn't know.

Instead, I do what I do best...I smirk and pretend nothing inside of me just caved in for a heartbeat. "No. Arson is frowned upon."

"Fine. We get a new house."

Now it's my turn to breathe since there's no way she noticed the way I reacted to her joke.

"That's not how renovations work, Scottie."

She huffs. "I know. But sometimes I think the house is winning."

"It's just because you're overwhelmed. And that's okay."

"I'm not overwhelmed," she lies.

"Right." I smirk. "And that's why you're threatening to commit felony arson."

She glares at me.

Even with the fire in her eyes, it's stupidly adorable.

I shake my head and avert my gaze. "Stop."

"Stop what?"

"Being—" *Beautiful. Funny. Soft where I'm all edges.* "You."

She blinks, mouth open. "Is that an insult?"

"Depends on the day."

"Oh, really?" She moves around the kitchen to stand in front of me, hands on her hips in defiance. "Then what day is today?"

"Today?" I lean in until our faces are only a breath apart, keeping my voice low enough for only her to hear. "Today, you're driving me insane."

In every sense of the word.

She's the kind of insane that gets into your bloodstream and rewires your heartbeat. The kind that makes you forget how careful you've kept your world small.

One smile, and suddenly everything feels too bright.

She doesn't even realize she's doing it.

She has no idea she's dragging light into places I boarded shut years ago. And I have no idea what the hell I'm supposed to do if she keeps going.

But the look on her face—eyes wide, tells me that I've said too much and not enough at the same time.

The cameraman clears his throat, reminding us he's still standing there, forcing us to both take a step away from each other.

"Cut," Andrea calls, and we both snap our heads to her in confusion. She walks over to where we stand, gaze bouncing between the two of us. "This is great. All of it. But I think with all this insane electricity my crew and I are feeling from watching you two, now might be a good time to do some of the fake dating filming before we move on."

Scottie tilts her head in confusion. "Huh?"

"You know, some of the relationship stuff."

Scottie groans. "You say it like we're about to perform a circus trick for the cameras."

"Maybe we are," I say.

She elbows me right in the ribs. "Just act normal."

"This *is* my normal."

She rolls her eyes. "That explains so much."

"Eek!" Andrea squeals. "This is so good. You two are *sooo* good. I'd like to get a few shots of you two really selling it."

Since the moment I met Andrea, something about her has felt off. I can't figure out why but watching her stop us just to get a few shots for the fake dating bit, makes irritation crawl up my spine. We already lost nearly a full week to rain delays. A week we easily could've worked through. My crew is trained for worse than what we had.

And now that we have a clear window, she's more focused on capturing the chemistry than getting the renovation back on schedule.

The cameraman moves his tripod closer to us. We step into the frame, and Scottie leans into me—closer than necessary.

"Now face each other," Andrea says.

And we do. Scottie looks up at me, and it knocks the wind right out of my lungs.

"Tucker, put your hand on her waist. Pull her in and sell the romance," Andrea orders.

Ready to play along, my hand finds her waist, and something electric snaps under my skin. Her breath stutters and mine damn near stops. Leaning in closer, I feel her warmth pressed against me. I lift my hand and let my fingers trace her jaw. Her skin is soft beneath my thumb. She tilts her head just slightly. Call it trust or instinct, but it pulls me in like a gravitational force that I don't stand a chance against.

There isn't a camera in the world that could convince me this is fake.

I slide my hand under her jaw, tilting her face toward mine. I lean in, ready to claim her lips as mine. My thumb moves to brush the corner of her mouth.

She inhales sharply, and I feel it. *Feel her.* Every trembling breath against my skin and every inch of air tightening between us like it's ready to snap.

Her gaze flicks to my mouth, telling me she feels it, too.

The way she's looking at me right now unravels something in me that I didn't know was still tied tight. Scottie has no idea what she does to me. The other night in my driveway, and now this? She has no idea how close I am to giving in. No idea that if she asked me, just once, to stop pretending, I'd kiss her like it's the only thing I've ever been meant to do.

"Tucker," she whispers.

Her breath hits my mouth and it damn near wrecks me.

I cup her face fully now, palms framing her cheeks like she's something precious that I'm terrified will break. "Hi," I whisper.

Her mouth parts like she's about to say something else, but instead, her eyes soften.

And that almost undoes me more than the way she was looking at my mouth a second ago.

"Hi," she whispers back, her smile barely there…like it's just for me.

"Perfect! Cut!" Andrea shouts.

But I don't move. Not right away.

Not until Scottie blinks, as if waking up from something we shouldn't have started.

She steps back, making the space between us feel cold. She brings her hand to her lips like she needs confirmation that all of that really happened.

And I smile like I'm fine and as if this was all for show.

Without another word, she turns and disappears from the kitchen. And I let her go because I have to.

Because this is fake.

Because she deserves more than I can give her.

At least that's what I tell myself.

CHAPTER 16

IT WASN'T NOTHING.

SCOTTIE

Standing in the bathroom with my palms bracing the edge of the sink, I stare at my reflection like the mirror might give me an answer I don't already know. I didn't even realize I was smiling until my cheeks started to ache. It's as if my body is still convinced I was kissed even though I wasn't.

It's stupid. It's reckless.

It's not what I'm supposed to be here for.

Andrea yelling "cut" still rings in my head like a warning bell.

The moment the words rang through the air he didn't pull away or drop his hands. He stood there, touching me, and close enough that my breath hit his mouth, and I felt him inhale like he was starving.

I panicked and ran.

Now I'm here, in *his* apartment over the garage, trying to convince my heart rate to return to a normal pace. It's been almost two hours since that moment and it still hasn't slowed. Of course it hasn't, because this is Tucker.

I've already convinced myself he's over it. He's probably working his shift at the bar right now laughing with the patrons and rolling his eyes at the dramatic influencer who bolted the moment things felt a little too real.

Maybe he's relieved.

I drag my hands down my face before reaching for the wash-cloth to wash the mess of the day off. I should probably eat something. I should do anything other than stand here re-living the exact moment his thumb brushed the corner of my mouth like he already knew what it tasted like.

Groaning to myself, I scrub my face enough that it's red.

As soon as I'm done, my phone buzzes on the bathroom counter. The name on the screen makes my stomach drop so hard it feels like it hit the tile. The universe never fails to remind me that peace is only temporary.

"Hi, Mom," I say, answering the phone reluctantly.

"Scottlyn," she says, her voice sharp like she's already annoyed with me for simply existing. "Is this a good time?"

I want to say no.

It's never a good time when you call.

"Yes," I say instead, because the truth is a luxury I don't get with my mom. "Yeah, it's fine."

"Your father and I were just discussing the project. I haven't seen much content posted from you. Is the production behind?"

I step out of the bathroom and into the small living space, pacing automatically like movement might drain the anxiety out of me. "I've been very busy with the house and filming," I say carefully. "But we did have some minor delays with the weather."

It's not a lie. My social media accounts have taken a backseat during this project. Not to mention, I can't share too much online until the show airs on TV. They gave me the go-ahead to share very little behind the scenes, but I can't share videos or things of me renovating the house yet. I've focused on just sharing pictures here and there to keep the account alive.

"And how is that going?" she asks. "Are they showcasing the right things? This is very important for your image."

My image.

The version of me my mom can quietly measure against my cousin. Against what she thinks a successful life is supposed to look like. The version that makes me…enough in her eyes.

"I know." I sigh, but keep my voice as bright as possible.

"Hmm," my mom hums, unconvinced. "So, how is the house coming along anyway? It's going to be a success when all is said and done, right?"

And there it is.

Not *how are you*? Or *are you okay*?

It's the same question she always asks dressed up in different words: Are you succeeding in a way that reflects well on us?

"It's going really good," I lie smoothly. "We're even ahead of schedule."

"I knew she could do it," I hear my father in the background, making my gut churn. If there's anyone I don't want to disappoint with this, it's him. As much as I tend to resent how easily he believes in me the way my mom never could, it also means I carry that belief around like something fragile. Like it's mine to protect.

"That's great, honey," my mother says. "I just worry this is a lot for you. You know that failure isn't an option here. Not with the world watching you."

My fingers grip my phone so tight that I almost snap it in half.

"I got this," I say, forcing a laugh to ease the tension. "Everything is going fine."

I allow my mom to talk for another minute about timelines. She tells me how I need to make sure I stay polished and to keep my posture during filming until my head feels like it's filled with cotton and my throat aches from holding in everything I want to scream.

"Okay, I have to go," I finally say. "We're starting early in the living room in a few days."

"Don't stay up too late, honey. You'll get dark circles under your eyes."

"Okay."

Then I end the call before I can hear another word.

Tossing my phone on the couch, I fall back onto it and feel the tremble in my hands. No matter how far away I go, I still feel like I'm standing in their living room after graduation and being told to apply for corporate jobs because it's my only option. Being told to be more like my cousin who has a better career and close friends.

My eyes blur enough that I close them, fighting the burn because crying is useless.

Crying won't change anything.

I sit up with my elbows on my thighs, pressing the heel of my palm against my eyes and breathe through the sting. The weight of the conversation and thinking about the timeline of the project sits so heavy on my mind that I feel I'm seconds from spiraling.

Then there's a knock on my door.

Two firm raps that cut through my spiral, and I freeze. I already know who it is. I can feel him like the air changes when he's near. Like my body clocks him before my brain does.

When I don't move, I stare at the door, willing him to walk away.

It's late, which means Tucker must have just gotten home from his shift at the bar. I want to hear his footsteps retreat back to his place, but they don't. Instead he knocks again, slower this time, like he's giving me space to choose.

I walk to the door on legs that don't feel steady and rest my hand on the knob without opening it.

"Scottie."

His voice is low and rough. It doesn't sound like the playful Tucker I've been working with or the one who calls me babe and smirks for the camera. His voice sounds like he's holding something back.

"Open the door," he says. "Please."

I squeeze my eyes shut and I press my forehead to the back of the door. "Tucker—"

"You don't get to run away from me."

I rear back, eyes flying open at his sharp tone. I swing the door open and come face to face with Tucker standing on the other side. He has one hand on the door frame and the other in the pocket of his jeans, resting casually.

"You were doing too much," I snap. "Faking for the cameras or not, that can't happen again."

"Too much?"

"Yes. Too much." My voice rises. "You don't get to say things like that and touch me like that when you don't mean it. That's not what this is, and it's giving me mixed signals. I can't afford to sit and think about it for too long because we're already behind schedule on the renovation!"

My throat burns with every word. The second the sentence leaves my mouth, my pulse is already punishing me for it, hammering in my ears. My fingers clamp harder around the edge of the door like it's the only thing keeping me upright.

Tucker doesn't move. He stands there, clenching his jaw so tight the muscle ticks in his cheek, like I've slapped him instead of throwing words.

"It wasn't nothing," he grits out.

My stomach flips like my body heard him before my brain could catch up. Heat crawls up my neck with part embarrassment, part anger, and part something far worse.

The space between us feels...crowded. Not with bodies, but with everything we're refusing to say. It presses into my lungs until I have to remind myself to breathe. His eyes are hard, but not cold. There's something raw under the anger and it terrifies me more than if he'd smirk. I swallow, but it doesn't help. My mouth feels dry the longer his eyes bore into mine.

"Scottie."

The way he says my name should be illegal.

It shouldn't sound like a warning and a plea all at once.

"I'm fine," I lie automatically.

"You're not," he says, still unmoving from where he stands. "You're doing that thing."

"What thing?"

"The thing where you pretend you don't feel anything."

My fingers tighten on the door I'm still holding. My skin is too aware of everything right now. It still feels the warmth lingering where he touched me earlier.

I want to tell him I can't handle this.

I want to tell him I *can*.

But my voice is lodged somewhere between my ribs and my pride.

He shifts a half step forward, barely anything, but my body reacts like it's a full lunge. My instinct screams to close the door, lock it, and go to bed. But my feet don't move—they can't.

I'm quite literally frozen in place by the same stupid thing that always gets me in trouble.

Want.

"Maybe I don't feel anything," I snap, keeping an even composure.

His gaze drops to my mouth for a fraction of a second, and my breath catches like I've just been caught stealing from the grocery store.

"Bullshit."

Tucker fills the doorway like he was made to. Broad shoulders, dark shirt, jeans, and work boots. His hair is mussed like he's been dragging his hands through it. And his eyes...they aren't teasing. They're stormy and focused on me like I'm the only thing he can see.

"Are you done?" he asks.

"Why do you even care, Tucker?"

The words hang between us.

He narrows his eyes. "Do you really want me to answer that?"

My entire body goes hot and cold at once while my chest rises too fast.

"I want you to leave," I lie, and my voice wavers at the end.

"Then tell me to."

I swallow hard as his gaze flicks over my face, reading me like a blueprint.

But I can't say the words. I've held myself back a dozen times, and every time he gets close, the only thing keeping me upright is sheer willpower and the fear of what wanting him will cost me. I've been restraining myself since the second I got into town and he looked at me like I was something worth having.

Restraint when he drove me home from the bar.

Restraint when I found the porch swing he put in for me.

Restraint when he stood too close in the kitchen and I could feel the heat rolling off him.

Restraint with every look in my direction.

Restraint today when his hand slid to my waist under the camera lights and my breath stuttered like my body forgot how to function.

Every fucking time, I've held back.

Every time, I've said *no* when I wanted to say *yes*.

Tucker steps inside without permission, closing the door behind him with a soft click.

"It wasn't nothing," he repeats his words from earlier with a little less rage with each word. "And for the record, I don't say things I don't mean."

I shake my head. "You can't say things like that," I whisper, the anger draining out of me. "Not if you're not going too—"

"Not going to what?" he challenges, but his voice cracks.

I hate that my eyes sting.

I hate that my chest feels tight.

I hate that I'm seconds away from either crying or kissing him, and neither option is acceptable.

When I don't answer him, his jaw flexes again. For a moment I think he's going to open the door and leave. I assume he's going to do the thing men always do when things get compli-cated and turn this into a joke.

But he doesn't.

He exhales. "I'm not trying to act like nothing happened back there at the house." With every word, his tone rises and my heart stutters. "I'm fucking trying here and every moment with you kills me more and more. You keep acting like you're alone in this but—"

"I am!" I cut him off before he can finish the thought forming on his face. Every time support came with rules and expecta-tions. My mom showing up only when I performed well. My dad believing in me but failing to protect me from my mother's constant disapproval.

A career where I had to work extra hard to be taken seriously.

His face shifts like I hit something, but then his gaze turns darker.

The air between us shifts. I open my mouth to apologize for my outburst or say anything else, but steps closer. "You ran today." I shake my head. "You ran because you felt it."

"Felt what?"

His eyes lock on mine harder than before. "Me."

My breath leaves my body and he takes another step closer. And another. I should move and put space between us but my body betrays me and stays right where it is.

"You have to stop saying things like that," I whisper with a bit of an edge to my tone.

"Why?"

"Because..."

"Because it scares you, Scottie?" he finishes for me. He waits a moment for me to say something, but when I open my mouth, nothing comes out. "It fucking scares me, too. You scare me. Every time you look at me it terrifies me because you unknow-ingly knock down another wall I've put up to protect myself from this exact thing."

"Tucker," I breathe out, looking away from him.

"No," he says, gripping my chin hard and forcing me to look at him. "Look at me."

I am.

I can't find it in me anymore to look anywhere else.

His hand lifts, hovering near my waist without touching me. It feels like he's asking and giving me a choice. Despite what my head is telling me, my skin aches for his contact.

"I'm going to need you to tell me to fucking stop. Because I don't know if I can on my own. Not this time. Not again."

I should.

I should use the same restraint I've used before, but... "I can't," I whisper.

His eyes flick down to my mouth again while his hand lands on my waist. Heat flashes through me instantly. My entire body reacts like it recognizes him as something dangerous and familiar all at once. His grip isn't harsh, but it's firm.

It's claiming.

"Tucker," I breathe out, my voice sounds like a warning.

My hand lifts before I can think about it, fisting the fabric of his shirt for something solid to hold onto. He leans in, close enough that his breath brushes my cheek. I can't tell if the apartment is too hot or if I'm just too close to him. His mouth hovers near my ear, not touching, but close enough that every breath against my skin sends chills up my spine.

"I know why you did it," he says against my skin. "You ran because it felt real. For a second, you forgot about the cameras and the plan. You forgot what this was supposed to be."

"I—I didn't forget."

"Liar."

Heat crawls up my neck and I hate that he can read me like this.

I hate that he's right.

"I ran because I didn't know what to do with it," I admit.

"With what?"

"With..." I swallow. "With you."

My confession hands between us, trembling like glass.

Tucker goes still before he exhales—a slow and controlled breath. "You don't have to know what to do with me," he murmurs, leaning in until his forehead is pressed against mine. "Just stop pretending you don't feel this thing between us outside of the show."

"But that's not what this is."

"Really?" he challenges, pressing his body into mine and my lips part on a shaky inhale. My body feels like it can melt right in front of him from just the contact. The ache between my legs throbs without even trying. "Because this doesn't feel fake and I don't see anyone staring at us here." His thumb strokes the side of my waist, and I swear my body answers him before my mind can. "Nothing about you feels fake," he breathes against my lips.

He's right.

My god, he's fucking right.

My breath catches and the sound is enough to tilt his control into something darker. His eyes flash and his mouth drops closer. Close enough that his lips graze the corner of my mouth with a whisper of contact. A test that jolts my whole body like he struck a match inside of me.

"You're fucking killing me," he snaps.

I gasp, and it's over. Tucker makes a low sound in his throat before his mouth is on mine. It's not gentle or soft. It's controlled only by how badly he's trying not to consume me whole. His hand tightens at my waist, pulling me flush against him and every inch of air between us disappears.

I kiss him back without restraint—without permission.

My fingers twist in his shirt harder, pulling him into me as if there's any space left. He deepens the kiss like he feels me choosing him and can't stop himself from taking more. He kisses like he's been waiting. Like every joke, every smirk, and every teasing comment was just him trying to survive wanting me.

My knees feel weak, but Tucker catches me. Wrapping an arm around my waist before spinning me and slamming my back against the door. My hands fly to his hair, tangling them in there as his tongue swipes against my bottom lip. I open for him, allowing him in completely. The kiss turns hungrier as if he can't decide if he wants to ruin me or keep me safe. Maybe both.

I should be panicking.

I should be pulling away.

Instead, I lift my chin, chasing his mouth again like he's the air I need to breathe. My hips rock forward, pressing into him as I moan into his mouth. His hand moves from my waist, slipping to the back of my neck as fingers tangle in my hair. He groans softly against my lips, and the vibration goes straight through me.

"Fuck," he says, pulling away just a fraction. "You have no idea what you do to me."

My chest is rising and falling too fast. "Do you want to stop?"

He shakes his head. "Not a fucking chance, Scottie." His mouth hovers mine again. "I want to keep going until you forget every single voice that ever told you that you have to be perfect to deserve what you want."

I blink, unable to process what he's saying.

He sees right through me. Of course he does.

"You can't say things like that."

His eyes soften. "I can, because it's true."

And for one terrifying second, I see it. I see what it would feel like to let him.

To stop holding myself together.

To stop performing.

To let someone else carry me for once.

The idea is so foreign it hurts.

Instead of thinking too much into it, I grip his shirt, pulling him down to meet my lips again, and allow myself to get lost in this moment with him.

Even if just for tonight.

CHAPTER 17

TO YOU, THIS IS ALL PRETEND AND FOR SHOW, BUT...

TUCKER

This kiss feels like an escape.

My words touched a nerve she didn't want to wake up, and I can feel it in the way her lips press against mine. I pull back, still pressing my body against hers on the door.

"Scottie."

She shakes her head, the emotions written on her face. "Stop. Don't. Just…keep doing this before I change my mind."

I step back, putting distance between us and hating how cold the room feels without her skin on mine. She looks up at me, shocked that I did.

"I meant what I said. You have no idea what you do to me," I say, pointing at her, feeling some type of irrational rage inside of me. "You drive me insane with the back and forth game. You don't move when I get close or touch you, leading me to think something is there. I know, to you this is all pretend and for show, but…" My words trail off, fearing I've already said too much and might scare her away.

I'm so gone for this woman.

There's no mistaking that.

She crosses her arms over her chest. "What you said before. About forgetting the voices."

"Yeah?"

"How?" she asks. "You don't even know me."

I step into her again. My body pulling me toward her on its own. I lift my hand, cupping her face before my hand slides from her jaw to her throat, stopping where her pulse jumps under my palm. My eyes land there and then lift back up to hers.

"Then let me. Let me be the one who does."

Something inside her cracks just enough that her body relaxes. Her hands find my chest, softly. No urgency in the way she touches me this time. No chasing away the feelings she was trying to hide.

I lean down, pressing my lips to hers to quiet any racing thoughts.

My hands slide to her hips, firm, pulling her closer until she's fully pressed against me again. Close enough that I can feel the heat of her through my clothes. She grinds her hips into me. Reaching down, but not releasing her mouth from mine, I grip her behind her legs to lift her. As soon as I do, both legs wrap tightly around my waist. I slam her back into the wall, as if a primal need to claim her in so many ways rips through me.

I thrust toward her, and she moans against my lips. My cock is bursting at the seams of my jeans. Everything about Scottie turns me on. The way she sounds. The way she's clawing at my back. The way she's angling her head just right to allow me to deepen the kiss.

I pull back and she whimpers at the loss of contact. "I'm not going to apologize for wanting you," I say, breathlessly, thrusting my hips into her. "I'm fucking done pretending I don't."

Something flashes in her eyes right then and there.

I see it.

I see the shift in her thoughts without meaning to. The way she's looking from my eyes, to my lips, and back up. Her arms wrapped around my neck and legs still around my waist. She's done pretending, too.

"So, what now?" I ask.

"What now," she whispers, unwrapping her legs to stand in front of me, "is you stop talking."

My hands cup both sides of her face, and I kiss her again—slow and deliberate this time. Savoring her. This time, she spins me, slamming my back to the door. I grip her waist, pulling her flush into me. Her hands work frantically between us, trying to undo the belt of my jeans.

"Scottie," I say into her mouth.

"Shh."

"Fuck," I murmur, kissing her again.

She undoes my belt, pulling it from the loop before tossing it to the floor beside me.

"What are you doing?"

"I'm done pretending, too, Tucker," she says against my lips before dropping to the floor in front of me.

She keeps her eyes locked on mine, and when she reaches up to unbutton my jeans, pushing them down my legs, I suck in a breath. It's not what I came here for. Kissing Scottie so she knows I'm done pretending was enough for me.

But this…seeing her on her knees for me…

"Fuck," I draw out as she pulls my boxer briefs down my legs. "You're going to ruin me."

"Good."

She grips my cock in her hand, and I hiss at the contact but don't take my eyes off every move she makes. Her hand slides up and down from base to tip, coating her palm with my precum. I already know I'm not going to last. There's no way with how perfect she looks right now.

She rises, just enough, and licks up my cock, swirling her tongue over the head. A groan vibrates through my body at the same time she takes me into her mouth. The world around me goes fuzzy and I feel like I can't breathe. Her eyes never leave mine as she bobs her head up and down, eager to suck my cock.

I place one hand on the back of her head, thrusting my hips forward. Her legs squirm under her, rubbing together as if she's getting pleasure from doing this.

"You look damn good on your knees for me, baby."

Her eyes flutter until they close, letting my words settle into her, but I reach down, taking her face between my hands, and force her to look at me.

"Eyes open. I want you to look at me while you suck my cock. I want you to see how it makes me feel."

She nods in approval, picking up her pace. She reaches one hand down between her legs, rubbing herself over the fabric of her leggings.

"This is usually the part where I tell you not to touch yourself," I growl. "The part where I tell you that only *I* will be touching that perfect pussy and making you come. But..." My words fall from my lips as her other hand comes up to cup my balls and she sucks my cock harder. "Fuck. Reach into your pants. Show me how wet you are."

She does as I ask, moaning around my length as she touches herself. She starts rubbing faster circles around her clit and I watch as her eyes flutter closed.

"Now show me."

Lifting two glistening fingers up, she shows me how fucking turned on she is.

"Good girl."

She releases my cock from her mouth with a pop, before smearing the two fingers over the head. I nearly fall over the edge from that alone. *Jesus Christ, that's hot.*

"Scottie," I warn.

She smirks up at me. "Now fuck my mouth, Tucker."

"My pleasure."

My hand reaches the back of her head, and she takes me in her mouth, bobbing up and down before I hold her in place. My hips thrust over and over again and I feel my cock hit the back of her throat. She doesn't gag but takes me like I'm made for her.

"I'm going to come, Scottie," I rasp, feeling my stomach tighten. "Unless you want my cum down the back of your throat, I'd stop. *Now*."

She doesn't move or release me from her mouth, and I see the smirk form on her lips as she looks up at me. It's enough to send me over the edge completely. My orgasm rocks me sharp and fast. The tension that's been coiled tight inside of me since she first came into town snaps all at once, and I can't hold it back even if I try. Every muscle locks and my mind goes white around the edges.

All I can think about is her.

Scottie's name is stuck in my throat like a prayer as I spill down her throat.

My chest rises and falls as I look down at her. She's still looking up at me as she wipes her lips with the back of her finger. I pull her up quickly, and she squeals with a laugh before I kiss her again. Tasting myself on her lips is enough to make me hard all over again.

I reach between her, cupping her pussy through her pants and feel the wetness through the fabric on my hand. "Jesus. You're dripping."

She nods repeatedly. "Yes. I'm so turned on. I can't even think straight."

I reach into her leggings while she claws at my shoulders. Her lips part as soon as I reach her clit. Putting just the right amount of pressure before rubbing slow circles.

"Did sucking my cock turn you on?"

"Yes," she moans. "God, yes."

She releases her hold on me, enough to hook her fingers into the waistband of her leggings, shimmying them to the floor. She opens wider for me, letting me in. The memory of exploring her body comes back almost instantly.

Because I know her body.

I spent hours upon hours studying every curve that night in the hotel room.

I learned what drives her crazy and sends her over the edge.

Dipping my head down, she tilts her head to the side, giving me access to her neck. I press my lips to it once. "This is one of my favorite versions of you. Unfiltered. Messy. Dripping for me." I press another kiss to her neck, this time sucking the skin above her pulse while my finger picks up the pace above her clit. "Wild and carefree." My teeth graze her skin and she moans when I insert two fingers deep inside of her. "My girl."

"Fuck. Tucker!"

"Say it."

"Say what?" she pants.

"Say you're my girl, Scottie. Say I'm yours, and I'll make you come right here against this door."

She fists my shirt in her hands, pulling me into her and slamming her lips to mine. Silent confirmation—I think. But I devour her moans, her breaths, and every gasp she releases as I fuck her with my fingers. Hard and fast.

She releases my mouth by biting my bottom lip playfully. "Are you threatening to hold back an orgasm if I don't say it?" She grins. "Don't forget, I know how to handle myself."

Ah. There's my sassy Scottie.

I reach deeper inside of her pussy, hooking a finger at just the right angle to make her eyes close and lips part in pleasure.

"I'm insufferable, remember?" I say breathlessly against her mouth. "I know you can handle yourself. But it's my turn now."

I bring my thumb to her clit and add pressure to really drive her crazy.

"Fuck," she murmurs, her body melting into me as her legs tremble barely able to hold herself up. "You are insufferable. But you're..." She pauses, feeling me hook my finger again. "Jesus. That's hot."

"If you want to come, just say the words."

"Say please."

I smirk. Fuck, this girl is going to absolutely ruin me. "Please, baby."

"You're so hot when you beg," she breathes out, rolling her hips against my hand. She reaches down between us, circling her hand around my wrist and picks up her pace. She fucks herself against my hand and all I can do is stare down between us in fascination.

Christ. She's perfect.

"Yes. I'm coming," she moans, letting her head fall back as her orgasm rocks her.

I move my fingers in and out of her quickly, feeling her pussy clench around me. It's enough to make me come again right in my hand, but I don't. I hold it in. Memorizing the way her face looks when she allows herself to tip over the edge, so I can think about it every night before going to bed.

Scottie may have not said it, but she's mine in every sense of the word.

As soon as the thought enters my mind, panic takes over.

Mine means letting her in.

Mine means she gets close enough to see what I keep buried.

So, when she comes down from her orgasm, I take her face in mine, pressing a kiss to her lips again, and hope like hell she doesn't feel the rising panic inside of me. Like I can convince myself I didn't just ruin this. I yank up my jeans, wordlessly and she does the same.

Fuck. Fuck. Fuck.

I crossed the line with her.

A line I've wanted to cross, because I'm so gone for her.

So why does it feel like regret clawing up my throat?

I freeze halfway through pulling on my shirt because this is the part where I would disappear without a word, but I don't. When my eyes find hers, I can see it in her face. She's expecting *me* to run the way I did the first time.

But I'm not.

"Hey," I say quietly. She looks up at me with soft eyes that wreck me. "I'm not doing what I did last time. I'm not running from you."

I see the relief flash across her face, and that alone hits me harder than the panic moments ago of us blurring the lines. Stepping closer to her, I take her face in my hands and press my forehead against hers. "I meant everything I said tonight. Don't run from me, because I'm not running from you." I kiss her once. "Let *me* be the one who knows you. All of you." I kiss her again.

She nods, cheeks shift to the perfect shade of pink.

"I'll see you tomorrow, Scottie."

"Tomorrow."

I walk out of the apartment with my lungs burning, because the truth is simple and brutal—Scottie deserves something steady.

And I'm the kind of man who ruins good things by touching them.

EPISODE FOUR

HOLDING IT TOGETHER

On today's episode of Nailed It or Failed It, *we're moving on to the living room. Years of water damage have left the ceiling sagging and the stakes sky-high.*

As Scottie pushes bold design and Tucker fights for structural sanity, things get...intense. And when a ladder misstep sends one of them tumbling, the real shock isn't the fall. It's the way they catch each other.

Let's just say...the ceiling isn't the only thing under pressure.

CHAPTER 18
THAT'S WHAT PEOPLE SAY RIGHT
BEFORE I HAVE TO CALL AN AMBULANCE.

TUCKER

We're making really good progress on the renovation.

The kitchen finally looks real. The cabinets are done, the floors replaced, the butcher-block counters installed, and the new range hood mounted. My crew has been through all the different parts of this house over the last few days. The stairs leading to the second floor have been replaced, allowing the crew to complete some of the smaller rooms upstairs.

Scottie has been in and out of the house the last couple of days. My crew worked on the outside of the house bracing the bricks of the chimney so it no longer leans, and she focused on a few of the smaller rooms upstairs, painting. Our paths have crossed a few times, but I've struggled to read her. I'm worried I went too far with her. But she's been acting…normal.

Easy smiles. Quick hellos. Like we didn't unravel each other in the apartment.

We haven't been able to really talk because I'm pulled one way with my crew and she's pulled the other by producers. I can't tell if she's giving me space or she's already learned how to bury what happened in her mind.

But every time I think about it, my body remembers before

my brain can catch up. The heat. Her mouth. The way she sounded when she said my name like she meant it.

And then the panic hits because I didn't just cross a line. I sprinted over it like it wasn't even there.

A part of me wants her—wants her to stay and see what we can be outside of this charade. The other part of me is terrified. So instead, I focus on what needs to be done on the house.

Progress, the one thing keeping me sane.

It's the only thing I can control.

Nails. Boards. Drywall. Angles and measurements.

But not her. Not the way she slips under my skin like she's always belonged there.

Now, the living room? It's still a war zone. Half of the drywall is ripped out, and the water-damaged section of the ceiling looks like it might come down just because it's tired of existing.

I thought the kitchen would be the worst of all the projects Scottie had planned. Turns out it's this. Which is why we're here extra early to get a head start.

Levi kicks a chunk of molding aside. "What do you think? Did this leak start in the '70s?"

"Don't care," I grunt out, dragging the ladder into the middle of the living room. "We're fixing this before she gets here today."

Before I have to look at her and pretend my hands don't remember the shape of her.

He snorts. "Right. Because all you care about is preventing mold. Not impressing the pretty influencer who makes you forget how to speak in full sentences."

I flip him off.

He grins. "Touchy."

Levi has always been one of my favorite guys to work with. He's fast and steady. But he's also annoyingly perceptive. And lately, it feels like the whole damn world can see the problem stamped across my face.

I don my work gloves and climb the ladder. Bracing myself, I reach down, and Levi hands me the crowbar, shaking his head like he's giving a chainsaw to a toddler.

"Try not to rip your shoulder out."

"I'm fine."

"Sureee," he draws out.

"Levi." I say his name as a warning.

"Yes?"

"Shut up."

Looking overhead, I assess the ceiling. The plaster is already cracked into a spider web that seems to spread more by the minute, with a water stain painted on like a bruise. It's ugly in the way something ignored always is. Like the house got tired of begging and decided to scream instead.

"Okay," I say, more to myself than him. "Let's get this down."

Levi backs away so he's not stuck under the debris when it falls. "Go on then, Hulk."

I wedge the edge of the crowbar into one of the cracks between joists, brace myself on the ladder, and pull hard. The first section gives with a sharp snap. Dust rains down like old ghosts, and chunks of plaster break loose, crashing to the floor. The sound is violent but satisfying.

Levi lets out a low whistle. "Damn. She really let this place rot."

I don't answer, but shove the crowbar again, harder, ripping out another section. More insulation spills out, exposing water rotted wood. Each pull is a release of something tense and ancient in the room.

And maybe in me.

Because the mess feels familiar. Something that should've been dealt with a long time ago, but wasn't.

"You good?"

"I'm fine."

I'm not, but saying it out loud right now feels wrong.

"Are you sure? Because you're going at the ceiling like it's personally responsible for hurting you."

"It kind of is."

He laughs again, but not as loud, like he's not sure if it's joke territory.

The truth is…demolition has always been the easiest part because it's controlled. You know what's coming, what stays up, and what you can salvage. You plan the damage.

People aren't like that.

Relationships sure as hell aren't.

Levi coughs. "Remind me to never piss you off."

"You already piss me off daily," I counter.

"Yeah, but mildly. I'd like to avoid this"—he twirls his finger in the air—"full rage version of Tucker."

"This isn't rage."

He gestures to the carnage. "Then what is this?"

I prop the crowbar on my shoulder and look up at the ceiling. Assessing the beams that are exposed to the light again.

"It's just…" I exhale slowly. "Getting rid of what's been holding the place back."

Because I know what rot does if you leave it long enough.

It spreads.

It ruins everything around it.

"Very poetic of you."

I flip him off again, and he grins. "So, is this the part where you pretend you're not losing it over her?"

Levi isn't stupid. He may not know what happened with Scottie, but I know he can tell something has changed. I've always been a hard worker and try to fix the things no one wants to touch. What's new is the intensity to it.

"I'm not losing it."

I'm containing it. There's a difference.

The room goes quiet, and Levi doesn't argue back. The only sound is the nail gun in the distance from the rest of the crew working, and the shuffle of debris as Levi moves around the living room.

It's almost peaceful.

And then I hear the front door creak open. I feel her before I see her, turning my head to the entryway of the living room, waiting for her to emerge.

Scottie stops at the edge of the hallway, looking between Levi and me, probably wondering what the hell is happening.

I open my mouth to ask her why she's here earlier than usual, but all the words fall from my tongue, because she looks like sunshine today—the way she always does.

Her hair is down, loose curls fall down the front of her chest. She's wearing a pair of loose-fitting jeans and a V-neck T-shirt tucked in at the front. Her shirt is a bright royal blue that brings out the color of her eyes.

It's intoxicating.

Levi breaks the silence. "I thought we weren't filming today," he says at the base of the ladder, keeping his voice low.

"We're not," I answer him, looking at her.

"Oh boy," Levi mutters under his breath, and I shoot him a warning glare.

"What are you doing here so early?" I ask. It comes out rougher than intended.

Her eyes glaze over the room, taking in the missing drywall and exposed wood in the ceiling. "I wanted to know what caused it," she says softly. "The water stain. I knew you guys were starting this today, and I couldn't stop thinking about it. Wanted to make sure it wasn't still leaking from anywhere."

"Don't worry," I say, reaching up to slap the wood in the ceiling, almost losing my footing on the ladder. "I've got it handled."

"Right." She crosses her arms over her chest, eying the ladder. "That's what people say right before someone has to call an ambulance."

Levi chuckles under his breath. "She's got you there."

"Why don't you go to the truck and get my measuring tape?"

He narrows his eyes. "Why do you need that?"

"Levi." I give him a knowing look, slightly tipping my head toward Scottie.

"Oh, right." He salutes me dramatically and disappears from the room.

Scottie still stands where she was, so I turn around to pull more of the ceiling down. I feel her move closer, hovering just enough that I can feel her presence like static on my skin. My legs tremble slightly on the ladder for half a second.

"Should we be saving this stuff for when we film?" she asks.

"We could." I shrug, pulling another piece off the ceiling and tossing it away from her. "I just figured this would save us some time. If Levi and I gut it today, the production crew won't be tripping over the ugly parts tomorrow."

"Right."

"Trust me. The cameras will appreciate us doing the messy work when they're not watching. It's a dust storm in here." I glance down at her. "And as much as I like having you here, I don't love the idea the ceiling might fall on you."

"Yeah," she says softly, looking around at the debris on the ground. "I'm not really worried about the ceiling."

I pause with one hand braced on the ladder, staring at her while she continues looking down.

"About the other night…" she starts, pausing as she twists her fingers together in front of her. My body goes rigid and I feel my heartbeat slam against my ribs. Her gaze trails up to meet mine. "You really meant it, didn't you?"

She means about me disappearing again.

She doesn't need to say it for me to know what she's asking.

I nod. "I meant what I said, Scottie. Every word."

Her shoulders drop in relief, like she's been holding that for too long. "Good."

I exhale, feeling the doubt that I went too far with her, slipping away. Quiet stretches between us in a way that makes it feel like we should probably say something else, but neither of us know how to without tipping it into something bigger.

She glances at the ladder, and then back to me.

"You shouldn't be up the ladder by yourself."

"Levi is here."

She huffs. "You sent him away to get something. What if you fell while he was gone?"

"You don't trust me on the ladder, Scottie?" I tease.

"Of course I don't," she scoffs. "You do dumb things."

I turn my head, looking down at her. "I do?"

She crosses her arms. "Don't think the crew didn't tell me about you climbing a ladder just like this while holding a circular saw yesterday."

I breathe a sigh of relief that she didn't think one of the dumb things I did was show up and make her come all over my hand. I roll my eyes. "That was one time."

"You're basically a trip to the hospital waiting to happen."

I prop my hip on the tallest part of the ladder, grinning down at her like a fool. "You worried about me, babe?"

The word slips out way too easily. The second I hear it leave my lips, something warm flickers through my chest because I didn't call her that for the cameras. I said it because it felt natural.

"Don't flatter yourself," she huffs, averting her gaze the moment her cheeks turn pink. "I'd just be annoyed if you got hurt. This whole show would fall apart."

My smile grows wider, and I adjust my body again on the ladder. It wobbles, just slightly. But Scottie reaches forward to grab my calf to hold me steady—gasping.

Everything in me stills.

Her fingers grip tight, and I can feel the shaking of her hands through my jeans.

"Careful," she blurts out quickly. "If you fall, I..." The words die as she bites back the rest of the sentence.

"What? Do you think I'll sue?" I offer the joke to calm her panic.

She exhales. "I'll have to find another contractor."

"Touching," I deadpan.

She flusters. "You're barely replaceable. Don't let it get to your head."

"Barely?" I shoot her a lopsided grin and shrug. "I'll take it."

Her eyes remain fixed on where her hands grip my calves, before she slowly trails them up my body until they settle on mine. They don't sparkle, but there's something in them I've only seen twice with her.

Unguarded.

Vulnerable.

It's the first time I've seen concern on her face that isn't wrapped in sarcasm. This is real concern that sucker-punches me right in the stomach.

I move my foot to step down the ladder, and her hands fall away reluctantly, like she didn't realize she was still touching me. When I reach the floor, I step closer to her, putting only inches between us.

"Are you okay?"

She nods repeatedly. "I didn't think the ladder would actually wobble like that. I was only joking about the whole falling thing, and—"

I bring both hands up, cupping her upper arms. "You're shaking."

"No. I'm just cold."

"It's warm in here."

"It's drafty."

"There's no draft."

Her jaw tightens, no doubt because she hates being seen. It's not the polished version of Scottie she gives the cameras.

I should step back. I should turn away before I fall into the same spell we put ourselves in back at the apartment. Instead, my hand instinctively lifts from her arm, reaching for her face. My hand hovers under her chin, wanting to tilt her face up and assure her I'm okay.

But Levi appears, clearing his throat. "Am I interrupting?"

Scottie steps back like she's been electrocuted, and I exhale. "Perfect timing, *buddy*."

My hands fall to my sides like they don't know what to do when I'm not touching her.

His grin says he knows exactly what he walked in on. He lifts his head to the ceiling. "Lord save me from slow burn fools."

Scottie tucks a strand of hair behind her ear, hiking a thumb over her shoulder. "I-I should go. I just came to check in."

I nod, watching as she takes one, two steps backward before turning on her heel toward the hallway. Before she disappears, she looks back. Her eyes drag over me—my hands, my body, then to the ladder and the ceiling. Worry lingers in her stare, no matter how hard she tries to hide it.

"Be careful," she says softly. "You're…important to this project."

And there it is. The loophole she gives herself.

Project. Not me.

But I hear the part she doesn't say anyway.

I swallow down the dozens of things I want to say to that, and offer her a nod instead. "Always am."

She presses her lips together in a flat line and leaves.

The silence that follows feels huge.

"Dude. She's gone," Levi says, snapping me out of my stare.

"I know."

"You can breathe now."

"I am breathing," I fire back sharply.

"Sure," he draws out. "If that's what we're calling whatever the hell you're doing."

I shake my head, climbing back up the ladder. Where moments ago I was steady and sure, now my hands tremble.

I can't tell if it's from the wobble or her reaction.

She cares about *me*.

And I'm pretending, *really pretending,* that thought alone doesn't completely undo me.

CHAPTER 19
WHAT EXACTLY ARE THEY NOTICING?

SCOTTIE

BLAIR

Girls' night at my place tonight.

BLAIR

Griffin is working at the bar.

LILY

I'm so in.

POPPY

I'm going to stay in tonight. I promised Sage a pedicure date.

LILY

You get a pass because we love Sage.

ME

I just got done filming for the day. I'm exhausted.

BLAIR

Sweatpants mandatory.

LILY

And I'll bring cookies and a bottle of sangria.

It's already dark out by the time I make it to Blair's place.

I almost texted them that I changed my mind after the long day of filming we had.

Tucker was right yesterday when he said we were better off gutting the living room before the camera crew came into the space. The ceiling and the debris were completely gone when I showed up this morning. Apparently, the water stain was from a loose pipe beneath the master bathroom that was slowly leaking over the years, creating that ugly brown halo in the ceiling.

Tucker and Levi fixed the problem before we re-insulated and patched the drywall in front of the camera today. Then we moved to refinishing the brick around the fireplace from its natural red to a rustic white and then put built-in bookshelves around that. Just when I thought we were going to call it a day, they insisted we paint the walls and the ceiling.

I swore up and down that I could paint the room myself.

But Tucker fought back with his perfect smile, saying he was going to help.

My issue is, I still don't know what to think about what happened a few days ago in my apartment. The way he made me feel. The way the moment now lives under my skin.

I saw the panic in his eyes when we finished.

I know because I felt that same rising panic, but it wasn't over the fear of him leaving without a word, it was because of the fear of him regretting it knowing I set clear rules for us outside of this fake dating charade on screen. I told myself I could tuck it away in the same box I kept every other messy thing I can't afford to feel while the cameras are rolling.

Only Tucker changed.

It's the small things, really.

The way he watched me work today—the way he smiled or the way his hands brushed mine in passing or the way I could feel his eyes on me from across the room whenever I was working on something.

The worst part is, somewhere deep in my gut, I want it to happen again.

Knowing damn well it can't. I can't afford the distraction any more than he has already given me. Not when I've fought so hard to build this version of myself to land this show.

The porch light glows softly, and I hear the sound of laughter coming from inside the house the moment I step out of my car. Lantern lights hang along the front railing, and there's a little flower box sitting on the top of the steps overflowing with wildflowers.

I grip the six-pack of hard cider I grabbed at the General Store in one hand, and knock with the other.

The door swings open before my hand is even at my side.

"There she is," Lily says. She's wearing sweatpants, bare feet, and an oversized cardigan that hangs to her knees. "Get in here, girl."

She hooks an arm around my shoulders and guides me inside. Blair appears in the hallway, tossing a dishtowel over one shoulder. "Yay! You made it."

Her tone is almost relieved, like she didn't think I'd come.

"Of course," I say, holding up the cider. "I brought gifts."

Lily plucks the six pack from my hand. "She comes bearing alcohol. We keep her."

I laugh and follow her inside. I take my sneakers off, set them by the front door, and follow Lily into the kitchen. It's beautiful. An open concept room with the kitchen sitting on one side, the island separating it from the living room.

"Okay. Love those socks. Ten out of ten. And they match!" Her hand flies to her chest as if she didn't expect it.

I look down at my feet and wiggle my toes. They are bright pink fuzzy socks with little flamingos scattered across them.

I laugh. "My personality may be bold and chaotic, but my socks are organized."

"Put that on a shirt," Blair says, pointing the wine opener in my direction.

Lily guides me into the living room, and it's exactly what I expect from Blair. It's cozy with mismatched throw pillows, a faded quilt over the back, and a stack of romance books on the end table. She has a candle lit that smells like vanilla and amber.

Two wineglasses and one cider bottle already sit on the coasters of the coffee table. There's a plate of what looks like…

"Are those—"

"Twisted cinnamon knots," Lily finishes for me, proudly. "Blair and I were experimenting tonight since Griffin is working at the bar. He's too tempted to eat everything if he's here, so we do it when he's out." She laughs. "And you're the guinea pig for these tonight."

"I will make the sacrifice for the bakery cause," I say, my mouth watering as I drop onto the couch.

"Good. It will make me feel better since I'm still struggling with emotional damage from last week."

Blair laughs, curling herself into the couch across from me, tucking one leg under her. "Ignore her, Scottie. She's been dramatic since Dallas made her cry over a board game."

"He cheated!" Lily protests.

"No. He strategized."

"Same thing."

I lean back on the couch, the tension between my shoulder blades easing. "Okay, now I have questions about this board game."

"Okay, so—" Lily starts.

"No," Blair cuts her off. "We aren't going there again." She turns to face us. "Instead, we want to hear about how the renovation is going. You said there was a mystery water stain. Did you find out what it was?"

I smile, because Lily and Blair have been very eager to hear all the progress whenever I stop by the bakery on my way in to work on the house. The last time I saw them was when I was on my way to ask Tucker about it yesterday.

"It was a nightmare. No one knew exactly where it was coming from at first. But once Tucker got in there yesterday, he noticed the slow drip from the boards. The primary bathroom tub piping was leaking. It was so slow that no one caught it when my grandmother was alive. But over time, it's just grown larger and larger."

Blair grimaces. "Yikes."

"Yeah," I say. "Tucker had to replace the whole section before replacing the ceiling."

Lily pours sangria into a glass and hands it to me. "But it's not leaking anymore, right?"

I take the glass from her and shake my head. "It's all new now. It'll look good on camera." I try to smile like that's all that matters.

Blair tilts her head, watching me. "And off camera?"

I fiddle with the stem of my wineglass. "Off camera, it's just a ceiling that almost gave out and is fixed now."

"Well," Lily says, sitting up straighter on the couch next to me. "We are very pro ceiling not caving in on your head."

"Same." I nod. "My head is already working overtime for this show."

They laugh, and the moment passes.

But not entirely, because for me it lingers in the corners. Thinking about how much my head is really working overtime, not just with the project and wanting it to be successful, but with Tucker.

With what this place is starting to mean.

With what happens when it's over.

The show has an end date. I've been so focused on it that I haven't even let myself think about what comes after the last scene and everyone packs up their equipment.

Do I stay?

Do I leave?

The idea of leaving used to feel obvious—renovate the house, prove myself, and move on. But lately, the thought of going back to my old life feels…off. Like I'll be stepping back into a version of myself that doesn't quite fit anymore. And staying would means choosing this town and choosing a house I'm still learning about.

We settle in, laughing over drinks and snacks. Determining that the cinnamon twists are a must carry at the bakery, Blair tells me the story about how she met Griffin. My sides hurt from laughing so hard when she brought up the story about screaming bloody murder over a moose creeping outside the window while she was in the shower, and Griffin barging in like a Neanderthal to "save her."

Lily reaches for a paperback from the stack and waves it vaguely. "Okay, next order of business. We've decided you need to join our book club. It's nothing official. Just Blair and me. Sometimes Poppy."

I shrug, reaching for the book. "What's it about?"

"We can't give *all* the details away, but it's a hockey romance."

"It's soooo good," Blair adds. "It follows a team called the Boston Rebels. It's chef's kiss!"

I look down at the cover, with the couple's character art on the front, and shrug. "I could use a little escape from reality. If I can find time."

Lily leans in. "That's why we wanted to recommend it to you. We thought it might…I don't know…" She pauses. "Be good for you."

Fear grips my chest, thinking they can see through me. I worry that these two already notice how unhappy I am inside; hidden behind the sunny mask I hope no one can see through.

"I like happy endings," I say. "On-screen ones. You know, watching them."

Blair's gaze sharpens. "What about off-screen? Do you get them in your life, too?"

"Blair." Lily whispers her name like she's prying too much.

I swirl the sangria in my glass, and the silence between us lingers in the air. They don't push, they just wait. I've never had this before. The people who come into my life fall into two circles: the ones who don't notice the seams, and the ones who rush to pull at them.

Blair and Lily are letting me decide.

The choice makes me feel dizzy.

I clear my throat and attempt to change the subject. "So. How many tragic board game deaths did Dallas cause last week besides yours?"

Lily groans dramatically, flopping back against the couch. "He bought hotels on all the orange properties and destroyed me."

Blair lifts her glass. "Rest in peace, your savings."

"It's fine," Lily says, sitting up again with a devious smile on her face. "I got my revenge when I made him try my new experimental muffins before they were ready."

"What was wrong with them?"

"They were…dense."

Blair chokes on a laugh. "That's putting it mildly. They could've been used as building materials."

"Perfect for Tucker," I say with a laugh.

Blair's eyes flicker at his name. Lily's do too.

"Speaking of Tucker," Lily says first. "I'm telling you this with love, but the entire town is talking about you two."

My stomach bottoms out. "Talking about us, how?"

Blair scoffs. "How do you think? He's the head contractor on your team, you two are working *very* closely together all day, and you argue like it's foreplay—"

"Blair!" Lily cuts her off.

"And a few people saw you stay late at the bar after karaoke night," Blair continues. "Someone even thought you two were already engaged by the way Tucker was looking at you."

I turn and give Lily a knowing look, because she was the

reason I was still there waiting for a ride, but she averts her gaze and tightens her lips. "To be fair, that same woman thinks anyone within six inches of each other is engaged. But still, people are noticing."

"What exactly are they noticing?" I ask.

Blair sighs. "They're noticing the same thing the producers noticed. The chemistry. The spark! And there's no denying the way Tucker looks at you when he thinks no one is watching."

My breath shudders, barely noticeable but enough to betray me. My brain is now doing backflips because, of course, they noticed. Of course, *everyone* noticed. Tucker doesn't exactly do subtle when he's staring at me like I'm the only person in the room. I know the look everyone sees, I've felt it burn along my skin when the cameras weren't rolling, and I've seen it soften behind closed doors when he's done pretending.

But hearing them say it?

Hearing someone else notice it?

I shake my head, heat crawling up my neck. "I don't...I mean, I'm not—"

Lily holds up a hand. "I know you're freaking out, but you should also know we're thrilled about it."

"For what it's worth..." Blair starts, smiling, "Tucker's different around you. Even before we knew any of this."

"The only time both of us have ever been around you two together is that night at Seven Stools though."

"It was all we needed to see," Lily says softly.

We sit in silence for a moment, the conversation stalling while Tucker's name flows through my head.

But I know, deep down, it isn't really about him.

It's about how easily Blair and Lily saw something real when I've spent years making sure everything in my life looked controlled and impressive enough to defend.

Even my feelings.

Especially my feelings.

And for the past two weeks, working on the house, everything has felt off. It has nothing to do with Tucker and everything to do with the unsettling truth that I still can't feel this place the way I keep telling everyone I do. I haven't figured out a way to voice my feelings, but this moment feels right.

I keep my eyes on the glass in my hands. "Can I tell you something…without judgment or pity?"

I lift my eyes to see their reaction, and they both go still and then slowly nod.

"No pity here," Lily says, placing a hand on my thigh. "Just vibes and maybe some sarcasm."

I inhale, and it feels like inhaling broken glass. "I don't feel… what I thought I would."

Blair tilts her head.

"You mean with the fake relationship on screen with Tucker?" Lily asks.

I shake my head. "With the house. This project." Blair sits forward in her seat, worry on her face and I let out a nervous laughter. "I know…this is very opposite of what we were just talking about. But it's been something I've needed to get out."

"You're safe with us," Blair assures me.

I offer her a thankful smile. "You see…my dad told me a story about how when my grandfather died before I was born, the house lost its shine. So, coming to Bluestone Lakes and taking on this project for the show, I made that my goal."

"I love that," Lily says with a smile.

I pick at the invisible thread of my sweatpants. "I've gone through every room of that house. Some of them we've already completed. Every cabinet and every closet," I say. "And there are no photos, no boxes, no old letters, no *nothing*. Nothing that I can connect with. It's…just a house."

Blair frowns. "That's kind of sad."

"It is," I whisper. "I was hoping for even the smallest bit of memories to be here when I showed up. I didn't even know she died when I was thirteen."

"What?" Lily gasps.

I nod. "My dad told me when I got offered this season of *Nailed It or Failed It*. I didn't know I needed to supply a house for the project and he told me about this one and how it was left to *me*. I was left a house by a grandparent I can't even remember for the life of me."

"Scottie," Blair whispers sympathetically.

I point a finger at her and force a smile. "Hey, I said no pity."

She holds up her hands in defense. "I can't help it. I feel things deeply, okay?"

We laugh lightly—and it feels good.

"My issue is that I keep saying I'm doing this for her. For my grandmother. To make it shine again like it's some big, emotional full circle moment."

"But?" Lily asks gently.

"But this house…it doesn't feel like anything more than a project to help me prove to my mom that renovation and DIY work is more than a hobby for me." I let my eyes trail down to my fingers clasped together in my lap as the familiar ache creeps into my ribs. "And I fucking hate that feeling."

Lily reaches over, taking my hand in hers. "I am so sorry you've had to go through that. From watching you work here on this house and stalking you on social media—shamelessly," she says, looking at Blair who nods her head in approval as if she made sure Lily saw my work. She turns to face me again. "I can tell you love what you do. You put your heart and soul into it, and *that* alone tells us this isn't a hobby for you. It's your life. It's your job. And you're able to make sage green cabinets look like the eighth wonder of the world."

I choke on a laugh, completely unexpected. "But they *are* the eighth wonder of the world."

"You're right," Lily smiles widely. "So let's not let anyone convince you otherwise."

"It helps when your two worlds collide, too," Blair cuts in. "When I first moved here, baking was my hobby. I loved it and lived in my kitchen back in the city. After I met Lily when I got to town and she offered me a job at Batter Up, I nearly kissed her feet."

"It's true," Lily agrees.

Blair exhales and leans back in her chair. "Look, all I'm saying is that everyone acts like the only real careers are the ones that look miserable from the outside. But most people who actually make it big? They start with the thing they'd do for free. They just refuse to stop when everyone else tells them it's not practical or realistic."

"That's…" I start, but shake my head in disbelief. "That's exactly what I've heard over and over again from my mom."

Lily squeezes my hand. "A hobby doesn't stay a hobby when you build a life around it. It becomes a craft. A career. A calling." Her words get louder with every one she says.

"Are you going to keep going?" Blair asks.

"A gift. A message," she continues with rapid and dramatic hand movements.

"We get it, Lil." Blair says to her and then faces me. "What I think she's trying to say is that a hobby is what you do when you're bored. A career is what you build when you're brave enough to bet on yourself."

Brave enough to bet on yourself.

I've spent so long trying to prove this to my mom that I didn't stop to consider whether I believed it, too. And for the first time since I got here, it doesn't feel like I'm defending my dream, it feels like I'm standing in it.

"And about the house," Lily says. "If you haven't been able to find a single thing, you should talk to Nan. She knows every single thing about this town and the people in it or used to be in it."

"Really?"

She nods. "I'm sure she can help you find what you're looking for and probably has pictures around somewhere, knowing her."

"Thank you. This means a lot to me. I will definitely have to talk to her as soon as I can."

"Anytime," Lily says, leaning back. I go to take a sip of my drink and the devilish grin is back on her face. "Sooo, circling back to our prior conversation. You like Tucker?"

I nearly choke on my drink and groan. "Lily, we were having such a nice moment."

"And now we're having this moment."

"I don't like him."

"You liar."

"I am…" I pause, thinking about it, not ready to tell them about the night he showed up to my place. "I'm professionally wary of him," I settle on.

"And yet, you didn't deny what everyone in town is seeing from you two."

I sigh. "He makes me nervous," I admit. "In a good way. Which is the problem."

Lily kicks her feet up on the coffee table. "Oh, girl. That's not a problem. That's foreplay."

I smack her leg. "Stop it."

"You stop pretending you don't think he's hot," Lily fires back.

"Lily." Blair wrinkles her face in disgust. "That's your cousin."

"Blair. Do not make me throw up, please." She waves her hands in disgust. "Those cinnamon twists tasted good going down, and I *do not* want to taste them coming back up. I'm just saying that Scottie thinks he's hot."

Blair laughs, and then directs her attention back to me. "Okay, but does your pulse do that thing when he looks at you? You know. Does it get all jumpy and do back flips?"

I automatically hate that I know the feeling she's talking about. I feel it every time he's around me. I flatten my lips and look away from her. "I'm not answering that."

"You don't have to," Lily says. "Your face already did."

It's quiet for a second before all three of us dissolve into laughter.

"You two are the worst."

"Correction," Lily says with her pointer finger in the air. "We're the best."

I smile, settling back on the couch. The conversation quickly changes to the two of them discussing book boyfriends and that one time Dallas cried at the end of a romance novel Poppy forced him to read, only to pretend it was allergies.

Then they move to arguing about who gets to recommend what I read next. And somewhere in the middle of all of it, the thought hits me. The problem isn't that I'm unsure of my feelings for Tucker. It's that I'm feeling too much at once.

For Tucker.

For this house.

For the town that keeps making space for me.

For the first time in a long time, I'm not sure who Scottie Monroe is without the perfect polished persona I've always been told to keep in place. But sitting here, with cinnamon sugar on my fingers, sangria in my glass, and two women who have already decided I belong, I think maybe...just maybe, I want to find out.

EPISODE FIVE

A PINK BATHTUB BATTLE

Today on Nailed It or Failed It, *we're tackling the pink-tiled primary bathroom. In this room, Tucker and Scottie can't seem to agree on anything except the fact that the entire bathroom needs a miracle.*

It should be a straightforward renovation.

But nothing is ever simple when these two are involved.

And when you put two people in a small space, things get…well, complicated.

CHAPTER 20

YOU KIDS WANT RATINGS OR NOT?

You want to know what's grinding my gears today?

It's not the fact that I'm sweating before the cameras even start rolling because this bathroom is the size of a shoe box. And it's not because Tucker Daniels is standing in it wearing a white tank that's practically painted on him, allowing me to see every muscle of his stomach through the fabric.

No.

It's the fact that I wasn't smart enough to say *"Hey, let's get the air conditioner in this house working before we do all the work."*

Which has snowballed to the above mentions and today's sour mood.

I'm supposed to just act normal while working under these conditions?

"I've never seen a primary bathroom this small," Tucker says. "I'm not even sure how they fit this tub in here."

I keep my eyes down on the bathroom tile. He's right, it's barely big enough for a toddler, much less a primary bathroom. It feels claustrophobic with him standing at the doorway, leaning on the frame with his arms crossed and one leg over the other. So casual. So hot. Damn him.

"I can do this project myself."

He smirks, pressing off the doorway to stand next to me. "Cameras want us close."

Of course they do.

Andrea waves behind the cameraman set up in the doorway for us to begin. I straighten my shoulders and put on my *show time* ready smile.

"Our mission today is to tackle this." I gesture behind me while talking to the camera. "As you can see, it's small. It's not your average primary bathroom, but it has potential. I want to replace the double sink with a single sink to give it a little more space."

"Or we can remove the tub," Tucker says.

I turn to face him, hands on my hips. "We're not removing it."

"It's cracked."

"It has character."

"It's unnecessary."

"It's vintage."

He doesn't argue back. We both just stare at each other. His expression is unreadable, while mine is clearly annoyed.

After what feels like minutes, I face the camera again. "The pink clawfoot tub is staying," I say with conviction, kneeling beside the vintage porcelain tub. It's the one bright thing in this Barbie nightmare of pink tile. "It may be stained with age and cracked, but it's beautiful. A thing worth saving," I say, running my fingers along the edge.

I almost laugh at the irony. I don't even know what's worth saving in this house because I don't remember anything here. I don't know if this tub mattered to my grandmother the way it seems to matter to me. Would she have fought to keep it, too?

Tucker crouches next to me, shoulder brushing mine. An accidental touch that feels anything but accidental. He glances at the camera crew, at the way they're laser-focused on us, waiting for the sparks.

And then he leans in closer, dropping his voice low. "A beautiful thing worth saving."

I snap my head to face him, putting his mouth a breath away from mine. I suck in a sharp breath, and his lips curve into a smile. My heart picking this moment to forget how to behave.

Andrea makes a pleased sound. "Perfect, keep that energy."

Tucker does. Shifting his weight just enough that his jeans brush my thigh. The tools on his belt clink against the tub, and the scent of cedar and soap wraps around me like something I'd lean into if I were brave enough.

This is all for the show. This is all fake, Scottie, I remind myself.

I stand up, putting distance between us. "Let's start with pulling out this double sink, and then we can start the demolition on the tile from the wall behind this tub," I say, pointing at the tile.

Tucker opens his mouth to respond, but a loud voice from the hallway pulls our attention.

"Did someone say demolition?"

Nan marches through the doorway wearing steel-toe work boots that look older than her, denim overalls stained with what I *pray* is paint, and a red bandana tied around her head like she's leading a rebellion. But what really makes my eyes widen is the sledgehammer over her shoulder. It's so big that I'm genuinely concerned for the structural integrity of the whole town.

Nan grins. "So, what wall needs to die first?"

"Nan…" I start.

She waves me off. "Don't you worry about me. I signed a waiver once. Somewhere."

Tucker chokes on a laugh. "Nan, this is kind of a controlled job site."

"Oh, my sweet Tucker," she says, walking over to him and patting his cheek with her free hand. "The only thing controlled in this town is my blood pressure medication, and even *that's* questionable some days."

She adjusts the sledgehammer on her shoulder. "Now, step

aside. I've been itchin' to knock down a wall since my lawyer back in the day told me I wasn't allowed."

I stare at her—blinking.

Is this really happening? I have to be dreaming.

"Nan," Tucker says, voice stern. "You can't just—"

"You kids want ratings or not?"

I lean to my side where Tucker stands. "Should we…I don't know, take the hammer from her?"

He shakes his head. "There's no stopping Nan if she's determined."

Nan cracks her neck. Like, actually cracks it. "All right. Someone tell me what damn wall I'm knockin' down."

Tucker places a hand on my shoulder. "I got this." And then he walks to stand in front of her. "Nan, we are not knocking down a wall. But since you want to knock something down so bad, why don't you help us get rid of this double sink?"

She pauses for a second, her free hand coming to her chin to think about it. "But I brought this thing." She gestures to the hammer in her hands.

I actually feel bad for how disappointed she sounds.

"And we're going to use it," Tucker reassures her, and then points to the sink. "Want to help us destroy this instead?"

She eyes the sink and smirks. "Hell yeah!" She adjusts her grip and angles the hammer like she's ready to charge. "All right, let's remodel this bathroom the same way I do my life— with zero planning and maximum destruction."

With that, she charges toward the double sink like she's trained for this her whole life.

I slip out of the bathroom and let her have this moment. In the hallway, I feel like I can breathe again knowing the cameras aren't on me and I'm not dangerously close to Tucker. I rest my palm against the wall and close my eyes for a breath, letting the noise of Nan's demolition fade into something distant.

Straightening my spine, I take a few more steps down the hall, the floorboards dipping under my weight the same way they've done since I first walked through this place. When I skim my fingers along the wall as I walk, they catch on something I didn't notice before. I stop, staring at it with my head tilted to the side. I crouch down and notice a square cut out with a small metal pull ring I never noticed before.

I pull the ring slowly, revealing a shallow crawl space tucked in the wall. It seems to be a storage space of some sort, just wide enough to slide a box or two through and nothing more.

My heart starts to beat faster as I kneel lower and look around. My eyes land on a cardboard box. Reaching for it with shaky hands, I drag the dusty box toward me and pull it free from the wall. It isn't labeled and the tape along the edges is brittle from age.

I gasp when I lift the lid and the first thing I see is a crocheted blanket. It's small and folded into a neat square. The yarn is worn thin in places, the colors softened into a pale pink but the pattern hits me right in the chest.

This was one of my baby blankets.

I've seen dozens of *my* baby pictures—and so many of them have this blanket in them. Were we here in those photos? And why are there none with my grandmother in them?

When I pull it out, I find a ceramic mug under it. White with a tiny hand-painted sun on one side. The handle is cracked but carefully glued back together. I turn it slowly in my hands and lose my breath when I see *my* name scribbled on the other side with backward letters and the year next to my name means I was in kindergarten when I made this.

Tears threaten to spill in my eyes because *this* is exactly what I was looking for. Something. *Anything* that makes me feel connected to this home. And it's right here in my hands.

I look down again and find pieces of papers tied together with twine. Lifting them carefully, I turn them over, not wanting to pull the twine just yet and that's when I notice it's a stack of handwritten recipes. At the bottom of every one it says *Millie's*

Favorite, I almost laugh because there has to be at least thirty or forty pieces of paper stacked together.

"So this is where you disappeared to."

Tucker's voice forces me to snap my head in his direction. I find him standing with both hands tucked into the front pocket of his jeans, his expression softer than I've seen it in a while.

"What did you find?"

I lift the blanket slightly. "A crawl space. I think it was used for storage. I don't know how we missed it."

He steps closer, crouching down beside me, careful not to touch anything. "Looks like someone hid the good stuff."

"My grandmother," I whisper, looking down at the blanket still in my hand. "I don't remember her," I admit. "I've been trying…" My words trail off, not ready to share any more than that.

Not that I don't want Tucker to know how I feel about my connection to this place—or lack of connection. To admit all of that when I've been talking about making it shine again, but treating this house like a checklist—a timeline.

Being honest about that right here and now, feels like standing in a half-finished room with no walls to hide behind.

I look up at him, opening my mouth to change the subject when I find he's already looking at me. Not the box or the blanket in my hand, but at me. A soft smile on his lips.

"I know you're trying, Scottie," he says as if he can read my mind. "You should know that you don't need to know every-thing about her or this home to take care of what she left behind."

I'm ready to thank him for that when a loud crash rattles the ceiling. My hands come up to cover my head and Tucker hovers over me as if we're both bracing for the blow.

But it doesn't come.

He stands, extending his hand to help me up. "We should probably go rescue the rest of the house from Nan." He snatches his hand back quickly, bringing it to his chin as if deep in thought. "Unless we leave her be and she can go at that vintage tub with the hammer."

"Don't talk about my tub like that."

He laughs and I do too.

He extends his hand again, this time leaving it there. "Come on, Scottie."

I nod, carefully closing the box and pushing it back into the storage space before I take his hand. The moment our palms connect, the warmth surges through me.

This time when I walk toward the crew and where everyone is, it's not because of a schedule or a cue. I step forward because, *finally*, this house feels like it's opening itself up to me.

I stand in the middle of the bathroom with my hands on my hips.

The tile is finally gone. We let Nan stay to take out some of her built-up rage on those, which means we got them removed in record time. The dumpster outside is now full of pink debris that felt impossible this morning, but is now gone, giving me a fresh slate for this room.

Before Nan left I wanted to ask her questions, but she claimed a hot shower and recorded soaps operas were calling her name. I don't blame her because she put in a lot of work helping us get rid of the tile.

I wipe sweat from my eyebrows with the back of my wrist. The bathroom feels naked, like it's showing us its bones.

The heels clicking in the hallway force me to turn my head to the empty doorway. Seconds later, Andrea fills the space, phone in hand, clicking away. She finally lifts her head. "All right. We've got the demo footage we need. The chemistry and banter are reading well on camera. I figured we could tackle installing the single sink and the flooring tomorrow. Does that work?"

I bite my tongue so hard, I almost taste blood. I'm so sick and tired of hearing about the chemistry between Tucker and I instead of the good progress we're making on the house.

"Yep," I settle on.

"Perfect! See you tomorrow, Scottie."

I watch her leave and listen for the click of her heels to fade before I sigh, relaxing my shoulders. I take a few steps to the window over the toilet, leaning forward to look out and notice the incredible view from up here. It's been so long since I've stayed this late after filming—embracing the quiet of this house without any drills or hammers around me.

It's peaceful in a way I'm not used to. The lake in the distance sits low and glassy, catching the last streaks of sunlight in its reflection, and the mountains rise behind it in soft blue layers that don't even look real.

This house feels like my home, even half torn apart.

But could I live here?

When I first came to Bluestone Lakes, I didn't know if I saw myself staying here when the project was over. I knew I wanted a place to call my own, but could this really be it? Do I want it to be it?

I stand upright and step away from the window, my body crashes against someone, and I let out a shriek. When I turn around, I see Tucker standing there, arms crossed and grinning.

"You scared the shit out of me," I tell him. "Don't you have to leave to go to work?"

"Griffin is covering the bar tonight."

My heart kicks into overdrive again. He's *choosing* to stay here with me. Or maybe I'm just looking into it too much. Oh my god, *what is wrong with me?*

"The plan is flooring tomorrow?" he asks, and I nod. "I hope you're prepared to pick a grout color so we don't have to argue about it."

I aim to kick him in the shin, but he dodges, laughing under his breath. My stomach does a traitorous flip at the sound. It's the kind of laugh that screams trouble and tells you to stay away before you're sucked in too far again.

Before I can say anything back, he points to the tub. "Want to start scrubbing the tub? It's going to take a while, and we can at least get it cleaned up at least before we need to re-glaze it."

I swallow. "Uh. Yeah. We can do that."

He moves to a box of tools off to the corner of the bathroom, digging through it before pulling out a package of candy. He looks over at me before tossing me the pack. I'm unsure what to think, catching it with ease as I roll it over in my hands. I notice it's already open.

"Are you a fan of Sour Patch Kids, too?" I ask with a laugh. "Feels like half the bag is gone."

"I'm more of a sweets guy," he says, still digging through the box in front of him. "Donuts and cinnamon buns are definitely my thing."

I tilt my head to the side, and look into the package of candy. I stare down and notice there's no yellow or green. My fingers go cold around the bag. It's such a stupid thing. It's candy. It's Sour Patch Kids. It's the kind of detail that shouldn't matter in a space where we're supposed to be worried about the pink tub that's offended him.

But it matters.

Because it means he remembered I don't eat the yellow or green ones.

"So...the yellows and greens just vanished on their own?"

Tucker finally looks up, shrugging like it's nothing. "Figured you wouldn't miss them."

I swallow, blinking. "You remember that?"

He hesitates—just for a moment and then nods. "Yeah. I remember."

I look down at the candy again, picking out a blue and popping it in my mouth. "Thank you," I say quietly.

"You're welcome," he says, going back to digging in his box.

I stuff the rest of the candy in the pocket of my overalls as he finds a couple of sponges. He tosses me one, and I catch it even though I'm caught off guard.

I kneel by the tub and he takes the spot next to me.

Too close.

Always too close.

We start scrubbing in silence, tension swirls around us. It's so thick that I'm having difficulty breathing. Every so often, his arm brushes mine by accident, heating my skin. I feel myself scrubbing harder and faster. Subconsciously, I think I just want to get this done faster, so I can stop pretending. I've been doing it all fucking day, and I'm exhausted. I want to breathe.

"You're going to ruin the finish if you keep scrubbing that hard," Tucker says.

I stop scrubbing and narrow my eyes at him. "Why do you care? You hate this tub."

"Because you do."

The words come out so quickly, like he didn't have to think about them. He cares because *I care* about this tub.

"That…uh, that doesn't make sense."

"All I'm saying is, try to be a little more gentler on the tub. Otherwise, you're going to scrub the pink off. Consider it constructive feedback." He reaches down into the tub where some water sits and flicks it up at me.

I gasp. "Did you just…attack me? With dirty water?"

He shrugs, smirking.

"Oh, it's so on."

I reach down, cupping a palm full of water and splash it toward him with full force. He freezes, and my eyes widen. Water drips from his jaw onto his thin, white tank that he's still wearing. My hands cover my mouth as he looks down at the "damage" I caused, and then slowly lifts his head, eyes narrowing. "You just declared war."

"I dare you."

We both stare at each other for a beat before we reach down, splashing each other with whatever water is there, barely able to keep our eyes open. We find small buckets in the corner, taking this water fight to the next level. Now, we're slipping around on the floor, but neither of us gives up. His laugh vibrates off the walls. I aim for his face every time, but he shields it like we're in battle. We're both now completely drenched and breathless. It's almost ridiculous.

But then, I slip. Just enough for my stomach to drop and my arms to flail. Tucker catches my waist instantly, like he's been waiting for me to fall so he could prove he'd be there to hold me up. His grip is solid, but the heat of his touch brands my skin through the soaked cotton. My body is pressed against his. It's hard enough to feel the rise and fall of his chest against mine, and soft enough that neither of us pulls away.

"If you wanted me closer, you just had to say the word," he says, breaking the silence.

Everything inside me goes quiet. The air thickens and my pulse slams so loud it echoes in my ears.

I don't move.

I can't.

"Are you okay?" he murmurs, his voice low.

I'm learning quickly that I can fake a polished look for millions of people online, but one look from Tucker and it all unravels.

"Yeah," I lie, standing straight but not putting distance between us. "I thought you'd let me fall. But you…caught me."

With his hand still on my waist, he squeezes me. "I always will."

I don't know how to take those three simple words.

His eyes bore into mine, and darkness washes over them. Desire pools in my gut as his fingers dig into my hips like he's trying to decide whether to let go or pull me closer. He leans in, letting his breath brush my cheek, and suddenly the water on my skin feels ice cold compared to the heat spiraling through my body.

"Don't look at me like that," I whisper.

He tilts his head. "Like what?"

"Like you're about to kiss me."

His gaze drops to my mouth and lingers, just enough to send heat crawling up my spine. Then his eyes are back on mine, and Christ, I can't fucking breathe.

My pulse trips over itself.

My chest feels heavy.

Everything inside of me pulls tight and sharp, lighting up in places I forgot existed.

"Maybe I am."

If he kisses me right now, I'll break.

If he doesn't, I'll break anyway.

His hand slides to the back of my neck, looking at me like I'm his next breath. "You have *no idea* what you do to me, do you?"

I shake my head, and he leans in.

"I've been dying to kiss you again. Every single fucking time I'm around you."

I no longer have the power in me to stop him. Despite my head screaming for me to step away from him, I can't. I lean in too, closing my eyes in anticipation of feeling his lips on mine again.

The sound of my phone blaring on the floor near the door pulls us apart like we just got caught doing something we shouldn't be doing.

I rush to my phone, looking down at the screen. "It's...my mom."

When I look up at Tucker, there's an expression on his face I can't quite make out. It's something that resembles pain.

"I'll give you privacy," he says, brushing past me and leaving me alone in the bathroom.

An ache forms in my chest, and I can't figure out why.

I answer the video call, trying not to sound like I was one second from kissing a man.

My mom's faces appear on the screen.

"Hi, Mom."

My mom squints, coming closer to the phone as if that will help her see better. "Scottlyn, you look…messy. I thought you were supposed to be maintaining your image out there for the show."

I pull the phone far away from my face and circle the bathroom to show her. "We just gutted the bathroom and it was a lot of work. It's hot today."

My dad comes into view, and I light up when I see him.

"Hi, honey," he says, taking the phone from my mom. "How's the house coming along?"

"Good," I say, nodding repeatedly. "We're going to finish up the bathroom tomorrow."

"That's great," he says, and I feel pride just from hearing his words.

Then my mom takes the phone from him. "That tank top is not flattering, honey. And why is your hair soaking wet?"

My stomach sinks. "I've been working."

"Working is no excuse to look like you just rolled out of a dumpster. This show is a big deal for you. I just don't want you to embarrass us, okay?"

My jaw tightens, and this is one of the many moments I wish my dad would step in, but he doesn't. So I fake a smile. "Sure. I won't."

My mom changes the subject to ask me what I plan to wear for the rest of the filming process. Asking me if I have enough outfits so I'm not repeating anything. She tosses in some comments about things I should add to the house during the process, despite my telling her my blueprints were done before we even started.

"I know your dad asked you how the house was coming along already, but will you make the deadline for the show so they can call it a success?" my mom asks. "People will never take you seriously if you don't nail it. Or whatever the show says." She rolls her eyes.

My stomach drops thinking about how I only have about two

weeks left. "Yeah. Right on time," I tell her, even if I don't know for sure what will happen by the end of this project.

By the time the call ends, my cheeks hurt from faking a smile. I drop the phone back down where it was before. When I stand up and turn around, I catch my reflection in the mirror that's still mounted on the wall. I don't recognize the girl staring back at me.

"I can't do this anymore," I whisper to no one.

I feel like I'm caught between the version of myself I'm supposed to be and the one I'm scared I might actually become. Tears burn the corners of my eyes as my mom's words echo in my head, scraping at a part of me I thought I could bury beneath filters and perfect lighting.

I've spent so much of my life performing perfection that I barely recognize myself without it.

The person I was on that call? She's built for approval.

But the person staring back at me in the mirror? She's real.

She's messy, but she's human.

And for the first time, I wish my parents saw me the way Tucker almost did.

Like I'm someone worth choosing, even without the performance.

CHAPTER 21

YOU CAN PUT IT DOWN.

TUCKER

It's been two days.

Two days of replaying our evening in the bathroom on loop.

Thankfully, the bar is busy tonight, as it always is on Friday nights. But even with the packed room and a bar full of regulars, nothing could drown out the memory of Scottie's breath on my mouth seconds before her phone rang.

Or the look on her face when she came out of that call, a different person than before she picked up. Even today, working on the house all day before I left to come to Seven Stools to work my evening shift, she wasn't the same Scottie.

I fought all day to ask her about it.

Hell, I cracked more jokes than usual to try to get a rise out of her.

Nothing.

Scottie gets under my skin in ways no one ever could. Every wall she builds I want to knock down. It's been a constant battle with myself to get to this point, because one minute I felt a ping of regret for crossing the line, knowing she would see the deeper parts of me. Then the next minute, I want her to see everything. I want to give her everything.

I pull into my driveway and sit there for a second while I let the quiet hum of the truck drown out my racing thoughts. I turn my head toward my garage loft, where a single lamp glows behind the curtains of the window facing my house. It looks way too inviting for a man who should know better by now.

I tell myself I'm just checking to make sure she's okay.

I kill the engine, step out of the truck and shut the door behind me. The night is cooler than usual, and crickets buzz somewhere in the woods. I look toward my house, the dark shape against the sky, with not a single lamp left on. It's not as inviting as the loft apartment. When I turn around again to face the loft, off to the other side of the property line, it feels like its own little world.

Her little world, for now.

I'm just about to turn for my house when I pause, doing a double take when I see her.

She's not in the window looking outside. She's sitting on the bottom step of the staircase with her legs pulled up and her arms wrapped around her shins like she's holding herself together by sheer force. She is wearing cotton shorts and an oversized sweatshirt, and her hair is pulled into a messy bun.

She looks…tired.

"Scottie?"

Her head jerks up. Even in the dim light shining from the top of the stairs, I can see it—red-rimmed eyes and a shine of tear tracks down her cheek. She scrubs at her cheeks quickly, like she can erase the evidence before I catch it.

"Hey," she says, voice cracking as I walk across the driveway to where she sits. "Sorry. I didn't mean to be out here and bother you after working all day. There's no seating on the deck, and I wanted to be outside for a bit."

Shit. I should have put some chairs up there for her.

I should have told her she can use the ones on my porch.

"Bothering me?" I stop in front of her, crouching down until

I'm eye level with her. "You're sitting on the stairs, and I was the one who called your name."

A tiny huff of sound leaves her that resembles a ghost of a laugh. Then it dies, and the weight settles back in her shoulders.

"I figured you'd be asleep," I continue, trending carefully but also wanting to make her laugh. "Or inside, plotting new ways to bully me about wall color."

She stares down at the ground for a moment and then shakes her head.

This is *not* the Scottie I know.

I reach forward, resting a hand on her knee. My palm on her bare skin sends chills through my body at the same time her head snaps up, eyes meeting mine. She looks so fucking tired.

"What's going on, Scottie?"

She sighs. "I just can't sleep."

"Why?"

She eyes me curiously, like she's not sure if she's ready to tell me more. Like she's not ready to open up to me. I don't blame her. We have an agreement for the show and nothing more.

"Is this about the show?" I ask when she doesn't answer.

"All of it," she says, swallowing. "We have so much left to do in the next two weeks. It's starting to hit me that maybe I won't be able to do this and that I'm in over my head."

"You can," I say before I can stop myself.

Her eyes flick up, startled.

I move to sit down beside her on the bottom step, leaving a few inches of space between us. Close enough to feel the heat radiating off her. Close enough to smell the soap she used in the shower and whatever floral thing she uses in her hair.

"The tile demo is done, the leak in the ceiling is fixed, and the tub is on its way to resurrection," I tell her honestly. "You've knocked all the big projects off the list. You're doing it."

She laughs, but it's forced. "It's not enough."

"It is," I counter.

She shakes her head, wrapping her arms tighter around her

legs. "You don't get it. It can't just be okay. This has to be incredible. The design, the reveal, all of it. If it's not perfect, the network won't care, but my mom will say she told me so."

And there it is.

That last part drops heavier than the rest.

"I spent my life making sure everything I did was enough," she whispers, pain laced in her voice as she looks at the ground between us. "I've been working so damn hard to be taken seriously in this industry and I feel like no matter what I do, it's never going to be enough."

"Scottie," I say sharply, urging her to look at me and she does. "You are enough."

Her body goes tense, even without my hands on her, I can feel it.

"You don't know that."

I grip her chin between my fingers so she doesn't look away. "I don't have to know your whole story to see your worth."

Her lips part, and I can see the argument building in her eyes the longer she stares back at me. I see all the ways she wants to say I'm wrong.

But she doesn't.

"I-I hate this," she says, releasing a trembling breath. "I hate that everyone expects me to be polished and happy at all times. And now, here I am, crying on a staircase."

"Most people cry on much worse furniture."

A startled laugh slips free. She presses her lips together quickly though, as if she didn't mean to let it out.

I feel my mouth curve into a smile. "See? Still human."

She scoffs. "I don't think I'm allowed to be that. Certain expectations have been set for me and I have to fight like hell to live up to them."

"That doesn't sound exhausting at all," I say sarcastically.

That earns me a genuine smile, one that doesn't feel fake and averts her gaze from me—eyes bouncing between her hands and the driveway.

"It's so tiring, Tucker. I went from making sure the world saw me for what they want, to getting this show and the producers telling me to be myself. But what they really want is the version they can sell." She blinks, a single tear escaping her eyes. "And if I mess up, it's not just a bad day. It's going to be on everyone's TV screen. Then I'll have a lengthy phone call with my mom saying 'I told you this was too big for you.'"

The words tumble out of her like a dam that just broke.

"I'm terrified I won't finish on time," she goes on. "The time-line is already so tight. We still have to work on that mess of a yard, the master bedroom, the entryway, and that ridiculous wallpaper. There's...so much." She drags in a shaky breath, facing me again. "What if we can't pull it off? What if this whole town, the crew, you...what if you all see me fail and realize I never deserved any of this?"

She breaks when she says it—*deserved*.

Her hands cover her face, and she releases every emotion she's held in for probably the first time in front of someone. It fucking destroys me inside that this is everything she's been thinking about since she got here. She's bottled up all these emotions and kept them to herself so no one would see her differently.

But I see her.

I fucking see all of her.

I don't think after that, I just move. I shift slowly, closing the gap between us before she can flinch away. Sliding an arm around her waist, I guide her gently onto my lap. She stiffens and gasps in surprise, but doesn't fight me. Her hands bunch in my shirt, holding on like it's the only solid thing left in the world.

"Hey," I murmur, one hand splayed across her back and the other cupping the back of her head. "Breathe for me, babe."

She does—ragged and catching on every inhale. She's half on my lap and half curled against my chest with her head ducking into my neck. It should feel like too much, but it doesn't.

It feels inevitable.

It feels like some part of me has been waiting to hold her exactly like this.

"Strong looks good on you, Scottie," I whisper against her hair. She pulls back, tear filled eyes meeting mine. "But you can put it down."

"And what if you see too much?"

"I already have," I answer honestly, reaching up to swipe a loose tear from her cheek with the back of my finger. "And I'm still here."

Her eyes search mine, looking for the lie and hoping she doesn't find one. She won't because it's the truth.

I'm still here.

I want to be here.

I'm finding that I've slowly become addicted to her.

"You know you're allowed to just…be," I say honestly, making sure she understands she can be herself with me. "Mess included."

She stares at me as if she's trying to decide whether she believes me. My heart pounds loudly in my chest, and I know she can feel it. Her hand lifts, and she hesitates before cupping the side of my face. Her touch is so light, but it's undeniable.

"Everyone gets a version of me. Mostly the put-together one."

"And what do I get?"

She swallows, still holding me. "The one I'm scared to hand over."

"That's the one I want."

"Even if it's ugly?"

I reach up, this time taking her head between my hands. Hers fall from my face and I bring our mouths inches apart. "Especially if it's ugly, Scottie."

Her breath catches in her throat.

The air between us sparkles with electricity. Sharp enough to raise goose bumps along my skin.

"I don't know who I am when the cameras are gone."

"Then let me be the place you find out."

She shifts again, just enough that the movement pulls her closer to me. Her thighs press against my hips, sending blood right to my cock. My fingers tighten in her hair. Everything in me narrows to the shape of her mouth, the tremble in her breath, and the way her eyes search mine like she's waiting for permission.

"That time upstairs…when we crossed the line. Do you think it was a mistake?" she asks, the question nearly knocking the air out of me.

"No," I answer quickly, shaking my head. "You're…" I pause, trying to find the right words. "You're the first thing that's ever felt as if you could wreck me and save me in the same breath."

She looks at me with wide, glassy eyes. The ones that make me want to fix every crack in her even though some part of me knows she's not mine to fix. Her hands fist in my shirt near my collarbone, knuckles brushing my skin, still holding on like she doesn't know how to let go.

And god help me, I don't know how to either.

I want to kiss her.

I want to take the fear out of her voice.

I want to make her forget anyone who's ever made her doubt herself.

"Tucker…" she whispers, lips parted.

And something inside me snaps the second she whispers my name, like it's both a question and an answer. I lean forward before I can talk myself out of it. Our noses brush, and she gasps—a tiny sound that nearly ruins me. My thumb strokes slow circles beneath her ear, the other hand now pressing at her lower back to keep her close because if she pulls away now, I might come apart at the seams.

She closes the space between us, but freezes and pulls back again.

"Scottie…" I breathe.

"Fuck," she mutters under her breath and attempts to get off my lap, but I grip both of her hips to keep her in place. "I'm sorry."

"Explain to me what's happening inside that head of yours."

Her body relaxes, melting into my lap again. She places both hands on my shoulders, and I can't tell if it's her way of keeping herself at a safe distance or for me.

"If I let you in…I won't know how to stop."

It's real—too damn real.

And real means dangerous.

I rest my forehead against hers, trying to breathe past the chaos in my chest.

"Then don't fucking stop."

Her breath hitches, and I feel it on my lips. She's so close I feel like she's testing just how weak my resolve really is.

"Then let's stop pretending," she adds.

Jesus Christ. Something that resembles a curse or a prayer slips out of me because she has no idea what she's asking for. My hands move to cup both sides of her face, holding her there because she feels like the only thing keeping me steady.

"You've had a day, Scottie," I manage, forcing the words out. "You're tired and…your walls are down. I'm not going to take advantage of that."

She blinks, confusion shifting into something like hurt as she looks down at the space between us, thinking I don't want this.

She has no fucking idea.

I lift her chin slightly, making sure she sees the truth in my eyes.

"I want you." I swallow. "Can't you see it, Scottie? I want you in a way that includes every version of you. Especially the ones you think I'd run from." My thumb drags softly at her hip like I'm trying to anchor myself. "In a way that makes me want to be good to you, careful with you, like you're something holy."

Her lips part, not prepared for the truth to sound like that.

But she doesn't pull away, not even a fraction.

"I want you in a way that ruins my ability to pretend with you anymore."

"Tucker," she says, barely audible.

"You think if you let me in, you won't know how to stop." I grip her hips tighter, pressing my forehead to hers. "But…now you know, I can't fucking stop with you. I can't breathe when we're in the same room. I can't think. I can't do anything but want you in a way that scares the shit out of me."

Painfully slow, I undo her fingers from my shirt and guide her off my lap, steadying her when her legs tremble. She stands in front of me, eyes searching mine, trying to understand the parts I don't know how to say out loud.

If I kiss her again tonight, I stop pretending.

And once I stop pretending, I don't know how to go back.

"I told you I'm not running from you, but you need sleep," I say quietly.

She nods, but she continues watching me. Memorizing something about this moment before it's gone.

"You said you can't breathe when we're in the same room." She pauses, blinking once. "I hope you know you make it easier for me to breathe."

I avert my gaze because I'm afraid of the look on my own face if I don't. I'm afraid she'll see that I believe her. I'm afraid she'll know that she's starting to matter too much.

I stand and step back, giving her space to climb the stairs to the loft. She hesitates for a second before going up, and I don't move until she disappears inside. My muscles feel tight as I head back to the main house.

Inside, I kick off my boots and drop onto the couch, staring at the ceiling. Only then do I allow myself to breathe.

I want her.

I want her so badly it's becoming a problem.

It makes me want to help ease some of this mess in her head. She's stressed—worried about the timeline of things. That's something I can help with.

I pull my phone out, staring at the blank screen for a good thirty seconds before opening my messages.

I don't do this.

I don't reach out for help.

I handle things on my own.

But after seeing how much of a mess she is over this and thinking about everything we still need to finish, I admit to myself something that feels a lot like surrender.

We need some help.

I click Griffin's name and send him a text before I can talk myself out of it.

ME

I need your help.

EPISODE SIX

NEIGHBORHOOD WATCH

Welcome back to Nailed It or Failed It! *We're taking things outside on today's episode, because it turns out the yard is just as wild as the chemistry between these two.*

An overgrown yard and a few stubborn roots make this a project much bigger than expected. But don't worry, this small town believes in community. You never know who might wander over with a power washer...or an opinion.

Let's just say, when the locals show up, so do a few surprises.

Sometimes the ones that surface aren't plants at all.

So grab your gloves and your shovels.

It's time for a makeover none of us saw coming.

CHAPTER 22

YOU'RE FLIRTING WITH DANGER, SCOTTIE.

SCOTTIE

I spend the morning doing a walk around in the house, taking mental note of the big projects we should tackle as soon as possible, in case we run out of time. To my surprise, we really have gotten far with this house. While there's a lot left that has to be done, it feels like a whole new house. The same bones are still alive, but on the surface…it's starting to shine.

I hate that I let my mother's voice get to me as much as it did the last few days. But her words left me spiraling—feeling inadequate. This house felt like a jigsaw puzzle dumped on a table. It was a scattered mess. Once I started putting the pieces together and seeing it come to life and pushing the negative thoughts down, it got easier—it feels easier.

As I step into the foyer, I find Andrea and Jade there with a grin on their faces. It's mischievous, like they're up to no good.

"Andrea? Jade?"

Andrea shimmies her shoulders and claps her hands together like she's about to give a speech to a football team instead of another day of renovation chaos. "I'm sooo excited for today."

"What's today?"

"We're heading outside today. Yard clean up, curb appeal, the works," Jade answers, the last two words with show hands high in the air.

I blink. "The yard?"

Jade beams like the sun personally blessed this moment. "We're making the viewers fall in love from the outside today."

"But we need to put the finishing touches on the bathroom," I argue, arms crossed. "And we have to lay the floors in the hallway upstairs. And I have to paint that other spare bedroom still. Don't you think we should finish the inside before—"

"We're waiting on a few supply shipments still," Andrea says with a bright smile that makes me want to gently strangle something. "This will keep the momentum going." She pulls out her phone and taps away on the screen. "Don't worry. I think we're still making good time."

She doesn't even look at me again before walking away and Jade follows.

She *thinks* we're still making good time?

If this fails, she moves on to the next show—the next season. I'm the one who becomes the cautionary tale of the DIY influencer buried under a heap of pink tile. I feel my breath begin to quicken, and for a moment I think I might snap again.

Then Tucker's voice from a few nights ago sounds in my head.

Strong looks good on you, Scottie. But you can put it down.

With his arms around me, and the safety in his words, I believe him.

I breathe.

Okay. I guess it's yard day.

I can handle a yard.

Maybe.

I step outside, the sunlight hitting my face enough to make me squint. I lift a hand to shield my eyes and take in the yard. It's obviously not the first time I've seen it, but it feels like it. The grass is almost to my waist in some spots and the driveway is coated in slick green moss.

Off to the side of the property, half swallowed by overgrown weeds, a metal swing glider sits hidden by a crooked tree. The paint is chipped down to bare steel in places and one of the chains hangs lower than the other, but the frame is still solid. Still standing.

I can picture someone sitting there with a cup of coffee and a folded blanket over their lap. The image lands in my chest before I can stop it. Inside the small storage space, I found what my grandmother kept. Out here, I can see where she might have used that coffee mug.

With every day that passes, it feels like the house is showing me how she lived.

Finally.

Just as I'm about to make my way closer to the glider, a voice slices through the moment.

"Hey, Scottie!" Lily says. I turn to find her bouncing toward me, bright as ever, and holding a bakery box. She stops in front of me, lifting it. "I brought carbs for courage."

"You're a lifesaver."

Blair follows behind her, wearing athletic leggings and a shirt that says *Demo Day*. I scan the rest of the property, and my jaw falls to the floor when I see Griffin and Dallas waving from where they are, unloading equipment from the back of a truck.

I continue scanning the rapidly-growing crowd.

More and more familiar faces scatter across the yard. The clerk from the General Store pulls a lawn mower out of another truck, Autumn from the coffee shop sets up a table with to-go cups of coffee, and kids in matching baseball hats stand in a circle putting on gardening gloves, with Nan pointing in different directions at what needs to be done.

It's like the entire town decided to show up and dig my dirt.

It's mid-morning. Did businesses close? For this?

Tucker stops beside me, handing me a pair of gloves. "I told you this place just needed a little love."

When I turn toward him, he has a satisfied grin plastered on his face. The kind you wear when something you believed in turns out exactly the way you said it would.

"Why are you smiling like that?" I ask.

Slowly, as if the world just came to a stop on its axis, he turns to face me. The look on his face is enough to make me lose my breath. Again. He leans in close, enough that if he wanted to, he could press his lips to mine and—

"Because the alternative is kissing you," he admits. He reaches up, wanting to brush any hair away from my face, but stops himself. "And I'm trying to behave."

My heart skips about ten beats, and I force myself to breathe. But Nan bustles past us, dragging an entire shrub behind her in one hand like it offended her so much that she had to murder it. The hedge clippers swing wildly in her free hand. "This bush was blocking the view out the front window," she declares, huffing like a warrior queen.

She's been here for all of ten minutes and has already removed an entire bush and has dirt streaked under her eyes resembling war paint.

"Nan!" Tucker calls after her. "You can't just dig up anything you see. There are water lines under those bushes."

"Good!" Nan shouts over her shoulder. "The plants are thirsty."

"I think I love her."

He chuckles, and it does something to my knees.

For the next hour, the entire town gets to work as the sun climbs higher in the sky. The camera crew and Andrea make their way through every inch of the yard, catching everything without getting in the way.

Dallas and Griffin coax the kids into hauling the fallen branches into neat piles close to the curb, turning it into a mini competition. I learned that the kids are all a part of a little league in town that Dallas coaches. I can see the way they nod in response to anything he says, and how they respect and listen to him.

Lily walks around the yard with Autumn next to her, fueling the entire town with caffeine and baked goods.

Poppy and Blair are in the driveway. Poppy has her hands on her knees and is laughing hysterically at Blair wrestling the power washer while Blair continues to say she knows what she's doing, telling everyone she learned how to power wash her tiny home herself when she first showed up in town.

I make my way to where they stand to see if I can help.

"I got this," Blair repeats. "Poppy, flip the power on this bitch. Let's do it."

I hold my breath, stepping back to avoid being impaled by the pressure.

She aims it down and takes a ready stance. Poppy flips the power on, and Blair remains in control as the moss lifts like magic.

I laugh—a real laugh.

And it has everything to do with everyone being here.

Suddenly, belonging doesn't feel like a foreign language.

I'm smiling, but inside, I'm choking up. The emotions sit on the edge, waiting to break free at the people who aren't my family, who are here to help me with this project. They believe in me more than anyone has ever believed in me before.

I want to soak up every minute in.

I want to remember this feeling forever.

The spell is broken when something roars to life behind me. I spin around to find Tucker starting up the weed wacker. My eyes trail his body—his very exposed body. He's wearing a pair of worn jeans with his tank top hanging out of the back pocket. I can see every rigid muscle between his abdomen and his flexed muscle in his arms. Not to mention, the baseball cap sitting backward on his head should be illegal. I can't stop staring at him—even though I know I shouldn't.

We're towing a thin, fragile line that burns hotter every time we pretend it isn't there.

I want to cross it all over again. Over and over.

I want to step right over it, grab him, and revisit *exactly* what it feels like when it's not acting for the cameras. I have to straighten my spine and pretend the way he looks doesn't unravel me as I step closer to him.

The problem is…neither of us are fooling anyone.

"I can do that," I say, reaching for the weed wacker in his hands.

He raises a brow. "You sure?"

I nod. "You can teach me."

"This thing bites."

"I bet it does," I say, winking, but quickly straighten my lips.

I don't even know where that came from. I feel myself staring at him, waiting for a reaction to the unexpected words out of my mouth.

Am I flirting with Tucker?

Oh my god, I definitely am.

He hands it over, and I feel relieved that he didn't read too much into it. The moment I hold it in my hands, I nearly sever my own ankles. The machine jerks, kicking like a wild animal.

"I think this thing has a vendetta against me!" I shout over the noise.

"You're supposed to control it, not dance with it."

"Easy for you to say, Mr. Muscles!" I say, gesturing to his arms.

He steps behind me before I can protest, reaching around me, covering my hands with his on the handle. He presses his chest to my back, and I feel the heat of his body everywhere. My heart rate starts doing gymnastics with every breath he takes and every shift of his body.

"Like this," he murmurs close to my ear, guiding the movement. "Let it work for you."

Hand over mine, we glide over the grass, clipping away at what was once a jungle out here. I clear my throat, trying not to sound affected by his presence. "You're awfully good at this."

I misstep to the side, forcing me to fall into him closer than I was. His arms tighten around me to hold me in place.

"Scottie," he growls out, but I don't move. My hips press into him, and I can feel everything—and I mean *everything*—against my back. The only thing it does is sharpen this reckless pull I already have for Tucker. This reckless gravity dragging me over the line again.

His lips brush the shell of my ear, and it takes everything in me not to melt straight into the grass. One breath against my skin and I'm already unraveling—willing to bring myself to my knees again for this man.

"Careful. You're flirting with danger, Scottie."

I smirk, turning my head to make eye contact with him over my shoulder, and he's so close. God, he's so close.

After thinking about everything the last few nights—the way he admitted he didn't regret crossing the line with me and the way he said it without flinching like the truth didn't scare him as much as pretending did. He was also the first person who ever looked at me and told me I was enough without attaching a condition to it. He's let me be myself with him, and I finally understand what I've been doing all these years—shrinking what I feel so everyone else can stay comfortable.

I don't want to do that anymore.

For once, I'm choosing me. And I'm choosing him.

"No, I'm flirting with you. The danger is just a bonus."

Tucker throws his head back and groans.

Stepping away from me, I feel the loss of his touch everywhere, but I keep moving the weed wacker how he showed me. With more control, I clip down all the high parts of the grass around the edges of the house with Tucker watching me as if to protect me from slicing my ankles in half.

Just as I'm about to finish, I spot the glider swing off to the side of the property again. Taking large steps over the still tall grass patches, I stop in front of it.

Tucker stops beside me, close enough that his arm brushes mine. "We can fix this up," he says softly, pulling his shirt over his head. "The swing. We don't have to throw it out."

I stare at it for another long moment, letting my fingers brush along the armrest. The metal shifting under my touch like it remembers being used. When I turn to face him again, his eyes are steady and show no judgment for why I'm staring at a swing with so many questions.

"Thank you," I say, surprising myself with how much the words matter. "I don't even remember it, if I'm being honest. It's been so long since visited this house that not even one memory has come back to me since being back here. But there's something about this swing…I just…I wish I remembered more."

"Whether you remember or not, this swing meant something to someone you loved." I turn to face him, shocked by his words. He shrugs. "That has to count for something. Besides…" He pauses, walking to the other side of the swing, gripping the chains. "Sometimes memories come back in pieces. Sometimes not at all. That doesn't make them any less yours."

I swallow, staring down at my hand. I think about how Tucker doesn't know about how I've been feeling toward this place. How I'm missing that connection to the house.

"I told you the other day in the hallway that I don't remember my grandmother," I say, not wanting to look at him as I continue. "I've been trying so hard these last few weeks to find a connection to this place—this house. It doesn't feel like mine. It's been nothing more than a checklist for me, and I hate that I don't remember a single memory I've had here."

Tucker crosses in front of the swing, coming to a stop in front of me, lifting my head with the back of his finger under my chin.

"Maybe it's not about what you used to feel. Maybe it's about what you feel now."

I look up at him, surprised by how steady his eyes are. "And what if I still feel nothing?"

He smiles. "Then we start from nothing. You rebuild it—the house and the memories. Whatever you want this place to mean again."

My chest tightens at the warmth behind his words. "You make it sound easy," I whisper.

"It won't be," he says honestly, letting his fingers trail along my jaw and down my neck. "But you won't be doing any of it alone."

The air between us pulls tight, charged in a way that makes my breath catch.

Tucker is looking at me like I'm not just some girl trying to remember a childhood swing. Like I'm something he wants to reach for.

I want to kiss him, right now in the open. The thought sparks through me so fast it leaves my knees unsteady. His eyes flick down to my mouth, and it's enough to make my pulse surge to life.

"Tucker Daniels!" a voice shouts from the yard.

We step apart, both of our heads snap toward the sound, and we spot Nan storming over to where we stand, offended and dramatic. She's waving a pair of gardening gloves over her head like she's signaling a passing plane.

"Tucker Daniels," she repeats, stopping between us. She pokes him hard in his chest, forcing his hands to fly up in defense. "I just found out a little something-something."

"Huh?"

She crosses her arms over her chest. "You really texted *Griffin* for help with all of this, but not me? I'm wounded." She pokes his chest again. "I'm offended." Another poke. "I feel so betrayed."

"Whoa, Nan," he says, holding her by both shoulders and leveling his stare with hers. "You. Don't. Text. Remember?"

She gasps. "I do too! I sent you a picture of my rose bush last month!"

"That was a letter," Tucker deadpans. "You mailed me a printed photo as if you don't see me every single day at the bar or around town."

Nan waves him off. "Details. You still should have alerted me. You know, I could have organized this little plan you had."

This plan?

Wait, did—

"And I could've been more prepared and brought my chainsaw," she huffs.

"No chainsaw," Tucker and I say in unison.

"Fine. But next time, you talk to me *first*," she says. Tucker nods, and she lifts her chin in victory. "Now, back to whatever you two were doin'."

As she stomps away, something in my brain clicks into place.

All of this—the town, the help, the overwhelming feeling that I'm not alone.

This was Tucker.

He called them for me.

He cares enough to assemble an army to help me win this battle against the jungle that is my yard, so I didn't feel so behind. My heart does a weird flip, and I press a hand to it like I can calm it with just my touch.

"You okay?" Tucker asks.

I nod, but my voice is trapped somewhere in my chest. "It's just...a lot." I gesture to everything around us with my hand. "Everyone is helping today as if it matters to them.

"It does matter to them."

"It feels like..." I pause, searching for the right word. "Like belonging."

"You already do." His gaze softens. "Whatever you need from here on out, you tell me. I'll make it happen. You want to make sure we're on time? I can do that. You want a break? Consider it done. No more stressing about this project alone."

My eyes sting with hope as everything inside me shifts.

Tucker held me when I cried on his porch, and today, he made sure I wouldn't have to do any of this alone. He reminded me that I won't ever have to.

He breaks our stare first, not because he's cutting off the moment, but because he's giving me space to feel it.

But I'm not hiding from it anymore.

Not from him.

My eyes sting with hope as everything inside me shifts.

The yard slowly settles into a rhythm with the town working together and the hum of conversation blending with the buzz of power tools.

I find Nan by the porch, directing two kids who look terrified of disappointing her, while attempting to untangle a hose that has seen better days. Once they get it done and Nan looks satisfied, they smile and run off.

I step closer, glancing back toward the yard where Tucker stands laughing at something Griffin is saying. I smile and return my attention back to Nan.

"Hey, Nan."

"Ah. There she is. How ya holdin' up?"

I shrug. "Not too bad. But I want to ask you something."

"If it's about ripping up that bush, it needed to go."

I laugh, shaking my head. "Definitely not about the bush. That really did need to go. It...smelled funny."

"Like cat piss? Yeah. You're right." Her expression shifts— not dramatic, but softer when she notices my lack of reaction. "Now, since it's not about the bush, what's going on in that head?"

I hesitate. For someone who can flirt with danger five minutes ago, this feels so much harder.

"What was she like?" I ask. "My grandmother."

Nan stares at me, registering my words. For a moment I don't think she's going to tell me. Then she reaches toward me and wipes a smudge of dirt from my cheek with her thumb. The gesture feels so maternal it nearly undoes me.

"You don't remember her at all?" she asks gently.

For a bull-in-a-china-shop type of woman, this softness from her feels so different.

I shake my head. "I keep trying. I keep thinking if I stand in the right room or touch the right thing, it'll just…click." I swallow, looking from her to the house behind her. "But it doesn't."

"She was stubborn."

I blink. "Stubborn?"

"Lord, yes. That woman once argued with the city for three months about a mailbox regulation. *Three months*, Scottie. Over the angle of the post." I laugh, but she continues. "But she was the kind of stubborn that meant she didn't quit on people and things. Ever. If she loved you, she loved you all the way through. No conditions."

I look from Nan to the ground, unsure of what to make of all this.

If she didn't quit on me, then why did I stop coming here?

Why did my mom, my dad, *and* I, stop coming here?

Turning my head to the side, my eyes land on the swing off to the edge of the property where I stood with Tucker an hour ago.

"She sat on that swing every morning," Nan says, noticing what I'm looking at. "Coffee in a chipped mug she refused to replace. The swing used to sit right here." Nan walks toward the spot in the grass just off the side of the porch and I follow her. She stops, circling where the swing used to sit. "She'd wave at everyone who drove by, which wasn't many people on this side of town." She laughs.

"She sounds…" I struggle for the word.

"Like someone who knew exactly where she belonged," she says with certainty.

The words settle over me, hitting me right to the core.

Nan looks from me to the house, turning my body to face it with her. "She loved this house. Not because it was perfect. Lord knows it wasn't. But she loved it because it was hers."

I think about the way I've been looking at this house like it's a project.

A checklist.

A deadline.

"I don't feel that," I admit, facing her again. "I feel like I'm borrowing it. Like I'm renovating someone else's story for a show."

Nan studies me carefully. "You know…memories don't always show up the way we expect them to. Sometimes they're not pictures in your head. Sometimes they're instincts."

"Instincts?"

She nods. "The way you stand in a room and already know how it should the look. The way you don't want to throw that swing away. The way you fight for this place even when you say you don't feel connected."

My throat tightens and I feel my eyes burn with tears. "You think that's her?"

"I think," Nan says firmly, "that you are more like her than you realize."

A breeze rushes through the air, rustling the pieces of tall grass that hasn't been cut yet. We both look down at it and then Nan looks up to the sky smiling. "Millie used to say 'just because you can't remember something doesn't mean it didn't shape you.'"

"She said that?"

Nan shrugs. "Among a lot of other things. Some of which I can't repeat in polite company."

I force a laugh because I know she's trying to bring me back to the present. She's trying to help me get my head out of this space I'm currently trapped in. But her words cling to me. I've been treating my missing memories like a failure. Like if I can't replay a scene in my mind or hear her voice clearly, then maybe I didn't love her enough. Clearly, Mimi Millie loved me enough to leave this house to me, but there's nothing else she left behind for me to piece together the missing parts.

But what if love doesn't work like that?

What if it's quieter?

What if it's in the way I refuse to throw out the swing. In the way I couldn't get rid of the pink bathtub. In the way I still need pieces of the house to stay the same so that I can make it shine again for her.

"Nan?" I ask, pulling her from her face to the sky moment. "What if I fix this place up and it still doesn't feel like mine?"

She smiles, stepping closer to me. "Then you keep living in it until it does. Homes aren't built from memory, Scottie girl. They're built from moments."

My gaze drifts back to the yard—to Tucker adjusting his backward baseball cap now in deep conversation with Levi, to Lily smiling and handing out pastries, and to Dallas pretending not to let the kids win in whatever game he's playing with them.

To belonging.

"She would've liked him," Nan says. My eyes snap to her and then follow her line to sight to Tucker.

I nearly choke. "Nan."

"I may be old, but I ain't blind. Millie always liked people who show up," she continues. "And that boy? He shows up."

I scoff. "I have no idea what I'm doing."

"With the house, or with him?"

"Yes."

Nan laughs so loudly that half the yard turns to face us. "Well," she says, squeezing my shoulder. "Good thing neither of those things are finished yet." She starts to step away and then pauses. "Oh, and Scottie?"

"Yeah?"

"She would be really damn proud of you."

Nan says it with such certainty that I believe it. I smile because I can't help it, and she pats my cheek once before turning back toward the chaos of the yard, already shouting at someone about proper shrub planting techniques.

I stand there a moment longer.

The house doesn't feel empty and hollow anymore.

It feels…in progress.

And maybe that's enough for now.

CHAPTER 23
WHY ARE YOU TELLING ME THIS NOW?

TUCKER

Two full days, and the overgrown weeds are gone, the driveway isn't covered with green moss, and the hedges around the house are trimmed instead of trying to become one with the house.

It actually looks like it's turning into a home instead of a cautionary tale of neglect.

I got the vibes today that the producers didn't expect we could finish the yard in such a short time. Truth be told, if we didn't have the help of the town, I'm not sure we would have. The vibes I get from Andrea are still off. There's this deep feeling in my gut she would rather see this season be a failure than a success…or a *Nailed It* as the show calls it. But by the end of the day, the looks shifted to something of wonder.

They didn't expect our community to show up the way they did.

They didn't expect to get the shots they did so that viewers would fall in love with Scottie and this project.

But they did. They are. They will.

Bluestone Lakes is more than just a community—we're family. When someone's in need, we do what we need to help.

When word spreads, people come. It's what the producers didn't say, but I heard anyway: *the yard alone could've eaten the schedule alive if we let it.*

But it didn't.

It's done.

We bought Scottie breathing room.

And that part matters more than anything.

By the time the last van pulls away, the house feels quiet. It reminds me of the time before all of this started where this property was my peace. My safe place to sit and think. In a way, it still is. Even when dozens of people are hammering away or painting walls, it's still the peace I've always come here for—it's still the place I can hear myself clearly.

I step across the yard, dragging leftover lumber toward the side of the house. It doesn't need moving, but my hands feel restless, and movement keeps the thoughts from getting too loud. I reposition them in neat stacks where we will need them for the next project we tackle.

"You know it's still going to be here tomorrow, right?"

Griffin's voice comes from behind me, but I don't turn around. "I'm aware."

I bend down to pick up a stray nail that isn't in anyone's way and toss it into the bed of my truck, before rounding my truck, opening the passenger door and organizing my tool belt on the seat.

"I feel like this doesn't need to be said," Griffin says, still behind me and resting a hand on my shoulder. "But in case you need the reminder, you don't ever have to pretend to be strong around me. You know I'm always here for whatever you need."

"I don't know what you mean?" I say in a semi teasing tone over my shoulder. "I'm not pretending."

He studies me, eyes flicking over the way I reorganize my tool belt. "Right."

"I'm not," I repeat. "I'm just cleaning things up here before heading to the bar."

"You work too much. You don't give yourself a break."

I shrug, turning to face him. "I like working. You know this."

He rolls his eyes. "No one likes working *this* much."

I lift my chin, trying to keep the conversation light and even teasing to avoid wherever my gut thinks Griffin is going with this. "Well…I do."

He exhales through his nose. "I'm not here to drag up old shit. I'm not here to call you out or argue with you about how much you like working. I'm here to be your friend—your cousin. And because of that, I know when a break is needed." His gaze drifts toward the house looming behind us. "Tonight, you need one. You're off."

"You just gave me a night off recently," I argue.

"And maybe it's time for another," he says, his tone softer but he doesn't back down. "You can pretend all you want with the show, with life, and with whatever is going on between you and Scottie. But you can't pretend with me."

I look down at the grass at my feet no longer clawing its way up my ankles, trying to come up with something funny to say back and make him take it back so I can work. Keep the jokes going as I always do, to maintain a light, optimistic mood. But nothing comes up. My jaw tightens, and *nothing comes up.*

He gestures toward my truck parked behind me. "Go home, Tucker."

And before I can say anything more, he walks away.

Part of me is glad he did, because I know anything that would have come out of my mouth would have been bullshit. Griffin knows all about my past. The trauma. The devastation. The way my life changed entirely in one single night.

The night I lost everything.

I swallow hard, dragging my sweaty palms down my jeans as if it will wipe away the feelings. Something stirs beneath the surface of my mind. The memories push, demanding space I refuse to give them.

Flashes of light.

Heat.

Screaming.

I shove them back down where they belong so they can't touch me, because letting them rise only makes me feel things I don't want to feel. I've spent far too fucking long building walls strong enough to keep it buried, and I'm not about to let a moment like this crack them open.

Maybe I do need this night off after all.

But when I get back to my house, everything feels wrong. I shower and throw on a pair of sweatpants and an old T-shirt. Then I find myself walking around the living room and kitchen like I don't belong here, like a stranger in my own space. It feels like I'm forgetting to clock in somewhere. I'm not used to being here when the sun is still in the sky; even if it's cresting over the mountain for sunset, it's still illuminating my place just enough that I forget what it looked like before tonight.

I move around the kitchen more by muscle memory than by intention. Pulling out a pan and some things stuffed away in my refrigerator, I get to making dinner. It's not until I'm standing over my sink that I catch the light turning on in the apartment above my garage. My movement stills because I was so lost in my own head when I got home, that I didn't even look up the stairs the way I find myself doing every night when I get home from the bar.

I tell myself I'm just watching the window to make sure she's okay.

But the moment the light switches off and I see her making her way down the stairs, I bolt for the door, ready to invite her in for dinner because it's basic courtesy to offer her food.

I scoff to myself. It's a lie, and even I don't buy it.

I want to see her.

Without people hovering over us or working on the house.

Just...her.

She stops at the middle of the steps, looking down at her phone and sending a message. She looks from the street and back to her phone as if she's waiting for someone. Jealousy roars to life for no damn reason.

I step outside, and the closer I get to the stairs, my stupid heart reacts like it's hearing its favorite song. She looks like she's dressed to go out—hair down straight, falling over her shoulders. She's wearing a pair of tight jeans and a flowy brown tank top tucked into the front of them. The colors aren't as vibrant as the day I met her, but even muted, she's still…bright.

"Hey," I say, stopping a safe distance from her.

It startles her, and she snaps her head up, hand flying to her chest. "Christ, Tucker. You scared the shit out of me."

"I thought you heard me coming. My boots are never quiet."

"I guess you're right." She smiles, body relaxing. "I was busy reading a text from Lily that she's running late."

"That sounds about right for her." I laugh. "Are you… heading out?"

I don't know why I paused asking her that. I'm not entirely sure I have the right to know what she's doing. But a deeper part of me wants her to stay, when my heart is screaming to let her go. It's screaming to not to get too close.

She nods, taking one more step down. "We're going to Seven Stools for some dinner and drinks. I thought you'd be working."

I try not to read too much into that.

Did she want to see me tonight?

"I've been demoted to the guy who stays home and cooks. Griffin forced me to take the night off."

Her brow furrows. "This is the second night off for you since I've been here."

I shrug like it's not a big deal.

But inside? It makes my heart beat double time that she notices.

"You work a lot," she adds, studying me in that way she's started doing lately, like she's trying to figure out what's underneath my jokes. "It might make someone think you're running from something."

It lands harder than it should.

I hold her gaze for half a second too long before forcing a crooked smile. "Or maybe I just really enjoy my own cooking."

She doesn't smile back.

"Why do you do that?" she asks, eyes narrowed and head tilted to the side as she makes her way to the bottom step of the stairs. "Why do you always hide behind jokes?"

Her question catches me off guard because she doesn't say it accusingly, she says it like she's genuinely curious. I huff out a quiet laugh and glance away from her. The idea of letting her see that? It kicks my heart rate up a notch.

"If I stop joking," I say, bringing my eyes back to hers. "Then people start to see the parts of me I can't fix. The cracks that don't sand smooth. The stuff duct tape doesn't hold or spackle won't cover." I swallow, wanting to look away but I can't. "I know how to fix houses, but I don't know how to fix people. Especially myself."

Something softens in her expression and I see the faintest smile form on her lips. She steps toward me, stopping in front of me. "Maybe you don't have to fix everything."

"That thought keeps me up at night."

The words hang thick between us, and neither of us looks away. Her eyes keep searching mine for a better answer. She wants the truth I don't let anyone close enough to see.

The words sit on the tip of my tongue to ask her to come inside, and ask her to skip dinner with Lily and stay here with me. I want to pretend it's casual, but I know better. Not with the way she's still looking at me, and not with the way my chest tightens at the thought of choosing a night with her over working at the bar for once.

This is the moment I should crack a joke and keep things easy.

But easy doesn't look like this.

"I'm...uh..." I start, clearing my throat and hiking a thumb over my shoulder toward my house. "I'm about to make some dinner if you want to come inside."

She hesitates but then nods. "Yeah. Dinner without the loudness of the bar sounds nice."

I grin wider than I should, stepping to the side and putting my arm out to guide her into my home. She reaches for her phone, likely sending a quick text to Lily about her change in plans. Once we get to my door, she takes off her shoes by the door without me asking, then pauses like she's conscious of every step into my life.

I try to see the place through her eyes as she looks everywhere, taking it all in. It's different from the loft—old, scuffed floors, hand-me-down furniture, and a couple of framed photos on the wall of me, Griffin, and Dallas, and then some of me with Lily and Poppy. Her hand covers her mouth in a chuckle when she spots Nan alone in a picture. One that she demanded I have in this place.

"This place suits you."

"Does that mean you don't think it's a disaster?"

She shoots me a pointed stare. "No. It means it's real."

I swallow around the lump suddenly lodged in my throat and retreat to the safer territory of the stove. "I was just getting dinner started."

She follows me, sliding into one of the stools at the small island, resting her elbows on the counter. I can feel her eyes on me as I move, preparing the chicken and vegetables.

"How long have you lived here?" she asks.

"I've been in Wyoming all my life. But moved to Bluestone Lakes when I was twelve, and then I got this place when I turned nineteen," I say, flipping the chicken and listening to the satisfying sizzle. "My uncle helped me buy it. It needed a lot of work, but it's what I like doing, so I didn't mind."

"You did a good job," she says, looking around at the walls. "I'd never be able to tell this house was anything other than this. I like it. It feels…safe."

"I like safe."

"Yeah," she says softly. "Me too."

We fall into a conversation that feels different from the ones we have on set while I finish cooking. It feels slower because no one is waiting off-camera to yell cut. It feels natural.

I set the plate down and slide it across the island in front of her.

She stares at it for a moment before she grins. "So, you mean to tell me that you can build things *and* cook?"

I plate my food, rounding the island and taking the seat next to her. "I contain multitudes."

Turning my head to the side, I watch as she takes the first bite. I bite down on my bottom lip as I watch her eyes fall closed as all the flavor hits her at once. When she opens her eyes, she swats my forearm with the back of her hand. "Don't do that."

"Do what?"

"Look pleased with yourself."

I shrug. "It's not my fault you're easy to impress."

She narrows her eyes. "I'm not impressed. I'm…adequately fed."

I lean back on the chair, draping one arm over the back of hers. "You made a sound when you tasted that."

She lifts the fork to her mouth, but she pauses with it an inch from her face when my words register. I didn't mean them the way she's taking them. I can see by the way her eyes widen just barely, and she stares down at the food on the fork.

"It was a happy sound," I add.

She moves then, taking another bite, slower this time. Swallowing, she pats her mouth with a napkin. "This is really good, though. I'm impressed. What is this called?"

"Marry Me Chicken." Her gaze snaps to me, and I can't help but laugh. "That's really the name of the recipe. It's said the way to a man's heart is through his stomach. So, whoever came up with it meant for whoever eats it to fall in love with the others cooking."

She stares at me for a beat, and now I fear I've *really* said too much.

That's not why I made this recipe, though. It's just the easiest thing I know how to make here at home without a screenshot of a recipe on my phone. I can make this dish from memory.

"At least that's what the internet says," I continue, shrugging and facing my food.

Out of the corner of my eye I see her take another bite while we sit in silence. I should have told her it was called something else. It's just…a stupid recipe that's making me overthink this way too much. My brain though? A fucking traitor, because what if…

Not what if I were to marry her—god, not that fast. Just this flash of her in my space in a way that isn't temporary. Her laughing at something dumb I say while she's barefoot in a kitchen that's ours. Her leaving a mug in the sink like she belongs here. Her looking at me like she already knows the version of me I'm trying so hard not to show.

My chest tightens on reflex.

The old instinct that says: *Careful. Careful. Careful.*

If she sees it all, she'll do what everyone does.

She'll leave.

Yet here I am…letting her fucking in. I don't let people in. I don't have people over. I don't give them the kind of access where they can bruise me without trying.

When I face her again, she's watching me with that same careful focus she uses when working on her grandparents' house, like she knows what I'm thinking, and she's trying not to pry too hard.

We eat in silence for a stretch. It's not an awkward silence, though. She breaks it when she makes some joke about Nan's battle with the bushes during filming, and I'm relieved for a different topic of conversation. Then I tell her about the time Levi almost fell through a ceiling because he didn't think the rotten spot was that big. We both fall into *easy* laughter, and I feel something inside me soften in a way that scares me more than any unsafe building structure ever could.

Finishing up the last bite of food on my plate, I stand and round the counter to put my dish in the sink. When I see she's done, she moves to stand but I stop her by grabbing the plate and putting it with mine.

I take a moment, watching her as she rests her elbows on the island and props her chin in her hands. The two of us with eyes locked on each other and so many things left unsaid.

I feel the shift in mood before she says, "Can I ask you something?"

I smirk. "You already are."

She rolls her eyes, but her mouth is trembling a little at the corners. "I meant to ask you that night you found me on the stairs outside. But I need to know…" She pauses, fidgeting with her hands. "Why did you do it?"

"Do what?"

"Leave," she says, looking down at her hands on the counter. "That morning in San Francisco, you just…left without a word."

The kitchen feels smaller all of a sudden.

I could lie. I could make a joke and shrug it off. But I can feel that this is where we draw the line. The place where I decide whether I keep pretending or finally tell her something true."

"I wanted to wake you up," I say, my voice low.

Her brows crease. "But you didn't."

"I know."

I scrub a hand over the back of my neck, searching for the words that don't make me sound like a coward. "I was in San Francisco for two nights. Well, it was supposed to be two nights. Dallas had a meeting with his former team out there, and I was at Between the Buns waiting for him to finish. Never expecting to run into you…" I pause, feeling my body relax. "I had a dozen or so texts on my phone when I woke up in your hotel room that he needed to leave as soon as possible to come back to Bluestone

Lakes. And he sent it urgently, pushing through my Do Not Disturb on my phone." I laugh lightly. "I got dressed and—"

The memory comes to me so vividly. Her hair splayed across the pillow, and her bare skin was exposed on her back where the covers fell. The only thing on my mind was that there was no way I deserved someone as beautiful and perfect as her.

"I stood there," I continue. "And I thought, if I wake you I'm going to want to stay. If I stay, I'll find a reason. And if I find a reason, I'll start thinking I'm allowed to have something I want just because I want it."

She stares at me, unspoken words on her face like I just rewired gravity.

"So I did what I'm good at. I left."

She swallows. "That's not an answer."

I force myself to hold her eyes. "It's the only one I've got. I didn't leave because you didn't matter, Scottie. I left because you *did*."

The silence that follows is thick, humming with something I can't put a name to. Her hands are on the counter between us, and I watch them flex.

"I've done a lot of things I don't think about too hard. Usually, it's related to my job, but walking out of that hotel room without waking you up?" I shake my head. "If life ever started handing out second chances, that's the first one I'd ask for back."

"Why are you telling me this now?" she whispers, looking down at her hands.

"Because you asked," I say quickly. "And because I'm fucking tired of you thinking you weren't worth a goodbye. Because you were. You *are*. It's why that night we slipped in the apartment, I made a point to tell you *I wasn't* running."

The air between us snaps tight.

She stands up from the stool, rounding the island between us. I stay where I am with my back against the counter. My heart pounds in my chest with every step she takes. Stopping in front of me, she looks up at me with a mix of anger and hurt—something molten that steals the oxygen from the room.

"You made me feel disposable," she says. "You know that, right?"

"And I fucking hate myself for it."

"Good," she breathes out, chest rising and falling. "You should."

We both stand there, staring at each other. The space between is charged enough to light the whole damn town. She's so close that I can see every fleck of color in her eyes. They bore into mine, filled with so much heat.

"I haven't stopped thinking about the last time I kissed you," I admit, the words pouring out of me like a confession. "Because it was the first time I didn't feel like running. I think that's what wrecked me, because I don't let people get close like this. But you keep…" I shake my head. "You keep finding every fucking crack."

"Is that a bad thing?"

"I haven't decided yet."

Her gaze drops to my mouth then snaps back to my eyes like she's angry for even thinking about it. The look on her face is pure conflict. But then her eyes go dark—a warning and a challenge all at once. The kind of look that says *don't you fucking do this to me again*. Her breathing is shallow, but her voice doesn't come.

Something snaps in me. I reach for her, hands coming up to frame her face. Her skin is warm under my palms. She sucks in a breath, fingers flying to my wrists. It's not meant to push me away, but to hold on.

"All I think about is how your mouth felt on mine and how much I didn't want it to end," I say, my breath against her lips and she doesn't move. Instead, her body moves an inch closer to me, pressing her body against mine. "Last chance to change your mind, Scottie."

"Don't you dare."

I lower my mouth to hers.

The world narrows when I feel her lips against mine. A soft sound escapes from the back of her throat before her hands move from my wrists to my chest, fisting my shirt like she needs this as much as I do. I pull her in hard until there's not a breath of space left between us, one hand sliding into her hair, and the other across the small of her back.

She melts, kissing me back with a kind of desperate relief. I stumble her backward a few steps until her hips hit the edge of the counter. My thumb strokes along the line of her jaw, tilting her head to deepen the kiss.

She lets out a soft, broken sound that goes straight to my knees.

When her fingers slide under the hem of my shirt, heat sparks across my skin. I groan softly into her mouth before I can stop myself. My grip tightens on her waist as if I can anchor both of us to this moment before it spins out of control. Her body *fits* against mine. Every curve presses close, familiar in a way that makes it hard to breathe.

I lift her to the counter, and her legs open instinctively so I can step between them. The movement pulls a laugh from her, but I swallow it when my lips are back on hers. This kiss isn't frantic anymore. It's slow and deliberate as we both acknowlededge every feeling we've been fighting to hold back.

Her hands slide up my arms, fingers digging into my shoulders, and it nearly undoes me.

"I don't think I can stop," I murmur against her mouth, letting my thumb trace the curve of her jaw. "You need to tell me to stop if any part of you doesn't want this right now."

She wraps both arms around my neck, pressing her forehead to mine. "I don't want you to stop."

I kiss her again. Each one is heavier until I'm painfully aware of every place we're touching. I move, peppering kisses along her jaw. She tips her head to the side, allowing me full access to the sensitive spot on her neck. Pulling down one of the straps of her tank top, I trail my lips along her collarbone.

"Tucker," she practically moans.

"Yes, babe?"

"More."

I pull back to look at her. I see the woman who makes me want things I swore I didn't need. The woman who keeps stepping closer to the cracks I've forced shut. Something settles in my chest when I cup her face. My lips brush hers in a kiss that feels like a promise.

"This doesn't stay fake anymore," I tell her, my voice rough. "Not tonight. Not ever again."

She reaches for the hem of my shirt and pulls it over my head.

"Good."

CHAPTER 24

PROMISES, PROMISES.

SCOTTIE

I toss Tucker's shirt aside and he tracks its movement.

When his eyes are back on mine, he has one brow raised and a smirk on his face. This was not what I had planned for the night, but I'm glad I took him up on his offer for dinner. I didn't expect to ask Tucker about San Francisco, but the words just rolled out of me. Now I'm sitting here, with him standing between my legs, and begging him for more.

He hasn't moved since tossing his shirt to the side, and my body feels like it's on the edge of combustion. He stares at me, trying to figure out if I mean the words I'm saying.

"I don't want to pretend anymore," I say, hoping he understands.

A muscle in his jaw tightens before he steps closer. The space between us disappears, and the rest of the world fades into static, and I suck in a sharp breath the moment I feel his cock press against me.

I shouldn't want this the way I do.

The night in the apartment left me feeling the same way I did after waking up in the hotel room alone, like he regretted it. I brushed it off to the heat of the moment and loneliness. Something I'd laugh off later and call it a mistake so we didn't have to call it real.

But there's no way it wasn't.

He looked at me then the same way he's looking at me now, like he's starving. He says my name like it belongs on his lips. I've tried to pretend, along with the rest of the facade, that I don't crave it.

The way his hands touched me.

The words he said.

The intense feeling of his eyes on mine the entire time.

But I'm already gone.

This time, I'm not slipping or worried about what's going to happen after tonight. This time, I'm choosing him.

"I'm glad we're on the same page. Because I'm fucking done acting like I don't want all of you," he growls. "I'm also done pretending I don't want to sink my cock into your tight pussy again and hear you scream my name when I make you come over and over and over again."

The gasp that escapes me is answered by the way his eyes darken. He closes the distance, stealing the breath from my lungs as his hands settle on my hips in a grounding way. He kisses me again. It's deep and sure and hungry. I kiss him back, as both of our hands roam each other's body, memorizing each other.

This isn't adrenaline.

This isn't fake chemistry.

This is want.

I hook my legs around his waist, and his grip tightens before his hips jerk into me. I moan at the intense feeling of pleasure of feeling his cock against the throb between my legs. My hips roll on instinct, chasing the feeling through my jeans, but it's not enough.

"Tucker," I groan.

"Patience, baby," he whispers against the corner of my mouth. "Let me have this time to savor you before I worship you."

My head falls back, and he kisses the corner of my lips, down my neck again until he reaches my chest, just above where the line of my tank top sits. He pulls the straps down before pushing the rest of the shirt down, revealing my thin lace bra.

"Fuck," he mutters against my skin, taking both breasts in his hand. When he pulls it down, the air makes my nipples harden. The weight of his stare on my body only intensifies the feeling. He takes one in his mouth—sucking and biting before doing the same with the other. "Perfect. So. God. Damn. Perfect."

My hips move on the counter, my body's way of saying it wants more. No, it *needs* more.

He stands tall, reaching between us with a smirk on his face. "My girl is *begging* for a release, isn't she?"

I nod eagerly.

I feel the way he calls me *his girl* throughout my entire body.

He unbuttons my jeans, sliding the zipper down painfully slow. I look down, watching every deliberate movement before I adjust myself enough to allow him to yank the jeans off my legs. I pull the tank top over my head and toss my lace bra to the side. I meet his eyes again, and they are already locked on me. I open my legs, willing him to step back between them.

But he doesn't.

He doesn't move.

His eyes trail every inch of exposed skin. This isn't the first time he's seen me naked, but it feels like it. I've never felt so vulnerable watching him watch me. But at the same time, it's exhilarating to have him looking at me the way he is.

I don't feel watched.

I feel chosen.

"You fucking undo me, Scottie."

"What are you planning to do about it?"

He smirks, sinking to his knees in front of me. My mouth opens, but closes quickly when he presses a kiss to my inner thigh. My body tenses for a moment before it morphs into pleasure.

"First," he says, kissing the inside of my opposite thigh. "I'm going to make you come on my tongue."

I bite down on my bottom lip as he trails his lips farther up my thighs. He stops just over my pussy. "And then," he says, his breath on the fabric of my panties only building the anticipation between my legs. "I'm going to sink my cock into you and make you come again, and again. I'm going to ruin you the way you've already ruined me."

"Promises, promises," I pant.

A devilish grin spreads on his lips as he looks up at me, hooking a finger into the side of my panties and pushing them to the side. Then he presses his face between my legs, sucking on the bundle of nerves wound so tight. I cry out almost instantly from the contact. My head falls back, and my hips rock forward against his face. He swipes his tongue across my clit before sucking it again.

"Tucker," I moan, unable to hold it in.

I open my legs wider for him, wanting to feel more. I reach forward, placing my hand on the back of his head, holding him in place as the pressure builds inside of me. Every swipe of his tongue only makes me that much closer to ecstasy.

"That feels so good," I tell him. "So good."

He presses one palm against my inner thigh, opening me up even more for him. I rest my foot on the edge of the counter, watching every move he makes. He reaches up with the other hand, inserting one finger in, and it's only then that my head falls back.

It's all too much.

"No," he says, still fucking me with his finger. "Keep watching, Scottie. I want you to see the way I'm devouring you." I look down between my legs, and the way he's looking up at me with my arousal coating his lips. "Such a good girl."

"More," I say breathlessly.

He replaces his finger with two, and it nearly makes me come right then and there. He swipes his tongue along my clit and fucks me hard with two fingers, hooking them to hit the spot that sends me over the edge.

Stars dance across my vision, and it feels like the world can't quite contain what's happening. My entire body feels like a fuse on the edge of an explosion. My breath shudders, quickening to the point I can't control it. Pleasure coils tight until it feels like I'm going to come undone entirely.

"Come for me, babe," Tucker rasps.

My thoughts scatter, dissolving into color and heat.

I tip right over the edge, screaming his name like a prayer. Over and over as my orgasm ripples through my body. For a heartbeat, I forget everything—fear and restraint. There's only release rippling through me in waves.

When it settles, I'm left breathless.

My thoughts come back, and fear grips my chest. If this is what real feels like, no wonder I've been afraid of it. This isn't about the way he's touched me or the lines we've crossed without looking back. It's about everything I've been holding at arm's length. The feelings that have simmered, waiting for the right second to crash in. And now they're here. Undeniable and barreling through me like a freight train.

"Talk to me," Tucker says, as if sensing the shift in my thoughts.

I look at him, and it's different, like something inside me has shifted permanently. I know the moment our eyes lock that whatever this is between us is not fleeting or casual.

I wrap my arms around his neck, pressing my lips to his and tasting myself on his tongue. It's eager and hungry and filled with the need for me. I need to feel Tucker in places only he can touch.

"Take me to your room," I say against his lips.

He wraps his arms around my waist, lifting me. I tighten my legs around his waist, refusing to break the kiss as he moves through his house. He kicks the door open, and despite just coming for him, I want it again.

"You're going to ruin me," he says, breathlessly against my lips.

"Good," I pant, setting myself down to my feet in the center of his room. "Because you've already ruined me."

He growls, and before he can do anything else, I press my palm to his chest, pushing him back onto his bed. He falls onto his back, holding himself up by his elbows and grinning. I watch him watch me as I slowly hook my fingers into the waistband of my panties and slide them down each leg.

"Fuck," he draws out.

I make my way to the edge of the bed. Leaning over him, I pull the waistband of his sweatpants and his boxer briefs down. His cock springs free, and he bites down on his bottom lip. I toss his pants to the side and wrap my hand around his shaft. I feel heat pool between my legs as I slide my hand up and down.

"You feel like something I didn't know I'm allowed to have," Tucker says low.

His words make everything inside me pause. His words have nothing to do with me and everything to do with whatever story he keeps locked behind that funny guy exterior. I've always had a feeling that something was there that he refuses to talk about.

But that one sentence tells me more than he ever has.

It tells me he thinks wanting is dangerous.

That he believes good things come with consequences.

That somewhere along the way, he decided he wasn't deserving of them.

"You have me now," I say, shifting myself over him, with one leg on each side of his. "You have me."

His hands come up to my hips, fingers curling tight as he closes his eyes to let the words sink in. I lean forward, cupping his face in my hands. He opens his eyes just before our lips meet, searching my face before I kiss him. Slowly, like he's something precious instead of something broken.

Like I'm not going anywhere.

He responds immediately, lifting his head to meet me and

deepening the kiss. It's not in a desperate way, but more like this is what he needs. Not the touch or the closeness, but the confirmation that I meant what I said.

That I choose him.

That I'm here.

"I need you," he whispers, and it's a stark contrast to the man he was in the kitchen. "Please."

"Condom?"

"Fuck," he groans. "I don't have any. If you can't tell, I don't do this often."

I feign shock. "You mean to tell me you don't invite women over for dinner and make them come on your counter all the time?"

He laughs, reaching behind me and playfully smacking my ass. But the way both of our bodies move is just enough that I feel his cock between my legs. My mouth opens from the needy feeling of wanting to feel him inside of me right now.

He steadies me—watching me as if he feels it, too.

"Scottie," he groans.

"I haven't been with anyone since you," I tell him. "And I'm on the pill."

He raises an eyebrow. "Are you asking me what I think you are?"

I nod. "I need you, Tucker."

"Fuck," he rasps, gripping my hips hard enough to leave a bruise. "I haven't been with anyone since you either."

In the past, I would have thought that's a lie.

I'd believe it was just another line someone would use to get what they want from me.

But I don't feel that with Tucker.

I lower myself on top of him, feeling his shaft against my clit. "Please."

"You're soaking my cock, and I'm not even inside of you."

"Then be inside of me."

He smirks, shaking his head. Reaching between us, he fists

his cock and swipes the tip across my arousal. "Watch," he orders. "Watch how my cock slides into you."

I bit down on my lip and lower myself on him. I feel him stretch me in the best way possible as I sink deeper and deeper.

"Jesus," he groans. "You're fucking perfect. You were made for me."

I move my body up and down, bouncing on his cock slowly at first, before picking up speed. I reach down, placing both hands on his chest to hold me up. He reaches forward, pinching my nipples between his fingers, and it only builds the pressure in my body. If I thought I was on the verge of combustion in the kitchen, then this is a whole nuclear explosion.

It's strange how quickly my body remembers him. There's no rush to this like there was that night. There's no need to prove anything, just careful slowness, like we're both afraid this might disappear if we move too fast.

Being with him like this again feels familiar and warm. It feels like exhaling after holding your breath underwater. It feels like coming home to something that still fits, even after all the damage.

"Ask me again, Tucker," I pant.

He tilts his head to the side in confusion, but I don't slow.

"What am I?"

He smirks, quickly understanding. "Say you're my girl, baby. Say I'm yours."

"You're mine, Tucker." I say, breathless from picking up speed and feeling the intensity build in my core. "And god, I'm all yours. You fucking have me."

He bites down on his bottom lip, and thrusts his hips up into me the moment the words leave my lips. I cry out his name, and he does it again. "*Ahh*," I moan. "I'm going to—"

"Yes, you are. I can feel it. You're fucking squeezing my cock."

I quicken my movements, going back and forth between bouncing up and down and rolling my hips forward. My breathing picks up as I struggle to keep it together. My body coils, and I know he's close by the look on his face, too.

"Come with me," I say through breaths. "Please, Tucker."

"You should already know by now." *Thrust.* "I'll do whatever you want me to do." *Thrust.* "I'm at your mercy, Scottie."

I fall on him, both arms on the side of his face as my fingers intertwine in his hair. I press my lips to his, taking in whatever he has to give me—breathing life into me again. I rock my hips, and he thrusts. It's hard and fast and rough. But it's enough to send me right over the edge. He doesn't let me release my mouth from his as I ride out the orgasm. I pant into his mouth, tongues dancing and stealing each other's oxygen just before he grunts into my lips, spilling his release inside of me.

I don't know how to explain this feeling to anyone.

I don't know what to make of it myself.

But I know for sure, this isn't just letting Tucker fuck me.

This is me letting him in *completely*.

My body relaxes on top of him, his chest rising and falling as he comes down from his release. Wrapping his arms around me, he holds me close. I turn my head, and I can feel the pounding of his heart on the side of my face.

"Tucker," I say softly.

"Mm-hmm?"

"Thank you."

He lifts my head with the back of his finger, his expression unreadable in the low light. "You don't have to thank me for sex."

I feel my cheeks heat. "That's not," I start, choking on a laugh. "That's not what I'm thanking you for, Tucker." He holds my gaze, tilting his head to the side. "Thank you for being honest. For not pretending. For letting me see the part of you that you keep tucked away from the world."

He spins us around until I'm flat on my back and he's hovering over me. He brushes the messy hair away from my face and then drops his forehead down to mine. I feel his uneven breaths against my lips.

"Every time, Scottie," he continues. "I may have fucked up the first time, but I'll choose you every time."

There's no hesitation in his words.

And it's at this moment that I believe him.

EPISODE SEVEN

MASTER OF THE SECRETS AND PAST

Welcome back! Today, we're stepping into the most personal space of the house. The master bedroom. It's not as bad as some of the other projects. We just have to tackle some water-stained plaster from a window that has been cracked for too long, warped floors, and a closet door that's seen better days. It's a room begging for a fresh start.

But not everything hidden is meant to be torn out.

And when Tucker and Scottie pull up the old flooring, they uncover more than damage. They find pieces of the past neither of them expect.

As emotions run high, Tucker becomes more than just the contractor holding it all together.

Some renovations change rooms.

Others change everything.

CHAPTER 25

DO WE THINK THIS
ROOM WILL FIGHT US?

TUCKER

Nothing about this house feels the same as it did last week.

Maybe it's because we spent a few days working on the yard, and now that we're back inside, we're seeing all the little jobs that got done during that time. Time is flying, and I hate to admit it, but I'm not sure how I'll feel when this project is over.

Is Scottie staying here at this house?

Is she planning to sell it and move back home?

These are the kind of unknowns that have consumed my mind since she stayed at my house the other night. The night we crossed the line where there's no coming back from. There's no denying that both of us were sprinting toward it, though. There was no awkwardness about it either. There was no discussion about whether she should sleep over or what it meant. She just… stayed—curled to my side like it's where she's belonged all along. And I stayed awake longer than I should have, taking it all in.

It felt like a dream.

I was afraid that if I closed my eyes, she wouldn't be there.

But when I woke up, she was. Scottie didn't rush out the

door the next morning, or pretend it didn't happen. Instead, she stole my shirt, complained that my coffee wasn't as good as Cozy Cup's, and kissed me like it was the most natural thing in the world.

It was easy in a way that scared the hell out of me.

And now, we're back at the house for another day of filming.

Walking through the first floor of the house, my head is on a swivel trying to find her. When I saw Levi outside, he said she was already working. I don't even know what the plans are for the day. When I don't find Scottie immediately, I head upstairs, poking my head in the smaller bedrooms before I find her in the master bedroom.

"Hi," I say, knocking on the doorframe once.

She snaps her head toward me as if I've startled her, and then softens when she eyes the two cups of coffee in my hand. "Hi."

I step into the room and try to hand her a cup, but she doesn't take it. Instead, she presses onto her toes, wrapping her hands around my neck. I wish like hell I wasn't holding these stupid cups so I wrap both arms around her.

"I can't tell if this is because I brought you caffeine or because you're starting to like me." I laugh into her neck.

She pulls back, arms still wrapped around my neck, and gives me a look. "It's a mix of both, if you must know."

"Hmm," I say, smiling as I lean down and press a kiss to her lips.

She doesn't pull back or stop me either. She melts into the kiss like it's a routine we've been doing for years. The way she looks at me isn't careful anymore, it's warm and open.

"You look happy today," I say.

She laughs against my mouth. "You say that like it's suspicious."

"It is when you're usually pretending when we're here."

She pauses, studying me before she shrugs and whispers, "Aren't we done with pretending?"

"Well, this works," Andrea says from the doorframe. I step back away from Scottie to put space between us, but she doesn't move. "Practice is good for the camera, even though we only have two more episodes to film. I like this. You two are really playing the part."

Scottie barely reacts, then looks at me and winks.

For the first time since this show started, she doesn't care what it looks like.

If they think this is us *practicing*, then we're going to roll with it.

"What's the plan for this room?" Andrea asks, phone in her hand.

Scottie turns around, taking in the master bedroom. "I want it to feel calm, like a place where you can exhale after a long day. Soft lighting and…" She pauses, looking around the room before pointing to a bare corner. "Maybe an electric fireplace over here to keep the cozy effect going."

I feel my insides tighten over a stupid electric fireplace. Nothing about that feels fucking safe, but I'm not going to burst her bubble right now.

Andrea nods, typing out notes on her phone. "Any large changes for this space we anticipate? Walls coming down? A crazy lady from town swooping in with a hammer?"

Scottie and I laugh because we know who she means.

But her first question nearly stops me from being able to laugh in the first place. When we worked on the outside of the house, I kept having this feeling she *wanted* to see Scottie fail. I feel it again at this moment, and I hate that I do.

I won't fucking allow it.

This is going to work and be done on time.

"No big changes," Scottie says, laughter dying down. "I'd just like to repair what's broken and keep the space as it is."

I look around, taking it in for the first time.

The room looks tired and worn down. The kind that comes from holding weight for too long without anyone noticing.

There's a water stain across the ceiling that matches the one we repaired in the living room, except this one means it's coming from the roof. As I walk around the room, my steps are uneven, and I realize the floor dips in multiple spots, enough to tell me the subfloor has been compromised. The closet door is hanging crooked, but that's probably the easiest thing to fix.

Nothing in this room can be fixed with cosmetics.

This room needs reinforcement.

I glance at Scottie, who's still talking to Andrea with her hands out as if painting a picture. I can tell by the brightness in her face that she sees potential for this room.

I fucking hate that all I see is risk.

"Light floors and clean walls to go with the soft lighting," Scottie says. "Nothing a little love can't fix."

I run my eyes along the ceiling and baseboards. "It needs more than that."

She glances at me, amused. "You always say that."

"And usually, I'm right."

"Usually."

I circle the room again, taking in every single inch of it—surveying and assessing. My skin crawls with everything this room needs. "We're gutting this room," I announce after a few minutes.

Scottie's smile falters. "Tucker—"

"This room is full of water damage, likely an issue with the roof, which is something we need to check out as soon as possible." I fucking cringe as the words leave my mouth because the last thing I want is these producers to think they won by making this season a fail. "The subflooring is uneven, and I don't trust what's behind those walls regarding the electrical work that will be needed," I say, feeling my fingers tingle, eager to reach for the pry bar. "We don't half fix rooms like this. We go all in."

She studies me for a moment. I see the disappointment in her face. But when I lock eyes with her, I beg her to read what I'm saying without any more words. I beg her to trust me on this.

She nods. "Okay, I trust you."

That shouldn't hit as hard as it does, but I've never been more thankful to hear it.

"Is that going to take more time?" Andrea asks.

My eyes snap to her, anger bubbling. Because when she asked us if there were any big changes we anticipated, my brain immediately went to the feeling I keep having when Andrea is around—she *wants* to see Scottie fail.

I won't fucking allow it.

This is going to work and be done on time.

"Nope," I answer her, popping the *P*.

My crew moves around us effortlessly to remove all the old furniture left in the room. It wasn't much—an old bedside table, a rusted metal-framed bed, and a chair in the corner that smelled of mold. Even with the little that was left, the room already feels bigger.

Scottie steps back in first, hands on her hips, surveying the room. "Okay. Do we think this room will fight us?"

I scoff. "Everything in this house does."

"Figures." She laughs and then shoots me a wicked grin. "Good thing I like a challenge."

"I've noticed," I say, watching her move toward the closet.

She waves a hand in a *come here* motion. "Try to keep up, Tucker."

I shake my head and make my way to her.

I couldn't stop myself if I tried.

We get to work without a plan beyond instinct. She peels back the trim while I score the seams. When the first section of drywall gives way, it comes down in a rough chunk, and we both step back at the same time.

"Nice catch," she says when I steady the falling edge before it falls on her.

Placing it on the ground, I turn to her. "You okay?"

"Always."

After that, we move around together too easily. I hold the

crowbar out behind me without looking, and she takes it. She ducks under my arm instead of asking me to move. At one point, she backs into me while tugging at a stubborn nail, and I brace her with both hands on her hips without thinking.

The banter's still there between us, but it's muted now.

It's less jokes for the sake of noise, and more small touches that feel intentional even when we don't acknowledge them.

When I move to tackle the water-stained ceiling, I climb the ladder. It's a feeling of déjà vu, except things are different between us now. She's not hovering, just there. When a chunk finally gives way, she startles and her hands fly to my calves to steady me.

"Careful," she teases. "If this falls on you, I'll have to find another contractor."

I glance down at her because she's definitely said this before. "And you'd miss me."

"Obviously."

I'm staring into her eyes, feeling a stab to my chest with feelings. Ones I've never allowed myself to have that keep coming back more and more with Scottie. Every look and every quiet moment between us chips away at the rules I built to survive. This isn't lust anymore. It's the kind of feeling that asks you to stay when your instinct is to run.

I should look away.

I should break the moment or crack a joke before I say something I can't take back.

The crack of plaster over my head cuts through my thoughts instead. Scottie's eyes go wide, and I cover my head to brace for impact. Dust rains down around me in a gray cloud.

"Scottie!" I shout, flying off the ladder to get to her.

She's crouched down with her hands behind her neck to protect herself from the falling debris. I place my hand on her shoulder, hoping like hell she's all right, because I won't be able to live with myself if someone I lo—

No. That's not what this is.

I care about her.

Fuck.

"Scottie?" I ask, my voice softer this time.

She releases her hands from behind her, looking up and around at the mess. Her hair is covered in dust and drywall pieces, but she's okay.

Thank god, she's okay.

"I'm glad I trusted you," she says, placing a shaky hand on my forearm. "If we didn't gut this room, who knows when that would have fallen down."

"Are you two okay?" Andrea says from the doorway. Her eyes are wide as she takes in the room. Scottie looks at Andrea, but my eyes are only on my girl. "I was downstairs and heard a crash. I thought that crazy lady was back, busting down walls."

"We're okay," Scottie answers for us. "Looks like this room needs more work than I thought."

"Are you sure you're okay?" I ask Scottie in a low tone, not acknowledging that Andrea is still in the room. "You're shaking."

She nods. "Just shaken up. I didn't expect the ceiling to give way like that."

Reaching down, I pick up a larger piece of the ceiling that fell and toss it toward the door so Levi and the rest of the crew can discard it with what we've already removed.

When I turn around, Scottie is crouched down, picking something up.

I freeze when she gasps.

Unwrapping it carefully, I see her holding a wooden box, worn with age, before she opens it slowly. She pulls out a stack of papers that looks like a mixture of letters and photographs.

Her breath shudders.

"Are you getting this?" I hear Andrea whisper to the man behind the camera.

"These were..." Scottie whispers, pausing before she faces me as if she just found treasure. "These were my grandparents."

I kneel beside her without thinking, resting my hand on her back. She leans into me just enough to tell me she's thankful I'm here. She flips through them, and I can feel the tension radiating off her under the palm of my hand. She looks up at the hole in the ceiling and back down, shaking her head. "I didn't even know there was an attic." She laughs softly. "I would have never found these if we didn't gut this room."

"Looks like they wanted it found."

She flips through everything—memories of her grandparents, captured in photos and letters. The pictures aren't the staged ones you would frame on mantels. They are all candid. One of her grandmother laughing with her head thrown back and barefoot in the yard. Another of her grandfather holding up a fish at Bluestone Lake. There are pictures of road trips and the two of them laughing on the way to dinner. They look young and in love.

Scottie wipes at her eyes, laughing quietly. "I love seeing them like this. I wish I'd gotten the chance to truly know them."

Something in my chest shifts at the pain I feel for her, never really knowing them the way she wanted to.

"Sometimes people leave the best parts of themselves tucked away."

The pain I feel for her morphs into a pain at the memories of my past I keep hidden from the world. The ones I'm keeping hidden from *her*.

She looks up at me, eyes shining. "You know, you're really good at this."

"At letting ceilings fall?"

She shakes her head. "At being here."

I swallow, not expecting that from this moment. "So are you, Scottie."

She hugs me suddenly, arms tight around me, while we're both crouched down in the middle of the room. I hold her like it's instinct. Like it's always been this way.

It stays that way for minutes that feel like hours.

I realize then, that I don't want a version of my life where she isn't in it.

And wanting her in that sense means opening the door to the one thing I've spent my life keeping locked.

The day everything burned down.

CHAPTER 26

LA LA LA.

SCOTTIE

There's something different about being in my grandparents' house after the cameras leave and the construction crew drives away. This sense of peace settles over me, almost making me feel like I can see myself here forever.

When I first got here, I didn't have a plan.

Hell, I still don't.

Do I finish fixing it up and sell it?

Do I take the money from the sale and show to buy in another town?

Or do I stay and let it become mine the way Nan said it could? Homes aren't built from memory. They're built from moments. I didn't understand what she meant that day when we stood in the yard staring at a rusted swing. But standing here now, I think maybe this is what she meant. Not some lightning bolt recognition or a sudden rush of childhood memories.

Just the slow, steady layering of new ones.

The kind you choose.

Tucker flashes through my head at that thought. Things with him have become easy. In a matter of weeks, I've gone from pissed off that he's the head contractor and having to fake date him, to feeling myself falling for him more and more with every day that passes.

Sometimes it knocks me off my feet, because how can a one-night stand consume my mind this much? It doesn't feel right, but at the same time it feels like what I need—what I want.

I make my way upstairs as the golden glow of the sunset sweeps through all the open windows. The master bedroom is taped off, with a hole in the ceiling covered with plastic until tomorrow. I stand in the doorway and my eyes find the box of my grandparents' memories sitting in the corner.

Lifting the caution tape, I duck under it and make my way toward the box. I sink down against the wall beside it. My hands hover over the lid of the wooden box. I've been trying so hard to find something that gave me a deeper connection to this house—something to make it feel like it's mine and not just a project. But now that I've found it, I'm afraid of what happens if I look even closer than I did before.

I open the box hesitantly, and staring back at me is a single photo of Mimi Millie, smiling at the camera. And it feels like she's smiling at *me*. My fingers tremble as I lift it. I stare into her eyes through the image, as if I can see her now. As if she's here in this home with me. I flip it to the back of the stack, coming to the next picture. It's the house from years ago with flowers blooming along the porch and that old swing glider that's now against the edge of the property line, sitting in the front grass right next to it.

Flipping again to the next one, I freeze, sucking in a sharp breath.

Because that's me.

A little girl with messy hair sitting cross-legged on the porch floor.

I flip to the next picture. It's me again, bundled in the same blanket I found in the crawl space, and Millie's head is thrown back in laughter as I make a funny face at her.

Another picture.

I'm tucked into the corner of the living room, knees pulled to my chest, the blanket wrapped around my shoulders while old cartons flicker on a small box television. I had to be about three in that picture.

I keep flipping and flipping—picture after picture. So many more memories of me and her. Photos of her and my grandfather. And I don't remember any of these moments. Despite the proof sitting in the palm of my hands, I don't fucking remember.

I press the photos to my heart and let my head fall back against the wall behind me as tears slip down my face. I don't bother trying to stop them. I'm crying for the memories I didn't know I had. Crying for the years I didn't ask questions. Crying because this house didn't just belong to her, it belonged to *us*.

All this time, I've been trying to force a connection.

But it was already here.

It was just waiting for me to look.

I sit upright, digging in my pocket for my phone. Lifting it to my ear, it rings twice before my dad answers.

"Hi, honey."

"Dad," I say, my voice breaking as I say it. "Why? Why did we stop coming here?"

There's silence on the other end and he doesn't answer.

"I found pictures," I add quickly. "Dozens and dozens of me. Of Mimi Millie and Pop Pop. I don't remember any of it, but I was here. A lot."

Another long stretch of silence, and I feel anger bubbling inside of me as more tears drip down my cheeks. I close my eyes with the phone to my head and my head falls back against the wall again.

"Why?" I ask again, barely above a whisper this time.

I hear movement on the other end of the phone, a chair scraping and footsteps as the TV in the background fades away like he's moving. And then I hear my mom's voice. "Who is that?" she asks him, but it's faint.

My dad lowers his voice. "We can talk about this another time, Scottie."

"Dad."

He exhales—heavy and hesitant. "I promise, honey. I will tell you everything."

"Billy?" my mom asks in the background, much closer this time.

"Talk soon," he says and then hangs up.

My grip tightens around my phone as I bring it to my lap, and without him saying it, I know. I know now it had to be Mom.

My gaze shifts to the photos still in my lap. The top one being me sitting on that rusted swing in a different outfit like it was a different day, laughing like I belonged here.

Because now, I believe I did.

I'm finally walking out of the house for the day when my phone buzzes in the back pocket of my overalls. Pulling it out, I find a string of texts from the girls.

LILY

Dinner and drinks tonight? My place?

BLAIR

I'm in! Griffin is headed to Seven Stools tonight to meet with an old friend.

LILY

Who?

BLAIR

I don't know. He said he went to high school with him, and he's back in town.

POPPY

I would love to, but I already made dinner and promised Sage a movie night.

LILY

Okay, Sage wins. Again.

LILY

Blair, can you find out who for me?

BLAIR

I'll get right on it.

ME

Dinner and drinks sound so good after this day.

LILY

Yay!! See you in an hour.

LILY

And Blair, don't show up without the information.

I should be exhausted. I mean, physically I am. My body aches in places I didn't know it could, and I know my hair smells like dust from the collapse. But my mind refuses to slow down. Today was just too much. From the ceiling falling on top of me, to Tucker flying off the ladder without thinking to make sure I was okay. The way his voice changed when he said my name. To the phone call with my dad. The intensity of it all is making me feel so much so fast.

Locking up the house, I don't even bother going home. Once I get to Lily's place, I check the mirror in my car before going in. Okay, bad idea. Maybe I should have at least taken a quick shower. But there's no time to second-guess because Lily is already on her porch, bouncing with excitement the way she always is.

It's the first time I've been at her place, and it's cute. It's on an adorable dead-end street named Waterlily Circle. One side of the street is a few houses, spread far apart, and the other side of the road offers an insane view of Bluestone Lake. I almost have to do a double take at how beautiful it is. It's almost like a secret oasis of the lake compared to the view on the drive into town.

I can definitely see why she chose to live here.

"I'm so glad you're here!" She beams when I cross the pathway leading to her front steps. "I don't cook often, but you're in for a treat tonight."

"Is it your birthday and you didn't tell me?"

She scoffs. "Trust me, you'd know when it's my birthday. Griffin makes a huge deal about it at Seven Stools. It passed a few months ago."

Entering her house, the smell of sugar, cinnamon, and something warm in the oven hits me first. Lily passes me a glass of sangria almost immediately before her eyes scan my face with the kind of attention that feels like care.

"Sit," she orders nicely. "You look like you went twelve rounds with sheetrock."

"I kind of did." I laugh.

"Wait, what?"

"The ceiling in the master bedroom sort of fell right on top of me today. It was way worse than I thought it would be."

"Jesus," Lily says with wide eyes. She reaches for my hair, fingers picking out a piece of dust that's stuck there. "I'm glad you're okay."

"Thanks. I'm definitely okay. It wasn't as heavy as I thought it was. It was more embarrassing than anything. Because *you know…*" I exaggerate the word, almost rolling my eyes. "The camera got the whole thing on film."

She sits up tall, smiling. "Well, at least you can look back when the project is finished and know you went through literal hell for the masterpiece of a room that's to come."

The front door opens, and Blair walks through the house as if she lives here, too, dropping her purse on the counter and settling on the couch next to me.

"Well," Lily urges her. "Did you come with the information?"

Blair shakes her head. "He never texted me back. You know how he is with texting. And you know you're not inviting me for dinner and drinks, only to take back the invite *you* sent if I show up without information."

Lily groans, falling back on the couch.

"All he said was that it's a friend from high school in town for the night. And said something about them catching up."

"He had a lot of friends in high school, Blair."

Blair shrugs. "I don't know what to tell you." Her eyes narrow into slits. "Is there a reason you need this information, *Lily*?"

"No reason." She turns her head away from us.

"Then why do you look like you're about to fake a phone call and leave the country?" I say to Lily.

"I do not," Lily argues. "I just…I didn't know Griffin was still in touch with people from high school. Besides, he said it was a friend and didn't specify which one."

"Okay, no," Blair says with a pointed finger in the air. "You don't get to dodge like that. Who do you think it is? Should I be worried?"

Lily shakes her head. "I don't want to get into it tonight, but one of his friends didn't believe in goodbyes." She shrugs like it's nothing, but I can see it means everything. "But it was a lifetime ago."

I tilt my head. "Are you spiraling right now?" I face Blair. "Is this Lily spiraling?"

Blair laughs. "I don't know anymore. But I have so many questions."

"I can't stand either of you." Lily lifts her glass in the air. "Let's just toast to unresolved feelings staying unresolved, yeah?"

Both Blair and I look at each other, silent before we raise our glasses and leave the topic be. I know I don't want to push Lily into talking about something she doesn't want to talk about, and from the look of concern laced with understanding on Blair's face, she won't either.

"So," Blair says to me. "How are things with Tucker?"

Nice change of subject.

But not the subject I'd like to discuss.

I take a sip from my glass and swallow. "Fine."

Blair's eyes widen. "Oh."

Lily's mouth curves into a knowing smile. "*OH!*"

I groan, standing from the couch and start pacing the small living room. "Okay, fine. Let's get this off my chest." I stop pacing. "You know what? I *need* to get this off my chest."

Both of them sit taller on the couch, scooting closer to the edges of their seats.

"We crossed a line. A *big* line. The line of all lines," I ramble, arms waving in the air. "When I got here, I couldn't stand him. I was pissed that I saw him again. I was angry that he walked out on me without even a goodbye after a one-night stand—"

"He walked out on you?" Lily gasps.

"*Shh.* Let her finish," Blair says.

"Yes. I almost told you two that night at Blair's house when we had girls' night." I finally stop pacing, shoulders slumped. "I met him before coming here when I was in San Francisco for my interview. I believe it's the reason the producers saw the chemistry they did. It's the reason why I said I didn't like him. But even then, I was definitely forcing myself to hate him."

"I want to get this all out now," Lily says, cheeks turning red. "We sort of already knew."

"What?"

"Dallas was with Tucker in the city. That's why Tucker was even there. And one night at the bar, it came up how you two first met."

I sigh. "Okay, so I'm pacing for nothing? Nervous to tell you for nothing?"

She grins, showing her teeth like she's sorry.

"Forget that. What's changed?" Blair asks.

"You're going to laugh."

"No, we won't."

I fall back on the couch, staring at the ceiling. "I think it's a combination of spending so much time together, and then we had sex…again." I hold up a pointer finger like I'm waving the white flag of defeat. "It's ruined me." They both chuckle, and I snap my head up, glaring. "Not funny."

"It kind of is," Blair says. "But I mean that in the nicest way possible because I can relate."

Lily plugs both of her ears with her fingers. "La la la."

"The first time with Griffin was so out of this world, it changed me. I was forever altered by it. There were feelings for him simmering under the surface, but all it took was *one time* for me to know he was it for me."

"I wouldn't say I'm forever altered by Tucker, but…yeah, the feelings have been tucked nice and deep here."

"No pun intended," Blair says, waggling her eyebrows, and I laugh.

"La la la," Lily continues.

Blair ignores her. "I'm just saying it's possible. You two have a history, from the one-night stand to working together on the house, and putting on this show *for the show*. See what I did there?" She winks. "It's probably a reason for these feelings to surface for you."

"Are you two done?" Lily asks, removing her fingers from her ear. "I really don't care to hear about my brother and my cousin having sex."

Blair rolls her eyes. "We're done, Lily."

I sigh. "I don't know. When I came here, it was solely for this show. I didn't have a plan for after. I didn't know if I'd stay or how I would feel about living in a house my grandparents owned when they were basically strangers to me."

Blair smiles, softly and genuinely. "This town has a way of changing you."

She's right.

Somewhere along the way, I stopped needing to shine so loud. The bright colors and polished smiles are still a part of me, but they aren't the only part anymore. I used to think people wanted perfection. That they wanted a woman who had it all together. But in this town, in that house, with these people, I have realized how much I love the in-between.

And maybe that's what this town has done for me.

It's made me see that while I'm imperfect, I'm whole.

"I need to ask you something," Lily says, and the worried look on her face has my body tensing. I nod, letting her continue. "Has Tucker said anything to you about his past and why he came to Bluestone Lakes?"

"No...why?"

"I was just wondering," she says, averting her gaze from mine.

"Lily," I warn.

"Really. I'm just curious. That's all," she says, placing a reassuring hand on my thigh. "He will tell you when the time is right. It's his story to tell, not mine. And I'm not saying this to make you nervous. But just know that when he does, it means he cares a lot about you and wants you in his life. It means he has real feelings for you, too. I think the Barlow family are the only people in town who know what he's been through."

The oven timer dings, and just like that, the conversation is gone.

We settle into random conversations over dinner after that. I listen as they talk about a book they recently read or the shenanigans Nan has been up to.

But my mind is only stuck on Tucker and what he hasn't told me yet.

It isn't until I leave Lily's house later that night that I realize whatever Tucker is hiding isn't small.

This isn't a story he's avoiding.

It's one he's surviving.

CHAPTER 27

YOU'RE SAFE.

TUCKER

After we wrapped up at the house for the day, I made my way to the bar for my evening shift the way I always do. But the weight of the day sat on my chest like a brick, and I couldn't shake it. Griffin took one look at me when I walked in and told me to go home.

I tried to argue, but he fought back harder.

While he insisted over and over that he had it covered, I stood there staring at him, the same way I'm sitting here in my living room now, staring at a blank wall in silence.

This house is quiet in a way that presses into me instead of comforts me. There's no music filtering through the house from the kitchen and my TV is off. The only noise is the low hum of the fridge in the other room and my own racing thoughts.

I look down at my hands clasped together in my lap.

I can't stop replaying the day my world changed since watching Scottie dig up her own memories. I don't have the luxury of digging up my memories. Every single one burned to the ground the same night my life did.

I squeeze my eyes shut, finally releasing my hands from one

another to press my palms into my eyes. My throat tightens and I feel everything as if it only happened yesterday.

And that's the thing about memories, they don't care if you're ready for them or not.

They show up without warning.

My eyes fly open, and smoke crawls across the ceiling faster than it should. It's thick enough to make it hard to breathe, swallowing the light from the hallway.

"Mom?" I barely manage to get out before I start choking.

It's a fire.

The house is on fire.

The air burns my lungs and every inhale scrapes my throat like glass. Then something crashes down the hall, like wood splitting or something giving way, and the sound punches through me.

"Dad!" I shout, my throat raw.

I scramble off my bed, circling in one spot to try and find an opening or a way out.

"Tucker!" I hear my dad shout in the distance. "You need to get out. Now."

"I don't know where to go," I cry out as loud as my lungs let me, tears spilling from my eyes.

"Find a way out!" My mom shouts from what sounds like another part of the house.

Fear freezes me in place and my hands fly out to the side as if bracing for impact, when I hear another crash followed by what sounds like my mom screaming.

"Mom! MOM!" I shout, rushing for the door. But when my hands land on it, it burns my palms, forcing me to jump back. "No. No. No," I mutter. The heat in the room presses in from all sides now.

Stop, drop, and roll? No, I'm not on fire.

I snap my head around to my window, and I see an opening. I rush toward it, needing to get out of this room so I can fix this. If I move fast enough, if I choose right, if I hold everything together with my bare hands, the house will listen.

It doesn't.

The smoke thickens around me.

There's another crash, followed by the sounds of my dad and baby brother screaming.

"No!" I scream, straddling the window. "Dad! Brady!"

There's no response.

I fumble with the latch, a cough ripping through my chest.

If I can just get out of my room, I can save them.

My eyes sting and my vision is blurred as I wrench the window open. The rush of air is immediate and for half a second everything goes still as the room inhales a deep, violent gulp of oxygen.

Heat punches the air behind me with a force so strong that it knocks the breath from my lungs. The walls groan before something else gives way. I know suddenly, with sick certainty, that this is bigger than me.

It's no longer safe here.

I fight back the bile rising from my throat.

Instinct takes over and I swing a leg over the ledge and throw myself out without thinking, barely registering the drop before I hit the ground and roll. The smell is everywhere, sinking into my clothes—my bones. I leap up, stumbling across the lawn before turning around to take in the house. My eyes scan every inch of the yard, looking for my mom, my dad, my baby brother. Anyone.

They had to have gotten out, right?

But I see no one.

No one is here.

The blast follows as a thunderous crack splits the air as flames burst outward.

The house doesn't just burn.

It collapses.

Everything crumbles to the ground with my family nowhere in sight.

"NOOOO!" I scream loud enough for the whole town to hear.

But I can barely hear my own voice as I shout because all I can hear is the ringing in my ears.

I didn't just fail to save my family.

I stand up from my chair fast with the same sound from years ago ringing in my ears as if it's happening right now. Pacing my living room and wiping the tears from my eyes with rage. The fucking memory of that night haunts me when I'm alone with my thoughts like this. I hate that it haunts me this way.

It's been so long since I've allowed it to come to the surface like that.

So long since I've allowed those feelings to consume me.

I tell myself I'm safe here.

I tell myself I'm older and stronger now.

I tell myself *I was just a kid. I didn't fucking know what opening that window would do.*

But my body doesn't listen. It never does.

I was only a teenage boy when I last heard my mom and dad's voices shouting at me to get out. The last memory I have of them is hearing their screams as the house fell on top of them with my baby brother inside.

"*FUCK!*" I scream in my empty room, rage flowing through my body, ready to punch a hole in the wall. "It's not fucking fair," I grit out, falling to my knees in the middle of my living room.

As if anyone can hear me.

As if I'd let anyone hear this.

This right here, is the part of me that no one will ever see. Not Griffin, Lily, Poppy, or any other members of my extended family.

I remember so vividly sitting on the edge of the hospital bed, staring at the flooring below me and my clothes covered in black —staining me with darkness. I didn't register them telling me I was okay. Them telling me I didn't have any major injuries. And most of all, them telling me everyone in the house...but me... died.

The only thing I kept thinking was…*why am I still breathing?*

My chest aches now in the present, like there's still smoke trapped in my lungs. I look down at my hands and they shake. They don't look like the hands of someone who has carried a house fire behind corny jokes and a light mood for years.

But I have.

I carry it in a way the bell above Seven Stools tells me how many people are in the place and how many people I'd need to make sure are *out* in the event of a fire.

I carry it in a way that I check every home I work on for safety.

I carry it in a way that I've spent so long trying to be someone worth sparing.

Because it's nights like tonight, when the memories creep in so vividly, and when the world finally stops demanding things from me, the thought comes in soft as a lullaby: *you should've been with them.*

It's not that I want to die.

It's that I'm so tired of being the one left behind and dealing with the aftermath alone. I'm tired of carrying names in my mouth like broken glass, tasting them every time I try to laugh to cover up the pain.

How long is a person is supposed to pay for surviving something they never asked for?

I press my palm to my chest to calm my racing heart. I stand up, letting my body fall back on the chair. I stare down at my shaking leg as I try to calm myself, but it doesn't work. It never works when the memory hits this hard.

A car door slamming outside cuts through the anger.

My body stills completely as I look at the wall between me and the outside world.

Scottie's home.

Please don't come here. Don't see me like this.

I sit there for a moment longer to allow the present to bleed back in.

My head falls to the back of the chair, and I close my eyes. For a moment, I pretend rest is possible. I pretend that if I stay still long enough, the thoughts won't find me again tonight. But I know they will. Grief is tattooed into my bones like something I never agreed to hold onto but can't seem to put down.

It's not fucking fair.

Finally, as if I've snapped out of the temporary bubble, I push myself out of the chair and out my front door. The night air hits my face as soon as I step outside, and I inhale in an effort to clear some of the smoke from my head.

Looking up, I see the light over the apartment door is on.

I cross the driveway and take the stairs two at a time before I can talk myself out of it. I raise my fist, knocking once because if I don't see her now, I'm not sure I'll make it through the night without breaking something I can't put back together.

Not because she can fix it.

Not because she can erase the past.

Because if I'm alone right now, I'm going to drown in it.

I fucking need her.

More than I ever thought was possible.

The door opens, and Scottie stands on the other side with confusion on her face at why I'm knocking on her door. She's probably wondering why I'm not at the bar tonight. My eyes scan her up and down, and she's wearing sleep shorts and a thin tank top, her hair loose around her shoulders. The sight of her hits me harder than any memory ever could.

"Tucker?" she says softly. "Is everything okay?"

No.

Yes.

I don't know.

"I just—" I swallow. She moves back to let me in, and I step inside. Looking around the space, it's smaller than I remember, and it smells like her shampoo and clean sheets. I face her again, my chest rising and falling. "I need you."

Her expression softens instantly and she doesn't even hesitate. Scottie moves toward me and I fall into her arms. My forehead hits her shoulder, and I don't even try to hold it together anymore. My breath shudders at the same time my legs weaken. We both fall to the floor on our knees. Her arms under mine, holding me up as if she can carry my weight effortlessly.

"I'm here," she says, moving her hands to find the back of my neck.

"I can't—" The words don't come out as I shake my head against her. "I can't do this alone."

She pulls back, taking my face in her hands. My vision blurry from the tears refusing to breach the surface. "Look at me," she says calmly, warm hands bracketing my face to hold my head upright.

But I close them, not wanting to see the look on her face.

Not wanting to feel embarrassment for this weakness. As much as I *needed her*, the guilt for bringing her into this is suddenly too much.

"Hey," she says again, gentle but firm. I open my eyes, taking her in. "There you are," she murmurs low, like she's found me in the dark.

I open my mouth, but… "I can't breathe."

"Yes, you can," she says, her thumb stroking my jaw. She moves to circle my wrist with her hand, and she brings my palm to rest on her chest, right over her beating heart. She mirrors the movement with her palm on my chest. "I'm here, babe. I'm right here."

My breath catches as the word "babe" slips out of her like it's natural, like she's said it a hundred times before this moment. Somehow that small, steady sound cuts through the noise in my head. The panic is clawing at my chest, still tightening its grip around my lungs, but her voice anchors me. Her touch keeps me steady. Her beating heart under my hand reminds me I can breathe again. I drag in a shaky breath and hold it before forcing a long exhale.

"That's it. You're here," she says, leveling her eyes with mine. "You're safe."

I'm safe.

I'm here.

She's here.

After a minute of inhaling and exhaling, I sit back on my knees. I drag a hand through my hair. "I'm sorry to show up like this. I—uh…I had a bad day."

Her expression softens. "You don't ever have to apologize for coming to me."

"I don't…" I release a long, drawn out exhale. "I don't like people seeing me like this."

Her thumb strokes slow over my chest. "Thank you for letting *me*."

I stare into her eyes, letting the silence stretch between us. Her hand moves to rest lightly on my forearm. I look down at the contact and then back up to her face, at the understanding already there.

She's not waiting for me to explain more.

She's just…here.

It's more than I could have ever asked.

I lean closer without realizing it and press my forehead to hers. "Fuck. I don't want to mess this up."

Her hand slides from my arm to my chest. "You're not. You can't mess this up even if you tried."

"Scottie," I say barely above a whisper. "I don't know how to let someone in without…" I pause, shaking my head. "Without everything else coming with it. But I can't make myself stop wanting you."

Her eyes don't leave mine. "I'm not going anywhere."

Her words land somewhere deep.

I reach for her, hands framing her face. Scottie leans into my touch as her eyes flutter shut for a brief second before opening again. The understanding and patience written all over her face nearly undoes me.

I want to tell her—I need to tell her and let her in.

But the words don't want to come out.

The wound is too fresh tonight.

"I can't do it," I breathe against her lips. "I'm not ready to explain what just happened. But I want you to know I'm trying. I'm fucking trying," I say, my voice strained as I fight back the emotions.

She presses up, kissing the corner of my lips. "I know you are. You don't have to tell me anything right now."

"This is all…it's all new for me. I don't do this. I meant what I said, I don't let people see this part of me."

"I know."

"But you, Scottie…" I say, my voice breaking where I didn't expect it to. "You didn't just get close. You fucking pushed your way in."

The words coming out, cracking something open in me, and I don't fight it. A tear slips free finally, but I don't wipe it away or hide it.

Not from her.

"I've spent my whole life teaching myself how to survive on my own and not relying on anyone else. And yet somehow, you walked in without asking, without forcing anything, and now you're *everywhere*." I shake my head, almost laughing at myself. "I hear your voice in my head before I go to sleep. I hear your laughter echo in the walls of every room I'm in, no matter where it is. You're the person I want to run to." She sucks in a breath, and I hold her there with her face between my hands, angling her to keep her eyes locked on mine. "I didn't plan for this, but you're etched into me now. It scares the hell out of me because it means whatever happens next, I'm already yours."

The words I just said should scare me.

It should make me want to run because I've said too much.

It should make *her* want to run at how fast it feels.

But she's not leaving.

Instead, her hands come up—gentle and steady as her thumb

brushes away the tear. I avert my gaze, letting the humiliation of everything and being a grown man crying in front of her, settle in.

"Look at me," she says.

I do.

"You scare me, too, Tucker," she admits, then pauses. She averts her gaze for just a brief moment, telling me she's hesitant to say more. I brace for whatever she's about to say, and my body tightens to prepare for disappointment. "I've been trying like hell to keep you at a safe distance—told myself not to fall for you," she says softly. "Since I got here. Since the beginning. I told myself it was the timing of everything. It hadn't been that long since you walked out on me." I wince at her words, but she continues. "The show and the mess of everything. I told myself it would be easier if I kept you at arm's length. Yet, you kept showing up for me in every moment, from the quiet ones to the hard ones to the ones that mattered." She smiles, shaking her head. "Do you remember what you said to me at the bar back in San Francisco?"

I tilt my head to the side in confusion.

"I said a lot of things, Scottie." I smirk, feeling the tension slip from my body.

She playfully smacks my chest. "Not any of that. But we talked about the meaning of home…" She stops, assessing me to see if I remember. Truthfully, I don't. "You said that home is just walls and a roof where you live and a structure with belongings and memories, but then you said it was more than that. You said it's who's inside those walls. It's where you feel whole." Her fingers skim my jaw, anchoring me in the present. "That night, you said it like you believed it. Like you were trying to convince yourself it could still be true."

My throat works around a lump so sharp it feels like I could choke.

"I thought I was just saying words to help you with your interview."

Scottie smiles. "You were. But you meant them."

She shifts, standing and reaching for my hand to lift me off the floor. She tugs me to the couch next to her so we're not folded into the floor like something broken. Keeping her hands on me, she's reminding my body it's allowed to be here.

I look down, my jaw tight. "I keep thinking…" I pause, swallowing and looking down at her hand on my thigh. "I keep thinking I don't deserve anything. Any—" My voice catches. "Any of this. You."

She lifts off the couch, straddling my lap, again—grounding me without even trying. "Then I'm going to do everything I can to show you that you do."

I pull her into me, not gentle this time. I pull her like I'm afraid if I loosen my grip, she'll vanish. She wraps herself around my shoulders, fitting against me like she always belonged there.

"Stay," I whisper into the crook of her neck. "Stay with me tonight."

"Okay."

My eyes close as my body finally lets go of the fight to stand alone. Somewhere in my chest, the fire still crackles. The grief still breathes. But her arms are real, and the floor beneath my feet is solid, and her voice is a lighthouse in the dark.

When Scottie pulls back, pressing a kiss to my forehead, I realize something that makes my chest burn in an entirely different way.

Home isn't the place I lost.

It's the place I'm choosing.

It's her.

CHAPTER 28

YOU'RE LOOKING AT ME
LIKE YOU CAN FEEL IT.

SCOTTIE

Opening my eyes, I feel disoriented.

I blink a few times, registering that I'm in Tucker's bed. I knew I was in his bed. But because I didn't fall asleep until sometime early in the morning—and only slept for maybe an hour—everything feels off. Even with the comfort of him next to me, body tangled with mine, I couldn't shut my mind off.

The way his hands shook like his body had betrayed him.

The way his breathing turned sharp and panicked.

The way he'd looked at me with bloodshot, tear filled eyes.

And when his voice broke…it broke me.

Stay with me tonight.

I said yes without a second thought. Because the truth is, I don't know how to look at Tucker and not want to take all of his pain into my hands like something I can sand down and smooth over. I want to be there for him. I want to build something around him strong enough that it can't touch him anymore. I want to take whatever demons he's buried so deep and lock them behind an unbreakable door.

I don't even know what it is, or how I can help.

All I can do is be here.

I look to where he lies next to me on the bed. He has one hand flung over his head, and the other resting on his chest with fingers slightly curled as if his body is still holding on. Even asleep, he looks like he's carrying something heavy.

I don't move right away.

I just watch him—the rise and fall of his chest.

Sometime in the middle of the night, staring between him and the ceiling, I remember a conversation with Lily. The way her voice turned serious when she told me about him opening up. *If he does, it means he cares.* It's clear from what I witnessed last night that he doesn't let people see that part of him.

Not even when he's so deep into it.

He *let me* see it.

He didn't try to hide it or make a joke to cover anything up. He came to me and asked for comfort. He trusted I wouldn't run. He trusted I would be there.

My hand moves on its own, reaching across the small space between us to brush his hair back from his forehead. I move gently, afraid to wake him too fast. Afraid that the second he opens his eyes, he'll remember everything and shut down again.

His eyelids flutter open, and he exhales, stretching his arms over his head. His gaze finds mine immediately, unfocused for a moment before it sharpens with recognition. He stares at me like he's making sure I'm real.

I smile softly. "Hi."

His throat bobs as he swallows, slowly sitting up against the headboard. "Hi."

Neither of us move.

We just sit there, staring at each other.

Then Tucker's eyes trail my body, down to the shirt I'm wearing and back up. We left the loft in such a blur that I didn't even grab anything. So once he was asleep, I grabbed one of his shirts from the dresser.

The corner of his lip twists in what feels like relief.

"You stayed."

"I stayed," I whisper back.

Something that resembles a memory flashes through his eyes, forcing his jaw to harden. He looks down at his lap, and I know the memory of last night is crashing back in.

"I'm sorry about—" he starts.

I cut him off when I lean forward, tipping his chin up with the back of my finger. "Don't."

"Scottie."

"No," I say again, firmer this time. I adjust myself so I'm sitting closer to him—thighs brushing together. I move to cup his face between my palms. His eyes close for a moment, inhaling and exhaling before meeting mine again. "You don't apologize for being human. Not with me."

"I wasn't..." His voice catches but he clears his throat. "I wasn't okay."

"But you are now," I whisper.

His head tips to the side, leaning into my touch. He reaches up, circling one hand around my wrist, almost holding me there and anchoring himself. "Thank you."

"You don't need to thank me. I want to be here."

He blinks as if trying to keep control over whatever emotion wants to rise up and make him feel too much again. I drop my hand from his face and onto his thigh in a way to say I'm still here.

"You're looking at me like you can feel it," he says quietly.

"I can."

He smiles, but it's weak. "That's unsettling."

"It's called empathy," I tease.

Tucker watches me for a second longer, then his gaze drifts away toward the window. His thoughts running wild in his head. *I can feel it*. His shoulders rise and fall with a slow inhale. When he finally looks back at me, his eyes are clearer.

"My entire family died in a house fire. Except...me."

I suck in a breath, holding it there. My body stiffens, and goose bumps pebble across my skin. Of all things that crossed my mind through the night, that wasn't at all what I was expecting to hear.

"Tucker."

He shakes his head. "I got out, Scottie. I don't know how. Well, I do," he says, looking down at his lap and taking my hand between both of his. "I woke up in the middle of the night, choking on thick smoke. I couldn't breathe. I could barely see in front of me. I screamed for my mom. I screamed for my dad." I squeeze his hand when I notice the change in his breathing, assuring him I'm not going anywhere. "The last thing I heard was their screams as the house collapsed in front of me. My mom. My dad. My—" He chokes on his words. "My baby brother. He was barely a toddler."

I blink, tears streaking down my cheeks. He lifts his gaze, reaching up to wipe them away. "The fire. It was my fault. I had been complaining about an outlet that kept sparking in the downstairs hallway. But we didn't get to it. I was the last to go to bed that night and forgot to turn off the lamp plugged into that outlet. If I…" He pauses, shaking his head. "If I hadn't left it on, the fire wouldn't have happened. My family would be here."

"I…I don't even know what to say."

"You don't have to say anything. I just want you to know. I *need* you to know the demons I hide from the light. I didn't want you to see this. But this…" He pauses, swallowing and gripping my chin between his fingers. "Is the reason I don't let people in. It's why I walked out that morning. I may not have been completely honest with you when you asked me before. *That* was the truth. If I stayed, I would have started believing I'm allowed to have something I want just because I want it."

My stomach churns and I feel nauseous.

All that time I spent pissed that he left without warning— without a goodbye. It was all because Tucker believes he doesn't deserve the things he wants. I can feel my heart breaking as I sit here, staring at him with tears blurring my vision.

The pain this man has been through.

The demons he's carried through his life.

The guilt of surviving when everyone he loved is gone.

I reach forward, wrapping my arms around his shoulder. He holds me back, pulling me into his chest. "Thank you for telling me all of this. Thank you for letting me in." I pull back, meeting his eyes. "But you do deserve good things, Tucker."

"Good things don't happen to people who get to walk away."

"That's not true."

"It feels true…" He pauses, shaking his head before looking back out the window. "I can't lose anyone else."

I move, cutting his line of sight to the window. "I'm not going anywhere."

Reaching up with both hands, he brushes the messy strands of hair away from my face. His eyes bore into mine, and he's silent. My heart pounds against my ribcage, wondering what he's thinking right now.

He nods once. "Okay."

I'm not sure if that's what he truly wanted to say, but I'll take it. I won't push him, not when he's like this. All I can do is be here for him.

I stand from the bed, extending a hand. "Come on. Breakfast."

He takes my hand, following me into the kitchen. I can see him ready to move around with ease, as if he's ready to make his morning coffee and breakfast. But I sit him down at the stool on the island. He tilts his head in confusion as I jog to the front door.

Opening it, I find the package of cinnamon buns Lily dropped off early this morning. I smile and make my way back to where he sits.

"What is that?"

"Breakfast," I say, placing the box in front of him. "You said cinnamon buns are your favorite, right?"

He looks down at the hole in the top of the box, before up at me. He reaches for the hem of my oversized T-shirt, pulling me into his open legs on the stool. His arms wrap around my hips, and my body flushes with his as he looks up at me, smiling.

He's smiling, and I can't help but mirror it.

"I'm guessing that's a yes?" I say.

"I don't deserve you."

I tangle my hands in his hair at the back of his head and lean down. "You deserve the world, Tucker Daniels. And I'm going to make sure to remind you every chance I can."

His gaze holds mine, steady and quiet. I press my lips to his. Holding it there so my words can register—so that he doesn't think otherwise.

And I realize with a rush of clarity that I'm not just falling for him.

I already have.

CHAPTER 29

I'M JUST DOING IT IN MY TONE.

TUCKER

Feels weird to be at Seven Stools for lunch and *not* be in a rush to get to a job site.

I sit in my usual spot when I come in for lunch, but instead of Levi next to me, it's Dallas. Griffin stops in front of us with a scowl on his face and aggressively wipes down the counter that's already clean.

"You good?" Dallas asks him.

He shakes his head. "I can't fucking stand out of towners sometimes. That couple over there"—he tips his head to gesture to the table in the corner— "rude as hell. The woman criticized me for the limited choices we have on the menu and basically bashed the entire town in her rant."

"I've been telling you for years that you have—"

Griffin cuts me off with a low growl, while Dallas laughs behind his hand.

"I often wonder who these people think they are with their entitlement when they come to a small town like this," Griffin continues, pointing a finger in my direction before sliding an ice water across the bar for me. "You guys always wonder why I hate the out of towners? Well, here's example nine hundred."

I twist my head over my shoulder to get a good look at them. Just by looking at them, I can tell they're stuck-up in a way that says they're too good for a place like this. I hate people like that, too.

"Are you eating today?" Griffin asks. "You're running out of time because you don't have that long of a break."

"You know me so well." I smile widely. "But not today. I'm off. Tomorrow I'll go back to finish the siding on Scottie's property to be ready for the final episode."

He narrows his eyes.

"I…" I pause, shifting uncomfortably in my seat. "I needed a break, I guess."

He's not buying it. I can tell by the way he's still staring at me. The last time he offered me a break, I had to actually fight him on it.

"You do look like hell."

"It's *sooo* nice to see you too, Grumpy Griffin."

He smirks. "I'm serious. You look like you got into a fist fight with your own brain."

I stare down at the water in front of me, gripping the glass with both hands because his comment lands a little too close to the truth.

Dallas shifts next to me, clearing his throat. "Do you want to talk about it?"

"Or do you want me to keep insulting you until you crack?" Griffin adds.

This isn't unusual—the banter.

Because this is what they know me for. Even with knowing my past, I keep the rest hidden from the world. On purpose. Because this? I like this. I like joking back and forth until we all smile and laugh. I like being the reason people smile and laugh around me.

Because of that…I huff a quiet breath. "You're very supportive."

"I'm a gift," Griffin says, hand to his chest.

Dallas places a hand on my shoulder. "Now, talk."

I glance past Griffin at the bottles lining the wall, but I can see the way Griffin's shoulders go still, like he's bracing for whatever I might admit out loud.

And it's fucking weird.

I've been carrying it for so long myself that I don't know what it sounds like outside of my own head. It felt different talking to Scottie about it in the comfort of my own home.

"I'm not…" I clear my throat. "I'm not good. I haven't been for a while."

Dallas doesn't flinch or try to fix it. He just nods in understanding because he recently allowed me to open up on the anniversary of the house fire after a little league game we had.

"No shit," Griffin says flatly.

I shoot him a pointed look. "You're supposed to be comforting."

"I am. I'm just doing it in my tone."

I shake my head, feeling my shoulders relax a bit. This was exactly the response I didn't know I needed from him. Griffin is there, but in the way he knows I will respond to better.

When I don't answer, his jaw tightens. "How bad was it, Tucker?"

I hesitate even though the memory of it is so fresh. My body feels tense remembering the way my lungs refused to breathe for me, the way my body shook like it didn't belong to me, and the sickening panic like I was falling from the second story all over again.

"The darkest it's ever been," I say, barely loud enough for them to hear.

But they do.

They hear every word.

Dallas pauses with his glass halfway to his lips, and Griffin's hand stills on the towel he was just using to wipe his hands.

"Tucker," Griffin breathes out.

"Why didn't you call us?" Dallas says almost at the same time.

I shake my head. "I wasn't in the right frame of mind to even think logically. I knew I couldn't be alone. I knew I needed something. The closest person was Scottie."

Both of their features soften, bodies relaxing. Neither of them look surprised.

I can almost feel it again now.

My head on her shoulder and the way she held me.

Her hands on my face, anchoring me.

The way she didn't ask questions.

"She stayed with me," I continue. "She didn't ask questions or run."

I feel the emotions thick in my chest. The feelings coming to the surface I've been fighting for so long. Knowing she stayed, and saying it out loud is two different things.

It's acknowledging everything at once.

She fucking stayed.

Dallas whistles low. "Well, look at you. Emotionally vulnerable."

I smile at the teasing—again, exactly what I need. "Don't start."

"That's a big deal, Tucker," Griffin says, and when I turn to face him, his mouth is curved into a faint grin.

The bell over the entrance chimes, and Griffin groans.

But for the first time, I don't laugh. He notices. Of course he does.

Dallas elbows me. "You want to tell him? Or are we going to keep pretending you keep it up because you like pissing him off?"

"But I do like pissing him off."

Dallas laughs. "Oh, we know."

But when my gaze lands on Griffin, his face is hard, concerning.

"It's not *just* to piss you off," I say, trying like hell to keep the teasing tone. "I...uh...I like to keep track of how many people come in and out. I like to know that if there was ever an emergency here..." *Like a fire.* "Then I know how many people I need to get out."

Something like understanding morphs in Griffin's features.

But he doesn't say anything.

Instead, he drops the dish rag and walks away, right into the kitchen.

I run a hand through my hair, worried I said too much. Maybe I should have kept it to myself like everything else. He doesn't need to carry this the way I've always carried it. He doesn't need to think about what's going through my head every time he hears the chime of the bell now.

Dammit.

"Don't stress about him, Tucker," Dallas says next to me, hooking an arm around my neck and pulling me into him. "He just needs a breather. You know we got you."

"Are you hugging me? Is Dallas Westbrook really hugging me?"

He barks out a laugh. "There's my weird friend." He releases me from his hold, clapping a hand on my back. "For what it's worth, you know I'm always here for you. You know if you need anything, I'll drop whatever to be there in a heartbeat. We're family now."

I purse my lips. "Are you going to marry my cousin? Say yes." I throw up prayer hands.

He rolls his eyes. "Here I am trying to be a good friend."

I turn in my chair, fully facing him, and grab his face in mine. "You're my bestest friend, Dallas." I reach up and press a kiss to his forehead.

He backs away quickly, swatting me off. "If you ever fucking do that again, you're going to be demoted from that title real fast."

I laugh, and it feels so good.

It's not the fake kind that I put on for show either. This is my family, and they're doing exactly what they know I need. Lightening the mood. Making me laugh. Allowing me the chance to joke. Allowing me to be myself. It's not because they don't care, it's because they *do care*.

"Now, before Griff gets back. Scottie. Talk to me," Dallas says.

I sigh. "I wish I understood what I'm feeling, Dallas. Everything is so new for me. It's so intense. It's…"

"Love."

"How can you be so sure?"

"Do you think about her a lot?" I nod. "Do you find yourself wanting to do things with her—be near her?" I nod again. "Does your heart race when she touches you?"

"I'm not telling you about how she touches me, Dallas."

He rolls his eyes. "I actually fucking hate you."

"No, you don't. *You love me*," I singsong, but he ignores me, taking a sip of his drink. "Truly? My heart does circles when she's around me. It feels like it's going to beat out of my chest. My brain can't think unless she's in the room. When I see her, all I want is to be near her, hear her laugh, anything."

"As I said," he says, smirking over the rim of his glass. "Love, buddy. That's love."

I open my mouth to say more, but the kitchen doors swing open. So fast that they bounce against the wall, nearly hitting Griffin in the face again. He still looks angry, but…less? He stomps to where I'm sitting, forcing me to sit up straighter in my seat. Bracing himself with two hands on the bar, stance wide and demanding, I look him in the eyes.

"You listen to me, and you listen good," Griffin says, finger in my face.

"Oh boy," Dallas murmurs, almost turning his body away from us.

"I fucking love you," he states boldly. Reaching across the bar, he grips the neck of my shirt. "You hear that? I love you. You're the brother I never had, and never wanted," he says, relaxing a bit and almost laughing at himself.

"Slow down, Grizzly Griffin," Dallas says, placing a hand between us.

I snap a finger in his direction. "Oh, that was good, Dallas. We gotta tell Nan that one."

Griffin almost growls. "No. You aren't deflecting right now. And listen…" He pauses, gathering his thoughts, and his body relaxes a bit. "I'm not going to make this about me, because it isn't. This is about you. But you have no idea how much that pained me to hear, and everything you've been carrying all these years. *Years*, Tucker. We're family. If you have baggage, then it's our job to help you carry the load. Please. Fucking *please*, don't do this alone anymore."

For half a second, my body reacts like it always does. Deflect, grin, make a joke. Something easy to bring the conversation back to where it's safe.

But his words hit so hard, he may as well have punched me in the sternum.

I know Griffin's not angry *at me*.

He's angry at the years of silence and the fact I've been metaphorically bleeding out quietly and pretending I'm fine.

My eyes sting, and I blink hard, because absolutely fucking not. I will not cry at my place of employment. I will not cry in front of these two. But there's nothing that can stop it. "I promise," I choke out, swatting away anything rolling down my cheek. Looking anywhere but them. I clear my throat. "I promise. No more doing it alone."

"Brothers." Griffin nods.

"Brothers."

And deep down, I've always seen him that way.

He was never just a cousin to me.

"Now…Scottie."

"We went there already," Dallas cuts in, and Griffin raises an eyebrow.

I sigh. "Apparently, this is called love."

He smiles so wide, you'd think Blair walked into the bar, but she didn't.

"And did you tell her?"

I shake my head.

"You probably should." Griffin shrugs.

I feel air trap itself in my lungs at the idea of even telling her how I'm feeling when I can't even seem to describe it myself. This started off as a faking a relationship for her show. Harmless…fucking harmless.

I should have known that pretending with Scottie would lead to more—something real. But my only focus was on doing this for her and making her dream home come to life. So I can prove to people I'm reliable. I can prove to her I won't mess this up.

I don't know the first thing about love.

What do I do if she says she doesn't feel the same way?

There's only one way to find out.

EPISODE EIGHT

COLOR ME NERVOUS

With one episode to go, will these two finish the house enough for it to be a success? We're about to find out as we wrap up our final project: the floral entryway.

It's the one space in a home that's supposed to say welcome home, *and not turn back while you still can. Between the faded floral wallpaper and trim that's holding on by a thread, this makeover needs both style and structural sanity.*

Scottie is ready to bring the color and make a statement.

Tucker is begging for a timeless finish that won't haunt them.

With the cameras rolling and the season finale right around the corner, the pressure is officially on.

One front door.

One last makeover.

And the truth waiting on the other side.

CHAPTER 30
SORRY. BUSY MORNING.

TUCKER

Lying on my side, I watch the steady rise and fall of Scottie's chest.

Since that night a few days ago, she's spent every night here in my bed. I can't help but wonder what I did to deserve this. To deserve *her*.

But she's here.

As if feeling my eyes on her, her eyes flutter open, and she stretches her body the way she does every morning before taking in her surroundings. The moment her eyes land on mine, she smiles. And it does that thing again—where my heart rate picks up and my lips beg to be on hers.

I'm addicted to Scottie Monroe.

Maybe Dallas is right.

Scottie adjusts herself in bed, scooting closer to me and draping one leg over mine, and rests her head on my chest. I'm sure she can hear the pounding of my heart right now, and it only makes me hope she can *feel it*, because the words are lost on me.

I don't know how to tell someone I love them.

I don't know how to feel these things openly.

"Good morning," she says, bringing her hand up and rubbing circles over my stomach. I feel her touch throughout my body.

"Scottie," I say in a tone with a bit of warning. "We're going to be late to the house if you keep doing that."

She tilts her head up to look at me, a smirk on her face. "What if I want to be late?"

"It's the last day of filming."

"And?"

I flip her onto her back, forcing a little yelp and a laugh out of her. I hold myself up with my hands on each side of her head, hovering over her. I dip my hips down, my morning erection pressing between her legs. Her lips part and her back arches.

I grin. "This what you want, baby? You want my cock inside of you before the cameras are on you? Do you want to be thoroughly and properly fucked for the world to see?"

"Yes," she breathes out, gripping my waist to hold me to her. *"Please."*

I lean down, pressing my lips to her like I'm greedy for her. She meets me with equal hunger, and it only intensifies the kiss. I move from her mouth, to the corner of her lips, to the curve of her jaw, and down her neck.

"I need a morning taste first," I say before moving myself down her body. I lift up her T-shirt—*my T-shirt*—exposing her bare breasts for me. I groan in satisfaction before leaning down and taking a hardened nipple in my mouth. I flick my tongue over it and suck before doing the same to the other side. Scottie writhes beneath me, her legs rubbing together impatiently.

"Don't worry. Your pussy will get my tongue in just a minute. Your body is too perfect not to be worshiped first though."

She moans, a breath escaping her lips as her head presses farther into the pillow and she looks up at the ceiling.

My mouth explores each breast again, and I swear she wants to come already. I trail kisses down her stomach, constricting beneath me at the featherlight touch of my lips. I hold myself up on an elbow, using my hand to hook into her panties. I tug them down just enough to press a kiss to her hip bone.

"Tucker. Please," she whines.

I sit up on my heels. Both hands reach for her panties now, and slowly—*dangerously slow*—I pull them from her legs. Our eyes watch each other with such intensity the entire time that it only makes me crave burying myself in her that much more. We've done this every night since she's been here, but the morning light creeping through the blinds, and the half-awake daze on her face make this feel so different.

It only makes me want to say those three words that much more.

Once the panties are off, I toss them aside. Scottie places her hands on her thighs, opening herself for me, wide and begging for me to devour her. It's only then that I take my eyes off hers and look down.

I growl. "*Fuckkkk,*" I draw out. "You're dripping for me, baby. I can see it."

"So do something about it," she begs.

I bite my bottom lip, lowering myself between her thighs. I dip my head down, pressing a kiss to each inner thigh before swiping my tongue through her wetness. We both moan instantly. Her back arches off the bed the moment I put pressure on her clit —flicking it with my tongue before sucking it into my mouth.

"God," she pants.

"Baby, the name's Tucker."

She reaches forward, tangling her hands in my messy morning hair, gripping the ends to hold me down. I bury myself in her pussy. Fucking her with my tongue like I can't get enough of her. And it's true, I can't.

"Tucker. Yes. *Yes.*"

I pull back, a breath away from her skin. "Such a good fucking girl."

She bites her bottom lip, looking down at me, and my cock hardens even more if that's possible. "Make me come, please."

"I fully intend to. First on my tongue. Second on my cock."

She smirks. "Promises, promises."

My chest vibrates and I find her clit again with my mouth. I suck, putting just enough pressure there to send her over the edge. The moment her eyes leave mine, I reach between her, thrusting two fingers deep inside of her. Her back flies off the bed, and she screams a mix of profanities and my name.

I don't let up until I feel her pussy contract around my fingers.

She's tight. So tight that it almost makes me come in my pants. The way her body reacts to mine. The sounds she makes when she's close. The taste of her arousal on my tongue. It's enough to send *me* over the edge.

"Tucker. Tucker!"

And that does it. She tips over the edge, legs shaking around my head as she keeps screaming my name over and over again like a prayer. I don't stop until her body relaxes. I pull my fingers out of her, dripping with her cum. I put the two fingers in my mouth, sucking them clean, and she watches me with her lips slightly parted.

"Mmm."

"I think you're trying to kill me," she says through labored breaths, then grins. "But damn, what a way to go."

I laugh, pulling myself up, tugging my boxer briefs off before I hover over her. My cock is already so hard and dripping with precum when it rests between her thighs. And if I didn't want to come before, the feel of her soft skin barely grazing my cock might do it.

"I think it's you who's trying to kill me," I say, a breath away from her lips.

I kiss her again, deeper this time. The kind of kiss that has nothing to do with the heat of the moment and everything to do with devotion. Her fingers wrap around my head, curling into my hair, and I let myself sink into it.

Into her.

Into the feeling that I'm safe enough to want.

She opens her legs for me, and I rock my hips enough to slide my cock into her. She sucks in a breath with her lips on mine, successfully stealing the oxygen from my lungs. She doesn't stop kissing me though. Her lips part, and my tongue tangles with hers as my cock thrusts in and out of her slowly.

When I pick up speed, that's when she releases my mouth from hers. Pressing her head into the pillow as her hips meet me thrust for thrust. I hold myself up on my hands and look down at her. I stare into her eyes and everything in me stills, but I don't stop moving in her. I don't stop chasing the feeling of giving her pleasure. But the look on her face right now, mixed with the way her lips part and the sounds coming out of her mouth. It makes my chest constrict for a different meaning than just sex.

I...*fuck.*

I love this woman. Without an inkling of a doubt, she's it for me.

But the words still don't come out.

I feel myself picking up speed, driving in and out of her with a feral need mixed with anger at myself for not being able to say it. Not being able to tell her exactly what she means to me. In a way, I guess I have. I told her she's etched into me. I told her I can't breathe without her.

Is that the same thing?

No, it can't be.

"Say it," Scottie murmurs with panting breaths.

My movements slow, my cock still buried in her. "What?"

Her hand that was just clawing at my shoulders moves to my jaw line, where she brushes a thumb over my mouth. "Whatever you're holding back."

My throat tightens, and they're there...right fucking there.

I open my mouth, but nothing comes out.

She smiles, but doesn't push. Instead, she bucks her hips and bites down on her bottom lip to bring us back to the moment. Like she understands and is reading it in the way my body can't be away from her, and my eyes can't look away.

"Do me a favor?" she asks.

I tilt my head to the side.

"Ruin me."

My grin spreads slowly. "My pleasure."

I move down on my elbows, caging her in with my hands on the top of her head. My lips are a breath away from hers, but I don't kiss her. I need to see her face when I make her come. She's close, I can feel it in the way her pussy contracts around me. I'm close too, but I refuse to let it go. I refuse to feel anything unless she is to.

"Come for me, baby," I whisper. "Let me hear you scream my name while you soak my cock."

"Yes. Yes. Yes."

Her hips buck up, staying there. Holding herself at just the right angle to allow me to fuck her the way she wants. I feel it to my core. I feel my release building and building, and it's harder to hold it back.

"That's it. You're so good at showing me what you want."

She moves her hands around my waist, hands pressed to my lower back, fingers digging into me. With my cock all the way inside of her, she holds me there, forcing me to still. And that's when I feel it. I feel *everything*.

"Goddamn," I hiss, feeling her pussy *literally* squeeze me. It's pulsing. Driving me crazy. "Is that...*Scottie.* You're going to kill me." She smirks before she rolls her hips. "You'd better come in the next five seconds. I won't last."

"Then fuck me, Tucker. Hard."

And I do. I drive my hips out and thrust hard into her. One... two times before she's over the edge. Her body shakes and she moans. Stars dance in my vision, but I keep my focus on her and everything she's giving me. My abs contract seconds before I spill my release into her.

She doesn't take her eyes off me.

We stare at each other, and I can almost feel the two of us saying those three words to each other with our eyes. But it's not enough—it will never be enough.

Scottie deserves everything.

Even if I don't feel like I do, she makes me believe that there's a chance I deserve her.

"You two are late," Andrea says to us as we make our way down the driveway.

Scottie laughs, skipping to meet up with her. "Sorry. Busy morning."

Jade, standing next to her, arches a brow and looks at me.

I shrug, unable to hide the smile on my face.

Oblivious to anything, Andrea claps her hands once before turning to face the house. She holds out a hand like she's show-casing a work of art. In a way, she is. Scottie takes in the house while I stare at her. Her eyes widen, and the reaction tells me that she didn't even notice it when we walked down the driveway.

"Is that..." Her voice trails off as her body carries her a few steps closer.

"They got the siding completely finished in one day," Jade says, with a little pep to her voice. It's a tone that says *you're going to do this. You're going to nail it.*

When I look at Andrea, though, her expression is unreadable. Almost like she's pissed we finished it. I don't fucking get it.

Scottie spins around, facing me. "Did you do this? You and your crew?" I nod, and she rushes for me, jumping into my arms and wrapping herself around me.

"You said you wanted rustic charm."

She pulls back, giving me a knowing look. "It's so perfect that I didn't even know it was new siding."

"Levi was able to find the type that was used on this house years ago. It was a bitch to find, but we did. I know how much you wanted to keep the house as close to what it originally was while adding your own touches," I say, looking at the house. "We decided the best option was to find the same siding. This way it looks the same, just less…"

"Abandoned," Scottie finishes for me.

I nod.

Before she can say more, Andrea cuts in, clearing her throat. "So this is the last filming of working on the house before the big finale. Looking at the checklist," she says, tapping her pen against the clipboard in her hands. "The entryway was last on the list. Not sure why we left it for last."

"I think my thought process was that we would be going in and out of that door so much. Trekking in dirt, tools, and sawdust." Scottie shrugs. "Why do it first when we would just have to clean it up or touch it up later?"

"Hmm." Andrea nods in approval, but is clearly thinking about it. "I guess you have a point." She snaps out of it. "All right. The crew is ready. Let's get your microphones hooked up and ready to finish this today."

Once everything is done, we make our way inside the house.

The camera crew is already set up with lights positioned. Everyone stands around with a hungry focus like they're waiting for something to go wrong. Scottie doesn't waver, though. I can't tell if it's because she isn't picking up on the vibes I get from Andrea, or if because she's just that confident.

I'm going with the latter.

Scottie stands in the middle of the entryway. It's large for a house this old, but it shouldn't take long. She has her hands on her hips, looking around. She's dressed in her signature paint-stained overalls again, which have even more on them from before this started. She has her hair in a messy knot on the top of her head because we *were* running late this morning.

She catches me looking at her and grins. "Stop staring at me like that."

"You've got paint on your face," I lie.

"No, I don't."

"You do." I step forward, cupping the side of her face, eager to touch her again, even if my cock was inside of her an hour ago. I brush the apple of her cheek with my thumb, rubbing the imaginary paint away. The whole room seems to disappear at the moment. This is how I imagine telling her how I feel—in her element, where we both connected on a deeper level. But again, I fucking don't.

"There. Got it," I whisper.

When I pull my hand away, her body sways as if she didn't want me to let go.

Andrea clears her throat and shouts, "Okay. Last episode. Let's make it a good one."

Scottie turns to face the camera, instantly smiling brightly. "Over the last few episodes, I've learned a lot about this house. My goal from the start was to make it shine again because I know that's what my grandma would have wanted." She moves around the entryway, fingertips trailing along an old table sitting on one wall, and peeling wallpaper on another. "To me...crossing that front door into the entryway, it's the first thing you see when you step inside the house. It's where your guests get the first impression. Where they kick off their shoes and stay a while. But right now, it's giving...haunted ghost."

I snort, and so does half the crew.

She looks at me. "What?"

"Haunted ghost? Is that your professional design term?"

She reaches for a corner of the wallpaper, peeling it delicately as if it might bite her. "Look at this pattern. It's like the flowers are judging me."

I shrug. "Hey, maybe they are. They've been here longer than you."

"Tucker, do not side with the wallpaper." She narrows her eyes, stepping close to me. She covers the mic clipped on her with her hand as she whispers, "You're not being a very supportive fake boyfriend."

I bop her finger on her nose, leaning into her ear and away from my mic. "Good thing none of this is fake anymore." Her breath catches, but she doesn't move. "We moved past that stage a long time ago, baby. I can show everyone right now if you'd like."

Scottie laughs, red-cheeked, facing the camera. "Well—" She clears her throat just before running her hands down her pants. I can't help the smile on my face. "Anyway. We're going to rip down all of this wallpaper, freshen up the trim, and then we're going to paint something *bold*."

"Define…bold."

With her hands out in front of her, she paints a picture for the world to see. "A color that makes you feel something when you walk in."

"The entryway doesn't need to punch people in the face, you know? Everything else in the house is warm and calm and inviting."

"First impression, Tucker. Remember?"

I cross my arms. "Neutral also can set the tone for a welcoming environment."

I briefly see a look of disappointment cross her face. It's not enough for anyone else to see, but I see it. I always see it.

This is her project.

This is her house.

"What color were you thinking?" I ask before she says anything more.

She looks at me, unsure. "I'm thinking about a deep teal. Like a lake at midnight."

"That's…actually not terrible."

"Really?"

I shrug, trying to hold onto the skepticism even as she beams. "Don't let it get to your head."

For the next few hours, Scottie, myself, and my crew demo the entire room. The crew almost hauls away the entryway table, but Scottie insists she wants to keep it and work on it later. It's an old, light oak colored table that doesn't match. But she wants to sand it down and repurpose it.

We remove all the old trim and replace it with a more vibrant white to accent the flooring with the new wall color. All the old wallpaper is removed, and it feels like the smell of old perfume went with it.

By the time we finish that, Levi comes back with the paint can.

Once we crack it open and I get a good look at it, Scottie does a happy dance when she sees it's the exact one she wanted.

I do think the color will be right.

Mostly because the truth is, I would forego every neutral paint swatch in existence if it meant she stayed this happy.

We set up the drapes and rollers, and start painting.

Once we get the first coat on, she stands back to look at it.

"I love it," she whispers under her breath.

Yeah, well, I love you.

"Oh, you have more paint on your cheek," I say, reaching up and brushing it again. But this time, the paint on my hand rubs all over.

"You did not."

"I did," I admit with a playful smile.

"You're dead."

She lunges at me, and I catch her around the waist before she can tackle me into the baseboards. Her laugh rings through the air but I don't put her down. I hold her there, in my arms, because she fits here.

"Put me down," she huffs.

"No."

Her eyes flick to mine over her shoulder, heat sparkling there, and for a second, the cameras don't matter. Nothing except her matters.

"Yes, Tucker!" Andrea calls out. "That's it. That's the shot we've needed all season. Look at her like you're obsessed with her."

I don't have to fake that.

Scottie's cheeks flush, and she realizes it before she wiggles out of my grip, swatting my chest. "Focus."

I grip her chin in my hands, letting the crew see just how obsessed with her I am. "You should already know you make it impossible to focus on anything when you're in the room."

She rolls her eyes and steps away enough to reach for a paint-brush. She dips it into the teal paint can.

I step back, hands up. "If you ruin the floors, it's on you."

She lunges forward, smearing a tiny streak of paint on my forearm. I freeze, slowly looking down at the paint and back up to her in a dramatic fashion.

Scottie gasps. "Oh no."

"Oh, yes."

She backs up. "Tucker, don't. I didn't mean it."

I dip my fingers into the paint with deliberate slowness, never breaking eye contact. "You times now you're declaring battle."

"I did not start a—"

I streak teal across her chest and she shrieks, stumbling back-ward into the front doorway, laughing so hard she can barely breathe. When I reach again, she steps through the door and onto the front porch.

"Not my front porch, Tucker!"

She backs up, down the steps, and onto the grass. I chase her, paint on my fingers, and we both laugh openly, bright and wild. Her face lights up in a way that makes me love her that much more.

She stops, catching her breath. "This is the last episode before the finale. You can't have a paint fight with me in the front yard."

"Fine," I agree. I grip her waist, tugging her into me. The paint-stained hand reaches behind her, gripping her ass. "And now my handprint is permanently marked on these overalls."

Her smile is wide, and I want to lean down and kiss it.

And that's when I feel it. The sharp ping to my chest, the way my heart races completely unrelated to running around. It's seeing her in the open front yard, sun hitting her cheeks. The urge to say it has never been stronger.

I feel it on the tip of my tongue.

But when I open my mouth to say it, the universe chooses that moment to remind us that nothing stays perfect for long. A throat clears beside us, and Scottie turns. Her expression shifts, her face goes white, and her body goes still as stone.

She looks terrified.

She looks like she wants to run and hide.

The cameras close in on us, making me more uncomfortable than ever. I shift, facing the same direction she is, and I notice the couple Griffin was complaining about the other day at Seven Stools standing there.

Whoever these people are, they have shifted something in Scottie that makes me protective of her. I want to step in front of her and pummel these two people—whoever they are.

But I don't expect her to say what she does, barely above a whisper.

"Mom? Dad?"

CHAPTER 31

YOU'RE ABOUT TWO WORDS AWAY FROM NEEDIN' AN ESCORT BACK TO YOUR CAR!

SCOTTIE

The air outside shifts so fast it feels like we're trapped in a bubble.

One minute I'm full body laughing with Tucker, and the next my breath catches like I just ran into a wall. The paint roller goes heavy in my hand while the smile dies on my lips.

Because standing a foot away from me are my parents.

What the hell are they doing here?

"Well…" my mom says with displeasure in her voice. "This is…interesting."

Her eyes scan me up and down, noting my paint stained overalls. She's seen them before, but there's definitely more on them now that we're nearly done with the house. Then she looks at the paint on my skin before she looks at Tucker, speckled with teal paint. My stomach drops, and a thousand versions of myself filter through my brain.

Me in high school, fighting to be perfect.

Me in college, overachieving on something I didn't want until I couldn't breathe.

Me on camera, smiling until my cheeks hurt.

Me on FaceTime mid-project, trying not to look exhausted to avoid a lecture.

And now…me standing here on the porch laughing too loud —too freely with two large cameras pointed at me with teal paint on my cheeks.

"Are we interrupting something?" she continues, because I'm stunned silent.

I feel my body stiffen, and I still don't know what to say. I feel as if the cameras are actually zooming in on me without even moving. The crew is quiet, waiting and holding their breath.

"No," I manage to get out with a wide smile.

My mom takes off her sunglasses, tucking them into her purse before turning to take in the house. I literally hold my breath. I stand here, trying to hide the fact that my fingers are trembling because I already hear it coming.

"I thought you would do more with it," she says.

And there it is.

I clear my throat, knowing the producers are not cutting this. "The possibilities were endless. I could have gone a dozen different routes with the project. Ultimately, I wanted to preserve what was. I wanted to keep the bones of the house alive and make it shine again."

"Shine again?" she asks.

My eyes fly to my dad who's looking anywhere but at the two of us. Does my mom not know what he told me about this place? I wish he never hung up on me that day I called him so I can understand any of this—understand what she knows and what I don't.

I look back at my mom and nod, feeling like I'm going to throw up. "The house was very weathered and needed some serious work, but not everything was a complete gut job. We were able to maintain everything I wanted."

"And *this* is what you wanted?" She scoffs, extending an arm toward the house. "I thought you were supposed to be proving this isn't just a hobby. You wanted people to take you seriously.

This…this is just a sentimental fixer-upper instead of something professional."

The words hit like a slap to the face.

Not because they're true, but because the house looks incredible now. I love the things we've done with it because it was *my* vision and *my* project.

"But," she draws out, turning to face me again. "I can see why you chose to do the bare minimum." She looks from Tucker to me and leans in. "You were too busy goofing around instead of working."

I don't dare look at Tucker.

I have never felt so embarrassed, and I don't need to see the look in his eyes.

My familiar reflex kicks in. I straighten my spine, smile properly, and nod my head. The performance is muscle memory at this point, but the moment I snap it in place, I feel Tucker's hand on the small of my back.

I *still* don't look at him, but I know what he's silently telling me.

I know he's telling me that I'm stronger than this.

"Scottie, you look…" my dad starts, sympathy on his face because I know he hates when my mom is this way.

"Tired. Exhausted. *Definitely* not put together," she rattles off.

"That's enough, Laura," my dad says under his breath, so hopefully the cameras won't hear.

Tucker shifts behind me, and I feel him inhale like he's holding back and trying not to jump in. His hand presses more firmly on my back, and I know he's urging me to stand up for myself. Just his presence is enough to feel strong enough to do it.

My dad extends a hand to Tucker, a warm smile on his face. "Hi. I'm Billy. And you must be…"

"Tucker," he answers flatly, returning his greeting before his hand is back on my back.

"It's nice to meet you. I'm guessing by the tool belt you helped?"

Tucker nods. "I did, but she did most of the work."

"He's the head contractor. And…" I pause, looking from my mom to my dad. "He's important to me."

My mother's expression freezes.

My dad just smiles.

"But you aren't staying here," my mom says like it's a fact when she never even asked me. "And you need to think about how *this*"—she gestures between Tucker and I—"will look on the show. Everyone is going to be watching."

Something inside me snaps like a cord that's been fraying for years and on its last string.

Fuck this.

Just as I open my mouth to speak, the sound of an angry golf cart comes barreling down the driveway. I say angry because it sounds like the engine is on its last leg. One putt away from exploding.

And driving it like a banshee is Nan.

She skids to a stop, a grin on her face, before she reaches into the row behind her and pulls out a giant pot filled with assorted flowers. She stumbles over to us, barely able to hold it herself. "I brought you something to fix the vibes of the porch." She drops it to the ground with a thud, dusting her hands before taking in her surroundings. "This feels like a situation."

Tucker laughs from behind me but tries to hide it.

"Thank you so much for the flowers, Nan. You can bring them to the porch if you'd like," I say, trying to remove her from this conversation to avoid any more embarrassment.

She eyes my mom for a moment before nodding in my direction. "You got it," she says before walking away with the potted flower.

"She hasn't changed a bit." My dad laughs, shaking his head.

"No, but your daughter has," Mom huffs.

I take a step closer to my mom, which forces me out of Tucker's grounding hand. I angle myself so that it looks as if we're just two people looking at the house. I smile, leaning to my side just enough so I can keep my voice low. This time I don't bother covering the mic with my hand. "You were right."

"Usually I am. But entertain me."

"I do need to think about how this looks. Because it looks like I've spent my entire life trying to earn your approval." I face her completely now, cameras be damned. "It looks like I've been smiling through exhaustion and swallowing my feelings and performing perfection because I thought that was the only way to be loved."

"Scottlyn," she whispers, her eyes wide.

"I'm not done."

"Scottie, maybe when the cameras—" Dad starts.

I shake my head, cutting him off. "This is exactly the right time." My chest is heaving as the truth pours out before I can stop it. "I'm so damn tired of being the version of myself you can brag about. I'm tired of building a life that looks perfect but feels empty." My words grow louder with every one that slips free. "I'm *so damn tired* of chasing validation that always moves the second I get close. I'm done doing what *you* want me to do because it's never going to be enough!"

My mom looks offended. "I've only ever wanted what's best for you."

"No. You want what *looks* best for you," I nearly shout.

I feel something settle in me as the sentence spills from my mouth. Almost like the calm after a storm. My parents don't say anything back. My mom looks hurt by the truth, while my dad is torn between being proud of me for standing up for myself, and sticking by her. But either way, they both look at me like they don't recognize the person standing in front of them.

And maybe they don't.

Because I don't recognize her either.

But I fucking like her.

"I heard raised voices behind me and assumed someone was trying to ruin a perfectly good day," Nan says, coming to stand between us.

"Nan," Tucker says. "Not your fight."

Nan looks to him. "If it's in Bluestone Lakes and involves people I care about, you bet your ass it's my fight."

She turns to face my mom, scanning her up and down.

"Nan, it's okay," I say, placing a hand on her shoulder.

My mom faces my dad. "Now I remember why we stopped coming here. This town makes mediocrity feel like magic."

Nan straightens slowly, rolling her shoulders back. "Careful," she says evenly. "You're about two words away from needin' an escort back to your car."

"Nan," Tucker warns.

My mom huffs in response. "Oh, please. All I'm saying is I didn't want my daughter growing up thinking this was enough."

"Enough?" Nan repeats. "Millie's house wasn't enough?"

Mom shrugs. "She should have sold this after Pop died. She refused to, and then refused help. The house was falling apart, and I wasn't going to keep dragging Scottlyn back and forth to a house like that."

My stomach twists.

Nan's jaw hardens. "Lies."

"Nan," Tucker warns again, with more growl to his voice as if trying to force her to but out. But I hold a hand out in front of him, needing to hear what she's about to say.

Nan steps forward, pointing a finger in my mom's chest. "*You're* the reason Scottie never came back here. It's not because of the house falling apart. It's because you couldn't stand how free Millie lived her life." I hold my breath and Nan doesn't hold back. She pokes her again. "*You* never failed to judge her for the way she acted around Scottie. Allowing her to be a kid and playin' in the dirt. How she would run around the fields laughing and dancing. You hated it."

My mom's eyes flash with the truth being laid out in front of me.

I step forward. "Is that true?"

324

"No."

Nan lets out a humorless laugh. "You forget Millie was my best friend. We never left each other's side. I was there the day you gave her an ultimatum over the phone. You said sell the house, move closer, or you'd stop bringing Scottie to see her."

Silence fills the air.

I don't move. Tucker doesn't move, and neither does my dad.

My mom grinds her teeth together, looking beyond us at the house. "I was protecting her."

"From my mother?" my dad cuts in, and we all snap our heads to face him. "Scottie didn't need protection from *my mother.*"

"I wanted what's best for her!" my mom shouts.

My dad steps closer to her. "I love you, but I also love our daughter. So, please, listen to me for once. You have to stop with this need to push Scottie into something she doesn't want— something she doesn't believe in. You've been doing it for so long that it's time to let go of it."

"Billy," she says, gasping like she didn't expect that.

"The entire drive here, you've been talking about how my mom should have never left her this house." My eyes widen and I wait in bated breath for his next words. "She left Scottie this house because she knew exactly what she was doing. She believed in her more than either of us ever did. Even if she was too young when she died, she still believed that Scottie would carry the legacy of this place and make it a home."

I'm shocked by his words. My lips part as I listen to every word, afraid if I move or even blink, he might stop. He's never really defended me like this with Mom. But this isn't him being careful anymore. This is him choosing me—standing in front of her like a wall saying I was worth believing in all along.

"Millie didn't just leave her this house," Dad continues. "She left her a chance."

Tears sting my eyes at the same time Tucker places a hand on my lower back again.

"This house wasn't just something to do for the show," I cut in, voice cracking. "I learned somewhere along the way that it means more to me than proving that this isn't just a hobby for me. This is real for me, Mom." I face her again, heart hammering in my chest. "I'm sorry if it's not what you wanted—this show, the house, this town, all of it. But it's turned into everything I didn't know I needed. I've renovated *my* dream home. And, in the process, found people who love and care about me."

My dad steps up first with glassy eyes. I feel Tucker back away from me a moment before my dad wraps his arms around me for a tight embrace. "I'm so proud of you," he whispers in my ear.

"Thank you, Dad," I choke out, hugging him back tightly. When he releases me, I look to my mom, who has her eyes fixed on the grass at her feet. I walk over, placing a hand on her shoulder. "I can't live for your approval anymore. I don't want to perform perfection either. I'm choosing the messy. Even if it's loud and chaotic. Even if you don't like it. Even if it's never going to be enough for you."

For a moment, no one moves.

"I'm sorry, Scottie," my mom says, lifting her eyes to meet mine. I don't miss the way she called me Scottie instead of Scottlyn. "I guess I just always thought...if I pushed you hard enough, you'd never have to struggle."

"I did struggle. Just not in the way you think."

She exhales loudly like she wants to argue. Like she wants to fix it or reshape the conversation into something she understands.

But she doesn't.

And I can't help but offer her a soft smile because that might be the bravest thing she's ever done. Without another word, she turns around and walks back to her car parked on the street.

My dad offers me an apologetic smile and follows her.

We all watch as the car drives off. It's only then that I inhale and exhale, allowing my body to relax before I turn around.

"Now that the beige brigade is gone," Nan says, walking to me first. She looks me in the eyes—all the amusement she carries with her all day is gone. Just for a moment. "I'm fucking proud of you, my girl. And I know, without a shadow of a doubt, Millie is too."

And then she side steps me, getting into the golf cart and driving away.

Tucker stands back, unmoving. As if he can feel me looking at him, he lifts his head, and an unreadable expression crosses his face. Anguish? I can't tell, but it makes my stomach flip.

I don't move. I can't. Fear locks me in place.

Was this—my parents—too much for him?

Tucker takes slow, tentative steps toward me until stopping right in front of me. Heat creeps up my neck, bracing myself for what he's about to say.

"I—"

He holds up a hand to stop what I was about to say, but still doesn't say anything. Staring at him, I can see everything he wants to say, but can't, flashing through his mind.

"A lot of people think a home is composed of walls and a roof where you live. A structure that you fill with belongings and memories," he says, pausing, his words sounding so familiar. "But it's more than that."

"Tucker," I breathe out.

"It's who's inside those walls. It's a place where you're seen without needing to explain yourself. A place where you can breathe and your flaws don't need to be hidden. It's a place you don't have to pretend…"

"You can just be," I finish for him.

His words still land the way they did the first time he said them, back in San Francisco. I remember them vividly because they resonated with me.

"Where you feel whole," he adds the last part. "And I've learned over the last few weeks that *you* are what makes me feel whole." He reaches up, swiping a thumb across my cheek at the tear I didn't even feel escape. "I've spent years being the comic relief and the guy who filled any gap of silence with laughter just so no one would see the cracks. But not you. You saw everything. Even before I let you in, you saw it all."

He takes my face in his hands, angling my head up to meet his, and I melt into his touch. My eyes try to close, but the intensity of his stare keeps them open, looking at him and hearing every word he says.

"And now you've seen all of me."

A smile curves on his lips, and a light laugh escapes. "You know, this place...was my dream home." I tilt my head to the side in confusion. He looks from me to the house and back to me. "I used to come here to this house, and think. It was my escape and place to hide when I didn't know how to be anything else."

I don't say anything, because I can't.

He releases his hands from my face, turning around to face the house. He takes a few steps to the side yard, and I follow like a magnet pulling me with him. When he stops, I do too, facing the same way he is, and take in the vast mountainscape painted in my own backyard.

"I used to come here and tell myself that one day I'd have this place. And if I didn't, I'd build something on this street close enough, so I always had this view. Because this house...it was nearly identical to the one I lived in as a child."

My body tenses, and I feel the pain of his past for him all over again.

"It's what always drew me here. The memories, even painful, feel different on this property. I like to think it has to do with the wide open view of the stars at night. Like my mom, dad, and brother were looking down on me. But I never fully knew what kept drawing me to this house. Even falling apart, it was waiting for someone to remember it mattered."

My heart beats so wildly in my chest.

"I spent years imagining what it would look like if someone

loved it enough to bring it back." He swallows hard, looking at me. "I know it sounds ridiculous, but it became a thing for me. A secret goal. Like if I could fix *this*, then I could fix myself. But then you showed up." He smiles, but his voice breaks off. "You walked in with your ridiculous optimism and your blueprints of ideas. And you didn't just renovate it. You wanted to save it and make it shine again."

Hearing my words repeated back to me makes my heart skip ten beats.

Tucker reaches for me again, and this time my hands find his hips, gripping the hem of his T-shirt in my hands like I don't want him to move.

"I didn't know what to do with that," he admits. "With you. With the way you looked at me like I wasn't just hired help." He huffs out a laugh. "I mean, for a while you looked at me like you wanted to strangle me."

I feel my cheeks turn pink, and I try to avert my gaze with embarrassment, but he stops me. Holding me steady. Not letting me look anywhere but at him.

"But eventually, through the facade we put on for the camera, you started to look at me like I matter."

My hands lift to his forearms, holding on because suddenly it feels like my body needs proof that he's real. "You've always mattered," I whisper.

His gaze drops to my mouth for a brief second before he forces it back to my eyes. "I tried so fucking hard to tell myself this was just work. I was just the contractor. This was your house. And I got good at it—at keeping it professional."

I blink because I feel the same way.

"But then you started showing me more," he continues. "You started trusting me with your decisions. You laughed when I joked. You didn't make me feel stupid for caring about safety and structure when you knew *nothing* I was going through. Somewhere along the way, this stopped being a job. It stopped being a place to hide. And I know, without a doubt, it's because you were here."

It's on the tip of my tongue to cut him off.

It's my turn to say how I feel, but I still can't get words to come out.

Not when Tucker is baring himself to me.

"When I told you all of that back at that hole in the wall burger place, I thought I knew what home was. But then you walked into my life and somehow made it all mean something else. I didn't know what that something else was. I've never felt like this before, so I didn't understand it. But I do now."

My breath trembles as I stare at the man who has made everything lighter during this process. Who has allowed *me* to be myself in the process. And he's standing here, offering me the heaviest and most beautiful thing he owns.

Himself.

"I love you, Scottie. I'm so crazy and deeply in love with you that I don't remember what my life was like before you were in it."

A smile curves at my lips. I lift my hand, touching his cheek and feeling the dampness from the emotions he let out. "I love you, too," I whisper.

His eyes widen like he doesn't believe he's allowed to hear it back. But then he lets out a sound that is half laugh, half breath, and half something that might be relief.

"Can you say that again for me?"

"I love you, Tucker Daniels."

And before I can even get his full name out, his lips are on mine. Like he can't survive another second without it. Like he's been starving and didn't know it until I said it back. The kiss is slow, but then it deepens quickly, because Tucker doesn't know how to be careful with something that feels like salvation.

His hands slide into the back of my hair, holding me there. When we finally break apart, he stays close enough that I feel his breath on my lips.

"I think…" He pauses, pressing his forehead to mine. "I thought this house here was my dream home. But it turns out you are. You're the home I can run to when I need an escape, when I need to feel seen, and when I need something that's real."

I reach up, pressing my lips to his again.

His arms tighten around me, pulling me in until there's no space left for any doubt. No space left for fear.

Just us.

CHAPTER 32

I KNOW EXACTLY WHERE I'LL BE.

TUCKER

I've built houses that can stand a storm and not budge, but nothing has ever hit me the way those three words have. Nothing has ever made me feel like my entire life split open. Hearing the words back, after fearing saying them to her, feels like everything before her was grayscale and all the after finally has color.

She breaks away from the kiss, looking up at me with a soft smile.

"You used my full name," I murmur, voice rough from everything I've been holding in.

"I did," she whispers and shrugs. "Felt dramatic."

I laugh, hooking an arm around her neck to pull her to my chest. I know she can feel my racing heart. It hasn't calmed down since her parents showed up. Since I watched her stand tall in front of them and say everything she's been holding back for years.

I wanted to cut in a dozen times.

I wanted to tell them to fuck all the way off.

But she did it on her own.

I knew I loved her before that because the thoughts had been swimming in my head for days—probably weeks. Scottie is a different kind of strong. Not once has she ever flinched when things got ugly during this remodel. Not even when the producers suggested we fake a relationship for the show. She just…adjusts.

And I've been watching her do it like it's nothing.

Hearing the words spill out of her told me she's been waking up every morning of her life and talking herself into being brave. She makes it look easy, too, which must have been the biggest lie she told the world.

So, watching her stand tall only made me fall more in love with her.

Just as I'm about to lean in and claim her lips as mine again, I hear a throat clearing to the side, and I freeze. Scottie does, too, as her eyes widen.

We both turn our heads and remember the crew standing off to the side. One behind the camera, with Jade and Andrea on either side. The lens is still pointed on us, red light blinking.

But Scottie doesn't flinch.

Of course she doesn't.

For a split second, she just stands there with teal paint on her cheek and my hands around her. Then she laughs under her breath. "Oh my god."

Andrea clears her throat. "Cut." The camera turns off, and Andrea steps toward us. "Well, we got all of that."

Scottie looks up at me, eyes bright and wild like she's waiting for me to panic. Like she's waiting for me to yank my hands back and retreat to the safer version of myself.

I don't.

I tighten my hold on her instead, making her smile shift. "Keep it," she says to Andrea, still looking at me before she winks and faces Andrea. "All of it."

"Are you sure? That was…really personal."

Scottie nods. "I'm sure."

Scottie steps out of my hold and looks around at the house. I can see her eyes take in the yard that all of Bluestone Lakes helped her clean up. Then her eyes scan the porch, and a smile curves on her lips when they land on the porch swing. She looks back at Andrea and Jade like she's decided on something more.

"I'd also like you to go through all the film," Scottie says. "I want the real stuff. You can keep the polished stuff if it involves me sharing what we plan to do with each space. But everything else…make it real. The sweat. The frustration. All of it."

"But…"

Scottie cuts her off with a hand in the air. "I know you have clips where I mess up lines, look exhausted, and have sawdust covering my head. I know you have some where I'm laughing so hard I might pee my pants. I want it all on the show."

"Being the face of the season, people are going to expect—"

"Performance?" Scottie finishes with a raised eyebrow. I feel something crack open in my chest the way she says it. "And that's what I'm doing. Giving them one."

Andrea studies her for a long second, glancing at Jade before looking back at Scottie. I can see the calculation behind her eyes and gauge whether the audience will tolerate it. "I'll see what I can do."

"No. You'll do it. I want everything you edit together to be perfectly imperfect." Her smile is bigger now, making the corners around her eyes crinkle. "If this show is about homes, then it should be about the truth of building one. Not just the pretty reveal."

"Okay."

Scottie exhales, and some of the tension leaves her shoulders. She reaches up, pressing a kiss to the corner of my lips before walking away. "I'm going to do the second coat of paint," she announces. "I may be choosing authenticity over perfection, but I'm still choosing coverage."

We laugh this time as I watch her disappear inside.

The air changes into something sharp now that I'm left alone with Andrea and Jade. When I turn my head toward them, I can see their faces trying to look satisfied, and I realize with cold clarity that they want to frame this season to belong to them and not Scottie.

No more.

I take a step toward them, lowering my voice. "It was you."

"What?"

"You brought her parents here."

Her eyes flicker, but her smile doesn't move. "We didn't bring anyone. They said they wanted to—"

"Don't," I cut her off. Not angry, but controlled. "Don't lie to me."

"This is television, Tucker," she says, holding my gaze like she thinks she can win this stare down. "It's more than just the house. It's telling a story. Which is why you came in for the plot, too."

Now I'm feeling angry. "This is her life."

She shrugs like it's nothing. "We didn't know it would be drama."

I laugh, humorless. "You knew exactly what it would be. You just thought the fans would eat it up the same way you thought they would with a relationship between the two of us."

Her eyes narrow, and that's the part that flips something in me.

She's not entirely wrong.

They *will* eat it up. The fans will call it empowering. They'll post clips and caption them with quotes about healing and choosing yourself. They'll scream about the moment she snapped and stood up for herself. But none of them will feel the cost of it the way she did. None of them will have to carry her shaking hands after the cameras turn off.

I lean in slightly, voice dropping even lower. "You don't get to weaponize her pain for ratings."

"We gave her a platform."

"No. *She* gave you a season."

For a second, she looks like she might argue.

"Here's what's going to happen," I start, crossing my arms over my chest. "We're going to finish up today. In a few days, we're going to film the scheduled final reveal. And then you're going to fucking leave Bluestone Lakes like a bear is chasing you."

Jade laughs next to me, but stops when I glare at her.

"Got it?"

They both nod and walk away.

I watch them get in their van and drive off before making my way back inside, where Scottie is. She's crouched down, painting a lower part of the wall with her tongue sticking out in concentration. The sight of her like this, messy and focused, makes my lips curve into a smile.

I reach into my back pocket and pull out a bag of candy. Her eyes snap to mine as if she just heard me now. I discard the candy in my hand, picking out the green and yellow and putting them in my pocket loosely. I filter all the other colors back into the bag and hand it to her.

"Sugar?"

She stands up, dropping the paint brush to the drop cloth at her feet. She jumps into my arms, wrapping her body around me. I catch her, nearly dropping all the sour candy to the floor, but I keep my grip on them. She presses her face into my neck, and I tighten my hold on her, never wanting to let her go.

She pulls back, legs around my waist to look me in the eye. "I love you."

I bite my bottom lip into my mouth, fighting back the biggest and cheesiest smile because that's what she does to me. That's what hearing those words from her lips does to me. Never in my life did I think I was deserving of this. This kind of love. This person. This life.

But she's changed everything.

She's made me believe in everything again.

I lean in, pressing my forehead to hers and whisper, "I love you, too."

I hold her right there in the entryway of the house she rebuilt —that *we* rebuilt. The house that chose her. The house that shines again because she walked into it.

I know with certainty that when the cameras finally stop rolling, the crew packs up, and the world moves on to the next story, I know exactly where I'll be.

Right here with her.

Home.

FINALE
COMING TO AN END

We made it to the season finale of Nailed It or Failed It!

Today will be the final reveal of the house we've spent the last month renovating. And what a ride it's been. This season started with one inherited house in Bluestone Lakes and one influencer with a dream that suddenly felt too heavy to carry.

Scottie arrived with a vision and something to prove.

Tucker showed up with a tool belt and a smile sharp enough to hide every crack.

And from the very first day, the chemistry wasn't just noticeable, it was impossible to ignore.

Together they took on every project. But it wasn't just the house that changed. Somewhere between the dust and looming deadlines, Scottie stopped chasing perfection and started choosing what felt real. Tucker stopped hiding behind the jokes and started letting someone in.

Now, after all the work and all the risks, the only thing left is the reveal.

The doors are about to open for us to see the final transformation. The question that remains is: did they nail it? Or did they fail it?

EPILOGUE

TWO MONTHS LATER.

SCOTTIE

Pulling on a pair of my comfiest sweatpants, I give myself a once-over in the floor-length mirror sitting in the corner of my bedroom. It used to be a place where a box of memories sat that I found when renovating this house. Now it's filled, and the memories moved, scattered around the house in various frames.

I make my way downstairs, the floors no longer creaking in warning. The walls aren't holding their breath. The teal entryway shines under the warm light, and every time I walk past it, I still feel the same thing I did the day we painted it.

The day I chose myself, and the universe didn't collapse because of it.

I hear chatter from the living room and make my way toward it. But my phone buzzing in my hand makes me stop. Looking down, I see it's a text from my mom, and I can't help but smile. It's a selfie of her and my dad sitting on the couch together, smiling so big with the TV queued up behind them to the channel for the season finale.

MOM

> We're ready to watch them say you Nailed It.

ME

Thank you, Mom. Fingers crossed.

MOM

I already know that's what they will say
because the work you did is exceptional. It
deserves as much.

Reading that only makes me smile wider. It took a few days before I finally had the courage to sit down with my mom and talk about everything without cameras or a production crew hovering over us. It actually made the conversation a lot less tense. She allowed me to openly share how I felt without judgement and I listened to her. By the end of the few hours together, we were both crying and apologizing for things. It brought us a sense of peace that made me wish I had opened up *years* ago. And since then, she's been a whole new person. She's encouraging, cheering me on, and I have never felt more support from her than I do now.

ME

I love you both.

MOM

We love you too.

I lock my phone and continue making my way to the living room. It gets louder with every step I take. The TV is frozen and queued up for the watch party of the season finale of *Nailed It or Failed It*. There's a sign hanging slightly crooked under the TV that Lily insisted on. The coffee table is buried under an assortment of food. Lily brought baked goods, obviously. Poppy and Dallas brought a charcuterie board. Blair and Griffin brought drinks. And Nan brought something in a very old crockpot, announced it contained "something different," but refused to elaborate.

"All right," Nan announces, coming in from the kitchen and

clapping her hands. "Where's my seat? I need to see myself on this high definition TV."

Lily laughs. "Nan, you were in like two episodes. Briefly."

"Yeah, but I was also in the background of the front yard episode. You can see me hackin' away in the bushes. I stole the season."

Blair holds up the phone in her hand. "The internet agrees."

"I'm a star," Nan says, face lighting up.

Dallas points at Tucker standing in the archway of the kitchen, arms crossed. "You ready, Hollywood?"

"Don't call me that."

"Oh, come on," Dallas says, face pulled into a grin. "You're famous now. People are making edits of you all over social media."

Griffin reaches for a piece of cheese and a cracker. "He's been pretending he hasn't seen them."

"I haven't."

Blair grins. "You have."

"He has," Lily agrees.

Poppy leans in, stage-whispering like Tucker can't hear. "He definitely has."

Tucker shoots them all a flat look, then his gaze slides to me. His expression shifts instantly into something soft like the rest of the room fades when he finds me.

It's been strange watching our story turn into something other people consume. The house. The rooms. But more than that, watching us. Because the show aired exactly the way I asked Andrea for, with all the real and raw stuff. I watched every episode before this one and saw every part where my smile slipped when I thought the cameras weren't watching, the nights my hair was a mess and eyes puffy, the moments Tucker was far too close, touching me carefully, and every single mess that was made.

They showed me sweating through the porch demo.

They showed Tucker almost falling off the ladder, and my hands on his legs.

They showed the ceiling collapsing and memories falling from it.

They showed my parents.

That part still makes my stomach turn over on itself, even though I've watched the episode twice already. The internet didn't just watch with me, they felt it.

The comments on social media were overwhelming. People started sharing stories of their own families, of never being enough, and finally feeling seen through the show. People cheered for me like they were waiting for that moment my whole career.

After that episode aired, my mom and I cried on the phone for an hour about how we're so happy that was behind us. She hates that it was aired publicly, and part of me does, too. The internet has truly painted her in a terrible light because of it. The next day, I went online and shared a photo of her and I in front of the house with a long caption about conversation. She didn't ask me to do that, but she's made an effort to change. And the least I could do is show them that.

But what really surprised me, was how much they fell in love with Tucker.

They called him everything from hot to protective to steady to the funniest man alive. Someone even wrote what felt like an essay about how he touched my back every time my parents spoke, as if he were holding me together. Another person made a video titled *Tucker Daniels: Walking Green Flag*.

I still don't know whether I want to laugh or hide from it.

"I don't care what the internet thinks," he says simply, lifting his chin in the air.

"Here we go," Nan mutters.

His eyes are locked on mine from across the room. "I only have eyes for one person."

The room erupts. Blair squeals, and Lily throws her hands up in the air with excitement. Griffin mumbles something under his breath, and Dallas shoots Tucker a wink.

My face heats while a smile tugs at my mouth.

Tucker steps toward me, close enough that I feel the warmth of his presence envelope me without his hands even on me. He reaches up, brushing the hair away from my face. "You okay?"

I nod. "You?"

He exhales. "Ask me after."

I tilt my head. "Are you nervous, Hollywood?"

"No." I raise an eyebrow, and he sighs. "Okay, yes."

I smile, reaching to place a hand on his chest. "It's going to be fine. It's just a house reveal."

"I know," he says before leaning down and kissing me. "I just hope they say you nailed it."

Even now, two months later, we don't know how they will paint the finale of the show.

When we recorded the final walk through, that was all it was— a showcase of every room we did and every project accomplished. Not even Andrea or Jade could tell us if we nailed it. That was something they would have to piece together based on the film.

He's right to be nervous, because a part of me is, too.

It's the moment everything becomes official and permanent. The thing people will replay and clip together on the internet.

"Ready?" Lily asks, standing in the middle of the room with the remote in her hand. All eyes are on us. We smile at each other and then make our way to one of the couches and take a seat.

"Let's see it."

Tucker wraps an arm around the back of the couch, fingertips caressing my shoulder as the introduction plays from the host. The voice is dramatic and bright, recapping the season like it's a romance novel disguised as a renovation.

"So dramatic," Griffin grumbles, and Blair playfully smacks his arm with the back of her hand.

"Shh," she says.

We watch the reveal sequence roll out—the shot of the front porch into the entryway, then into the living room, the kitchen, and the master bedroom. The before-and-after videos transitioned together, and even I'm shocked to see it all. I'm sitting in the house we're watching on TV, but seeing them cut from the before to the after just makes me feel a sense of pride.

I did that.

We did that.

Lily gasps like she hasn't seen things herself, and Blair points to the screen when they show the pink restored tub on the screen. There's a brief clip of Nan taking her sledgehammer to the bathroom sink and then another of her dragging a bush across the yard with dirt smeared across her cheeks like battle paint. The entire living room explodes with laughter.

Dallas catches his breath first. "Nan, you look like you fought the shrubs and lost."

"The comments on the internet were right," Poppy adds. "You *are* unhinged."

Nan beams, bowing her head. "Thank you. Thank you."

Then the episode shifts as the music changes and tension builds. The last scene appears on screen, and there we are. Tucker and I are laughing together, our hands linked, and paint splattered on our faces. He looks at me the same way he's looking at me now. Like I'm the only thing in the room that matters.

It's a replay clip of my parents showing up.

Tucker's hands are on my back on screen.

I realize here and now how many times he's held me up before I even knew I was falling during this entire process. I blink hard, trying to keep the emotions of it down.

Tucker picks up on it, the way he always does. "Are you okay?"

I nod repeatedly. "I'm just...feeling all of it."

His thumb strokes my shoulder in slow circles. "Yeah. Me too."

The announcer's voice cuts in, making the entire room freeze. This is the moment. The end of the last episode—the end of the season. This is where they tell the world if the project was a success.

What began as an old abandoned inheritance for Scottie has turned into a full circle transformation. I say that because it's more than just the house's transformation. It was the town and two people brave enough to stop pretending. Scottie didn't just renovate this home in Bluestone Lakes…she found one. She found her people. She successfully showed us that perfection should never be the goal when it comes to something like this. It's about working together and putting everything you've got into what you want in life.

Along the way, Tucker showed us that the hardest renovations aren't always structural, but they're emotional. With honesty, this project became something more than a makeover.

It became a second chance.

Scottie Monroe…you not only found a home, but you Nailed It!

Everyone in the room leaps from where they sit, hands in the air, and cheering that we did it. I stay stuck in my seat with Tucker unmoving right next to me. My mouth is open, and I stare in shock as they continue to circle the outside of the house on camera and say more things I can't process.

But I did it.

I nailed it.

With tears in my eyes, I look at Tucker, who's already looking at me with glassy eyes himself, smiling down at me. "I'm so fucking proud of you, babe."

Turning my body, I take his face in my hands and kiss him hard. So hard his body tenses for a moment before relaxing. His hands reach around my waist, pulling me to him. I pull back, a breath away from his lips. "We did it," I whisper.

"*You* did it."

"I had a *really* good contractor to help me."

"Hmm. That guy was all right." Tucker smiles back, pressing another kiss to my lips.

"You two better get married and give me a grandbaby to spoil," Nan snaps from behind us.

I pull away from Tucker, heat creeping up my cheeks.

Tucker chokes on air. "Nan."

She shrugs. "I said what I said."

Griffin laughs and Dallas groans. Blair and Lily come up with arms out. I stand, accepting their embrace and words of praise.

I can't believe we actually did it. I mean, looking around the room and the house, living here since the project was done—it's home. Bluestone Lakes is home.

For the next half hour, the room buzzes with warmth and noise and the kind of love I didn't know existed outside of fictional stories. At least the ones Blair and Lily have had me reading lately.

"We should get going," Griffin says to Blair.

"The show literally just ended," Lily huffs.

"And you haven't tried my crockpot dish yet," Nan adds.

Griffin rolls his eyes. "I know. But I have to be up early to tackle some jobs on the ranch since Levi left to help with that hurricane relief in North Carolina."

Poppy gasps. "Wait. That's where you're from Dallas."

Dallas nods. "My hometown is more inland. It was the coast that got hit really hard."

"Oof," Nan says. "Levi is an angel."

"He's a good guy and a damn hard worker," Griffin sighs. "I've been slightly worried about how much I have to take on over at the ranch now. Even if he's only there a few hours after his construction shift ends, he does a lot of work for me."

"If you need help while he's gone, let me know," Dallas offers.

"I appreciate the offer. But an old friend of mine offered to help me out."

"Old friend?" Lily practically chokes.

Griffin nods. "Asher is coming back for a bit. He's staying in Bonneville, but it's close enough still that he's open to working for me while he's here."

My eyes continue to watch Lily. I notice her entire body stiffen, but she relaxes quickly, so no one catches it before she nods. "Gotcha," she finally says, but it comes out hoarse. Like it's the last thing she wanted to hear.

"Ash is coming back?" Nan gasps.

Griffin shrugs. "That's what it sounds like. I'm not sure what his deal is. I mean...I know why he left." He pauses, and the entire room falls quiet. I look around at everyone, and they have their heads down like they know, too. I have no idea what to think, but I'm curious. "I just don't know why he's coming back now, after all these years."

"It will be nice to have him around," Nan says. "That boy might have always been trouble, but I liked him more than I like all of you."

"That's a lie," Tucker says flatly.

"Is it?" Nan raises an eyebrow, smirking as she turns and walks into the kitchen.

I look at Lily, and I can tell the change of subject is welcome. I turn to Blair, and she's looking at her, too, with questions in her eyes, and I know the next time we get together it will be brought up.

The conversation shifts to Dallas for a bit about what it was like on the East Coast as we all clean up the food scattered around the tables.

Then everyone starts to leave.

Lily embraces me in a hug and whispers, "I'm so proud of you," in my ear.

I lean my head to whisper in hers. "Are you okay?"

She pulls back, a weak smile on her lips. "I hope so."

Dallas slaps Tucker on the shoulder. "Don't let fame go to your head."

Tucker smirks. "Never."

Poppy hooks an arm in Nan's elbow to physically guide her out before she can take home my throw pillows and leftover cheese.

Once everyone is gone, the house is empty and it's just Tucker and me.

The kind of quiet that used to scare him.

The kind of quiet that used to send my brain into overdrive.

Now it feels like peace.

I stand in the entryway for a moment, staring at the teal wall. Tucker steps behind me, close enough that I can feel his warmth without him touching me. When he finally reaches out, his hand slides around my waist, pulling me back against his chest.

"You stayed," he murmurs into my hair.

I smile softly, leaning into him because I know what he's saying. He's reminded me often since we finished the show and I moved into this house that I never knew existed.

I turn in his arms, looking up at him. His eyes are softer now than they've ever been. The hard edges he built to hide everything inside of him are worn down by comfort and the truth that he isn't alone anymore.

"I did. I stayed." I pause, the curve in my lips stretching higher. "I think you should, too." He tilts his head in confusion. "Here. With me. Stay here with me. I'm asking you to move in with me so you don't have to keep leaving when you don't have to."

His hands tighten around my waist, and he lowers his forehead to mine. "Here?"

I nod. "You said this was always your dream home, right?"

He pulls back, eyes boring into mine. And then his hands move to grip the sides of my face before pulling me in for a searing kiss. It's hard and rough and all-consuming. I melt into him while my fingers grip the hem of his T-shirt. I feel the kiss over every inch of my skin.

He pulls back, and there's a shine in his eye that wasn't there before.

A promise of sorts.

A look of hope on the horizon.

"This house. This land. It may have been my dream home before, but that was before you. Before I knew the true meaning of the words. Before I felt what it was like to love someone more than anything else. *You*, Scottie Monroe, are my dream home. Whether it's here or anywhere in the world. It's always fucking you."

My heart swells so full it feels like it might burst.

I rise to my toes and kiss him—slow and sure. He holds me close like he never wants to let go. When we break apart again, he stays close with his breath against my lips.

"You'll stay?" I ask again.

"Wherever you are is where I want to be, baby."

I smile so wide that it hurts. We kiss again, and this time it's the kind that says he means it. That he's here. That he's choosing this life. That he's choosing himself.

I pull back keeping my arms around his neck. "I guess you were right that night we met." Tucker looks at me with confusion in his eyes. "All great love stories really do start with a corny pickup line."

He smiles so wide that it makes me do the same. He scoops me up and I wrap myself around him and we laugh together while he walks me back to the living room.

Around us, the house settles into itself—quiet and warm and finally whole.

Not because every corner is perfect.

It never will be.

But because now, the people inside it are brave enough to be real.

We no longer have to wonder if we're enough. We don't have to hide behind armor or lock ourselves behind closed doors to feel at peace.

And this…this messy, beautiful, imperfect life we have built together is finally home.

Don't forget…

Sign up for Jenn's newsletter to be the first to hear the news on new releases, announcements, influencer opportunities, and more.

http://jennmcmahon.com

Acknowledgments

For you.

I can't start off these acknowledgments without thanking **my readers**. You not only supported me in the transition to small town romance, but you raved about it—screamed about it. You allowed me to be a part of this space without batting an eye. You've given me the drive to write what I *love* and didn't question me. Now three books in, I'm obsessed. I hope you are too because I might be stuck in my small town romance era for a little longer.

To team Jenn McMahon—*Emma and Jenna*. I'd be lost without you and everything you do for me. From making sure I'm on task, to making sure I'm on schedule with social media plan, to keeping everything running so I can write and edit and edit some more. You two are my lifeline.

To *Salma*—I said it before, and I'll say it again. You're amazing. Everything you touch turns to gold. You are the NO girl I need to turn this into a YES book. Your tough love will always be my favorite, and your listening ear when I'm crashing out will never be taken for granted.

My Alpha and Beta readers—*Rachel, Shima, Libby, Jenna, Jen, Ashley, and Isabella*. You put up with my hot mess self when I was in the early writing stages, always behind schedule. And then when I needed a fast, last minute beta read before it went to audio (because again, behind schedule and on the verge of a crash out) you showed up in ways I'll never be able to thank you enough for.

To *Caroline*—or Carol. Only I'm allowed to call you that. 'I can't stand you.' (Can that be all that needs to be said?) HA! In all seriousness, you worked with me on being late (I have a trend here if you're still reading this far into my thank you's) and my split manuscript being sent at random times. You've been my day one, and I couldn't ask for a better friend with me on this journey.

To *Mel*—this cover? CAN YOU EVEN? You already know I love everything you've ever done for me, but a thank you here is justified because at the last minute, you put up with me changing things, moving things, and flipping the title all over the place. Also, you'll always be my favorite podcast on my ride to work.

My sprinting girls—*Victoria Wilder, Julia Connors, Leah Brunner, and Ashley James.* You have quite literally been by my side for every word I wrote for this book. Every mental state I went through. Every high, every low, and everything in between. I love our group chat more than anything. Thank you for being my safe space and the reason people are even reading this book. There's no way it would have been done without you.

About the Author

Jenn McMahon is a Jersey Shore based romance author who lives by the ocean with her husband, two kids, and a trio of dogs. As a lifelong lover of romance novels, she's spent years engrossed in stories before writing her own book that debuted in April 2023.

Her work can be defined by its core themes of strong female friendships, found family, and making readers feel seen through the characters she writes—allowing readers to find a piece of themselves within the pages. She has been known to make readers laugh while occasionally shedding a tear through her stories.

When she's not writing, Jenn can be found rewatching her favorite comfort shows—Scandal, Grey's Anatomy, and Friends. If she's not doing that, she's definitely petting her dogs or heading to the beach with her kids.

Scan Here to access my socials, Facebook reader group, newsletter sign up and everything you need to stay connected.